THIEF
on ✝he
CROSS
TEMPLAR SECRETS IN AMERICA

A Novel by **David S. Brody**

Eyes That See Publishing
Westford, Massachusetts

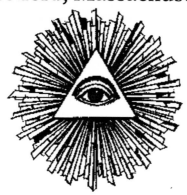

Thief on the Cross
Templar Secrets in America

Eyes That See Publishing
Westford, Massachusetts

ISBN 978-0-9820732-7-8

1st edition

Printed in USA

Praise for David S. Brody's Books

"Brody does a terrific job of wrapping his research in a fast-paced thrill ride that will feel far more like an action film than an academic paper."
—PUBLISHERS WEEKLY (*Cabal of the Westford Knight*)

"Strongly recommended for all collections."
—LIBRARY JOURNAL (*The Wrong Abraham*)

"Will keep you up even after you've put it down."
—Hallie Ephron, BOSTON GLOBE (*Blood of the Tribe*)

"A riveting, fascinating read."
—MIDWEST BOOK REVIEW (*The Wrong Abraham*)

"Best of the Coming Season."
—BOSTON MAGAZINE (*Unlawful Deeds*)

"A compelling suspense story and a searing murder mystery."
—THE BOSTON PHOENIX (*Blood of the Tribe*)

"A comparison to *The Da Vinci Code* and *National Treasure* is inevitable....The story rips the reader into a fast-paced adventure."
—FRESH FICTION (*Cabal of the Westford Knight*)

"An excellent historical conspiracy thriller. It builds on its most famous predecessor, *The Da Vinci Code*, and takes it one step farther—and across the Atlantic."
—MYSTERY BOOK NEWS (*Cabal of the Westford Knight*)

"The action and danger are non-stop, leaving you breathless. It is one hell of a read."
—ABOUT.COM Book Reviews (*Unlawful Deeds*)

"The year is early, but this book will be hard to beat; it's already on my 'Best of 2009' list."
—BARYON REVIEW (*Cabal of the Westford Knight*)

"Five Stars."
—Harriet Klausner, AMAZON (*The Wrong Abraham*)

"An enormously fun read, exceedingly hard to put down."
—The BOOKBROWSER (*Unlawful Deeds*)

"A feast."
—ARTS AROUND BOSTON (*Unlawful Deeds*)

About the Author

David S. Brody is a *Boston Globe* bestselling fiction writer recently named Boston's "Best Local Author" by the *Boston Phoenix* newspaper. He serves as a Director of the Westford Historic Society and is a former Director of the New England Antiquities Research Association (NEARA). A graduate of Tufts University and Georgetown Law School, he is an avid researcher in the subject of pre-Columbian exploration of America. In his spare time he coaches his two daughters' youth sports teams, skis, and plays on adult ice hockey and softball teams.

For more information, please visit:

DavidBrodyBooks.com

Also by the Author

Unlawful Deeds

Blood of the Tribe

The Wrong Abraham

Cabal of the Westford Knight: Templars at the Newport Tower

Preface

This novel is a continuation of the themes I first explored in *Cabal of the Westford Knight*. Specifically, did ancient explorers visit the shores of North America, and if so, why? Readers of *Cabal* will recognize its protagonists, Cameron and Amanda, as well as the Knights Templar themes. However, *The Thief on the Cross* is not a sequel to *Cabal* and readers who have not read *Cabal* should feel free to jump right in.

As in *Cabal*, the artifacts and art work pictured in this story are real. Readers may want to first visit the Author's Note at the end of this book for a more detailed discussion of the issue of artifact authenticity.

The research for this story has taken me to areas where, quite frankly, I never thought I'd go. A few years ago I knew very little about John the Baptist, the Book of Mormon, Leonardo da Vinci, the Mandan Indians, Burrows Cave and the divinity of Jesus Christ. Somehow these seemingly unrelated subjects weaved themselves together (along with the Templars) to produce this story. I hope readers find these subjects, and their possible connections to each other, as compelling as I do.

I recognize that, compelling or not, the themes explored in this story are controversial and may be offensive to readers with strong religious beliefs. I simply followed the path down which my research took me. I apologize in advance to readers who may be offended by this story.

—David S. Brody

Warning

This book contains themes that may be offensive to readers with strong Christian or other religious beliefs.

PROLOGUE

[Paris, December 25, 1309]

Gaul de Teus was not yet dead, but no longer alive. He had been holding on for months, his hatred for his French captors and their Vatican lackeys keeping his heart beating long after any spark of life burned in his soul. He forced open his eyes, a slit of sunlight barely visible in his underground cell. Finally the day had arrived.

"Tell them I will confess on Christmas morning," he had told his guards. He knew it likely King Philippe and the king's sickly pawn, Pope Clement V, would attend and view the confession as part of their holiday festivities. Neither would want to miss a good torture. Over the past two-plus years many of his brother Templars had died at the hands of their inquisitors. Others had withdrawn their confessions just before death. He would instead provide a confession his captors would wish they had never heard.

The guards came for him mid-morning, dragging him from his underground stone chamber, his feet too blistered and his kneecaps too shattered to support his weight. The cat-sized rats peered at him as he shuffled along, sniffing at the decay that hung over him, furious to see him leaving their lair. Only yesterday, or perhaps the day before, the guards had covered his face with rancid cheese, tied him down and allowed the rats to feast; he had clamped closed his mouth and eyes but most of the skin on his face and inside his nose had been gnawed away, replaced by a puss-filled, scabby paste of putrid flesh. The pain he had suffered was unimaginable. But the indignation fueled the loathing which kept him alive.

Outside, he gulped at the fresh winter air, almost reigniting the flame of life within him. He closed his mouth. None of that. Now was not the time to think about living.

They led him into a courtyard, the sunlight assaulting his eyes. A raised platform had been constructed along one wall, a dozen ornate chairs set side by side as a viewing station. A pile of coals, orange and angry, glowed in the center. A stockade stood near the flames. Later in the day that same flame would likely be used to roast the Yule boar for the evening feast. Apparently King Philippe viewed the roasting of his Templar prisoner as a mere appetizer. But it was the corrupt king and his spineless pope who would burn in hell.

The stockade stood eight feet tall. The guards stripped de Teus to his loincloth, hoisted him up and clamped his neck and wrists between the horizontal wooden bars. They wheeled the structure closer to the flames and spun it so he faced the viewing platform. "Tell his majesty the prisoner is in position," one of the guards called. The warmth of the coals below him actually felt good after months in the dungeon.

Squinting, he scanned the rooftops above the courtyard wall. A bearded man in a hood raised himself slightly above the parapet wall and nodded. *Thanks to the Blessed Mother.* His message had been received. He might at least avoid the final torture.

He watched King Philippe lead his retinue onto the viewing platform, the structure set tight against the courtyard wall to shelter the royal party from a would-be assassin's arrow. Philippe took the center chair, set throne-like on blocks above the others. A permanent scowl dominated the king's pale, sharp-featured visage. De Teus knew the face well; as the Templar treasurer he had overseen loans to the king totaling millions of francs. No doubt Philippe took extra joy in besting his former banker. To his right sat Pope Clement, a balding, meek man who avoided de Teus' glare and instead examined his cuticles and coughed into a bejeweled handkerchief. Clement had fled Rome and moved the papal court to Avignon, subjugating him to the whims of the French king. Philippe smirked at de Teus. "Your face disgusts me. Perhaps you should stop picking at your scabs."

De Teus mustered what little saliva he could in his mouth, lifted his head and spat at the leering monarch.

Philippe laughed and sipped from his goblet, his guests taking their cue and doing the same. He motioned to the guards, who splashed grease into the fire and slopped animal fat onto de Teus' legs using an oversized basting brush. The flames leapt at his ankles; he lifted his knees reflexively. "You spit at me now. Just as you and your fellow Templars spit on the cross and disparage our Lord Jesus Christ," Philippe said. It was a common charge against the Order, and not entirely untrue. It brought the eyes of Pope Clement off his fingernails. Philippe leaned forward. "I have been told you have something you'd like to tell us, de Teus?"

De Teus had rehearsed his words for weeks. There was no sense in delaying further. He raised his chin and filled his lungs. "I confess to this, and this alone: I worship the God in heaven. Upon my death my soul will reside in his kingdom." He shifted his eyes between Philippe and the Pope. "It is you who are the sinners. It is you who blaspheme the true God. It is you who profane the Lord by claiming divinity for the Thief on the Cross."

The Pope's eyes widened in fear; the royal party gasped. "The Thief on the Cross?" the Pope wheezed, turning to the French king. "What is this heresy?"

Philippe jumped to his feet and shouted to the guards. "Silence him! Make him stop!"

De Teus nodded to his brother Knight crouched on the roof beyond. A crossbow arrow sailed through the air, piercing de Teus' heart. He smiled as he took his final breath. "We know the truth. We have the bones," he exhaled, revealing the Vatican's most-guarded secret.

CHAPTER 1

[November, Modern Times]

Cameron Thorne leaned over the lectern and paused. A few seconds of well-timed silence drew attention more effectively than a raised voice. Not that the crowd of breakfasting Freemasons had been inattentive so far—they seemed fascinated by his description of artifacts evidencing exploration of America by the Knights Templar during medieval times. But Cam wanted to end strong.

The clanking of silverware in the crowded Holiday Inn function room ebbed. Cam smiled, reflecting on life's strange journey. Two years ago he toiled in a large Boston law firm, a thirty-something attorney trying to do something meaningful in a profession that so often rewarded the meaningless. Now he was part of a group of researchers helping to change the way Americans viewed their history. And having the time of his life. "As the Native Americans say, Christopher Columbus was the *last* person to discover America. And we have the ancient artifacts and sites to prove it."

He spoke staccato-like, counting off on the fingers of his left hand. "The Kensington Rune Stone. The Newport Tower. The Bat Creek Stone. The Spirit Pond Rune Stones. The Westford Knight." He held up five fingers. "That's five. I could give you 20 more. These artifacts are real, and their authenticity has been scientifically established. They didn't appear here by magic."

The eyes of his mostly-male audience locked on his. "The bottom line is that the archeologists and historians need to offer an explanation for these artifacts that's a bit more academically rigorous than putting their fingers in their ears and yelling 'Hoax!' every time they see one. Because that's not going to cut it any more."

Here it was, in a nutshell. "So, we say to these so-called experts: You are entitled to your own opinions." He slapped the podium with an open palm. "But you are not entitled to your own facts."

✠ ✠ ✠

A stooped, gray-haired man in a light blue golf shirt pushed his chair back from a table in the back of the function room even before the applause had subsided. "Mr. Thorne, will you accept a question?" His tone was light, almost playful—as if the man were a law professor challenging a prized student.

Cam smiled. "Of course."

"I attended Harvard in the 1970s and had the pleasure of taking a couple of history classes with Samuel Eliot Morison. He used to say that anyone who believed in European exploration of America before Columbus was a fool."

Cam scanned the room. "For those of you who don't know, in the early 1970s Morison wrote *The European Discovery of America*—it's considered the definitive book on European exploration of America. He won the Pulitzer Prize for it; there's even a statue of him in Boston on Commonwealth Avenue." Cam chuckled. "So I guess if someone is going to call me a fool, I should be happy it's him."

Cam faced the stooped questioner. "I'm actually glad you brought this up. In Morison's mind hiking to America from Asia makes perfect sense, but taking a boat from Europe is incomprehensible." Cam shrugged. "And since he was so prominent, nobody dared cross him."

Cam sipped his water. "So I went back to look at his writings. Specifically, I was curious how he dealt with the L'Anse aux Meadows settlement in Newfoundland. The Icelandic Sagas describe Leif Ericson and his crew traveling from Greenland to a land called Vinland a number of times in the 11th century. Morison was convinced the Newfoundland settlement is the ancient Vinland and that the Vikings sailed no further south than that. I think he's wrong. There are plenty of artifacts that show Vinland is on Cape Cod. Morison calls these artifacts fakes, which makes this discussion illustrative of the whole debate."

Cam had been talking for an hour; his audience needed to get to work. He rushed to make his point. "So let's look at the evidence. First, the Sagas talk about Leif and his party spending a snowless winter in Vinland, during which the cattle grazed daily.

6

Second, the Sagas describe Leif's men harvesting grapes and making wine, hence the 'Vinland' name." Cam spread his hands. "But they don't have snowless winters or grapevines in northern Newfoundland. So how did Morison reconcile all this?"

Cam let the question fester for a second. "Had Morison discovered some kind of aberrant climate pattern in the early 11th century? Or perhaps the translation of the Sagas into English was in error?" Cam shook his head. "No. I'm paraphrasing, but this is essentially what he concluded: '*We know that Leif Ericson's father, Eric the Red, was stretching the truth when he coined the name 'Greenland'—Greenland is barren and not at all green. Leif himself must have been lying when he described the snowless winter and grape vines of Vinland. Like father like son!*'" Cam spread his hands again. "And so, that's it. Morison basically throws a B.S. argument in our faces and calls us fools if we say it smells funny." He shook his head. "And for 40 years nobody's been willing to call him out on it." He glanced at the blue golf shirt. "Well, 40 years is long enough."

The man in the blue golf shirt smiled and offered a smart salute before turning and shuffling out of the room.

✙ ✙ ✙

A small girl, perhaps eight years old, tugged lightly on Amanda Spencer's sleeve. A pair of cobalt blue eyes framed by chestnut skin and braided, jet-black pigtails peered up at her. "Excuse me," the child said in a firm voice. "My mother is in the bathroom and she needs help. I think she fainted." Her lower lip trembled slightly.

Amanda knelt. She and her fiancé Cameron had just entered the soaring, glass-enclosed atrium of the Native American history museum at the Foxwoods casino in southern Connecticut. The terrified girl knew she was not supposed to talk to strangers, but the museum had just opened on a quiet Monday morning and there was nobody else to ask for help. "Of course, honey. What's your name?"

"Astarte," she said, enunciating each of the three syllables.

"That's a pretty name. My name is Amanda."

The girl studied her for a second, shifting her weight from foot to foot. "You talk funny. Like Mary Poppins. And you're pretty just like she is."

The comment struck Amanda as odd given the girl's mom was in peril, but it had been years since she spent time with eight-year-olds. "Well, thank you. I talk like her because I'm from a city called London, just like Mary Poppins." She took the girl's hand. "Now let's go check on your mum."

"I'll call 9-1-1," Cam interjected.

"Good idea." She kissed him quickly as he dialed. "Be right back."

Astarte pushed open the door and led Amanda into a well-lit, modern restroom with a bank of sinks along the right wall and stalls along the left. "Where's your mum, honey?" Amanda raised her voice over the noise of an electronic hand dryer.

"Over here." As the girl pulled her deeper into the room, a door to a nearby stall swung open and a large woman with hands jammed into her sweatshirt crossed behind Amanda toward the sinks. Astarte stopped short and turned, looking up. Amanda bent down to her; something in her face had changed—instead of fear, Amanda saw remorse in the girl's eyes.

A pair of strong arms bear-hugged Amanda, and a heavy boot kicked her feet out from under her. She landed hard on her hip as Astarte scrambled away. *What was happening?* Fear washed over her like a cold fog. A meaty hand shoved a rag over her nose and mouth. Amanda gagged, smelling something sweet like Juicy Fruit gum as she tried to turn to see her attacker. Her eyes watered and her fingers and toes began to tingle. *Some kind of chemical.*

A second body rushed from another stall, a second pair of strong hands and sharp fingernails grasping her arms. She writhed and lashed out with fists and elbows, but she felt like she was under water, her limbs moving in slow motion through the thick air. The weight of her first attacker stayed on her, collapsing her as the hand dryer and rag muffled her cries for help. Astarte cradled her head, preventing it from crashing to the tile floor as she toppled. And then the world went black.

✝ ✝ ✝

Cam watched the little girl lead Amanda away as he explained the situation to the dispatcher. Just over a year ago he had met Amanda; together they had uncovered a series of artifacts and sites scattered around New England that evidenced medieval exploration of America by the vestiges of Templar Knights fleeing Europe in the late 1300s. Since the discovery their lives had been a whirlwind—lectures, documentaries, a book deal. And recently an engagement ring. They had even been contacted by a Hollywood agent who wanted to make an action film chronicling their adventures. "Matt Damon would be perfect to play you, Cam," the agent had said. "And Emma Watson, with green contact lenses and her hair dyed blond, would be an ideal Amanda."

Cam shrugged. Might be fun to make a movie. And at least the agent had suggested someone decent-looking to play him, even though both Cam and Matt Damon were too old for Emma Watson. But for now they were having a great time traveling around the country fleshing out their research; Cam had cut back to three days a week at his uncle's law firm—he had left his downtown practice—while Amanda's new job as a reporter for the local newspaper also gave her flexibility to travel. They weren't getting rich, but he felt extraordinarily well-off.

Cam glanced at the bathroom door; he would wait another couple minutes before knocking. From his leather shoulder bag he pulled out the strange letter that had brought them to the museum. "Attorney Thorne," the letter began in a shaky, slanted cursive, as if written by an arthritic lefty. "My name is Jefferson January III, and I am a staunch admirer of your recent efforts to reveal our nation's long history of European exploration prior to Columbus. But you have only scratched the surface of this topic. I have a personal collection of artifacts that dwarfs what you have seen so far."

Though he had read the letter a half dozen times, Cam pulled the paper closer to his face, struggling to decipher the angled scrawl. "I almost died as a young man—during that time I traveled to heaven and back, receiving specific instructions from God as to my mission on earth. My mission, I am certain, will soon become your mission: to prove that America is meant to be God's New Jerusalem."

He smiled as he recalled Amanda's reaction to the missive. "Just what the world needs—another chap with God on his speed dial. I don't fancy I'll be drinking any Kool-Aid if he offers it." For some reason it seemed like the eccentrics usually ended up with the most interesting artifacts, perhaps because they were more open-minded about ideas that contradicted mainstream teachings. And January had followed up with a series of phone messages and emails, practically begging them to come. So, finally, they had carved out a few days prior to Thanksgiving to view his collection, which he was in the process of donating to the tribe's glitzy new museum. Cam doubted lightning would strike twice, that they would again stumble upon a series of sites and artifacts that would change the way Americans viewed their history. But he wondered what else existed out there, what other artifacts remained undiscovered or stashed away in private collections....

One thing had become clear: Thinking of the Atlantic Ocean as a barrier rather than a superhighway was as narrow-minded as medieval mapmakers who portrayed the Atlantic as the monster-laden edge of the world. Plenty of evidence showed that Phoenician navigators, sailing ships far larger than what Columbus navigated, had circumnavigated Africa; Thor Heyerdahl had sailed a reed boat from Africa to Barbados in 1970; and historians acknowledged that South America had been settled by ancient explorers sailing across the Pacific. So why did historians so blindly reject the idea of explorers venturing across the Atlantic before Columbus, both pre- and post-Viking?

Through a glass panel in the museum atrium Cam watched an ambulance and police car pull into the front drive; a young, fit policeman jogged through the revolving doors toward him as the paramedics grabbed their equipment. No doubt the equipment, like the museum facility, would be state of the art—the casino had almost overnight transformed the Pequot tribe into one of the wealthiest entities on the east coast, and they had built the massive glass- and chrome-faced museum as a repository for Native American culture and history. As a federally-recognized tribe, and therefore a sovereign nation, they also had their own police and fire departments.

Cam described the situation and pointed to the restroom door. Only a few minutes had passed. "Coming in," the officer announced as he cracked open the door. "Police." A hand dryer stopped, allowing Cam to hear the clop of the policeman's feet as the door swung closed behind him.

Cam checked his watch; Jefferson January was a half-hour late for their meeting, which seemed odd given how hard he had pushed Cam to make the drive to Connecticut. Cam tried his number and bounced to an answering machine. A few seconds later the policeman emerged from the ladies room. "Sir, are you sure this is the right room?"

Cam jolted upright. "Of course. I haven't moved."

"Well, there's nobody in there. It's empty."

"What? Did you look in the stalls?" It was an obvious question, but where else could Amanda and the girl be?

"All of them. Nobody is in there."

"Is there another exit?"

"Not that I'm aware of." He studied Cam. "But come on in, have a look yourself."

Cam pushed past the officer. The stall doors were all open—there was no place else to hide. "What's behind this door?" In the corner of the room the outline of a door sat recessed into the wall.

The officer shrugged. "I assume it's a closet." He pulled on a small knob. "It's locked."

"Well, can you get a key? They must be in there."

"In the locked closet? Sir, I—"

"Look, I know it sounds stupid. But can you find a key to that door? I saw my fiancée go in here with a little girl. They didn't just disappear."

Sighing, the officer led Cam back into the atrium. "You guys might as well stick around a few more minutes," he said to the paramedics. "Wait here," he ordered Cam as he began to walk away. "I'll see if I can find a key to that closet." He stopped and pulled out a notepad. "Actually, before I go, what was your name?"

✝ ✝ ✝

Amanda awoke in the back of a darkened van, disoriented. Her head rested on a pillow; a little girl clasped her hand and looked down at her with wide, blue-black eyes. The eyes triggered a memory—a cold numbness spread through her as she recalled the bathroom attack. "Do you feel okay, Miss Amanda?"

She tried to sit up but a wave of nausea forced her down to the pillow. "Where am I?" The taste of Juicy Fruit gum in her mouth made her want to gag.

"In my uncle's van."

"Who's your uncle?"

"Is she awake?" A woman's voice carried back from the middle of the van.

"Yes, Aunt Eliza."

A sharp-nosed, chinless woman with graying hair pulled behind her ears leaned over the seat and peered down at Amanda—not the woman who first grabbed her, but perhaps the one with the sharp fingernails. "You've met Astarte. My name is Eliza." She smiled caringly, as if soothing a lost kitten. But her teeth seemed too small for her mouth, and the spaces between them gave her face an ominous, rodent-like quality. "Please don't be frightened. We mean you no harm."

"Well then what do you bloody want with me?"

Sighing, Eliza reached down and touched Amanda's cheek with a cold hand. "God has sent you to us to help spread his word."

✝ ✝ ✝

Eliza had become adept at wearing her mask. Fellow congregants at the nearby church she and Jefferson attended saw her as a simple Mormon spinster—a devoted congregant who wore high-necked dresses and spent her free time baking for Church luncheons and reading the Book of Mormon. The Spencer woman probably had a similar impression of her as they bounced along in the van. If they only knew.

Outwardly, the only thing remarkable about her was that she had not married, choosing instead to run the household of her powerful brother. Decades ago she had silenced the whispers by spreading a rumor that as a child she had suffered a kick from a horse that made it impossible for her to bear children, and therefore was an unworthy bride. Not that many men had pushed the issue. Under the tenets of the Mormon religion, being unmarried made her ineligible for heaven. But she was certain she was doing God's work, assisting her brother Jefferson in ways even he could not imagine. He was a force of nature, storming his way across the country on his mission to change the way the world viewed the Mormon Church. What nobody knew, including Jefferson himself, was that he was guided by weather patterns only Eliza truly understood. Patterns Eliza sometimes even controlled.

✛ ✛ ✛

Cam paced, waiting for the police officer to return. He tried Amanda's cell phone, checked his own for messages and re-inspected the restroom for signs of a struggle or anything amiss. He tried to not let ugly thoughts creep into his consciousness, but it was like trying to swat away black flies on a summer night.

Finally the officer ambled down the hall, no particular urgency in his gait. "That door leads to a closet that also backs into the cafeteria kitchen. It's for cleaning supplies, stuff like that. You can get in from either side."

"Well, that must be where they went."

He held up his hand. "I questioned all three people working in the kitchen. They didn't see any woman or girl or anyone come through there. And they've been there for the past hour, getting ready for lunch."

"That's impossible." Fear churned inside his stomach. "Where else could they have gone?"

The officer crossed his arms; he was, like Cam, only medium height, but he tried his best to lift his chin and look down at Cam. "Mr. Thorne, is it possible your fiancée does not want you to find her?"

"What?" Cam took a deep breath, counted to five. Cops rarely responded to raised voices. "Look, if that's what she wanted, she could just drive away—she has the car keys in her purse."

"Well perhaps we should check the parking lot then."

What a waste of time. But he didn't have much choice. "Fine." Walking as fast as he could without actually jogging, he led the policeman through the revolving doors into the unseasonably warm fall air. They crossed the drop-off area and followed a path to the paved parking lot. Cam stopped short. The Subaru was gone. "Oh, shit."

✠ ✠ ✠

Cam hopped on a shuttle bus heading back to their hotel room. The police officer had allowed him to file a missing person report, but made it clear he had wasted enough of his day on what he believed to be some kind of lovers' quarrel.

Cam took a deep breath and pulled out the letter again. January had lured them to Foxwoods, but instead of showing up for their meeting had, apparently, abducted Amanda. But why? He tried Amanda's cell again, and then January's. Nothing.

The bus completed its short trip. "Final stop," the driver announced. Cam made his way toward the front exit. A couple of twenty-something guys in the front row watched him in the rearview mirror, their eyes darting away when he looked up. He continued past them. Why were they waiting for him to pass before getting off?

Bounding down the stairs of the bus, Cam took a dozen long strides across the parking lot toward the hotel. He then spun quickly and reversed course, as if he had forgotten something on the bus. The two guys were only a few yards behind him, directly in his path. He didn't believe in coincidence—if they were following him, it was related to Amanda's abduction.

His fists clenched in his pockets, Cam brushed lightly against a balding, pear-shaped man wearing a New York Jets sweatshirt. "Watch out, buddy," the man hissed.

Too much aggression for a light brush. Cam pushed it. He needed info. "Chill out. And you might feel better if you found a real football team to root for."

The second guy was bigger than the first, unshaven with blond hair and hard, bloodshot eyes. "Fuck you," he said, grabbing Cam's shoulder and spinning him around. Cam caught a whiff of last night's beer, partially masked by this morning's coffee.

Cam smiled up at him. He wouldn't normally have been such an ass, but he wanted to provoke his pursuers. Plus he really hated bullies. "Sorry, didn't mean to insult your girlfriend."

The big guy's face reddened and he drew back his fist. The guy outweighed Cam by at least forty pounds, but Cam had sparred a bit in the gym in college and he understood leverage and angles. As the thug wound up and lunged, Cam stepped straight at him, surprising him by moving inside the radius of the blow. Before his assailant could react Cam threw a quick right hand, fist landing squarely on nose. A torrent of blood gushed from his face as the man dropped to his knees.

Cam turned quickly to the Jets fan, ready to engage him as well. The smaller man staggered back. But Cam wanted answers. "Why were you following me? Is it January?"

The pear-shaped man's eyes widened and his face blanched. "We ... yeah ... what are you talking about?"

Cam moved toward him. "I hope you're not here to play poker. You're a shitty liar." The man was a link to Amanda. If Cam could get him alone he might learn where Amanda had been taken....

As Cam reached for the man's collar the bus driver stepped off the bus. "Hey, what are you doing?" The driver pulled out his cell phone; he must have seen the altercation. The last thing Cam needed was another encounter with the tribal police. He snapped the pear-shaped man's head back with a short jab to the chin, turned and began jogging away. After a few steps he spun. "Tell January if he hurts Amanda, I'll hunt him down and break his neck."

Five minutes later Cam was in his hotel room, his heart still racing. For the fourth time since Amanda disappeared he tried phoning both her and January; again he bounced to voice mail. He opened his laptop, hoping to Google January and learn more about the man. But the Internet connection in the room was down. "Damn it." He phoned the front desk, waiting six rings before hanging up in frustration.

Grabbing his laptop and the letter, he jogged down the hall to the elevator bank, waited thirty seconds for an elevator that never came, and finally kicked open the stairway door and ran down four flights of stairs to the lobby. He tried to keep the edge from his voice as he approached the front desk. "Hi. The Internet connection is down in my room."

A middle-aged woman with bags under her eyes nodded. "The whole hotel is off-line. A wire went down."

What else could go wrong? "Any idea when it will be back?" Had January arranged this also, along with the abduction and the see-nothing cafeteria workers and the car disappearance and the thugs on the bus?

She shrugged.

He fought to keep his manners. "Okay, thanks."

He couldn't just sit around waiting for his cell phone to ring. He called information and requested a listing for the local police department. "No, not the Pequot police. I'd like the number for the police in the closest Connecticut town to Foxwoods."

✝ ✝ ✝

A half-hour and a $35 cab fare later Cam entered the Ledyard police department. He explained the situation to an older, grey-haired sergeant with a round face and sun-burned nose. Cam guessed he had probably just come from the golf course. "No disrespect to the Pequot police force, but my fiancée just disappeared and they aren't doing anything about it." He didn't mention his altercation outside the bus.

The sergeant rubbed the nail of his index finger against a cuticle on this thumb. His eyes drifted out the window, probably wishing he were still on the course. "You seem like a bright guy. You ever hear of sovereign immunity?"

Cam hadn't mentioned he was a lawyer. He played dumb, but he had been afraid of the sovereign immunity issue. "Not really."

"Well, it means a policeman from Canada can't come into Vermont and make an arrest."

"Okay."

"And that's the situation we have over at Foxwoods. Technically, when you go onto Pequot land, you're going into a different country. That's why it's called the Eastern Pequot Tribal Nation. It's a nation, a country. They have their own laws, and their own law enforcement. Now they might invite us onto their land to help investigate a case, but we can't just go marching in there like John Wayne."

"So they can do whatever they want, like ignore a kidnapping?"

"Now that wouldn't be particularly good for their casino business, but, yes, pretty much, that's it. Especially in a case like this where there's really no evidence. You know that saying, 'What happens in Vegas stays in Vegas'? Well, it's even more true here—what happens at Foxwoods stays at Foxwoods. The state made a deal with the tribe because it wanted the gambling revenues. A deal with the devil, some say." He locked eyes with Cam. "Sounds like you might have to make some kind of deal with the devil yourself if you want to find that fiancée of yours."

CHAPTER 2

Amanda lay back on the pillow, analyzing her situation as the van weaved down some country road. Her teeth chattered, probably her body's reaction to the knock-out chemical. Or maybe just plain terror. Reaching around, her hand shaking, she tried to locate her purse—there was a can of mace tucked inside. No luck. They must have taken it from her, along with her cell phone. The muffled conversation of two men floated back from the front of the vehicle. Presumably the large woman who had first attacked her was in the middle seat with Eliza. Not likely Amanda could overpower them all and escape.

Yet she didn't seem to be in any immediate danger—Astarte continued to hold her hand, and Eliza continued to peer down at her with a frozen smile like some kind of Stepford Wife, albeit an unattractive one. Yet the fact remained she had been kidnapped and was bouncing along in the back of some windowless van.

Amanda fought to control the chattering. "You told me your mum was sick, Astarte. Where is she?" She couldn't help but stare into the girl's eyes—they were cobalt rather than olive, but they possessed the same haunting, imploring look as the green-eyed, Afghani refugee girl on the cover of National Geographic magazine back in the 1980s.

The girl frowned. "Uncle Jefferson told me it was okay to tell a lie if that's what God wanted."

Jefferson. So this wasn't random. Which should make it easier for the authorities to figure out. "What kind of lie?" Amanda expected Eliza to jump in and stop the inquiry, but instead she turned to the girl to await her response.

"My mother is dead. I don't remember her. But Aunt Eliza and Uncle Jefferson and God are my parents now. They take care of me. When I'm older I'll take care of them." She giggled. "Not God, of course. He takes care of himself. But I'll take care of all the others."

Amanda sat up, swallowing her nausea. Who were the others? "All by yourself?"

Astarte nodded emphatically, the vehicle's dome light reflecting in her dark eyes. "I'm the Fortieth Princess. That's my job."

✙ ✙ ✙

Cam took another cab, this time to an Avis rental lot. On his way, alone in the back seat, he pulled Amanda's picture up on his phone. The pose was classic—big smile, the wind blowing her blond hair, shamrock-green eyes alive and vibrant, head tilted playfully to one side. When he first met her she reminded him of something out of a fairy tale, a beautiful fair-skinned princess waiting to be rescued from a tower. It turned out she could take care of herself just fine. Except now, a year later, she really did need to be rescued.

He fought back a rising sense of panic. He needed to stay calm, stay rational.

From the Avis lot he drove to a Starbucks to use their WiFi connection. As a diabetic he needed to eat regularly, so he lunched on a bagel and banana. At some point whoever abducted Amanda—presumably January—would contact Cam with their demands. But in the meantime thoughts and visions of what might be happening to her tormented him. Grinding his teeth, he pushed his anxiety to the back of his mind. Worrying about her wouldn't help him find her. And she could take care of herself; she was probably hatching an escape plan already.

To find her he needed to learn more about Jefferson January, if that indeed was his real name. An Internet search turned up a year-old newspaper article detailing his plans to donate a portion of his collection of ancient American artifacts plus a large sum of money to the Pequot museum. But that's all he found. Cam reread January's letter and its strange message, wondering again what January wanted from him—obviously the stakes were higher than Cam had anticipated.

Cam turned his attention to the Polaroid photo clipped to January's letter. January had included it as bait, as an example of the kind of artifact he possessed in his collection. But what did it say about the man and his motivations? Cam examined the series of lines carved into an ovular black stone.

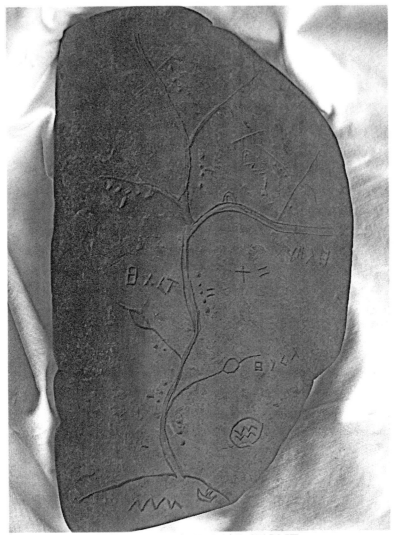

BURROWS CAVE MAP STONE

When he first examined the photo Cam thought the carving depicted a tree with branches running off it, but Amanda had suggested the lines portrayed a river system. "It could be a map of the Mississippi River basin," she said.

He had consulted an atlas—the trunk of the tree matched the path of the Mississippi River, the two main branches to the right tracked the Ohio and Illinois Rivers, and the large branch to the left mirrored the Missouri River. "Pretty good guess for a Brit."

"Just because most Americans couldn't find the Nile if they fell in it doesn't mean the rest of the world is ignorant about geography." She had kissed him quickly on the tip of his nose. "Not that we don't fancy you American cowboys."

He allowed the memory to gnaw at him for a few seconds— his nose still tingling from the touch of her lips—before returning to the map carving. They had decided the boat-like drawing at the bottom of the stone floated in what was probably the Gulf of Mexico, the igloo-shaped markings represented caves or other enclosures, and the letters looked like some kind of ancient script. But that's as far as they got.

He tried a few Google searches, hoping to learn more about the stone carving. After ten minutes he tossed the photo aside like a Frisbee. What he really wanted to do was jump in his car and race around the streets surrounding the casino, searching for Amanda. Using Google Earth, he looked down at the Foxwoods area from a satellite view. Woodlands surrounded the resort. Driving the streets aimlessly would be futile—January had carefully planned things out and perhaps even bought off the police. The two thugs on the shuttle bus were minor players and the amateurish encounter probably an aberration. This would be a chess match, not a street brawl. And to win Cam needed to better understand his opponent.

Cam pulled out the letter and reread January's words. "My mission, I am certain, will soon become your mission—to prove that America is meant to be God's New Jerusalem." He exhaled. Was that what this was all about? Had Amanda been abducted by some kook with a messiah complex?

✠ ✠ ✠

An electric garage door whirred open and the van bumped over a threshold before coming to a stop. Amanda guessed they had been driving for about 45 minutes, but that didn't count the time she was unconscious. And it felt like they had been driving in circles, probably to disorient her in case she woke up early in the trip. She sat up slowly, the nausea not as bad as it had been. But she still couldn't stop her teeth from chattering.

"Astarte, can you tell me where we are?"

"Uncle Jefferson's garage. Upstairs is where Aunt Eliza and I live."

The back door of the van swung open and the woman who had first attacked Amanda filled the space. Tall and thick and freckled, like the Midwestern farm girls they showed in the old American movies. "Come with me." Her words were flat and emotionless. Maybe some kind of military training.

"Where are you taking me?" Amanda considered grabbing the child as some kind of bargaining chip but Astarte scampered out of the van before she could act.

"I'll drag you out of there if I have to." Again, no emotion, just matter-of-fact. Amanda sighed, slowly sat up and scooched herself toward the back of the van, the bright lights of the garage harsh on her eyes. The garage was large and clean, with three bays and a row of power tools and yard implements hanging neatly against the back wall. At some point they might make a good weapon. Grabbing her by the elbow, the guard steered her toward an enclosed center staircase, Eliza following. Astarte skipped along ahead, her dark, braided pigtails swinging as she hummed what sounded like "A Spoonful of Sugar" from the Mary Poppins movie.

"Astarte, can you wait for me?" Amanda asked. The girl spun around, smiling, and skipped back a few steps. Amanda pulled her arm away from the guard, who surprised Amanda by loosening her grip, and reached down to take Astarte's hand. "Where are we going?"

"Upstairs to have some lunch. Uncle Jefferson says you're going to come live with us for awhile."

Amanda forced her teeth to unclench and her lips to curve into a smile. She did her best to hold the girl's cobalt eyes. "Astarte, I'd really fancy a short stroll outside. I'm still feeling a bit under the weather. Will you show me around?"

The female guard turned to Eliza as if looking for the woman to intervene, but Eliza merely shook her head slowly. Nobody said anything. Odd as it seemed, apparently the decision rested with Astarte alone. It was almost as if nobody wanted to cross the young princess. The girl considered the request, her finger on her chin and her lips pursed. She took a deep breath and delivered her verdict. "I'm sorry, but no. Uncle Jefferson said we were to go straight upstairs."

Amanda allowed the girl to see her disappointment—manipulating the little princess might be her best chance for escape. Astarte looked at her sadly before brightening into a smile. "I know. I can have Aunt Eliza make you some hot tea. That will make you feel better. We'll have a floating tea party, just like Jane and Michael Banks."

Another Mary Poppins reference. The children in the story longed for attention from the grownups in their cloistered world. Did Astarte see Amanda as some kind of magical English nanny come to nurture her? Or perhaps the girl was just lonely and in need of a playmate.

Astarte opened the door to a staircase. Amanda scanned the room for some way to escape. Everything she had ever read or heard about self-defense told her to fight back or scream or do something to prevent being brought to an isolated place, but she was badly outnumbered and outmuscled. Each step brought her closer to a kind of attic prison, like some princess in a medieval fairy tale. But in a surreal and scary twist, it was not the princess but rather herself, the commoner, being held captive by a small army that deferred to a little girl known as the Fortieth Princess.

✛ ✛ ✛

Jefferson January watched the windowless van pull into the three-bay garage from his simple ranch-style home across the compound. He was the only man he knew whose garage was larger than his home. Of course neither edifice was as spacious or lavish as the underground bunker containing his most treasured pre-Columbian artifacts. Which was only fitting—he was holding the artifacts in trust for God.

He fingered three of those artifacts now, wondering again if they were the correct choices. With Amanda Spencer's abduction he now had Cameron Thorne's full attention—January's clumsy henchman with the broken nose could attest to that. It would have been easier if Thorne had been more responsive to January's earlier correspondence; his indifference had left January no choice but to orchestrate Amanda's kidnapping. He simply didn't have the luxury of time, of waiting for Thorne to clear his schedule and make his way back to Connecticut a second time while the cancer ate away at January's organs. In the end it was probably for the best—Thorne would be angry, but he also would be focused. Now that he had Thorne's attention, the next step would be to seduce the man, to convert him into a passionate believer of the amazing story these artifacts told. A story that would change the way Americans viewed both their history and their God.

The map stone had been a wise choice as an opening salvo, like a sultry smile from the blond across the bar. And the mini-brawl in the parking lot, though not planned, had gotten Thorne's blood boiling. The seduction would continue later in the day when he whisked Thorne away to a secret locale—the trip would serve as a flirtatious repartee, a musky perfume, a brush of knee against knee. Finally he would consummate the romance by allowing Thorne to view the priceless artifacts.

January smiled. The truth was he had never spent much time in bars, the consumption of alcohol being against his Mormon religion. But as a wealthy widower and church leader he had been the target of many attempted seductions over the past decade, before the ravages of cancer left him emaciated and stooped and addicted to OxyContin. He understood and accepted that the disease was part of God's plan, that causing his once-powerful 58-year-old frame to shrivel and decay was a way to focus him on the sacred mission that had been ordained for him. Just as it had been God's plan to take his dear wife from him at such a young age before she could give him children, thus allowing January to devote his life to Astarte and the fulfillment of her destiny.

Struggling with the weight of the three shoebox-sized stones, he wrestled them one by one into a custom-made wheeled case.

He sank heavily into his desk chair and dabbed his face with a handkerchief as he fought to fill his lungs with air. It was early for his next pill, but he didn't want to be distracted by pain so he popped another OxyContin and downed it with a swig of bottled water. He had the advantage over Thorne for now, but the same extraordinary resourcefulness that made Thorne such a desirable ally could also make him a formidable adversary. Which was why it was a good thing God was on Jefferson's side.

✛ ✛ ✛

Cam spent another half-hour trying to decipher the map stone, but he finally couldn't sit still any longer and made his way back to the rental car. The bright daylight surprised him—it was still early afternoon. It felt like days had passed since Amanda's abduction.

As he unlocked the car door his cell phone rang. Finally. "This is Cam."

"And this is Jefferson January." A nasally voice, almost wheezy. And calling from a different number than the one Cam had been dialing. Probably untraceable.

Cam took a deep breath. "Where's Amanda?"

"She is quite safe. For now. And she will remain that way as long as you cooperate."

"If you hurt her I'll hunt you down. I promise it."

"I'm hopeful there'll be no need for that, Mr. Thorne." Perhaps a hint of a Midwestern accent.

"I'm listening."

"First off, no more visits to the local police. I know about your meeting in Ledyard. You'll find I know just about everything that goes on around here."

"Fair enough. Let Amanda go, and there'll be no need for the police."

January barked out a short laugh. "Nice try." He lowered his voice, as if taking Cam into his confidence. "Here's the thing, Mr. Thorne. I'm not a young man, and I'm doing the Good Lord's work. I have stage four colon cancer—I'll be dead in a matter of months, if not weeks. So you'll find the normal things that motivate people won't work with me. I have more money than I will ever be able to spend, I'm not healthy enough for girls, I'm not afraid of jail since I'll be dead before they can lock me up." He paused to catch his breath. "But I am in a rush. I don't have the luxury of time, of convincing people like you to help me or to fit me into their busy schedule. So I take certain shortcuts when necessary."

Cam forced the rage from his voice. "So what do you want from me?"

"I want your full and undivided attention. Which I now believe I have. So now, after a worthwhile delay, we can have that meeting we did not have this morning. Meet me at the museum at three o'clock."

"What, so your thugs can take another swing at me?"

January exhaled. "That was a mistake. They were only supposed to be following you. I assure you it will not happen again."

"All right, I'll come. But only if you bring Amanda."

Another bark of a laugh. "No, no Mr. Thorne. You are hardly in a position to make demands. Amanda will stay with me a bit longer." He paused. "And Mr. Thorne. All those things that have gone through your mind the past few hours, all the horrible things you have imagined happening to her, all the perverse images that have forced their way into your consciousness—she has suffered none of those degradations. Yet."

CHAPTER 3

Cam knew he shouldn't be rash, but he also knew he was running out of options. Amanda was in danger, the police couldn't—or wouldn't—help, and he himself had no idea how to find and rescue her. But he knew someone who specialized in this kind of thing. He agonized over the decision for twenty minutes, desperate to come up with some other way to rescue Amanda. Finally he scrolled through the address book of his phone until he found a Rhode Island number. He hesitated before finally pushing the transmit button.

Jacob Whitewolf Salazar answered on the third ring. "Cameron Thorne. I'm surprised you kept my number."

"My phone does it automatically."

"All right then, I'm surprised you called."

"Me too. But I'm desperate."

Salazar was a mercenary, a gun-for-hire, a Special Ops soldier who had taken his unique set of army-trained skills into the private marketplace. A year ago he had been hired by a Vatican splinter group to prevent Cam and Amanda from uncovering secrets revealed by medieval artifacts scattered around New England, secrets that had the potential to undermine the authority of the Catholic Church. Salazar had ultimately failed in his mission, though he would claim he chose to abandon it when he began to find it distasteful. In either event, Cam bore a scar in his upper arm attesting to Salazar's skill with a handgun and his willingness to use it. "I'm listening."

Cam took a deep breath. "What is it they say about strange bedfellows? I need your help."

"This personal or professional?"

"Personal for me, professional for you." Cam explained the details of Amanda's abduction. "I think January's holding her someplace near the casino, probably on Pequot land. Can you help me?"

"I'm between jobs—I'm spending Thanksgiving with Rosalita. So I've got a few days."

Cam considered asking about the girl, but he had no stomach for small talk. Or for pretending he really cared about the mercenary and his daughter. "You okay that this might involve the Pequot tribe?" Salazar was himself half Narragansett; Cam expected that the tribes were at least loosely allied.

"Not a problem. It might even help me get some answers." He paused. "By the way, did you get a new dog?"

One of Salazar's overly zealous cohorts had killed Cam's dog, Pegasus, a crime for which Salazar profusely apologized; by contrast, Salazar had viewed Cam's gunshot wound as just part of a day's work. "Yeah, a Labrador Retriever named Venus." It was a strange question. Maybe it was Salazar's way of showing he was still sorry about Pegasus. "Why do you ask?"

"No reason." Salazar coughed. "Also, are you guys married yet?"

"Engaged."

"Oh."

Cam wasn't sure how this was supposed to work. "So what next? Do you need money?"

"I'll drive up there in a few hours, call you when I arrive. Go to your meeting with January and see what he wants. As for money, my fee is a thousand dollars per day, plus expenses." He paused. "So far nobody's ever stiffed me."

✝ ✝ ✝

Cam arrived at the museum a few minutes before three o'clock. He parked in the fire lane next to a tow zone sign and slammed his door shut—a feeble but heartfelt statement of defiance.

A man who looked like he should be guarding the President strode toward him, a flicker of irritation flashing in his eyes at Cam's choice of parking spaces. "My name's Vincent. This way, Mr. Thorne." Stiff, clean-cut. White shirt and navy slacks—a professional, unlike the two punks from the shuttle bus. He led Cam into the soaring museum atrium, passed the ladies room where Amanda had been abducted, and down a hallway to an unmarked door. "I'll need you to step inside." He pushed the door open; lights went on automatically.

Cam peered into an empty conference room. "Where's January?"

"As I said, please step inside. I'm going to search you. Then I'll bring you to Mr. January. Please empty your pockets."

Cam sighed. "Whatever." He stepped inside and dropped his cell phone, keys, wallet and chewing gum on the table. From a pocket in his windbreaker he removed a couple of granola bars and a case containing his insulin supplies.

Using a wand similar to the ones they used at airports, Vincent scanned Cam. He froze as the wand passed over Cam's left hip. "What's that?"

"Insulin pump." Cam lifted his coat to show the pager-sized device clipped to his waistband. "I'm not taking it off."

Vincent nodded. "Okay. Follow me."

Vincent—was that his first name or last?—led Cam back down the hallway, through the atrium and back outside.

"Where's January?" Cam asked.

"I'm taking you to him." They approached a black Ford Explorer.

"I'm supposed to be meeting January at the museum."

Vincent shrugged. "My orders were to search you and then bring you to Mr. January." He held the door open.

Cam got in. For now, January was calling the shots.

Vincent followed Route 2 back to the interstate and turned north on Route 95. Cam had assumed January was holding Amanda someplace on the Pequot land, but they were now far outside its borders. "Why the interstate?"

"Like I said, I'm taking you to Mr. January."

Less than five minutes later they crossed the state border into Rhode Island, and ten minutes after that whizzed by a highway sign for T.F. Green Airport in Providence. Cam pulled out his cell phone, surprised Vincent had allowed him to keep it. Apparently January didn't feel threatened by Cam, which itself was a bit disquieting. Cam texted Salazar. "On way to Providence airport. Should I get on plane?"

Salazar texted back immediately. "I think not much choice. My buddy works at airport. Give me 5."

A few minutes later another text arrived. "January has jet on runway. Destination Olney, Illinois." Cam deleted the texts.

He had guessed right; they were headed to the airport. But why Olney, Illinois?

✛ ✛ ✛

Amanda sat cross-legged on a quilt on the floor across from Astarte, both of them sipping imaginary tea from small porcelain tea cups. The chemical seemed to have left her system—the nausea had abated and her teeth no longer chattered. But the cold fear that had first washed over her in the museum bathroom remained; every few minutes she shivered, her body attempting to warm itself through muscle burn.

The room, windowless other than a couple of sky lights, ran along the front of the garage building, the bed and a dresser tucked under the sloped roofline. It was a typical young girl's bedroom, except that the art on the walls—a poster of Pocahontas from the Disney movie and a framed quilt featuring a Native American medicine wheel—reflected her Native American culture. That and the fact that a guard stood outside the door.

Amanda pointed to a backpack-like object hanging above Astarte's bed. "What's that?"

The girl stood on her bed and pulled the item off its hook. "It's a cradleboard. We use them to hold our babies." Astarte slid a doll into a flowered pouch attached to a two-foot-high wooden slab and leaned the polished slab against a wall; it stood almost vertical, on small legs. "This way the baby can see the world."

Amanda nodded. It made sense. Why should a baby always have to look up into the sky?

Astarte then slipped a leather strap around her forehead and hung the board down her back. "The mom can also carry her baby like this." She smiled. "But it gives me a headache."

Amanda spent a couple hours playing with Astarte, figuring her best chance of escape was to somehow win the girl's trust. They chatted as they played, Amanda learning that the girl did not have any friends other than a few kids she saw at church and was home-schooled by Eliza. Her favorite toys were her collection of Native American dolls, but when she grew bored with them she downloaded a video game called SimCity to an Apple computer on her desk and showed Amanda how to create and manage virtual cities. "If I'm going to be the princess, I need to know about buildings," she explained as she tinkered with the city's infrastructure. Advanced stuff for an eight-year-old, but might she be better off in the long run riding a bike to the park with some friends?

"How did you get so good at computers?" Amanda asked.

"Uncle Jefferson taught me." She pulled out what looked to be some type of smart phone. "Aunt Eliza says I'm too young to have a phone but Uncle Jefferson says I need to learn about tech-...." She swallowed, making room in her mouth for the big word. "Technology."

Amanda also learned that January and Eliza were not her real aunt and uncle, but had somehow gained custody of her when her mother died when Astarte was a toddler. In fact, Eliza and January were siblings, not husband and wife. The girl didn't seem abused or neglected in any traditional sense of the word, though the isolation—not to mention the princess thing—was hardly a recipe for a healthy upbringing.

"I saw you kiss Mr. Thorne at the museum. He's very handsome. Are you two going to get married, like Ariel and Eric in *Little Mermaid*?"

"How do you know his name?"

Astarte shrugged. "Uncle Jefferson talks about him a lot. He needs Mr. Thorne's help."

That explained why she had been abducted. Not that it justified it in any way—why not just ask for help if they needed it? Amanda forced a smile. "In any event, I agree, he is very handsome. And I do intend to marry him." She studied the girl, whose view of the world seemed inordinately shaped by children's movies. "But I love him because of who he is inside." She moved closer. "Let me tell you a story. When I first met Cameron, I had a horrible rash on my face from being out in the sun too long. But he still liked me, even though I looked like a swamp monster."

Astarte nodded. "Sort of like *Beauty and the Beast,* right?"

"Yes, I suppose so."

"As a princess, I'll have to marry a prince someday. Probably someone who Uncle Jefferson selects for me. That's what happens with princesses."

Amanda considered this for a moment. "It's generally not a good thing to marry for reasons other than love, Astarte. For example, what if the man your uncle chooses for you fancies fishing and you do not—what would you do together?"

The girl put her finger on her chin and raised her eyes, as she seemed to do when weighing matters of importance. "Why," she said suddenly, "that's easy. I'd learn to fish so I could go with him."

Amanda couldn't help but respond with a small laugh. "Useful attitude, that."

During their tea party, Amanda could hear a television down the hall. Some preacher was making an impassioned plea for his audience to repent and be rescued by Jesus. Amanda would settle for just being rescued.

"Is the tea making you feel better, Miss Amanda?"

"Yes, much, thank you." Eliza had made her an actual cup, plus served them both egg salad sandwiches for lunch. She took another imaginary sip. She had spent enough time winning the girl's trust. She stood. "I think it's time for me to leave now. Can you please show me out?"

Astarte frowned. "I'm sorry, but you must stay. Uncle Jefferson insists on it. And he always gets what he wants."

"I see." Amanda tried another approach. "When I was a little girl my mother always sent me outside to play after lunch. I especially liked hopscotch."

Astarte's face brightened. "I love hopscotch!"

Amanda stood and reached for the girl's hand. "Well, let's go out and play." It was a long-shot, but she didn't exactly have a lot of options. Leaning down, she continued in a whisper. "But let's leave Eliza and the other adults here. It'll be just us two girls, right then?"

They grabbed their jackets and Astarte reached for a piece of chalk as she opened the door. The guard sat in a kitchen chair in the hallway. "Judith, you stay here," Astarte said. "We're going outside to play."

The sentry's eyes narrowed as she weighed her options. She had a small nose and mouth that made her face seem too petite for her oversized body. "Your uncle told me to stay with Miss Spencer." She stood.

Astarte crossed her arms in front of her chest. "And I'm telling you to stay here." She glared up at the woman for a second before taking Amanda's hand and leading her down a hallway to the kitchen of the above-garage apartment.

"Aunt Eliza, we are going outside," she repeated. "You and Judith can stay here."

Eliza, seated in front of a small television, shifted in her chair. "Are you certain Uncle would approve?"

"Yes," she said imperiously. "He likes me to get exercise."

A sliding glass door off the kitchen opened onto a small deck with a wooden staircase leading to the back yard below. Amanda's heart raced as the girl heaved the door open—was the guard really going to obey Astarte and let them go outside alone? And was Eliza really going to allow it? She listened for the sound of footsteps in the hallway. Nothing.

Ten seconds later they stood in the backyard, a grassy area a little smaller than a tennis court surrounded by trees on three sides and the garage on the fourth. Amanda peered through the trees, wondering what lay beyond. No doubt the guard was watching from a window above. But Amanda was a fast runner, an ex-gymnast who could still run a 5K race in well under 20 minutes. Not that she had a plan once she raced into the woods—she had no cell phone, didn't know where she was, and wasn't equipped to spend a November night in the wilderness. She shivered again.

Astarte skipped over to a concrete slab and began drawing a hopscotch board. "I know what you're thinking, Miss Amanda," she said matter-of-factly. "If you want to try to run away, I won't say anything. But I do wish you'd stay." A small tear glistened on the girl's eyelash.

Amanda crouched down so she was at eye level and took Astarte's hands. Could she leave this lonely girl alone with these odd people? "It was wrong of your uncle to bring me here without my permission. You said he did so because he needs our help. Do you know why?"

The girl shook her head, her pigtails swinging back and forth.

"Well, I promise I will come back as soon as I can," Amanda said as Astarte sniffled. "Do you know what's beyond those trees?"

"No. I've never gone back there. Aunt Eliza said there are bears in the woods."

No doubt lions and tigers as well. Amanda took a deep breath. "Well, wish me luck. I'll return as soon as I am able." She kissed Astarte quickly on the cheek. "I had a splendid time playing with you today."

A quick stretch of her legs, another deep breath and she turned and sprinted across the open yard toward the woods. She half-expected a shot to ring out, the guard taking aim at her from up on the balcony above like in those old World War II prisoner camp escape movies. Crouching and running in a zigzag pattern she quickly reached the edge of the woods and leapt over a short stone wall into a dense thicket. Barbed branches pulled at her legs and bit at her ankles as she pushed deeper, the canopy of trees diffusing what little late afternoon light remained. She chose speed over stealth, grunting and thrashing through the brush, one hand in front of her face to protect her eyes. After stumbling twice she changed her stride, lifting her knees high to prevent being tripped up again. Her ears strained for the sound of pursuers, but she was making too much noise herself to hear anything other than her own labored breathing and the angry snarls and snaps of the undergrowth as she fought through it.

She plowed along for almost a minute, the scratches and pricks scarring her skin just as hope grew in her heart. And then it was over. She almost ran face-first into a fence, the chain-links appearing seemingly out of nowhere in the darkened forest as she elbowed aside a tree branch. She got her arms up just in time, impaling the side of her wrist on barbed wire but fortunately sparing her eyes. "Damn!" She stopped, carefully twisted the rusted wire from her skin and peered up at the metal barrier. Probably eight feet high, with lines of barbed wire strung in loops along both the midpoint and the top to prevent anyone from attempting to climb over. Sucking on the blood seeping from her wrist, she walked along the fence line, kicking at the bottom, probing for an opening. But the fencing ran deep into the ground, the earth tamped down solid—she would need a shovel and a good hour of digging to make even the crudest of tunnels.

Desperate, she ran along the perimeter of the fence. It continued for about 50 yards before making a right-angle turn back toward the garage. She reversed, ran back to her starting point plus another 20 yards and hit another right angle turn. Apparently the fence surrounded the entire garage property, equally effective at keeping visitors both in and out. That must be why the guard hadn't come after her yet.

But she couldn't give up. The ground in this corner of the property was moist. She found a thick branch, dropped to her knees and stabbed at the soil beneath the fence, prying dirt away until she found the bottom row of the embedded chain links. Stabbing at the ground angrily, she loosened the dirt, scooping it away with a flat stone like a dog digging for a bone. After a couple of minutes she had dug a cavity the size of a cereal bowl beneath the barrier. Wedging the end of her branch as far under the fence as she could, she stood and pushed down on the branch, using it as a fulcrum to pry upward the bottom of the fence. It bent back a bit, but the bottom was too sharp for her to grab it firmly and really force it upward. She removed her tennis shoes and yanked off her sport socks, then rolled her socks into a ball and used them to pad her palms and fingers. Alternately working with the branch and her hands, she succeeded in raising the meshed fence a couple of inches and banked her gain by cramming a cobblestone between her branch and the sharp bottom of the fence. A cat could probably squeeze through now.

Rolling to her feet, she slid her shoes back on, quickly found another thick branch and dug in again next to the first branch, prying the fence open another couple of inches and again securing her work with a small fieldstone. Blood ran down her wrist and onto her hand but she didn't care. One more branch, plus another stone, and she had succeeded in wedging back a span of fence about 18 inches wide. Wide enough for her to squirm through once she made it deeper. Sweating profusely now, she rubbed a dirty hand across her brow and again rolled to her feet to find another branch—

"That's enough, honey."

Amanda's entire body sagged. Judith stood over her, a steel flashlight held menacingly at her hip. The guard pointed her chin up toward a security camera mounted high on a nearby tree. "I figured I'd let you finish digging your little hole before I came to get you."

Amanda had been too focused on the fence to look for cameras. "How very kind of you."

"It'd be easier for both of us if you walked. But I can drag your ass back to the compound if I have to."

Amanda stood. They were alone in the woods, and the guard no doubt had a cell phone. Judith seemed to sense her thoughts. "Don't try anything cute."

They walked a few steps, Judith half a stride ahead, when suddenly the brawny woman pivoted and thrust the butt of the steel flashlight backward, deep into Amanda's gut. Amanda didn't feel anything for a second or two, then it was as if her entire body short-circuited. Her muscles spasmed and she flopped to the ground, her heart and lungs shutting down for a few seconds as if someone had hit the off button on her central nervous system. It hurt like nothing she had ever felt before, her entire innards screaming in agony. She had once fallen off the uneven bars and landed on her back in a gymnastic meet and it felt like an elephant was sitting on her chest, but this was many times worse. She writhed on the ground, coughing and gasping, unable to even focus her eyes, until slowly her internal organs restarted themselves and a bit of air and blood began to flow through her body. From a long way off, high above her, she heard Judith's voice. "That's for trying to escape. If you try it again, you best be sure you succeed."

✛ ✛ ✛

The Explorer snaked its way into a back entrance to the airport, stopping near the tail of a mid-size jet with the markings

'Learjet 45' on its fuselage and a metal staircase leading to an open hatch. Vincent stepped out and motioned for Cam to follow. Cam checked his watch—almost four o'clock, the sun only a few degrees above the late November horizon. He zipped his windbreaker and trudged up the stairs.

"As soon as you take a seat, we'll be on our way," Vincent said.

"Where are we going?"

"As I said, to meet Mr. January."

Four grey leather seats ran along each side of the jet. Cam took the front seat on the left, Vincent the second seat on the right, probably so he could keep an eye on Cam. A maroon curtain separated the cockpit from the cabin. "Is January up there?" Cam asked Vincent. Vincent merely shrugged and opened a fishing magazine.

They took off immediately, flying toward the setting sun visible in the southwestern sky, the jet's speed almost keeping pace with the rotation of the earth to create a seemingly never-ending sunset. Turning his body in his seat so Vincent couldn't see what he was doing, Cam removed the picture of Amanda from his wallet. Was she okay? Frightened, no doubt. But was she actually being abused? By the time they began their descent an hour and a half later the sun was just beginning to kiss the horizon. Cam munched on an energy bar; he needed to pay attention to his blood sugar even as he focused on rescuing Amanda. Fifteen minutes later, and 25,000 feet lower, the glow of dusk illuminated their landing at a small airfield surrounded by miles of flat farm land, the landscape checkerboarded by dozens of narrow access roads cut into the crop fields.

As the jet rolled to a stop in front of a simple rectangular hangar building, the maroon cockpit curtain opened. A long-armed man wearing a light blue golf shirt sat slouched in the leather copilot seat. He smiled and gave Cam the same salute he had offered at yesterday's breakfast. "No doubt you have deduced that I am Jefferson January," he wheezed.

Cam studied him. His adversary appeared underinflated, as if the air had slowly leaked from his once-robust body and his shell had folded in on itself. His eyes, blue and dilated, protruded from a graying face marked by sharp crags, like bedrock blasted away alongside a superhighway. A few loose strands of gray hair were combed neatly back from his forehead. He pulled himself into a standing position and pushed his tall but bent frame past the curtain. "I suggest we get right to work."

"Where's Amanda?" Cam remained seated. As January approached Cam noticed a pungent odor, sort of the way old, wet grass clippings smelled as they began to decay. When he was a child, his cat died of leukemia and Cam had noticed that same smell in the weeks before her death.

January ignored the question. "Follow me. We have much to do." He coughed into a handkerchief as Vincent pushed open the cabin door, then used the back of the handkerchief to dab his brow. "I need your help. You want to ensure Miss Spencer's safety. The sooner we get our work done the sooner we both get what we want. It really is a simple equation."

Cam remained in his chair as the pilot followed Vincent out of the plane. January continued. "I am one hundred percent certain European explorers have been on this continent for over two thousand years, since before Jesus. And I have the artifacts to prove it." He gestured toward the open door, sighing as he saw Cam refusing to follow. "We both know, Mr. Thorne, that at some point you are going to get out of that seat, follow me down those stairs and be suitably impressed by my artifacts."

"Not true." Cam sprung from his chair and spun January by the shoulder, pulling him away from the door, and shoved him face-first against the concave bulkhead. He pushed against the man's back, pinning him in an awkward, arched position. The fury of the past day coursed through him, but the attack was a calculated one: Cam wanted to test the resolve of his enemy. "It's possible instead I'll squeeze your neck until your face turns purple." Vincent and the pilot had disembarked, so it was no idle threat.

January craned his neck to peer over his shoulder and offered a small, wet smile, his teeth long and yellowed. "No doubt you could. And no doubt you won't. In the end, you will do the rational thing. Which is why I saw no need for Mr. Vincent to stay. Now release me, Mr. Thorne. As I said, we have work to do."

The response had been logical and fearless. January understood that even if Cam could overpower him, Cam was still stuck in Illinois and Amanda would still be his captive. Cam shifted his weight and stepped back, releasing his adversary. January would not be easily intimidated. For now Cam had no choice but to play the dying man's game.

✠ ✠ ✠

Amanda allowed the hot water to pour over her body, washing away dirt and sweat and more than a few tears. No matter how hot the water, her body still shuddered periodically. Even worse, when she breathed deeply or turned suddenly a sharp pain shot through her core—the flashlight blow may have cracked a rib. Thankfully there was no blood in her urine. But worse than the pain was the fear that numbed her core. She wanted to be home, sitting in front of the fire playing Scrabble with Cam. Or kayaking on the lake. Or jogging along a wooded trail. Anything but … this.

Surely Cam had gone to the police, and surely he was trying to find her. But how seriously did police take these kinds of missing person reports, especially in a place like Foxwoods where alcohol and gambling frequently contributed to lovers' quarrels? She exhaled cautiously, wincing. Other than continuing to befriend Astarte, she really had no plan for escape. And she still had no clue what January wanted from her.

She stepped out of the bathroom wrapped in a towel, her teeth chattering. Eliza waited in the hallway. Bowing slightly, she handed Amanda her shoes, sweatpants, a sweatshirt and a new pair of socks and white underpants. "I'm washing your clothes. They should be dry in a half-hour."

Amanda crossed her arms over her chest, swallowing the stab of pain. "What do you want from me?" It was tough to appear menacing while shivering in a towel, but Amanda hoped her anger would come through.

Eliza's painted, small-toothed smile remained frozen on her face. "Astarte is doing her lessons. She should be back shortly." With that, she motioned Amanda to return to Astarte's bedroom across the hall, offered a small curtsey and walked away.

There was little chance there was anything in a young girl's bedroom that could be used as a weapon, but after dressing Amanda rifled through the drawers and bookcases looking for something that might come in handy. The best she came up with was some twine. She shuddered at the thought of wrapping the rope around Astarte's neck, even as a bluff. But she stuffed it in her pocket—at some point she might have to do something drastic to win her freedom.

Astarte burst in a few minutes later. "I brought you a cookie. Aunt Eliza didn't want me to but I insisted." With two hands she held out a sugar cookie balanced on a napkin.

Amanda couldn't help but smile. "Thank you." She gestured at a cot that had been brought into the room. "Am I meant to sleep here tonight?"

Astarte grinned. "Yes. Usually Aunt Eliza sleeps with me. But she snores."

"I'll do my best not to." Amanda sat on the cot. "Astarte, do you have any family other than Eliza and Mr. January? Cousins or anything?"

"No. They took care of me after my mom died. I was only two. That's when we moved to Connecticut." Her deep blue eyes clouded, but Amanda needed to learn more about the young princess.

"You mean you didn't always live here?"

"We used to live in Salty Lake."

"Do you mean Salt Lake City?"

The girl grinned. "Oops, yes. But I don't remember it."

"So you're not part of the Pequot tribe?"

"No. Uncle Jefferson is friends with the Pequot people—he's helping them with their museum. But I'm Mandan."

"Mandan?" That explained the blue eyes. Native American legend and oral history was one of the best sources of evidence of pre-Columbian visitation to America, so Amanda had read up on Native American history. The Mandan were the tribe of so-called White Indians. Lewis and Clark visited them in North Dakota in the early 1800s at the behest of President Jefferson who, because of the Mandan's European-like appearance and lifestyle, wondered if they might be one of the Lost Tribes of Israel. Others believed them to be descended from Prince Madoc, a 12th-century Welsh explorer said to have found his way into the central part of North America. Whatever their origins, the tribe was largely wiped out by smallpox in the mid-1800s; the few remaining members merged into other tribes. "Aren't the Mandan extinct?"

"Like the dinosaurs?"

"Yes, I suppose." Which means they hardly needed a princess. Unless Astarte's destiny was to rule peoples other than the Mandan.

The girl furrowed her brow. "That's silly, Miss Amanda. I'm not dead. I'm right here next to you."

CHAPTER 4

Cam followed January through the terminal building marked "Olney-Noble Airport." Vincent waited at the curb, his red Chevy pickup a beacon in the fading light. Cam noted it was a full-size, four-wheel drive model with the body riding high above 17-inch tires. Apparently they would be going off-road.

"Would you like me to drive, Mr. January?" The guard eyed Cam suspiciously.

"No. I'll drive. You stay here. Mr. Thorne and I have much to discuss. And much to see."

Cam climbed into the passenger seat. Too late now to turn back. Vincent pulled out a blindfold. "Should I put this on him?"

January shook his head. "No. I'm hoping Mr. Thorne is so impressed by what he sees that he wants to come back many times." He offered a wet smile. "To do that he'll need to know the way."

They drove for about twenty minutes, January's crooked body hunched over the steering wheel, his claw-like hands guiding the truck with surprising competence. The land looked much like it did from the sky—flat and colorless, the monotony interrupted only by an occasional farmhouse. As if reading Cam's thoughts, January spoke. "I'm not old, Mr. Thorne, I'm just dying." There was no self-pity in the comment. But Cam sensed an almost fanatic resolve in the man, a belief that true greatness was within his grasp if only he could survive long enough to make a final desperate stretch and ensnare it in his bony grasp. Cam still had no idea if his adversary was lucid or delusional. Either way, it seemed the best way to ensure Amanda's safety was to continue to placate him.

January snapped on a gospel music station and sang along, loud and off-key but full of passion. When, mercifully, the song ended, January spoke. "We are in southern Illinois, approximately 120 miles due east of St. Louis, not far from the Indiana border. Curiously, this area is known as Little Egypt. Some say it's because of the fertile farm land, similar to the Nile Delta." He shook his head. "That seems like a stretch to me. I believe it's because of the many Egyptian-like artifacts found in the area."

Cam had never been in this part of the country. "Which is why we're here."

"Precisely."

It was now dark, almost 6:00 local time. January turned onto a dirt road cutting through muddy fields of what had been stalks of corn. January coughed into his handkerchief. "I only come here at night." He flicked off his headlights as they bounced along. "We are, or soon will be, trespassing. I apologize in advance if some angry farmer plants a pitchfork in your backside. I usually wait until after midnight, but we are short on time."

A few times January careened off the road, but he quickly corrected his line and continued along, occasionally turning left or right as he made his way deeper along the maze-like route. January took a deep breath. "Have you ever studied the Burrows Cave artifacts?"

The artifacts weren't really relevant to Cam's Templar research, so he hadn't paid much attention to them. "No." But he guessed they hadn't flown to Olney, Illinois just to tour the corn fields.

"In some ways, that is surprising. You are one of the leading researchers of early exploration of America. Burrows Cave is as important to that study as the Kensington Rune Stone and the Newport Tower. I myself have spent years studying them."

"Is that where the map stone you sent me came from?"

"Yes. That and about 5,000 other artifacts." January wiped his chin with the back of his sleeve and took a deep breath. "In the 1980s a truck driver named Russell Burrows was walking through the woods looking for arrowheads and Civil War artifacts and stumbled into an underground cavern." A thick row of trees appeared dimly in the moonlight beyond the farmland out Cam's window; apparently some of the area remained uncultivated. January made a quick right turn, cutting through a narrow cornfield and heading straight for the wooded area.

January continued. "The cave was filled with carved stones, as if it served as some kind of ancient repository. The carvings reflected a hodgepodge of eastern Mediterranean cultures—Phoenician, Egyptian, early Christian, Jewish, Roman, Northern African. The one thing the artifacts had in common was they all dated from about 2,000 to 2,500 years ago. Over the next few years, Burrows removed thousands of artifacts from the cave."

Angry as he was, Cam was curious about the artifacts. "Didn't he show them to anyone?"

"He tried. In fact, he brought them to the state university, and also to the state archeologist. I don't have to tell you how that often goes—they laughed in his face."

Cam nodded. The find would have been so outside the scope of what mainstream archeologists believed about American history that they would have dismissed it almost reflexively. As a group, archeologists were the most close-minded people Cam had ever met. His comment to the Freemasons about archeologists putting their fingers in their ears and yelling hoax was only slightly hyperbolic. Even so, that didn't mean the Burrows Cave find was legit. "I have to believe that even the most skeptical archeologist would at least take a look at Burrows' pieces. Why did they dismiss them?"

"There was nothing suspicious about the pieces, other than the fact they belonged along the shores of the Mediterranean and were found instead in Illinois. But the experts all wanted Burrows to take them to the cave so they could see the artifacts *in situ*. You know how archeologists are—they don't trust anything they don't pull out of the ground themselves. Not that they're likely to ever find anything sitting on their asses in some office. Well, anyway, Burrows couldn't show them the cave. He was trespassing, like us, sneaking in at night to haul artifacts out. Including a few gold pieces. And there were some other gold figurines in the cave that were too big for him to get out. Obviously he wanted to keep those for himself. So he never showed anyone the cave. And so nobody believed it was real."

Who would put gold in a cave as part of a hoax? "What, did they think he was making this stuff in his basement?"

"Exactly. Not that they had any evidence." January flicked on the headlights and angled the truck from side to side, apparently using the lights to locate some kind of landmark in the trees. "Ah, there it is." He veered left and stopped in a small gap between two trees, one of which had a bicycle reflector nailed at eye level to its trunk. "Come on. Follow me." He slipped a daypack over his shoulders before reaching into the back seat and pulling out a shotgun. "Remington 1100, semi-automatic," he announced. "I'm not a big fan of pitchforks."

Stooped as he was, January showed surprising agility and energy, using the shotgun to swat away branches as he pushed through the underbrush and down a slight slope into the woods. They walked a quarter mile along a faded path, the topography less flat than the farm land they had passed through, the crunching of their feet on the carpet of leaves masking the nocturnal sounds of the forest. Just as on the plane, Cam could easily have overpowered his adversary, even with the shotgun, but then what? Instead he followed dutifully, January stopping occasionally to pan his flashlight in an arc before plowing along. "In the summer the mosquitoes are unbearable. I don't know how Burrows did it, coming out here almost every night to collect artifacts."

January was breathing hard and sweating even in the cool night air, the hike obviously a huge strain on his system. But his eyes shone with a feverish excitement as he walked in a circle at the crest of a ridge, kicking at the ground. The ridge overlooked a valley, and in the distance the moonlight glistened on the surface of a small river. Cam recalled the map stone and the series of rivers leading to the cave marked on the map.

After a few minutes of kicking the ground January dropped to his knees, rested his shotgun against a tree stump and brushed away a pile of leaves and branches. "Good. Nobody's disturbed it." His flashlight reflected off a round PVC tube sticking six inches out of the ground. "Took me nine years to find the cave. Still haven't found a way inside. Burrows dynamited the entrance shut and covered it with dirt."

"Why?"

"Because he's a smart S.O.B. He removed a fortune in gold and also a few thousand artifacts. If the landowner ever found out he would have accused Burrows of theft. But the landowner never knew he was here, never even knew there was a cave on his land. Still doesn't. By dynamiting the entrance, Burrows made sure nobody would ever find the crime scene."

"A victimless crime. So how did you find the cave?"

"I had a pretty good idea of the general area based on local scuttlebutt, but we were still talking hundreds of acres. So I brought in some mining experts. Ground penetrating radar. Seismic and resistivity testing. Hydrology maps. Basically the same kinds of things a mining company would do before drilling. Once we thought we found a promising spot, we drilled. Ever play Battleship when you were a kid? Eventually, if you take enough shots, you're bound to hit something. Cost me a fortune because we had to sneak out here at night, then pay the workers to keep quiet about it." He looked up at Cam. "Some that wouldn't keep quiet had to be dealt with in other ways."

January was obsessed, desperate and on a mission from God—no doubt he would not hesitate to kill those who crossed him. How far would Cam have to go with this to ensure Amanda's safety?

"I finally found the cave a few months ago," January continued. "But cancer found me around the same time. And the land owner refuses to sell; over time I could convince him, but that's the one thing I don't have."

January removed his backpack and bungee-corded his flashlight to an overhanging branch. From the pack he pulled out a stapler–sized plastic fish. The fish was attached to a black power cord; the other end connected to a video monitor he placed on a boulder near the PVC pipe. January had taped a small flashlight to the bottom of the fish. "This is a basic ice fishing camera. You drop it in through a hole in the ice and the image comes up on the monitor." He flicked on the power switch and flashlight and lowered the fish down the PVC pipe. "Pretty appropriate, since the fish is a symbol of Jesus." He barked out a short laugh. "I guess that makes me the Fisher King of the King Arthur legends, old and injured, and you my Galahad come to help me find the Holy Grail."

"The Holy Grail?"

"Not literally. But many theologians believe the Holy Grail is really a symbol of God's grace, available only to those who are spiritually advanced and pure. As I said, God chose me to find His true word. Perhaps He chose you as well."

Cam let the comment hang. Sometimes a fish was just a fish. Even when it was really a camera. "How far down is the cave?" He couldn't take his eyes off the monitor. Was he really standing atop a cave filled with ancient artifacts? He glanced quickly at the river in the distance—if the cave symbol on the map stone marked his present location, the river in the distance led to the Ohio River and eventually the Mississippi.

"About 30 feet." January eased the camera down the hole until the line went slack. "Bottom." He pulled the cord to raise the camera up a few feet and turned the monitor toward Cam. "Have a look."

Cam had craned his neck to view the monitor; he now knelt to view the images straight on. He almost jumped back as an angry face—teeth bared, nostrils flaring, eyes narrowed—stared back at him. The fearsome face was carved onto a wall of the cave like a prehistoric Jack-O-Lantern. Cam studied it. "He seems to have Negroid features."

"I think he's a sentry. The Phoenicians often employed Africans as guards and soldiers." January rotated the camera 90 degrees. "We're in a small room." The outline of an arched doorway led out to what was presumably the main cave complex.

"How big was that face?" It was tough to get any kind of scale.

"About two feet tall." January rotated the camera another 90 degrees. "There. Take a look at that."

A series of hieroglyphic-like markings appeared on the cave wall opposite the sentry. "This script matches a lot of the artifacts Burrows pulled out of the cave," January said. "It's a variation of Phoenician. But so much of it is covered with dust that I haven't been able to translate it." Whatever it was it didn't look like any Native American writings or carvings Cam had ever seen.

January raised the camera another foot. Above the writing the camera shone on a square alcove, the size of a small television, recessed into the cave wall. A pair of flat round pottery pieces sat inside the alcove. "Lamps?" Cam asked.

"Yes. Probably filled with oil." January flicked at the camera, the lens angle changing as the fish bounced slowly. "You can see the soot along the top of the niche."

"Makes sense. You'd need light in there, especially if you wanted to read what was written on the wall."

January rotated the camera another 90 degrees, aiming toward the back of the room. After fiddling for a few seconds he grunted. "There." A stone platform ran along the wall. As a cold wind blew across the ridge, Cam peered in, waiting for the image to settle. Atop the platform lay a skeleton, the skull turned toward the middle of the room, its eyes staring vacantly into the camera. Cam shivered, unable to tear his eyes away. "I see why you think the carving was a sentry."

"Yes. He's guarding the corpse. The writing is probably some kind of obituary. This is a crypt, one of a number Burrows found in the cave. He was careful not to disturb any of the bodies or burial sites."

Cam swallowed. The body probably hadn't been disturbed in 2,000 years. "If you can get that body, you can do DNA testing on the molars." Which, if January was correct, would totally rewrite history. Amazing.

"Exactly." January coughed into his handkerchief. "But it won't be me who gets the body, Mr. Thorne. It will have to be you."

For the first time Cam actually considered helping his adversary. January happened to be a nut case, but that didn't mean the cave itself was a hoax. He felt a moment of pity for the dying man. "So you won't ever know the truth about this—about the cave, about the body."

January grinned, his eyes dilated and afire. "Oh, that's not true. I'll know the truth long before you will. Where I'm going there are no secrets."

✛ ✛ ✛

The 7:30 display on the digital clock in January's pickup surprised Cam. Was it possible they had been at the cave site for only an hour? The images from the cave, and the apparent ramifications of the find, were enough to fill weeks of space in his brain. There was no longer any need for him to feign interest in January's artifacts as a ruse to protect Amanda. If the whole thing was a hoax, it was an incredibly elaborate one. And one that would seem to be beyond the capacity of a single Illinois truck driver. Cam had been tempted to grab a shovel and begin digging right then, in the dark.

January guided the pickup back through the cornfields toward the airport. "Like I said, Burrows was trespassing so he never brought anyone to the cave. But he took out thousands of artifacts, sold most of them for twenty, thirty bucks each to a local antiques dealer. Showed up at her door a couple of mornings every week, covered in dirt, with a satchel full of carved stones."

Decent money, but not enough to get rich on. Especially when you figure in the time it would have taken Burrows to carve the pieces, assuming it was a hoax. "Anybody ever study the stones? You know, scientifically?"

January nodded. "There were quite a few people, amateur historians, who believed Burrows' story. They bought the artifacts and studied them. What was interesting, and this is what first caught my attention, was that there was not a single piece of hard evidence that called into question the artifacts themselves—no microscopic debris from modern tools, no linguistic error on any text stone, no image inconsistent with ancient religious practices. All the skepticism was centered on Burrows himself."

"And the fact he wouldn't show anyone the cave."

"Which didn't make sense then, but makes perfect sense now that we know he was trespassing."

In the end, the Burrows side of the equation was really irrelevant; if the artifacts were tested and proven to be authentic, it didn't matter who found them. What was fascinating was the question of who carved the stones and how they got to Illinois. "So who were these cave people?"

"Good question, one I've spent 20 years trying to answer. I've retained many experts and paid them dearly over the years, but none of them can give me a definitive answer." January turned out of the cornfields and onto the main road. "The one thing they all agree on is that the pieces all tie back to the Mediterranean region, ranging from 500 BC to the time of Christ.

Somehow these explorers made their way to the Gulf of Mexico and then up the Mississippi River."

Cam sensed there was more to the story, or at least more to January's version of the story, than the man was letting on. For that matter, Cam still had no idea what exactly January wanted from him. As if sensing that Cam was about to ask questions he didn't want to answer, January pulled out his cell phone and called Vincent. "Have the plane ready to take off in ten minutes."

Cam had experienced firsthand how dismissive and narrow-minded the mainstream academic community could be. Even so, was it really possible Burrows had stumbled upon the greatest archeological find in the nation's history and that the experts had passed it off as a fraud or hoax without proper investigation?

Five minutes later they turned into the airport. The leather seats in the jet's cabin had been reconfigured so two of the seats on the right side faced each other, with a small table between them. A white cloth covered irregularly-shaped items on the table.

January dropped into the rear-facing seat and motioned for Cam to sit opposite. "If you were to research Burrows Cave on the Internet, you'd be hard-pressed to find any commentator supporting its authenticity."

"But I don't imagine they have seen the cave you just showed me."

"No. But let's put the cave aside for a minute. Fascinating as it is, there is nothing in there that would have been impossible for Burrows to fabricate. The carvings, the lamps, even the body could have been planted." He made an effort to lift himself higher in his chair. "In the end, we must examine the artifacts."

He folded the white cloth back onto itself, revealing a 12-inch high carving of a human head. "It is a piece of uncommon beauty and grace, a sculpture no amateur like Russell Burrows could hope to produce. Please hold it tightly as we are about to take off."

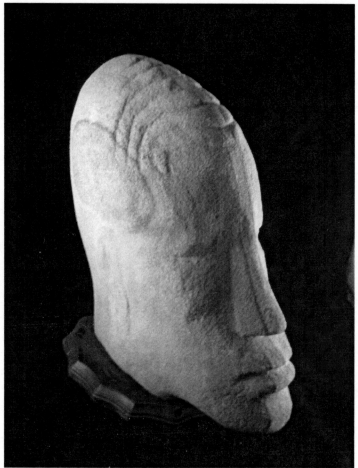

BURROWS CAVE STONE HEAD

Cam turned the sandstone sculpture toward him, slowly rotating it and examining it on all sides. As January said, the sculpture was a gracefully elongated, artistic rendition of an African—perhaps Egyptian—face. It was similar to the sentry carving in the cave, with the forehead slanting back, a long narrow nose and prominent lips. It reminded Cam of one of the giant carvings on Easter Island. But artistry didn't necessarily establish authenticity. If January was trying to make a case for the legitimacy of Burrows' pieces, he was going to have to do better. "My understanding is that sandstone is pretty easy to work with."

"For a trained sculptor, yes. Not for Russell Burrows. He was a truck driver and before that a prison guard."

"Hardly an airtight case. Maybe his wife did it."

January grinned, his yellowing teeth wet with saliva, seemingly oblivious to the plane hurtling down the runway. "Excellent, Mr. Thorne. I was hoping you'd be a tougher sell than that—extraordinary claims require extraordinary proof, and I want you to be completely convinced. How about this then? I've had the sandstone analyzed by a geologist. That type of sandstone predominates in northern Africa."

Cam nodded. It was unlikely Burrows would have imported the stone as part of a hoax. "So it was brought here by some Mediterranean seafarer?"

"Probably as some kind of funerary object. The head represented an ancestor, or even a god. But the features, and the stone itself, take us back to northern Africa and the Middle East."

"If you're talking seafarers from that area of the world, you're probably talking the Phoenicians, maybe 500 BC, right?"

January nodded, smiling, seemingly pleased Cam had chosen that date. "Precisely, yes." Hand shaking, he wrestled with the cap on a bottle of water. Finally he pried the top off and drank noisily, spilling a few drops down his chin as the plane nosed its way into the air. "Now, please take a look at the middle artifact, the small black stone."

Cam pulled the cloth back further and cupped a smooth, calculator-sized stone in his palm. Carved into it was a 7-stemmed candelabrum along with some form of ancient writing. "This looks like a Jewish menorah, except I think menorahs have nine arms instead of seven," Cam said.

BURROWS CAVE MENORAH STONE

January nodded. "Very astute. Continue."

Cam assumed more valuable he was to his manic host, the more leverage he would have to ensure Amanda's safety. "And the writing is the same style as on the wall of the cave." He paused. "And I think also the map stone."

"Again, correct."

"So what's the significance of this stone?"

"First, the fact the menorah has seven arms instead of nine is odd, but not unprecedented—it is a representation of the giant golden menorah that stood in the Temple of Solomon in ancient times. I suppose we could envision a scenario in which Burrows dug through some arcane library book and learned this fact and carved a menorah from biblical times rather than a modern one." January shrugged his bony shoulders. "Though I doubt it. But note the triangular base. This is very rare—most menorahs, even seven-stemmed ones from biblical times, stand on tripods, with a vertical bar above the triangle. There are only two known versions of menorahs with triangular bases without the vertical tripod bar, both from the first century B.C. Only the most expert scholars would know of these prototypes. It is next to impossible that Russell Burrows would."

"Maybe Burrows just got lucky with the triangular base."

"Please, Mr. Thorne. Neither of us believes in that kind of coincidence. That's not the way the world works."

Cam nodded; January was correct. He barely noticed they were now ascending. This was good, solid analysis. The kind of thing Cam could sell a jury on. "Does that mean the writing is also first century BC?" If not, then the argument would collapse on itself.

"Precisely. The writing is, again, Phoenician. It says 'Tyre,' an ancient port city south of modern-day Beirut. The Phoenicians had been conquered long before the first century BC, but their alphabet survived. What is especially interesting is that one of the letters, the circle with the vertical line bisecting it, appears at first glance to be a mistake—it should have both a vertical and horizontal line within the circle. But in certain areas of the Mediterranean the vertical line alone was used. You can count on one hand the number of experts in the world who possess this knowledge." His wet eyes held Cam's. "Needless to say, Russell Burrows is not one of them."

Cam lifted the third stone in the collection, a rectangular piece of white marble about the size and thickness of a hotel bible. A head, perhaps a Roman soldier, appeared carved in profile, along with a few letters of undecipherable script.

BURROWS CAVE ROMAN SOLDIER

January spoke as Cam studied the piece. "The marble itself is probably from the Mediterranean region, which is telling. But the important thing is the damage and erosion along the bottom half. Notice how it appears that the stone was partially submerged in water, which washed away much of the detail—and dirt—below the soldier's neck. This type of erosion occurs over many decades, perhaps centuries. My experts believe it probably occurred during periodic storms when the cave flooded and streams of water rushed through. It would be nearly impossible for Burrows to fabricate weathering and erosion like this."

Three different types of stone and three different types of carvings. And most importantly three different cultures represented—Phoenician, Jewish and Roman. No wonder the experts laughed in Burrows' face. But, paradoxically, in some ways the outlandishness of the collection was compelling evidence of its authenticity. Why would a hoaxster go to such elaborate lengths to make the pieces seem authentic and then so carelessly mix pieces of conflicting cultures together?

Cam rubbed his face with his hands. January was a nut and probably delusional, but his artifacts were stunning. They were either part of an incredibly elaborate hoax or one of the most important archeological finds in history. "So what is the story these pieces are telling?"

The old man sat back in his seat as the plane leveled. "They tell the story of an ancient people from the Middle East settling in the American heartland in the centuries before Christ was born." He took a deep breath, leaning his craggy face forward and locking his watery blue eyes on Cam's. "I am a dying man, and this has been my life's work. So I am admittedly biased. But the artifacts don't lie. I am convinced these people are one of the Lost Tribes of Israel. You can read all about them in the Book of Mormon."

CHAPTER 5

"You were smart to mention it. This January guy and his theories are just the kind of thing that could kill the Governor's chances." Georgia Johnston motioned to the waiter for a refill of her seltzer water. What she really wanted was a martini, but her Mormon companions didn't drink. It was a small but painful price to pay for saving the country from the liberal loonies.

"How so? If January has artifacts that prove the Book of Mormon, that helps the Governor, not hurts him. How can proving the validity of our sacred text be a negative?" Fred Bigelow was a humorless, stork-like attorney with the most prominent Adam's apple Georgia had ever seen. A senior partner at one of Boston's largest law firms, he was well-connected and normally pretty savvy. But he was about to step in front of a train with this Book of Mormon thing. Unless she stopped him.

Georgia chewed on an ice cube, formulating her response. She and her dozen cohorts, all men, had been meeting monthly for almost two years, alternating between Boston, Washington, D.C. and Salt Lake City, strategizing in preparation for the next Presidential election. They were seated around a large table in a private, wood-paneled room at Concord's Colonial Inn on the Monday night before Thanksgiving, a musket shot from where the battles of Concord and Lexington began. The choice to meet at the birthplace of the American Revolution was not a random one for a group that bled white and blue along with red. Trey Buckner, a short, square-jawed man with steely-gray eyes who rarely spoke, reported directly to the Mormon leadership in Salt Lake City. Others had gained the candidate's trust over the years either through business, politics or family connections, in addition to their religious ties. Whatever their connection to the candidate, all were committed to seeing him elected President.

"Look, what makes your guy such a good candidate," she began, "is that he looks like something out of a 1950s movie, Mr. All-America, someone you'd want to have as a neighbor." Or a lover. Not that she had a chance with a guy like him. In her prime Georgia would have been described as full-figured and brainy— not traits that were particularly popular to men in rural Texas, where she grew up. And her prime was a good 30 years in the rearview mirror. Unwilling to settle for just some guy, she had never married. Which left her plenty of time to indulge in her passion for politics as well as her second career—for the past two decades she had worked as a CIA analyst, her day job as one of the country's top political consultants providing the ideal cover for her spy work.

She continued. "But anything that reminds the voters he is somehow different from them is very dangerous. Obama won because he did a great job acting and sounding like your neighbor—you never heard him slide into ghetto lingo or jive like Jesse Jackson. So the less about Mormons and their church, the better."

Bigelow nodded, the protrusion on his neck bouncing as he did so. "You make a valid point." Even he must realize many people viewed the Mormons as some kind of cult, like Moonies or Hare Krishnas.

The Mormons were not exactly desperate to get the Governor elected—for the most part they lived pretty good lives, not just in Utah but around the country. But blue ribbon candidates didn't come around every day, and the election of a Mormon President would solidify their position in America's mainstream in much the way John F. Kennedy's election in the 1960s had quieted mistrust directed at Catholics. And Barack Obama's election proved that, in America, anyone could become President. So while not desperate, they wanted it badly. Badly enough to recruit non-Mormons like Georgia to help shape political strategy. And they sometimes even took her advice.

But why would she want to help them? Their policies toward women were anachronistic, and she immediately distrusted anyone she couldn't get drunk with. Yet her career as an intelligence operative had given her a profound understanding of Islamic hatred for Western culture and ideology—there was no way the Arab world would voluntarily end its holy war against the West. The U.S. was locked in a fight to the death, one that would be won with swords not plowshares. And she, along with most others in the intelligence community, viewed the Mormons as strong allies in this fight. Though she found their religious beliefs to be rigid and oftentimes paranoid in addition to chauvinistic, they were effective and loyal foot soldiers—no other group in America could be counted on to be more patriotic. They were, in some ways, a less violent version of the jihadists who comprised Islam's most ardent advocates.

She continued. "The Democrats aren't stupid—they're going to try to link the Governor with all the extremist Mormon beliefs they can, just like the Republicans used Obama's middle name and his ties to radical groups to try to turn Americans against him. The first thing they'll try to do is bring up the whole polygamy thing. But the Governor has such an All-American family that I don't think that will fly." She paused here, choosing her words carefully. "So they'll be looking for another way to show voters how the Book of Mormon really is far outside mainstream Christianity."

"Hold on for second. I don't understand your point." The speaker was a bow-tied elderly banker. "Why is it you think our religious teachings would be so distasteful to other Christians? We are just another branch of Christianity, just like the Catholics and Baptists and Methodists."

This was no time to pull any punches. "With all due respect, no, you're not. Since you asked, how many Americans do you think would vote for a candidate who is a devout follower of a religion founded by a convicted con man?" She paused. "A con man who claims to have been told by God to take at least 28 wives, some of whom were as young as fourteen? Where I come from, people who claim to have self-serving conversations like that with God are seen as either kooks or liars. And that's being kind."

She looked around. A few of the men's faces had turned red; most shifted uncomfortably in their chairs. Trey Buckner merely glared at her. "Look, sorry to be blunt, but you guys brought me in here to tell the truth. You have to face reality." She focused on the few men, including the banker, who seemed to be most bothered by her words. "And how about the Governor's belief, as a devout Mormon, that all other Christians—the very voters he is depending on—are in a state of permanent sin? Because, as much as you try to hide it, that's what your religion teaches. Just like it teaches that polygamy is practiced in heaven, where, by the way, unmarried women are not admitted. And how about a candidate who believes that ancient Israelites came here to fight a war against a race of giants, and that the descendants of these people became our Native Americans? News to most people. As is your belief that Jesus, after he was resurrected, ignored his followers in Jerusalem and instead descended to preach to the natives here in North America."

"Every religion has certain … extreme positions and unorthodox teachings," mumbled the banker. "Nobody condemns Hinduism just because its adherents believe they may have been a mosquito in a previous life."

"But Americans aren't being asked to put a Hindu in the White House," Georgia said. "Remember how the Republicans attacked Obama when they found out about his pastor's anti-American sermons? That was poison for him—he would have lost the election if he hadn't thrown that preacher under the bus. Well, the Governor's going to be in the same position if all the peculiar little details contained in the Book of Mormon become public. But unlike Obama, he can't just change pastors. He'd have to renounce his entire religion."

"Which simply is not going to happen." The attorney Bigelow clenched his jaw. "So what do you advise we do?"

"I can't guarantee it will work, but here's what I would suggest. The liberal press in this country is incredibly self-righteous—they won't bring up the religion issue head-on. That's why, once the Governor clearly stated his opposition to polygamy, Mormonism wasn't an issue last time he ran. But the press will happily report on a controversy involving religion once they get the whiff of that controversy brewing. And that's the danger of January and his artifacts—in order to cover a debate about whether the artifacts prove the authenticity of the Book of Mormon, the press will first have to summarize the truths stated in that Book." She raised her chin. "And then our candidate is done."

Bigelow squinted at her over a pair of reading glasses, impatience in his voice. "Perhaps I did not hear correctly. What

60

specifically is it you are suggesting?" She was glad she was not a female associate in his law firm.

Georgia sat back. This was one of those times when her CIA bosses might not approve of her political recommendations. But she did what she always did in these cases—she went with her gut. "Apparently I need to spell it out: You do whatever is necessary to bury January and his artifacts."

✜ ✜ ✜

Cam's cell phone rang as the corporate jet descended toward Providence. Salazar. January had returned to the cockpit so Cam answered.

"I'll be at Foxwoods in an hour."

"I'm probably flying over your head right now." Whispering, Cam quickly described his trip. He wasn't sure it was wise to ally himself with the mercenary, but after spending a few hours with January he knew he didn't have much choice. January was the most dangerous of adversaries—he believed he was doing God's will, and he wasn't afraid of death. "I can meet you around midnight. Assuming he lets me go."

Salazar considered this for a few seconds. "He doesn't gain anything by keeping two hostages. He'll let you go. By the way, I brought a friend."

"A friend?" One mercenary was bad enough.

"I'll let her say hi." After a few seconds a sharp bark echoed across the phone line.

"Is that Venus?" Cam and Amanda had left her in a kennel, expecting to pick her up after a night at Foxwoods.

"I think we might need her. She knows Amanda's scent."

"How'd you get her?"

"You told me her name and breed. I called the local kennels. Convinced them you asked me to pick her up."

"You could have just called me first." There was something overly ... familiar about the mercenary's actions. Sort of like an acquaintance who pulled up a chair at the dinner table uninvited.

"No need."

Hopefully he could spring Amanda just as efficiently. "Okay, whatever. So what next?"

"I'm pretty sure I know where January lives—an old army buddy owns a fence company and he remembers doing a job for a middle-aged guy near Foxwoods a few years ago. Not many residential jobs around there, so I think this is the property." He gave Cam directions to a Burger King not far from the highway. "Meet me there. Swing by your hotel first and get some of Amanda's dirty laundry, a sock or panties. Wear black and dress warm."

Cam hung up. He had no idea what they would be doing, but it would feel good to be doing something.

✝ ✝ ✝

Amanda did her best to remain an animated and energized playmate to the little girl, swallowing both the pain in her ribcage and the bitter taste of being held captive. Astarte was extremely bright—she read and wrote well above her third-grade level—and she seemed to have a good knowledge of current events and the world around her. What she lacked were playmates and the chance just to be a kid. Eliza had brought them popcorn, and now they sat on the floor and watched *The Little Mermaid*. It was ten o'clock, but apparently Astarte didn't have a bedtime.

"Aunt Eliza doesn't like this movie—she says Ariel misbehaved by disobeying her father. But Uncle Jefferson says it's okay because her destiny was to find her prince."

"Does he ever tell you who your prince might be?"

"No. He says only God knows."

On the screen, the mermaid Ariel swam to her secret hiding place. "When I was a girl in England," Amanda said, "I had a secret hiding place in my house that nobody else knew about. It was quite an old house, and it had a room hidden behind a closet." Not exactly true, but worth a try.

Astarte's eyes lit up. "Me too! There's a secret room where Uncle Jefferson keeps his important things. I'm the only person he lets go in there."

Amanda feigned disappointment. "Well, that doesn't really count. If you can't go in there without him, it's not really your special place." She turned back to the television.

Astarte's cobalt eyes fired. "I can too go in there myself! I know the combination and everything."

"Astarte," Amanda said, adopting her best Mary Poppins voice, "young ladies of proper breeding do not make up stories."

"I did not make it up!"

The girl was obviously not accustomed to being chastised. The collection was why Amanda had been abducted; it might also be a key to her escape. Eliza had said goodnight, and Judith sat guard outside the bedroom door, but otherwise the house seemed to be empty. Was there a way to access the private room without Judith intervening? "I find it hard to believe your uncle would entrust such important information to ... someone so young."

Astarte jumped to her feet, her long dark braids swinging in anger. "Follow me. I'll prove it."

Instead of heading toward the door, the girl stomped across the room and pulled a toy chest away from the wall next to her bed. Along this wall the roofline allowed only three feet of headroom. A small door was set into the low wall; Astarte yanked it open to reveal a narrow storage area tucked into the roof eaves running, apparently, the entire length of the building. Pulling a flashlight off her night table, Astarte stepped into the alcove. "Follow me. Unless you're afraid."

"One second." Amanda stuffed a couple of pillows under the blankets on both beds and turned the lights and television off; if Judith checked, it would look like they were asleep. "Okay, I'm ready."

Astarte was able to walk almost upright, while Amanda, trying to avoid twisting her ribcage, bent her knees and neck to squeeze her way along. They seemed to have moved along the entire length of the three-bay garage until, at the far end of the structure, Astarte's light illuminated another small door. "What's on the other side?" Amanda asked. She had no interest in meeting up with Judith's flashlight again.

Astarte's anger had faded, replaced by a giddy excitement. "It's the dining room. But we always eat at the kitchen table." She nudged the door open and ducked through. Amanda followed, cupping her hand over Astarte's flashlight. Moonlight illuminated the room as she strained her ears, listening for Judith. Nothing.

"Where to next?"

"This way." The girl passed into the kitchen and pointed to a deadbolt on a paneled door. "That lock is hard for me to open." Amanda snapped it sideways and slowly pulled the thick door toward her. A steep staircase descended in front of them, the same stairway that had brought Amanda to her upstairs prison. Astarte led the way with her flashlight. Amanda paused, her eye catching the glow of a cordless phone mounted on the wall next to the door. She lifted the receiver, slid it into her pocket and pulled the door closed behind them. Hopefully nobody would notice the phone missing.

Cool air and the faint smell of gasoline filled her nostrils as she followed the princess down the darkened stairwell. "Don't worry, we won't be in the garage for long. And it's warm in Uncle Jefferson's room." The girl must have noticed Amanda shivering. "He calls it his bunk-bed, but I don't know why."

Astarte actually had quite an elevated vocabulary for her age. "Do you mean 'bunker,' perhaps?"

The girl grinned. "Oops, bunker."

Astarte jumped off the bottom step and led Amanda to the back corner of the garage. She shone her light on a steel bulkhead door, the kind usually used to access basements from the back yard. Amanda reached down. "Shall I open it?"

"Yup. Just pull."

Another stairwell led them down another full flight, bringing them outside the footprint of the garage and into the space between—and below—the yard separating the compound's main house and the garage. Apparently either structure accessed the underground bunker. At the bottom of the stairs they reached a landing in front of a steel door. A keypad glowed green next to the door. "This is where we need the combination," Astarte announced.

Amanda didn't want to come this far only for the girl to have second thoughts. "I still have trouble believing your uncle gave you the combination."

"He didn't give it to me. I watched him push the buttons." She paused, her eyes sad. "Sometimes people think because I'm little, I'm not very smart."

Amanda resisted the urge to bend down and comfort the girl. Not yet. "Well, you must be quite smart if you really do remember the secret code."

Astarte reached up and flipped open the cover to the keypad. As Amanda watched, she carefully pressed the buttons one-by-one, her mouth silently forming the letters as she worked to spell the word correctly: P-R-I-N-C-E-S-S-4-0. The red light on the bottom of the keypad flashed green and a hidden deadbolt released. "There. I told you I could do it."

Amanda pushed the door open. "Well, it seems as if I owe you an apology!" She crouched and hugged Astarte. "Now let's go explore."

They passed through the door into a simple rectangular-shaped room with a series of museum-like, glass-covered display cases running down the middle and both side walls of the room. Amanda walked around, scanning the collection. Each case displayed a number of artifacts, most of them stone, and each artifact featured a small card with a typewritten explanation of its provenance and significance. There were probably hundreds of artifacts in total, arranged chronologically, with dates ranging from 500 BC to medieval times. "These are absolutely fabulous, Astarte." She would love to spend a week here. With Cam.

"Uncle Jefferson says this is the best collection in the world."

At the far side of the rectangular room another door and keypad entry system sat recessed in a wall. "What's behind that door?"

Astarte marched over and input the same code. "More artifacts." She pushed open the door and lights automatically came on as they walked in. This room was smaller, but as in the first room the artifacts were arranged chronologically. The display cases in this room were painted black, unlike the white-painted cases in the larger room. "Why are the cases painted different colors, Astarte?" For some reason it seemed important.

"Uncle Jefferson says the artifacts prove that God's people came to America a long time ago. He says rocks can't lie." She waited until Amanda looked her in the eye. "But some rocks were made by the devil to confuse us. So he keeps those ones in the black cases. Nobody's supposed to see the devil's rocks."

The girl said it matter-of-factly before turning and returning to the larger room. "Devil's rocks," Amanda whispered to herself. On impulse, she lifted the hinged cover of one of the display cases and slipped a carved white stone the size of a paperback book under her shirt.

CHAPTER 6

"How was your meeting, Uncle?" Astarte asked, her eyes wide with interest.

"Very good, my little princess. But I'm surprised you're still awake. It's past midnight." The two of them sat kitty-corner at January's small square kitchen table, like lovers at a Paris café.

"I heard your car come in. Aunt Eliza made me eat dinner without you. I wanted to wait."

A wave of warmth gushed through his decaying body. He and the girl always ate dinner together, just the two of them. It was his one chance to be alone with her, to share his knowledge, to tutor her on what she needed to know to fulfill her destiny. It was his favorite time of the day. And it was the thing that made him most sad about dying. "And how was your day with Miss Amanda?"

"We had fun playing. Then Miss Amanda tried to run away. But Judith brought her back."

January had heard this all already. "What is she doing now?" He picked at a piece of cold chicken.

"She's asleep." But he had not adequately answered her original question, and she was not to be dissuaded. She leaned closer. "You haven't told me anything about your meeting."

He sighed. "Well, Mr. Thorne—"

She pulled back and crinkled her nose. "Sorry, Uncle, but your breath is smelling worse."

He smiled sadly. You could always trust an eight-year-old to be brutally honest. "I'm sorry," he said, speaking out of the side of his mouth. "It's because my body is decaying on the inside."

Astarte took his hand. "It's okay, I don't mind
. I still love you." She leaned back in. "Please tell me about Mr. Thorne."

He blew his nose into a handkerchief. Somehow the love of this little girl had become the most compelling thing in his life. Other than his mission, of course. And thankfully the two were intimately intertwined. "So, our Mr. Thorne is a very capable fellow. Intelligent, but not the kind of intelligence you get just from reading books. He has the kind of intelligence you get from observing the world and learning from it."

"Is he going to help us?" She sped on before he could answer. "I hope so. Miss Amanda is very cross with you, and it would be better if we were all friends."

He answered the girl truthfully, as he usually did. "I don't know. Your people and my people are what we call minorities in this country, Astarte. That means there are very few of us compared to the others. Because of that, people don't always want to help us."

She chewed on this information for a few seconds while January coughed into his handkerchief. "If we tell Miss Amanda that God needs Mr. Thorne and her to help us, I think she'll do it."

"Remember what I told you. People sometimes don't believe you when you tell them you are doing God's work."

She nodded knowingly. "That's why you need to show them the special papers and rocks, right?

"Correct. I showed Mr. Thorne some of the rocks today. I'll show him the rest in the morning."

✛ ✛ ✛

Cam had expected some kind of muscle car, but Salazar waited for him in the Burger King parking lot in a gray minivan with an "I Support Youth Soccer" bumper sticker. "Better cover," Salazar said. He was not the type to use three words when two would do.

Cam climbed in and allowed a prancing Venus to lick his face. "Hi, baby." He buried his face in her fur, her familiar scent both a comfort and a reminder of how their lives had been upended. Venus sat on her haunches between the two front seats. Occasionally Salazar reached over and scratched her tawny back as he drove; after a few such gestures Cam casually pulled the dog out of Salazar's reach and onto the floor at his feet. The two men had similar builds—both were of average height and fit, like they belonged on a soccer field somewhere. But while Cam sported a goatee and an easy smile, the mercenary was clean-shaven and brooding, as if showing either stubble or joy would be a sign of weakness.

"The van also carries all my equipment. Infra-red goggles, parabolic listening devices, explosives, firearms."

Cam turned in his seat. He hadn't fired a gun since summer camp. "Are we planning to storm the compound?" He smiled.

Salazar shrugged, his features frozen. "You want to get Amanda out, right?"

The response hit Cam hard. He figured they would sneak in and pull Amanda to safety, maybe knock a guard over the head if they had to. But Salazar seemed to envision a commando raid. Maybe the Salazar thing wasn't such a good idea. "Well, let's just make sure she doesn't get hurt."

Salazar set his jaw. "Nothing will happen to Amanda." He took a deep breath, his eyes checking the rearview mirror. It was just after midnight, a tough time to tail someone without being seen. "My Rosalita still talks about the time she met Amanda at the Newport Tower." Amanda had shown the girl how the rising sun illuminated an egg-shaped keystone in the round stone tower on the morning of the winter solstice, symbolizing the rebirth of the earth as the days began to lengthen. "Amanda was real nice to her. Almost mother-like."

Cam knew the girl's mother had left Salazar when the girl was a baby. But didn't know how to respond to the 'almost mother-like' comment. "How old is she now?"

For the first time tonight the mercenary smiled. "Eight. Probably the same as this little girl you're dealing with."

Cam changed the subject. "So what's the plan for tonight?"

"First step is to make sure we've got the right place. Venus might help with that. Then we do some reconnaissance. Then we figure out a plan. Then I go in."

"You mean *we* go in."

"No. I only work with pros. Going in with amateurs gets you killed real quick."

The point didn't seem negotiable. But later Cam might revisit it. "I'd prefer sooner rather than later."

"Sometimes sooner means you screw up. As long as she's not in immediate danger, we'll take it slow." He turned to Cam. "You meeting January again tomorrow?"

"Yeah, first thing in the morning, at his compound. He wants to show me more of his collection."

"Don't piss him off. As long as he thinks you're cooperating, Amanda should be safe." Salazar adjusted the rearview window. "I read about you and Amanda last year after we ... parted company."

"You mean after you shot me and we escaped."

The mercenary shrugged. "Just doing my job. Besides, I let you go."

They rode in silence for a few minutes. "Do you really think the Knights Templar were here before Columbus?" Salazar asked.

Cam took a deep breath. At least it was a safe subject. "Yeah, I do. I'm not sure we have all the details exactly, but there were definitely groups of explorers here in the late 14th century, and they definitely had connections to the Templars. My guess is they knew at some point the Church would turn on them again, as they had done in 1307, and they'd need a safe refuge."

"But I thought the Templars were the army of the Church. Why did the Church turn on them?" It almost seemed like Salazar felt sorry for the medieval knights.

"Because the Templars figured out the Church was built on a bunch of lies. When they were in the Middle East in the early 12th century they found documents or artifacts or something that revealed the true history of the early Christians. In fact, that may have been why they went to Jerusalem to begin with, may have been why they called for the Crusades—the early Templars were made up of noble families from France, families who had kept alive the true teachings of the early Christians from before the Vatican took over. In fact, some of these families believed they descended directly from Mary Magdalene and Jesus. Later most of these families were wiped out in the Albigensian Crusade in the Provence region."

"Weren't they called Gnostics?"

Cam nodded. Salazar had been doing some reading. Which was not surprising—many military types were fascinated by the

Templars. "Yes, they rejected the need for the Church hierarchy. They felt they could be good Christians by praying directly to God, without a priest as an intermediary. So the Church massacred them." Cam paused. "But we're getting ahead of ourselves. When the Templars first went to Jerusalem in the early 1100s, I think they were looking for evidence that proved the stories that had been passed down through their families about Jesus and Mary Magdalene having children."

"And they found what they were looking for?"

"I think so. Or maybe they found other Church secrets about early Christianity. Either way, that's how they got so powerful so fast—they basically blackmailed the Church by threatening to reveal the truth."

"'Blackmail' is not really the right word." His knuckles had turned white on the steering wheel.

Cam barely knew the mercenary, but his memory of him was of a man in control of his emotions. That seemed to have changed. "Well, whatever word you want to use, it took the Church 200 years to avenge the … incident. Many Templar Knights were killed or imprisoned. But those that remained, the vestiges of the Templar Order, reorganized themselves and focused on North America as both a hiding spot and possible future settlement area."

Salazar turned onto a winding country road, ending the Templar discussion. Every few seconds he checked a GPS device, eventually slowing and pulling onto the shoulder. "We walk from here. Put Venus back on her leash and then come give me a hand with these packs. And rub some of this onto your face." He handed Cam a tube of black paste.

Each shouldering a backpack, they pushed through a wooded area, a nearly full moon illuminating the night. Salazar led, slashing through the thicket with a machete. "We've got about a half-mile hike; we'll need to stay quiet when we get closer. From what I learned from the tax rolls, January owns about 20 acres. We're coming in from the back." He checked his GPS. "There's some wetlands up here; we'll swing wide around them."

Salazar moved at a fast pace but Cam kept up easily, relieved to finally be in action. Venus seemed to sense his tension, her ears back and her eyes scanning the forest around them. Ten minutes later Salazar motioned for Cam to slow and keep quiet. "We're getting close. Stay low. My buddy said there's an eight-foot fence and cameras mounted every 50 feet."

Cam tugged lightly on Salazar's arm, intending to point out the thinning trees ahead. But the tug was like a trigger. Snake-like the mercenary uncoiled, shoved Cam in the chest and pulled a knife from his belt as he crouched in a fighting position. A feverish intensity in Salazar's eyes froze Cam, the knife pointing menacingly inches from his face. Cam held his hands up and pushed the words through his constricted windpipe. "Easy, Salazar."

Salazar clenched his teeth, gulping air through them. "You shouldn't ever touch me." His eyes, dark and dilated, slowly refocused. "I am a trained fighting machine," he said softly. He slid the knife back into its sheath.

Cam rotated his neck. What had he gotten himself into? Venus huddled by his feet.

"Wait here," Salazar ordered. He crawled ahead about 20 yards and returned, now seemingly calm and composed. "Just as my friend said. Time for Venus to go to work." He clipped an electronic tracking device onto the dog's collar.

"What's she supposed to do?"

"Did you bring an article of Amanda's clothes?"

Cam pulled a dirty sock out of his pocket.

"Good. Let her smell it. Then just let her go. She's a retriever, it should be instinctive."

Cam shrugged. "Okay." He removed the leash, put the sock at her nose, gave her a gentle push in the direction of the fence. "Go ahead, girl. It's okay. Go find Amanda."

Sniffing the ground, the dog zigzagged her way forward, angling to her left toward the fence. Thirty seconds passed. "She may have something," Salazar said as he peered through the trees with a pair of night-vision goggles.

They lost sight of her. Cam waited another half a minute. "I'm going to go look for her." Venus was only about 40 pounds; she had no chance against a coyote or even a fisher cat.

Salazar shook his head. "No. Give her a minute. We would have heard her bark if there was a problem. But it's a long fence." He handed Cam a palm-sized monitor. "You can track her on this. She's following the fence line down to our left." He paused, staring at the monitor. "It looks like she stopped."

The electronic dot on the screen pulsed in the same spot for about ten seconds before moving back along the fence line toward them at a fast pace. Another ten seconds passed and Venus came trotting through the brush with something in her mouth. She stopped at Cam's feet and, almost proudly, dropped Amanda's muddied pink and blue sock into Cam's hand.

Cam rubbed Venus' neck and glanced at Salazar. "I don't know how Amanda's sock made it out to the fence, but she's in there all right."

✠ ✠ ✠

Salazar surveyed the forest around him, at home here in the darkened woods. It would be simple to stick a hunting knife in Thorne's back. Then drive back to the Burger King, get Thorne's car, leave it here by the side of the road and hike back to the minivan. Nobody knew they were out here; nobody had seen them together.

But did his feelings for Amanda justify murder? He had long since come to grips with the moral ambiguity of mercenary work. He was a U.S. Army Ranger turned soldier of fortune; it was his job to kill. That he was now fighting on behalf of corporations and institutions rather than on behalf of nation-states was really a distinction without a difference: Killing was either immoral or it was not. And if it was acceptable for nations to wage war for economic or religious or political reasons, why was it any less moral for non-governmental entities to do the same? He no longer wrestled with the question. Taking others' lives had become an accepted part of living his.

But this was different. This was murder simply because he hadn't been able to stop thinking about a woman who was engaged to another man. This was a selfish, primordial need to possess a woman who was as close to the ideal female as he had ever encountered. This was about the needs of an alpha male to find an appropriate mate. In an earlier time, when men lived in the wilderness, walking the fine line between survival and death on a daily basis, the decision would have been a simple one. He would have killed Thorne and taken Amanda as his own. Had the fundamental nature of man truly changed? He shook his head in the dark.

He ran through the conversation he would have with the police, the story airtight even if they checked Thorne's cell phone records. *Yes, Thorne contacted me, asked for my help finding his fiancée. We were supposed to meet in the morning; he asked me to bring his dog. He said he had located January's compound and was going to scope it out overnight. He said he was being followed, had a fight in the parking lot with a couple of guys. Maybe they tracked him into the woods.*

Then, of course, he would rescue the remarkable Amanda. She would mourn the death of her lover, no doubt. He would expect nothing less. But in time she would get over Thorne. And he would be waiting.

✝ ✝ ✝

Salazar handed Cam a pair of night-vision goggles and, using the trees as cover, together they crept close to the fence. Venus, tied to a pine, was content chomping on a rawhide bone Salazar had the foresight to bring.

The mercenary surveyed the area. "Basic perimeter fence. Barbed wire, a few stationary cameras, no electricity, just like my buddy described. Keep kids and hunters and maybe a small-time burglar away." He pointed toward where Venus had retrieved Amanda's sock. "She tried to dig under."

"So what next?"

"We wait. You go to your meeting in the morning with January and get a feel for the place. Try to figure out where they're holding her. Then we go in tomorrow night."

Cam hated the idea of leaving Amanda un-rescued when they were so close, but he also saw the benefit of waiting a night to gather more information.

His cell phone buzzed, interrupting his thoughts. An unidentified Connecticut number flashed on the display. He moved deeper into the woods and answered in a low voice. "Hello."

"Cam, it's me."

"Amanda," he breathed. A pile of bricks floated off his chest as he exhaled in relief. "Are you all right?"

She spoke in a hushed voice. "Yes. But I can't talk for long. I'm being held in January's compound."

"I know. We're out in the woods behind the fence. We found your sock."

"My sock? And who's we?"

"I'm with Salazar. I need help to get you out of there; I think January paid off the cops." Salazar gave him a strange, almost cheerless look and his shoulders seemed to sag, but Cam was too excited to focus on it. "Where in the compound are you?"

"Above the garage, front room. But don't get me yet. I want to stay one more day."

"You what?"

"Trust me. That little girl needs me, and I'm perfectly safe. But I need to go now."

Now that they knew where she was being held, they should just go rescue her. "Are you sure you're okay. Are you hurt at all?"

"I'm fine. Really. But I need to go."

"All right. But be ready for us at four o'clock tomorrow morning."

"Got it. And Cam, I love you."

"I love you too. Just be safe."

✠ ✠ ✠

Cam and Salazar spent another half-hour walking the perimeter of the compound before heading back to Cam's hotel.

"I'm going to stay up listening to an all-night radio show," Cam said as they entered the lobby. The show often discussed exploration of America before Columbus and Cam planned to call in to see if anyone knew January or had any insights into the

Burrows Cave artifacts. "So you might want to get your own room." The truth was Cam had no interest in sharing a room with the mercenary.

Salazar nodded. "You're paying, so whatever." He bent over and patted Venus on the forehead. "Meet at seven in the lobby."

Cam showered quickly, checked his blood sugar, ordered a hamburger from room service and, the Internet connection now working, found the website for a radio show hosted by a researcher that focused on ancient American artifacts and history. The host was discussing how Native American oral history told of many waves of European exploration of North America prior to 1492. Cam dialed; the host and Cam had met a couple of times, and he put Cam on the air.

"I wanted to shift gears and try to get some info about Burrows Cave," Cam said. "There's a guy named Jefferson January who apparently has a pretty big collection of artifacts from the cave. Anybody have any opinions about whether these artifacts are legit or not?"

"In fact, January was a guest on my program a couple of years ago," the host said. "He's got some interesting theories. To understand where he's coming from you need to know a bit about the Book of Mormon." He explained that the book, which Mormons viewed as co-equal to the Bible in terms of importance and sanctity, detailed how a group of Israelites left Jerusalem circa 600 BC and sailed to America. Once there, they split into two groups, Nephites and Lamanites, who frequently warred with each other. Eventually the Lamanites destroyed the Nephites, whereupon the Lamanites broke into various tribes and became what are now identified as Native Americans. "Now, the book goes into some pretty specific geographic detail, which has led most Mormon historians to conclude that these ancient peoples originally lived in Central America and only later made their way north to what is now the United States and Canada."

"But not January," Cam responded.

"Not January. He believes the ancient lands were in the Great Lakes region. Remember, Lake Ontario isn't far from where Joseph Smith claimed to have found the golden plates containing the Book of Mormon. And January claims to have the artifacts that prove his theory."

"The Burrows Cave artifacts."

"But not just those. He claims to have other artifacts. A bunch of the Michigan Tablets, for example. They disappeared from a private collection years ago. Maybe he bought them up." The host explained that hundreds of engraved stones depicting Biblical scenes were dug up in the Detroit area in the 1890s. Most experts dismissed them as fraudulent. But, curiously, much of the ancient writing found almost 100 years later on the Burrows Cave stones matched the writing on the Michigan Tablets. Cam found an image of one of the stones.

A MICHIGAN TABLET STONE

The carvings were even more elaborate than the Burrows Cave stones. "Wait, you said the writing matches the Burrows Cave artifacts?" Cam said.

"I did. But there's more." The host made no effort to hide his passion for this topic. "The Ohio Decalogue Stone and the Bat

Creek Stone in Tennessee also support January's theory. Smithsonian experts originally believed the Bat Creek stone, discovered in the 1880s, depicts Cherokee writing. But about a hundred years later an amateur historian turned it upside down and immediately recognized it as an early form of Hebrew writing. It reads, 'Hail the Jews' and the form of the script dates back to the first couple of centuries A.D." Cam found an Internet image of this artifact as well.

THE BAT CREEK STONE

The host continued. "And the Ohio Decalogue Stone, found in a burial mound in 1860, displays the figure of Moses in the center of the stone with the text of the Ten Commandments inscribed along the perimeter. The script, again, is an ancient version of Hebrew. The burial mounds date roughly between 100 BC and 500 AD." Cam, once more, found an online image.

THE OHIO DECALOGUE STONE

Cam had seen pictures of both these stones before, but they suddenly took on added import in light of January's claims.

"January also hinted at finding something up in the Catskill Mountains in New York, but he wouldn't say what it was," the host said.

Cam had never heard of any finds in that area of New York. But it made sense that early explorers could have made their way up the Hudson River. "The Mormon Church doesn't agree with January's theory?"

"Their experts are not much different than experts in the rest of the country. They were all taught that the ancient lands are in Central America, so that's what they believe. No matter what the evidence says." The host laughed. "Many of our listeners know how that works."

"Anyway, I'm curious if you or any of your listeners have an opinion about the Burrows Cave pieces."

"I know a geologist who's examined hundreds of the carvings in his lab, including lots of January's pieces. He has some questions about one or two of them, but for the most part he says the weathering patterns are consistent with ancient artifacts and there's no evidence of modern tool usage." He chuckled. "Not to mention that there are thousands of them. Even the most ambitious hoaxster would stop at a few hundred."

"I'm getting a little tired of the hoax explanations," Cam said. The "hoax" refrain was the common response from the academic community when confronted with artifacts that didn't fit neatly into their version of history.

The host continued. "One of the things we don't pay enough attention to in this country is Native American legend and oral history, the theme of tonight's show. From what I've been told, the Yuchi tribe tells the story of a sealed mausoleum in southern Illinois containing gold and the archives of a lost people."

"Burrows took gold from the cave, right?" Cam asked.

"Supposedly quite a bit. Which is another argument against it being a hoax. Who throws gold in a cave and waits for some stranger to find it?"

Cam hung up. Sometimes things just boiled down to common sense.

✛ ✛ ✛

Astarte came bouncing into January's kitchen at seven o'clock, a bit later than normal, and kissed him on the cheek. "Good morning, Uncle Jefferson," she said brightly.

He smiled. "Did you oversleep, princess?" He had been up since four. No sense sleeping away the last hours of one's life.

She sipped at her orange juice. "Just a little. I was up thinking about what we talked about last night."

"Are you enjoying Miss Amanda?"

She set her glass down. "Yes, but I do think it is wrong to keep her here if she wants to leave."

"I agree. But sometimes God requires us to do ... difficult things in his service. I'm afraid this is one of those times."

She seemed to accept this. "Are you meeting with Mr. Thorne this morning?"

80

"Yes. And I received some bad news late last night which makes obtaining Mr. Thorne's cooperation even more crucial." Bigelow, the Boston lawyer, had gotten cold feet and was no longer willing to champion January's cause. For decades January had argued with historians in Salt Lake City that his artifacts proved the validity of the Book of Mormon, and for decades they had resisted his efforts because Mormon doctrine held that events described in the Book occurred in Central America, not in the Great Lakes region as January's artifacts clearly proved. In fact, if they knew what January was up to they would excommunicate him. Whatever the reason for Bigelow's change of heart, Cameron Thorne had become January's last and best chance.

Astarte nibbled on a bagel. "Can you tell me again how come I live with you and Aunt Eliza?"

"Was Miss Amanda asking?"

"Yes."

"All right. You can tell her. It all started almost two hundred years ago when your people, the Mandan Indians, lived in North Dakota. Originally the Mandan lived further south and east, in the Ohio River Valley, but as the European settlers came they took the Indians' land and pushed the tribes westward."

"That wasn't very nice of them."

"Well, honey, that's just the way the world is sometimes. When the Mandan first came to this country, they tried to push other people off their land. Back then the Mandan were called Lamanites, and the people they fought with were called Nephites."

"I thought the Mandan were called the White Indians."

"Yes, but that was later on. Originally they were called Lamanites."

"I've heard Aunt Eliza talk about Lamanites."

"Yes, their story is told in the Book of Mormon. But that is for another day. What is important for now is that the European settlers who came to North Dakota brought terrible diseases with them. One of them was called smallpox. The Mandan often traded with the settlers, which caused them to catch this disease. All of the Mandan in their villages in North Dakota died. But a few dozen Mandan were off on a trading mission when the sickness came and they survived. Most people don't know about them."

"That's what Miss Amanda thought. She said Mandan were ... stinked."

He smiled "Extinct."

"Yes, that's it."

"At around this same time, in the middle of the 1800s, my people, the Mormons, were living in Illinois, in a city called Nauvoo. They met the surviving Mandan, who had no place to go, and invited them to live with them. That's how my great-grandfather met your great-great-great-grandmother."

"Were they friends?"

He weighed the question. It was time for the girl to know the truth, or at least some of it. And he was running out of time to tell it. "More than friends. My great-grandfather was the prophet Joseph Smith, and he married your great-great-great grandmother." There was no need for the girl to know her ancestor was one of more than 20 wives taken by the Mormon leader. "She was apparently very beautiful, just like you. But her first husband died from smallpox."

"Was she the princess?"

"Yes, she was the 35th princess. Before she met Joseph Smith, she had a daughter, princess number 36. That's who you descend from. And after she married Joseph Smith they had a son. And that's who I descend from." He dabbed his mouth and smiled. "So, you see, you and I are actually cousins."

She giggled. "So now I shall call you Uncle Cousin!"

He yearned to tell her the entire truth, but it would serve no purpose other than to confuse her. "So, anyway, over time the Mandan people stayed in Illinois with the Mormons and became part of the community. After Joseph Smith died many Mormons went to Utah with Brigham Young. But some stayed in Illinois, including both of our families. Some of the Mandan married Mormons and other non-Mandans. Except the princesses. They always married full-blooded Mandan men, at least for their first husbands."

"So I shall also," she exclaimed.

He shook his head. "Actually, that would be impossible. Your mother was the last pure-blooded Mandan."

Astarte weighed this for a few seconds. "You mean I'm not a pure-blood?"

"No." He smiled. "Your father wasn't Mandan."

"He wasn't?" She paused. "Uncle, who was my father?"

Again he longed to tell her the truth. The bullet, still lodged near his spine, caused his stooped posture and brought constant pain. But that was nothing compared to the psychological scar of being shot in the back by his own father. Daddy never understood that January was just trying to fulfill God's will, to fulfill the prophecy of the Fortieth Princess. All Daddy saw was his middle-aged son, bare-assed, atop the young Mandan princess Daddy had raised as a daughter. "Astarte, your father was a Mormon, a descendant of the prophet Joseph Smith." January looked away. "Just like me."

"But who was he?"

He hated to lie to the girl. "I don't know. All I know is that he was a descendant of Joseph Smith."

Astarte spent a few seconds mulling this over. "So can I be a true princess if I'm not a pure-blood?"

He took another deep breath. "Actually, you are something much more important. Way back in the 12th century, over 800 years ago, it was prophesized that the Fortieth Princess would unite the peoples of the world under the true word of God. When it was time for your mother to have a baby, she chose a descendant of Joseph Smith to be its father. Your father. She thought it would help you fulfill the prophecy." It was true. It had been Astarte's mother's idea to unite the bloodlines. Not that Daddy ever believed it; he died less than a year later, never having forgiven his son.

"Is the prophecy about me written in the Book of Mormon also?"

"No. It was prophesized by a great princess named Marie-Claire, who came to America from the country of France with some brave men called the Knights Templar."

"How did you find the prophecy?"

How indeed? "It began almost 70 years ago, when my father was a young man doing missionary work in France just after World War II. He befriended a priest who gave him an ancient document that told of the voyage of Marie-Claire and the Templars to America. Eventually he gave me the document. Following clues left in this document has been my life's work ever since." That, and ensuring the prophecy would be fulfilled. "Soon it will be time for you to bring the prophecy to life."

She nibbled again on her bagel, weighing his words, her head down. When she looked up her eyes were wet with tears. "How will I know how to unite all the people?"

He took her hand and kissed it, holding it to his craggy cheek as he spoke, the gesture allowing him to hide his own tear-filled eyes from the girl. With all his heart he wished he could live to help her. But it was not to be. "There's nothing to fear, Astarte. God will take your hand and show you the way, just as I am holding it now."

✛ ✛ ✛

Amanda's first inclination had been to return the phone to the kitchen as she and Astarte snuck back from the bunker the night before, it being unrealistic to expect that nobody would notice it missing. But she decided to keep it; it was her only connection to the outside world. She was more concerned they would discover the missing artifact. So when Astarte left to have breakfast with January, Amanda locked herself in the bathroom, turned the water on and phoned Cam. He answered on the first ring. "Are you all right?" he blurted.

"I'm okay. Can't talk for long. But I think the password for the security system is the word princess followed by the numerals four and zero."

"You sure you're okay?"

"Honestly, I'm fine." Knowing he and Salazar were planning a rescue had dissipated some of her cold fear.

He exhaled. "Princess-four-zero, got it. I'm meeting January in an hour at the compound. I love you, honey. Please be careful."

"I love you too, Cam. See you at four in the morning. And please don't oversleep."

CHAPTER 7

January lingered over breakfast even after Astarte departed to return to Amanda. The whole thing with the attorney Bigelow gnawed at him—it didn't add up. It was one thing for Bigelow to slowly lose enthusiasm over time, but his turnabout had been so sudden, and the tone of his email so formal, that it seemed almost certain something had intervened to poison the well. And in the hierarchical world of the Mormon Church, that "something" was almost always a Church official in Salt Lake City. Perhaps January shouldn't have threatened to blow up the Museum of Church History and Art in Salt Lake City if the church historians didn't take a closer look at his evidence….

After forcing himself to choke down a piece of toast to settle his stomach, he popped three OxyContins and pushed himself out of his chair. Thorne was expecting to see more artifacts and January did not want to disappoint him. Before breakfast he had spent a few hours in his bunker gathering a dozen of his best pieces, the ones that most persuasively supported his theory. Of course, this did not include any of the devil's rocks—he kept those hidden and, in fact, had left clear instructions with Eliza that they were to be destroyed upon his death. He summoned a male security guard from the front gate to help him pack the pieces into a wheeled case and carry them up to the kitchen. He now removed a few choice stones from the case, arranged them on the table and covered them with a chamois cloth.

Forty-five minutes later January watched through the window as the same guard searched Thorne and his car before opening the gate. Thorne, tight-jawed, scanned the compound as he marched toward January's front door, no doubt searching for his fiancée. They would meet at the kitchen table, a casual setting that would stand in stark contrast to the secrets January would reveal around it.

Thorne pushed open the front door. "I would like to see Amanda."

January remained seated, gesturing to his guest to take the seat Astarte had recently vacated. "Must we go through this every time? She's safe. Now please sit down." He pushed a magazine across the table. "Have you seen this?"

Thorne remained standing. "No." He glanced at the article.

"More evidence of Mediterranean explorers coming to America in ancient times. It's pretty compelling—strong DNA links between the Cherokee Indians and the Jews. Did you know the ancient Cherokee name for their divine spirit is 'Yo-He-Wah, almost identical to the Jewish Yahweh? One would think this type of thing would get some play in the mainstream press. Especially after you kicked the door down and stormed the 'Columbus Was First' castle. But no. Nothing."

"You brought me here just to see this?"

"No. I just thought you'd be interested. As I said before, I brought you here because I need your help." January fought back a stab of heat in his gut, gritting his teeth until it passed. Even the drugs were losing their effectiveness. It would not be long now. He took a deep breath and wiped the saliva off his mouth. "Perhaps my approach was wrong. I truly felt that once you saw the cave and some artifacts your anger would fade and you would understand why I abducted Amanda. I meant no harm; it was done simply to get your undivided attention. Mr. Thorne, there is a story here that is bigger than both of us, a secret history that will force historians to rewrite our textbooks, force religions to reexamine their beliefs. Surely a few days of anxiety is nothing compared to being part of such a cataclysmic event." He settled his watery eyes on Thorne. "Your Prince Henry discovery opened people's eyes. This will knock them on their ass."

Thorne studied January for a few seconds. "Nothing justifies kidnapping Amanda. Not even close. But I'm here. I'm listening." He sat.

"Yes, you will hear me out, because despite your anger your curiosity is piqued." He shifted in his chair, trying to relieve the pain as the cancer gnawed away at his cells like millions of tiny piranha. "As you probably know, the Book of Mormon is based on inscribed golden plates found by Joseph Smith on the Hill Cumorah in upstate New York in the early 1800s. It tells of God's dealings with the ancient peoples of America from approximately 600 BC to 400 AD."

Thorne cut him off. "Look, I'm willing to be open-minded about Burrows Cave and your artifacts. But you're never going to convince me that angels gave some golden plates to Joseph Smith and that the Book of Mormon is a holy text."

January nodded. In some ways he welcomed Thorne's skepticism. If he could convince someone like Thorne he could convince almost anyone. "There was a time, in my youth, when I shared that opinion. But that was before I started looking at the evidence."

"You mean the artifacts."

"Of course."

"Just because your artifacts show that ancient explorers came to America doesn't mean those explorers were Mormons, or Nephites, or whatever you call them."

"On the contrary. The artifacts tell the exact story of the Book of Mormon. You are a lawyer. Once you see the evidence you will agree."

"Like I said, I'm listening."

January handed him a pen and a legal pad. "I think you'll want to take notes." He smiled. "In case you want to cross-examine me later." He began. "The Book of Mormon tells us the Nephites came to North America from Jerusalem in 589 BC."

Thorne scribbled "Nephites" and the date 589 BC on the pad.

January continued. "Most Mormon authorities believe these Nephite seafarers arrived in Central America. But I believe the ancient lands described in the Book of Mormon are actually in the southern Great Lakes region. So it makes sense we should find artifacts in the Great Lakes area that reflect the culture and history of people who came from the Middle East." He recited the line he had written and spoken dozens of times over the past few years. "Specifically, the artifacts should be culturally and historically consistent with Jewish life in the 6th century BC and also that of the Phoenicians, who logic would tell us were the ship owners and sailors and navigators who likely accompanied the Nephites. Agreed?"

"Okay so far. If anybody from that time could sail across the Atlantic it would have been the Phoenicians. Their boats were bigger than the ones Columbus sailed."

"Agreed. Now take a look at this." January pushed a Burrows Cave artifact across the table.

Thorne examined the carving, which portrayed a curved-bow ship on the water with the moon, the sun and what appeared to be some stars in the sky above it. "Is that the Little Dipper?"

BURROWS CAVE URSA MINOR STONE

"Yes. And this is an important point. The only ancient culture known to have used the Little Dipper, or Ursa Minor, as a navigational reference was the Phoenicians. In fact, no other ancient culture even sailed at night."

January continued. "And what we find on the Burrows Cave artifacts is Phoenician writing dating from exactly this period. And I've already shown you the sandstone head, which fits neatly into Phoenician religious practices of the day."

Thorne shifted in his chair. "You're going to need more than a couple of artifacts to prove your case."

"Fair enough." January bent down and, using all his strength, hoisted a keyboard-sized marble slab onto the table. The image displayed two seated bird-faced women facing each other in profile, each holding a cat on a leash. "The Egyptian male gods Horus and Ra-Horakhty are often depicted with bird heads, but no Egyptian goddesses have bird features. The use of the bird face on a female body indicates a Greek influence, which didn't pervade the Middle East until around 600 BC."

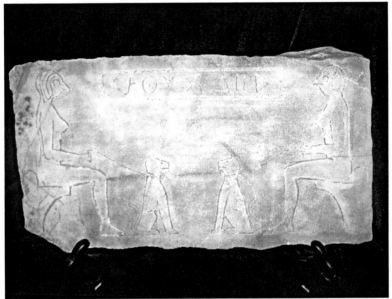

BURROWS CAVE BIRD-FACE STONE

January waited while Thorne studied the slab. "What's interesting about this carving," January said, "is the combination of Greek and Egyptian motifs: the bird-faces indicate a Greek influence while the use of cats is Egyptian. No similar examples exist in museums. Some would argue this shows the carvings to be the work of an amateur forger. I believe a forger who went to the trouble of carving thousands of pieces would not have been so careless as to make such a fundamental error; it would have been easy to simply copy from a book at the library. I believe instead this piece is unique and demonstrates a branch of religious worship—a hybrid—otherwise unknown to scholars."

"Unknown to scholars because the worshipers of this hybrid religion left the Middle East and came here."

"Precisely."

Thorne scribbled a few more notes. "So your evidence indicates there were Phoenicians here in the sixth century BC. But it doesn't show they were Mormons or Nephites or whatever you call them."

"That's a common misunderstanding. The Book of Mormon doesn't claim the Nephites were Mormons. It says they were Israelis, led by a man named Nephi. And it is likely, as we agreed, that there were Phoenicians in their traveling party. So these artifacts are perfectly consistent with the story told in the Book of Mormon."

Thorne stared out the window for a few seconds. He leaned forward. "So what's your problem then? If the artifacts fit so neatly with your theory, why do you need me?"

"Yes, why indeed? The answer is because they don't all fit so neatly. In addition to the Phoenician artifacts from the sixth century BC, there are a number of stones that exhibit scenes from the first century AD. Specifically, images of Jesus Christ and the destruction of the Temple in Jerusalem. Obviously, these events would not have been known to the Nephites journeying 500 years earlier."

"So how do you explain them? Divine intervention?"

Thorne was masking his curiosity with insolence. In his younger days January would have reached over and cuffed him. But there was no time for that stuff now. And his guest did have a right to be peeved. "No. I am a man of reason, though my faith is also strong. I have come to believe there were two waves of travelers. The second group came in the first century AD. Do you recall the map stone photo I mailed you?"

Thorne nodded. "It shows the Mississippi River and its tributaries."

"Correct. And I believe that was carved by the original wave of travelers. Here it is." He unwrapped the paperback-sized stone and handed it across the table to Thorne.

BURROWS CAVE MAP STONE

Thorne studied it, turning it in the light as January spoke.

"If this were a road map, and you were heading north on the Mississippi, I would tell you to take your second right onto the Ohio River, then a left onto the Wabash River and then another left. That would put you on the Embarras River in southern

Illinois, the river you saw in the distance last night. Note the symbols where that river ends. One is a horizontal line with four short vertical lines which I believe represents a stockade structure built for defensive purposes. The other figure, below the stockade as if being guarded by it, is igloo-shaped with an archway—this clearly symbolizes a cave. Burrows Cave."

"Okay, I'll buy that. But then what's the other cave marking south of it, on the Ohio River?"

"That's Cave-In-Rock, an enormous cave carved into the limestone by the river. It was famous during pioneering times as a haven for outlaws. But there are reports from the early 1800s of Egyptian and Roman hieroglyphs carved on its wall. Now it's covered by graffiti. No doubt those writings would have told an interesting story." January shrugged. "Who knows how many other artifacts have been lost to time?"

"Have you translated the writing?"

"The words are basically labels—'cave,' 'river branch,' 'village.' Each dot signifies a day's journey."

He allowed Thorne a few seconds to study the map. "You may note that the carving shows the Mississippi emptying into the Gulf of Mexico well east of its modern course. According to geologists, this map shows the river's ancient course." He smiled. "Pretty sophisticated work for a hoaxster, don't you think?"

Thorne ignored the question, though January sensed he was moved by the logic of the analysis. January continued. "As I said, this is an early map, representing the first wave of explorers. By the time the second wave came, the Nephites and Lamanites had spread eastward." He handed Thorne a second black stone, a bit larger than the first.

BURROWS CAVE MAP STONE

"You'll notice that Burrows Cave is again marked with the igloo shape, just below the stockade. But this time the map shows the entire Ohio River valley, all the way into Pennsylvania and southern New York. This is the historic home of the Mandan tribe, before they were pushed into North Dakota."

Thorne's eyes widened. "This is the region where the Bat Creek Stone and the Ohio Decalogue Stone were found."

"And many others you are not aware of. Eventually they will all be on display at the Foxwoods museum."

Thorne turned the map stone over. Along the top of the back of the map stone ran a series of slash marks, as if someone were keeping count. An equal number ran across the bottom. "What are these?" Thorne asked.

"If you count them you'll see that there are 40 slashes along the top and another 40 along the bottom. Each represents a generation. The stone has been in Astarte's family for 80 generations."

"Astarte?"

94

January smiled. "We're getting a bit ahead of ourselves. She's the little girl from the museum."

Thorne turned the map back over. "So you think this second map stone was carved in the first century by a group of refugees from the Mediterranean region."

"Yes." He paused, making sure Thorne's eyes were on his. "And I believe some of Jesus Christ's family members were part of this group."

"Which ones? I know they fled Jerusalem."

"Like many others, I believe Jesus and Mary Magdalene had a child, and that Mary brought that child, Sarah, to the south of France and raised her there. And this plays a part later in our story. But now I am talking about Jesus' niece, Anna, daughter of Jesus' brother Jude. She was named after her grandmother Hannah, mother of the Virgin Mary. After Jesus was crucified, Jude went to the northern African kingdom of Mauretania to preach—this is the present-day Morocco."

"I've never heard of Jude or Anna."

"The Church doesn't like to discuss or even acknowledge the family of Jesus—it makes him seem too human. But there are Roman accounts of the Desposyni, the family of Jesus. The Romans were very concerned his followers would rally around one of his brothers. Most of the family members were killed; a few fled Jerusalem. Jude ended up in Mauretania, as I said."

"Okay, continue."

"At that time Mauretania was ruled by King Juba II and Queen Cleopatra Selene, the daughter of the famous Cleopatra and Mark Anthony. Anna married into this Mauretanian royal family." He paused for effect. "Her marriage united the dynastic bloodlines of Jesus Christ and Queen Cleopatra."

Thorne sat back. "I never really think of Jesus and Cleopatra being of the same historical era. But it makes sense—they only lived, what, a generation apart?"

"Yes. She died in 30 BC."

"So these Mauretanian royals had some pretty impressive ancestors—Uncle Jesus and Grandma Cleopatra." He shook his head. "And you think these are the people who came to Burrows Cave."

"Correct. During the first century Mauretania was populated by merchants and refugees from all over Europe and the Mediterranean, much as Morocco is today. Eventually it became quite wealthy, predominantly from the sale of purple dye which Roman nobility prized for their garments. When the Roman Emperor Caligula began to run short of funds, some time around 40 AD, he sent an invading army to raid King Juba's treasury. But when the army arrived, a large segment of the population, including the royal family and many members of the merchant class, had fled. And the treasury was empty. The fleeing Mauretanians were never heard from again. One theory is that they followed ancient Phoenician maps and sailed across the Atlantic to the Gulf of Mexico, and from there up the Mississippi River. It makes sense they would have interacted and perhaps settled with other Mediterranean peoples once they got close to the Burrows Cave area."

"You're assuming your Book of Mormon is correct and there actually were other Mediterranean people here."

"Yes, I am assuming that. But the artifacts are consistent with that assumption."

Thorne nodded. "Okay. Your theory that would explain the eclectic nature of the artifacts. The merchants represented many different cultures and therefore carved many different kinds of artifacts—Roman, Jewish, Greek, African, Phoenician, Christian, whatever."

"Exactly. Artifacts that all date to the late first century." January sipped some water. His body ached, and he could feel his heart throbbing just to keep blood flowing to his organs. His fingers were white and cold. Not much longer. "The Book of Mormon speaks of a 'time of peace,' during which the two tribes—I forgot to mention that the Nephites split into two groups, the opposing group being called the Lamanites—finally stopped fighting each other. I believe this 'time of peace' was brought on by the arrival of the Mauretanian refugees, including the young bride Anna."

"The niece of Jesus," Thorne said.

"Yes. Anna's children were the first American royalty. Astarte's mother is Anna's direct descendant, her bloodline guarded and protected to prevent contamination." January paused. "Only once was a new line added to it. Only once in 2,000 years."

✙ ✙ ✙

"Only once," Thorne repeated, sighing. January knew Thorne's curiosity would allay his frustration and anger over Amanda's abduction. "All right, I'll bite. What was added to this royal bloodline? And when?"

For January, this was where it all began. He would need Thorne to finish the journey for him. "In the late 12th century a group of six Templar Knights, accompanied by a French noblewoman by the name of Marie-Claire, traveled across the Northern Atlantic in search of Anna's bloodline. They ended up in the Catskills region of New York." He smiled. "This, I'm sure, is not too hard for you to believe."

His guest shifted in his seat. "The trip itself is not hard for me to believe. I still have my doubts about the Anna bloodline stuff. I assume you have some evidence of this journey?"

"Of course." From his briefcase on the floor January pulled a burgundy leather folio the size a coffee table book. He carefully laid the object flat on the table and unclasped the brass latch. Inside rested about a dozen sheets of ancient parchment, each sleeved in a pocket of air-tight protective plastic. He pushed the folio toward Cam. "Please be gentle. The pages you are looking at are over 800 years old. We call it the Clairvaux Codex, after the Cistercian abbey where it was written. At one point the pages were bound in a book, which is why it's called a codex. It was given to my father by an old French village priest just after World War II. His church had been destroyed by the Nazis, and he himself was near death. It tells the story of the Templar journey to the Catskills in the year 1179." He pulled a loose-leaf notebook from the same briefcase. "This is a translation of the document, along with my notes—the original is in Latin. You can read it at your leisure." He leaned back, catching his breath as Thorne carefully examined the writings. "The parchment has been carbon-dated to the mid-1100s."

A few more seconds passed before Thorne looked up again, during which time January placed the stone artifacts back in the carrying case. "So what were these Templars doing here?"

"What indeed?" January supposed that Thorne himself could make some educated guesses, but wanted to learn what January knew. "I have spent the better part of the last 40 years—since I turned 18 and my father first shared the Clairvaux Codex with me—trying to determine just that. But it was worth the effort. In fact, it was when I realized I had spent exactly 40 years that I finally solved the mystery. As you may know, the number 40 is of critical importance in the Bible—the Jews wandered the desert 40 years, it rained 40 days and 40 nights, Moses was on Mount Sinai 40 days and 40 nights, Jesus fasted 40 days, kings reigned for 40 years--"

Thorne cut him off. "That's because it takes the planet Venus 40 years to complete a full cycle. Venus was sacred to ancient peoples who worshiped the Sacred Feminine; the writers of the Bible incorporated these ancient beliefs to make it more palatable to the people."

"Exactly. One of the reasons the Jewish rabbis of the time were so willing to accept Jesus as a prophet was because he descended from Abraham by 40 generations on his mother Mary's side. The community was waiting for a new king, a new leader, the next king in the Davidic line. It was time."

January sipped some water and caught his breath. "Once I focused on generations and life cycles and the number 40, the answer to the riddle became clear: Marie-Claire and the Templars came here to re-seed Jesus' bloodline. Exactly 40 generations had passed since the birth of Jesus; the cycle was over. Marie-Claire was part of the Jesus bloodline, descended from Mary Magdalene in the south of France. It was time for her to refresh and refortify the holy bloodline here in America." He would not insult Thorne's intelligence by explaining how important bloodlines were to ancient Europeans, especially those of noble or royal birth. In royal families, the family tree looked more like a vine, circling back on itself as cousin married cousin to keep the bloodline pure and free from contamination.

98

Thorne nodded. "The 40 slashes on the back of the stone." He stared out the window, apparently deep in thought. "Even if your theory about refreshing the bloodline is correct, why come to North America?"

"Because, as I said, Anna's branch of the Desposyni, of Jesus' family, ended up in North America in the first century. The Templars knew Anna's group had migrated eastward into the Ohio River Valley and southern New York, probably from their Scandinavian members who learned of it from the Viking voyages—we saw this migration on the map stone. And the Templars also feared the Church might turn on the bloodline families, seeing them as a threat to Rome's religious authority. It turns out they were correct to be afraid—the Church wiped out many of the French bloodline families, including Marie-Claire's, in the Albigensian Crusades in the early 1200s. But a branch of the bloodline would be safe here in America, far from the reach of the Vatican."

Thorne's eyes widened again—this explanation seemed to resonate with him, perhaps confirmed some of his own theories. "So Marie-Claire came all the way to New York with six Templar Knights just to get pregnant?"

"No. She already had a young son by her husband Aragon, one of her Templar escorts."

"I thought the Templars were celibate."

January waved the question away. "Most were nobleman who joined the order later in life, after marrying and fathering children. As was the case with Aragon. And even then some were less celibate than others." He gulped more water. "In any event, Aragon was a Spanish nobleman who actually descended directly from Mohammed—recall that the Moors ruled Spain during this time. Most Christians at the time loathed the Muslims. But the Templars had strong ties to the Islamic world and they believed that adding Mohammed's bloodline to that of Jesus and Cleopatra would cement these alliances. Even at that early date the Templars feared they would have to flee Europe for North America."

"As they eventually did."

"Yes. It was your research that helped me put all these pieces together."

"So this son of Marie-Claire and Aragon would then marry into the Jesus family bloodline in America?"

"Correct. Into Anna's line. Which could itself trace its blood directly back to Jesus and King David, and also to Cleopatra. The line was as pure as any European royal family. Today this family is known as the Mandan Indians."

Thorne nodded. "The Mandan. The White Indians. Lewis and Clark met them while heading west. Thomas Jefferson was obsessed with them."

"Yes, by the time of Lewis and Clark the Mandan had been pushed back west again by the settlers."

"I thought the Mandan were extinct."

"Not completely." January filled his lungs with air. His story was nearing its end. "And now, today, another 40 generations have passed. Another cycle is complete. It became time to refortify the bloodline."

Thorne blinked. "Astarte."

"Yes, she is the Fortieth Princess." January straightened himself in his chair and steeled his voice. "To Astarte's mother's royal bloodline, I have added the blood of the Prophet, Joseph Smith, my great-grandfather." There, he had said it. Admitted he had fathered Astarte. His own earthly father had almost killed him when he found out. But January had been obeying his heavenly father, who had appeared to him in a dream and decreed he mate with the Mandan princess.

The significance of his message empowered him, adding timbre and resonance to his voice, causing his words to reverberate and echo around the room. Thorne could not fail to heed their import. Or their divine inspiration. "Think what Astarte embodies, Mr. Thorne. She is the true princess of the Western world—more royal blood flows through her veins than through anyone else alive. Her kingdom shall be here in America, in God's New Jerusalem. The world is ready for a female spiritual leader—just as the world was ready to accept Jesus as the Age of Pisces began, so too will it be willing to accept a female messiah as the Age of Aquarius dawns."

Thorne looked at him blankly.

"Don't you see?" January said. "Aquarius, the sign for water—water is where life begins inside the womb. A woman is destined to rule!" He banged the table with an open hand. "Astarte. She unites the bloodlines of Judaism, Christianity, Islam and Mormonism with the ancient Egyptian cult of Isis and its worship of the Sacred Feminine. In fact, her very name—Astarte—is an ancient version of the Isis name. It is Astarte's destiny to bring the true word of God to all the earth's inhabitants. And that word is the Book of Mormon."

He sat back, exhausted, his sermon having sucked the energy from him.

"So that's what this is all about." Thorne shook his head. "You expect me to help you help her, what, take her throne? This is crazy. I promised to hear you out. Well I have. And you promised to free Amanda once I did."

"Help her take her throne?" January repeated. Somehow Thorne did not understand. "No, God will do that. I just want you to show the world these artifacts, to recover the ancient scroll the Templars left hidden in the Catskills. That is your destiny; God has chosen you for this mission. The artifacts themselves are compelling and convincing. All they need is a champion. You, Mr. Thorne, shall be that champion."

Thorne rolled his eyes. "God didn't choose me for anything. The only reason I'm here is because you kidnapped Amanda."

January took a deep breath. How had his words failed to convince his guest? He leaned forward. "No, Mr. Thorne, you are wrong. From the very first day you began to study the history of this continent God has been leading you down this path." He locked eyes with the young man. "You must not deny your destiny."

Thorne stood. "I promised to hear you out. And I have. Now I expect you to keep your promise and free Amanda."

January had hoped it wouldn't come to this. But God, in his infinite wisdom, had made sure January had a backup plan. With a sigh he bent slowly and removed a Glock 22 revolver from a paper bag under his chair, realizing as he did so that this had been God's plan all along, that Thorne was never going to be convinced by mere words. So be it. He waved the weapon a few times, Thorne's attention drawn involuntarily to the polished metal. Guns had a way of ending a debate that words could not resolve.

Thorne eyed him, his handsome face blanching. Did he fear the dying man would shoot him? His mind would reject the possibility, understanding that January needed him alive. But fear was a funny thing—like faith, it played by a different set of rules, ignoring reason and logic. January lifted the gun, the barrel flicking back and forth like a serpent tongue. Slowly he turned the weapon away from Thorne and toward his own mouth.

January had prepared for this final resolution for weeks, fought to keep his body alive just to get to this point. Instead of trepidation he felt only elation, as if the spirit of God had already cupped his soul in His gentle hands in preparation for the journey ahead. "You may not approve of my methods, or of my religion, but in the end you cannot ignore the evidence. The truth is here, in the artifacts and in this Clairvaux Codex and in the ancient scroll you will retrieve. And you are the one who is destined to reveal this truth." He held the gun steady. "Read the document and my notes, Mr. Thorne, follow the clues, climb the mountain and recover the last few artifacts and the scroll I am too close to death to recover. And then tell the world."

Thorne swallowed. "You're a sick man."

January nodded. "In fact, I am terminally ill. But that is irrelevant. You will see that what I have told you is true. I want your help. You'd prefer me dead—yes, I can see the contempt in your eyes. And, of course, you want your fiancée back. Well, perhaps we can both have what we want, Mr. Thorne. So here's my offer to you. A death wish, if you will."

With a theatrical panache January yanked a dishtowel away, revealing a small video monitor resting on the table between them. "Recognize anyone?"

Thorne leaned in, his face registering first relief and then fear at the sight of Amanda sitting at a kitchen table sipping tea. "Where is she?"

"She's close by, and she's safe. For now. But if you look closely, you'll see a small suitcase under the table near her feet." Of course, Astarte was being kept far from the kitchen.

Thorne nodded, swallowing.

"That case contains a dozen sticks of dynamite. And note the electric cord running from the wall to the case." January looked at his watch. "In precisely 43 seconds an electronic impulse will detonate the dynamite. I have no doubt it will be fatal to anyone nearby." He removed his watch, which was set to display in the timer mode, and dropped it on the table in front of Thorne.

Thorne's jaw tightened. "Make it stop."

January smiled. "Actually, you have that very power." He pointed to a light switch on the wall behind Thorne's chair. As he did so, he licked the thumb and forefinger of his left hand and inserted his wet fingers into an electrical socket on the wall next to his chair. "The circuit to this outlet is currently off. That light switch does two things—it deactivates the circuit running to the dynamite, and energizes the circuit to this outlet."

As Thorne cocked his head, January spoke. "So here is my offer: My death and Miss Spencer's life in exchange for your help. You have 12 seconds to decide." He inserted the Glock deep into his mouth, the barrel pointed up toward his brain. The wet fingers of his free hand remained in the outlet. The taste of metal spread thickly in his mouth.

Thorne's eyes darted between the monitor, the watch, the light switch, the outlet, and the gun. January sensed Thorne had figured out that flicking the switch would send an electric shock through January's body, causing January's muscles to contract and his finger to pull the trigger. Thorne had also figured he didn't have time to both disarm January and get back across the room to the light switch before the timer reached zero. Thorne half-stood. "Don't make me do this. Put the gun down."

January choked out the words. "Five seconds. Deal?" He closed his eyes. *Glory be to God.*

Thorne's chair scraped across the floor. January took a final breath before a piercing flame ignited his fingers and flashed through him. He felt a stab of cold pain in his head, but that was quickly washed away by the salving, gentle voice of God informing him that Thorne had accepted the deal.

CHAPTER 8

Cam dove across the table, hoping to yank the gun away from the deranged January. "Stop!" He felt nothing but contempt for his adversary, but no one should die like this. Yet January's simple engineering trick worked perfectly—the force of the shot snapped January's head back, showering Cam with bloody skull fragments. Slowly the lifeless body slid off the chair and crumpled to the floor.

Cam rolled off the table and stared at the monitor. He held his breath, a blood-red zero aglow on January's digital watch. Amanda sipped her tea, oblivious to the bomb at her feet. Cam peered at the monitor for a few more seconds before finally exhaling. He found a dish towel hanging on the refrigerator door and wiped January's blood off his face with a shaky hand. He closed his eyes and breathed deeply through his nose, fighting to keep from fleeing the carnage around him.

Opening his eyes slowly he checked the monitor again, not trusting that in the next few seconds the earth would not shake and his world be shattered forever. But, gloriously, the monitor displayed Amanda continuing to sip her tea. Another deep breath and he edged toward January, reaching tentatively for his lifeless wrist. No pulse. Now what? He lifted the phone off the counter, dialed 911 and gave the address. "Jefferson January just shot himself in the head. He's dead."

The security guard rushed in as Cam hung up. Seeing his boss crumpled on the floor, he pulled his revolver and leveled it at Cam. "What happened?"

Cam kept his voice calm and made sure the guard could see his hands. "January shot himself in the mouth." He swallowed. "I just called 911." He steadied himself against the refrigerator.

The guard was young, maybe early twenties, possibly just back from a tour of duty in Iraq or Afghanistan. Composed, but clearly in battle mode as he studied the scene.

Cam took a deep breath; he felt clammy. He hadn't eaten in a few hours and was starting to get shaky, probably from the adrenaline rush. "Look, you searched me and my car when I came in. You know I'm unarmed. And the gun is still in his hand."

The guard nodded. "That's his Glock all right." He lowered his weapon.

A commotion in the parking lot drew their attention. Cam moved past the guard and pulled open the front door. A large muscular woman—presumably another member of the security staff—sprinted toward him. Amanda, hand-in-hand with the little girl, followed. She spotted him. "Cam! Are you all right? Someone said they heard a gunshot."

He moved aside for the female guard and folded Amanda in his arms, his heart thumping against her chest. "I'm fine." He moved his mouth to her ear. "Keep the girl away," he whispered. "January shot himself." He inhaled her scent. At least she was okay.

Amanda's body went limp for an instant. "How horrible." She kissed him tenderly on the mouth. "You're shaking."

He closed his eyes, his joy at seeing her irreconcilable with the gruesomeness of January's suicide. Or was it a homicide? He fought to control his breathing, the floral scent of her hair slowly calming him. He squeezed her to him.

She recoiled. "Easy. I hurt my rib."

He pulled back. "Are you okay?"

"I am now." She leaned back into him, her fingers digging into his back.

He smiled sadly. "Me too."

After a few seconds she gently pulled away. "Cameron, this is Astarte."

He did his best to smile. "Nice to meet you."

She stared up at him with dark, questioning eyes that belonged on an older face. "Hello."

Cam and Astarte stared at each other for a few seconds before Amanda re-grasped Astarte's hand and began to lead her away from January's house.

"Wait," Cam said. "Take these with you. Put them in the trunk of my rental car out there; it's unlocked." He handed her the wheeled carrying case containing the stone artifacts and the leather-bound folio. The gesture seemed at once both petty and crucially important. He whispered, "They were important enough for January to die for."

She nodded and kissed him again before turning back to Astarte. "Come with me honey." She pulled the case. "We can't stay here."

The girl looked up sadly. Somehow she knew. "Is Uncle Jefferson dead?"

"He may be hurt. But the police are coming and they will take care of everything. For now we need to go back to your room." She spotted Venus, her nose pressed against the car window and her paws scratching excitedly at the glass at the site of Amanda. "Better yet, come to the car so you can meet Venus. Though I'm not sure how she got here."

"Does she bite?"

"No," Amanda smiled. "But she licks."

✚ ✚ ✚

The text message came just as Judith bent over January's dead body. This was not how she expected this mission to end. Not that she even understood what the mission was all about. All she knew was that her bosses in Virginia had arranged for her to take a mundane security job with some crazy Mormon, to gather as much information about his activities as she could, and to wait for further instructions. That was two months ago. And until this week it had been about as exciting as watching someone play solitaire.

She displayed the message. "Eliminate Amanda Spencer. Eagle777." *What?* She stared at the screen. There was nothing ambiguous about it, and the Eagle777 sign-off attested to its authenticity. But it made no sense. Orders to murder, especially civilians on U.S. soil, were almost never given—and only then to protect national security. She walked into the living room and texted back. "Please repeat." She had helped out with the kidnapping because she didn't want to blow her cover, but this....

Her supervisor, a man named Jabil Hayek whom she spoke with weekly but had never actually met, would not appreciate her insubordination. She had killed in combat before, but she wasn't going to assassinate a civilian unless she was 100% certain of the order. And even then she might have second thoughts.

The response came seconds later. "A matter of TOP national security. Eliminate Amanda Spencer."

Shit. What in the world could Mary Poppins have done to deserve this? Judith had reported to Hayek that the girl and Amanda had snuck into January's bunker full of artifacts. But did that warrant death? She sighed. She had signed on for a life in the intelligence community. And that meant secrecy and violence and ugliness. And most of all it meant blind obedience to orders coming from Virginia. Even if they seemed to make no sense whatsoever.

She peered out the window. The local police had just arrived; Eliza was leading them to January's kitchen. They would want to interview Thorne, which would take a while. But apparently he hadn't killed January so at some point he and Amanda would get in the car and drive away. Which meant she only had a few minutes to carry out her orders and then get the hell out of there. Slipping out a side door, she walked as casually as she could across the compound before sprinting up the stairs to her bedroom above the garage. She quickly packed everything she would need to survive in the woods into a small backpack.

Descending the stairs three at a time, she barged into the garage and grabbed a pair of bolt cutters hanging with the other tools on the back wall. She sprinted through the rear yard and along a path toward the security fence, stopping at an area of fencing brushed by the low branches of a pine tree. She snapped at the metal, grinding and twisting the blades; she folded back a section of fence. Once on the other side she would fold the fence section back into place and camouflage the breach with the tree branches, hopefully delaying her pursuers. After that her superior fitness and survival skills should keep her alive. She checked her watch. Nineteen minutes had passed since she received her orders. She sprinted back to her bedroom above the garage.

Sweat ran down her armpits and pooled along the waistband of her blue workpants as she pulled the curtain aside and rested the stand of her Remington M40 sniper rifle on the window ledge. She had a clear shot at Thorne's car parked 100 feet away. It was a shot she could nail from five times the distance, her biathlon training making her an expert markswoman even with an elevated heart rate. She rubbed a clammy hand over her face and exhaled slowly. What in the world had Mary Poppins done?

✝ ✝ ✝

Jabil Hayek sat behind a nondescript desk in a nondescript office within a nondescript office building in suburban Virginia. He sucked his cigarette—his fifth of the morning—down to the filter and crushed it into a navy blue "World's Best Dad" coffee mug he now used as an ashtray. Some dad. He'd be lucky to make it to Thanksgiving dinner at this rate. And he wouldn't feel much like celebrating if he did. If heavy hangs the head that wears the crown, then heavier still hangs the head that keeps the secrets—and makes the difficult decisions—that protect the peace. But maintaining the peace was paramount—no child should have to grow up the way he did, or witness the things he witnessed, after Lebanon exploded into civil war in 1975. If a few must die so the rest can live in peace, well, such is the ugly but unavoidable cost of living in a civilized society. The needs of the many outweigh the needs of the one.

He rubbed his face and lit another cigarette. He had chosen this career, chosen to serve his adopted country in this way. Life as an intelligence officer was good work, necessary work, honorable work. Even if sometimes, like today, he had to make decisions that might leave blood on his hands.

Not that he had expected today to be the day the Clairvaux Codex resurfaced after more than 60 years, in the possession of a nut like Jefferson January no less. But that's the way things often worked in the intelligence world—information bubbled to the surface from strange places at strange times. And then it had to be dealt with.

McDevitt had warned him the Clairvaux Codex might someday reemerge. The crusty, steel-eyed World War II veteran had called him into his office on a warm fall afternoon in November, 1989, the day the Berlin Wall fell. "I always said I'd stay at my desk until we finally beat the Commies. Well, they're done. So I'm off to do some fishing. Just a couple of things you should know about before I go."

McDevitt had held up a yellowed manila folder, with the words CLAIRVAUX CODEX written in block letters on the tab. "For your eyes only. Nobody else knows about this."

"Why me?"

McDevitt was a near-legend at Langley for his instincts and insight—he had the rare ability to see three or four moves into the future, to see what was coming around the corner. But he tended to work alone, and Hayek had only limited contact with him.

"Two reasons. First, everyone likes Klinger."

"Klinger?"

"Yup. From M*A*S*H. Because of him Americans like the Lebanese. They don't think of them as Arabs or towel heads or terrorists. And that includes the Americans here at the Agency."

"Okay, I guess."

"Second, who always loses when there's a war in the Mid-East?"

"The Jews. Even when they win, they lose because everyone hates them."

"Correct. And who else?"

"The Lebanese. We end up getting caught in the middle. Usually our homeland is the battle field."

"Exactly. That's why I picked you. You have a horse in this race—the last thing you want to see is another war in the Middle East. And you won't be perceived as biased or paranoid like some Jewish agent might be. People will trust you, like they trust Klinger."

"I don't have to wear a dress, do I?"

McDevitt had responded with a rare smile. "So. The Clairvaux Codex. It's supposedly a medieval document, though nobody's seen it in almost half a century. The Nazis were obsessed with it. And if the Nazis wanted it that badly, there must be some pretty good stuff in there. Templar stuff. The Nazis had a whole unit researching the Templars and their secrets."

Hayek lifted the manila folder, leaned back in his chair and recalled McDevitt describing the interview he had conducted with the young German clerk in 1945:

"First of all, I always wore a big Jewish star when I was questioning those Nazi bastards. Scared the shit out of them—they didn't know I was an Irish-Catholic kid from Boston. This one Kraut was young, maybe 20 or 21. Just a simple clerk. Whole life ahead of him. But afraid of what we were going to do to him, of course. He had been stationed up in northwest Italy in a place called Seborga. Seborga is one of those principalities, sort of like Monaco—it's part of Italy, but they have their own government and currency. When the war ended, the kid hiked over to France and surrendered."

The young Nazi clerk had explained to McDevitt how his unit had been sent to that area of Italy to search for Templar artifacts—specifically, documents and religious relics the Templars may have discovered while excavating beneath King Solomon's Temple in Jerusalem in the 12th century, during the Crusades. "Apparently the nine original Templar knights had gathered at the Cistercian monastery in Seborga before crossing to Jerusalem in the early 1100s," McDevitt had recounted. "It was one of their key strongholds. So it made sense that Templar secrets would be hidden there. One thing in particular caught my attention: The kid said there was some kind of document that would undermine the foundations of Western religion." He had tapped a tobacco-stained finger on the manila folder. "That would have been a big deal for the Nazis—getting rid of religion, and replacing it with Nazism, was a fundamental part of Hitler's plan. The state would become the new religion. That's why so many Catholic priests ended up in concentration camps. So they were interested in anything that would undermine Christianity."

But according to McDevitt the Nazis never found what they were looking for. They tortured a nun into admitting she had seen a leather-bound folio containing medieval writings. She had heard that the folio told of an ancient parchment scroll hidden in a cave many weeks sail west of Europe. An old priest had fled with the manuscript into the hills before the Germans arrived, and the war ended before the Nazis tracked down the priest.

The discovery of the Dead Sea Scrolls in the late 1940s had prompted McDevitt to occasionally update the file with a few newspaper clippings, but otherwise the file had remained dormant for 60 years. Until now.

Hayek fingered the short report Judith had filed early this morning, summarizing the Spencer woman's activities. Almost in passing Judith mentioned that January possessed some medieval writings he called the Clairvaux documents—it was nothing more than dumb luck that he had assigned the young agent to January in the first place, based on some threats January had made when the Mormon leadership refused to support his theories about ancient Mormon history. Now it looked as if January had found the ancient manuscript the Nazis had hunted. If so, had he also found the ancient scroll the Nazis believed would bring down the Western religions?

McDevitt was long since dead, but his instructions echoed inside Hayek's head. "Documents like that have a way of bubbling up at the worst times. Keep an eye out for anything about Clairvaux and the Templars. Someday those papers will turn up again. And it'll be your job to bury them."

✠ ✠ ✠

Cam killed half an hour answering questions from the Pequot deputy police chief, a sixty-something guy whose gruff, street-smart demeanor was softened by a pair of dark, caring eyes. A detective from the state police force took notes. They had moved to January's dining room table, Cam snacking on an apple from January's kitchen. He and the deputy chief sat across from each other while the cop who originally investigated Amanda's disappearance from the museum stood nearby also taking notes. They were on Pequot land so the tribe police had jurisdiction.

Cam kept it simple—January shot himself. No need to get into the whole light switch and electrical outlet machinations; nobody seemed to notice the burn marks on January's thumb and finger. And Cam's story checked out. Still, nobody seemed to want to take responsibility for letting him go. Cam stood. "Look, if you think I took the guy's gun, pried his mouth open and blew his brains out, all without anyone hearing a commotion, then arrest me. Otherwise I'd like to be done with this."

The cop from the museum responded. "You had a motive. The guy kidnapped your fiancée."

"Really? According to you, she just got cold feet."

"And you have blood splattered on your clothes."

"Like I said, I dove across the table to try to stop him. Check the gun—you won't find my fingerprints on it."

"Maybe you wore gloves and then later put the gun in Mr. January's hand."

"Maybe you've been watching too much TV."

The officer took a step toward Cam.

"Enough," the deputy chief spat. He kicked at the carpet and studied his shoes, as if he could find the truth in the creases of the leather like some kind of carnival palm reader. Finally he sighed. "Mr. Thorne, you can go."

Cam didn't give them time to reconsider. He grabbed his coat and jogged to the car. Amanda and Astarte were throwing a tennis ball to Venus in the parking lot. A woman whom Cam had been told was January's sister watched them from a picnic table on the lawn between the garage and January's house. "I don't know about you, but I'm ready to get out of here," he said to Amanda.

"Definitely," Amanda responded. She took Cam's hand and turned to Astarte. "It's time for us to go, love."

The girl frowned. "Can't I come with you?"

Amanda shook her head. "You belong here, with your Aunt Eliza." January's sister had gotten off the picnic bench and was walking briskly toward them. "But I promise to come back for a visit."

"Is Uncle Jefferson dead?"

Amanda dropped to her knees, her eyes level with Astarte's. "I'm afraid so."

The girl sagged. "I was afraid that would happen." The little princess hugged Amanda, resisting Eliza's efforts to pull her away. "All the people I love end up dying," she sobbed. "First my mommy. Then Uncle Jefferson."

Amanda stood and released the girl to her aunt. Two seconds later a gunshot echoed through the compound, the reverberation a haunting exclamation point to the little girl's prophecy.

CHAPTER 9

Georgia had been a CIA operative for almost 20 years and only once before, immediately after 9/11, had she been ordered to drop everything and head straight to Washington for an urgent meeting. Even though it was the Tuesday before Thanksgiving, she had little trouble finding a flight; D.C. was one of those places people flew out of rather than into during the holidays.

She landed at Reagan National late morning and hailed a taxi. These meetings always made her uncomfortable. She understood politics and politicians—it was all about spin and messages and news cycles. Form over substance. But the intelligence community didn't work that way. For them substance—data and information—was everything. The problem was that, as an operative, she was rarely given enough context by her superiors to understand how the information she obtained fit into a bigger picture. It was like working on only a small portion of a jigsaw puzzle.

A half-hour later the cab dropped Georgia off in front of a modern, X-shaped building in Tysons Corner, a northern Virginia suburb of Washington. It was her first visit to the new ODNI headquarters—the Office of the Director of National Intelligence had been created after 9/11 to oversee and coordinate the nation's various intelligence communities. She crossed a dark blue industrial carpet into a large conference room overlooking a parking lot and the highway in the distance. She wasn't surprised to see half a dozen staffers seated around the table; typically the FBI, Homeland Security and Defense Department, along with the CIA, would be represented in any ODNI operation. But she was surprised to see the stern, square-jawed face of Trey Buckner from the Mormon campaign group staring back at her—she had assumed he answered to Salt Lake City, not Washington. Maybe it was both. So this must somehow involve the Governor's Presidential campaign. Or perhaps Jefferson January.

Apparently the group had been waiting for her. A tall, paunchy man with olive skin, tightly curled dark hair and puffiness under a pair of dark brown eyes sat at the head of the table. No doubt he had once been handsome; in fact, with a little sleep and a few visits to the gym he still could be. As he cleared his throat and took a puff on a cigarette, she squinted at his badge—'Jabil Hayek.' She recognized the Hayek name as a prominent Lebanese one. He was perhaps ten years younger than Georgia, making him almost a contemporary; most of the others in the room looked young enough to be her children.

He didn't bother with the formalities. And the fact he was smoking in a government building indicated he ruled this little fiefdom. "We have a situation that has been festering for a number of years. Our job is to make sure things don't begin to rot." He turned to Georgia. "Perhaps you recall the advice you gave to the campaign group up in Massachusetts?"

It seemed that Trey had already briefed the group. "Regarding Jefferson January?"

"Yes." His tone was matter-of-fact, not warm but not unkind either.

"I believe my exact words were to do whatever was necessary to bury January and his artifacts."

"Well, the first part is taken care of. January shot himself in the head earlier this morning."

"Shot himself?" It was a bit too convenient.

Hayek snorted. "Believe it or not, yes. But not before he took a number of steps to ensure the continuation of his mission or quest or prophecy or whatever he calls it."

Georgia's mind raced. She hadn't even realized they had January under surveillance. Apparently not her corner of the jigsaw.

Hayek explained how a woman had gained access to the artifacts housed in January's underground bunker. He looked at his notes. "Her name is Amanda Spencer."

Georgia interrupted. "The one who's doing all the research on the Templars in New England?"

Hayek looked back at her blankly. "I'm, um, not aware of her background." He glared at a young male assistant.

"The Spencer woman and a guy named Cameron Thorne are part of a group that has been studying a bunch of runic inscriptions and other artifacts that seem to tell the story of the Knights Templar coming to America in the late 1300s." She had attended a conference they spoke at in Newport, Rhode Island last spring, and even shared a spiced rum with them at the bar afterward. Nice people. They had even paid for her drink.

"Wait," Hayek said. "What's this about the Templars in America?"

Georgia knew they had gone off on a tangent, but her superior seemed interested so she continued. "The theory is the Templars came over to escape the Church, both for economic and religious reasons. They make a pretty compelling case that the Templars were actually worshipers of the Goddess."

"What goddess?" Hayek asked.

"You know, Mother Earth."

"You mean they were pagans?"

Georgia bit her tongue. "I suppose you could use that word. Others would say they were looking for a duality in the godhead, a balance of both male attributes and female attributes. Obviously the Church during medieval times was about as patriarchal as you can get. The Templars may also have been protecting the bloodline, the offspring of Jesus and Mary Magdalene."

"Did they ever mention anything about an ancient scroll, or about a Cistercian abbey in Clairvaux?"

She shrugged. "Not that I ever heard."

Hayek waved the Templar discussion aside. "Back to the issue at hand, Ms. Spencer's expertise in the Templars might explain why she was at January's compound." He lowered his voice. "At some point—in fact, only about ten minutes ago—our agent targeted Ms. Spencer."

"Wait. Your operative took a shot at Amanda Spencer? Just because she, what, saw some carved stones?"

✝ ✝ ✝

Judith threw the backpack over her shoulders and raced toward the rear staircase, the Remington still warm in her hand. The 15 pounds of metal felt like an anchor as she took the stairs three at a time and then leaped the final six. But she would need the rifle both to survive in the woods and as protection against those pursuing her. Assuming she survived, she would then have to go underground and somehow reinvent herself, give herself a new identity, start a whole new life.

All because she couldn't bring herself to fire the bullet that would turn Mary Poppins' skull into Humpty Dumpty.

She pushed through the hole in the fence and trekked perhaps a mile into the woods. Would it be enough of a head start?

The police would of course want to catch the sniper.

And her CIA superiors would want to know how—or more importantly why—she missed her target. If they even bothered to ask.

✛ ✛ ✛

Cam's mind clicked through the images as if turning the pages of an old superhero comic book. A gunshot ringing off the side of the car. Voices screaming. Amanda diving into the back seat. Himself crawling to the driver's side door. Police running from January's house with guns drawn. Screeching out of the compound. Crashing through the metal security gate. Bam. Whack. Pow. Screw the cops. He wasn't going to stick around and serve as target practice.

He gulped some air as they reached the main road, his fingers white against the black steering wheel. "Amanda, you okay?"

Her trembling hand squeezed his shoulder. "We're fine. Just frightened to death."

"Who was shooting at us?" He tried to control his breathing, forcing himself to inhale only through his nose.

"I have no idea. But I heard it whiz by my ear. I'm still shaking."

Amanda's earlier comment echoed back to him. "Wait, did you say 'we' are fine?" He looked in the rearview mirror to see a pair of cobalt eyes peering back at him.

"I dragged her into the car. Bloody certain I wasn't going to leave her out there."

"Of course." He accelerated, one eye on the side mirror as he sped along the state highway. Nobody seemed to be pursuing.

Amanda put her arm protectively around the girl. "It's obviously not safe for her back at the compound."

"Agreed. We'll have to bring her to the police or social services or something."

The young princess whimpered. "But I want to stay with you. I'm afraid." She stared at Cam in the mirror, her eyes wet and beseeching. "I need a prince to rescue me."

✟ ✟ ✟

Georgia repeated the question. "Your operative took a shot at Amanda Spencer?"

"Fortunately, she missed," Hayek said.

Georgia seemed to be the only one who noticed Trey's sharp intake of breath. "Missed?" she asked. "Completely?"

Hayek nodded. "Yes." Hayek leveled his brown eyes on Georgia's. "And I want to make it clear that I issued no such order. To do so would be a clear violation of U.S. law." She couldn't decide if he was telling the truth or just trying to cover his ass. "But our agent knew we did not want the Spencer woman prancing out of the compound with January's artifacts and papers. Apparently the agent got a bit overzealous and made an attempt to … incapacitate … Ms. Spencer. But she was acting on her own."

Incapacitate. One of the reasons ODNI was created was that it operated in a gray area, answerable to the President and empowered to take actions on domestic soil that were otherwise forbidden. Actions such as assassination. But how could it be necessary in this case? "What in the world would make your agent think it was necessary to kill an innocent civilian over some carved stones?"

A few younger staffers shifted; apparently they were not used to anyone questioning Hayek. And any of them with half a brain knew this talk of assassination could put them in front of a Congressional inquiry. Or worse. "I'm not at all sure she thought that. Again, my guess is she just panicked. But this all happened only minutes ago; I just got off the phone with the local police."

"So what happened next?"

"According to one of the security guards, in the commotion Ms. Spencer and this Cameron Thorne fellow you mentioned—he is now apparently her fiancé—ended up fleeing with a suitcase full of artifacts. More importantly, they also ended up with a medieval document from January's collection." He sucked on his cigarette. "The Nazis were searching for this document during World War II. They believed its contents could undermine Western religion. It is called the Clairvaux Codex."

Trey cleared his throat. "Which artifacts did they take?"

Georgia wished he had not interrupted; she wanted to hear more about this Clairvaux Codex.

"I don't know for sure. But apparently January had been meeting with Thorne, trying to enlist his aid. This fits in with what Georgia was just telling us. I think we have to assume they have the best of the bunch, whatever January thought was important."

"By important, you mean whatever proves his theories?" Georgia said.

"Yes." Hayek looked around the table. "Those artifacts, and in particular the Clairvaux Codex, could destabilize the entire Middle East. It's not important that you know what secrets the artifacts reveal. What's important is that we need to get them back." He ground his cigarette into an ashtray. "Unfortunately, Spencer and Thorne are spooked, so they will not be easy to find." He exhaled. "This mushroomed on us quickly. It is now a top priority. As I said, this stuff could further destabilize the Middle East—not that anyone over there needs another excuse."

"Wait," Georgia said. "So you think January is right? These artifacts validate the Book of Mormon?" If so, it would be an astounding revelation. But how would that destabilize the Middle East? Hayek hadn't given them any details.

Hayek chewed his lip. "I wish that was all we were talking about. The Book of Mormon is the least of our problems."

✠ ✠ ✠

Astarte tried not to cry. Adults didn't like cry-babies. But she felt very sad. Uncle Jefferson was dead, and Mr. Thorne didn't want to keep her. The police would bring her back to Aunt Eliza. But she didn't want to live at the compound without Uncle Jefferson, especially because Aunt Eliza wasn't a very nice person once you got to know her.

Mr. Thorne was talking on the speaker phone to a man named Salazar as they drove on the highway. "This doesn't make any sense. That shot hit right next to Amanda; I was about ten feet away. But why try to kill her? I'm the one January gave the artifacts to. I'm the one he brought to the cave. I'm the one he wants to solve the mystery. If someone wanted that kept quiet, they would have shot at me instead."

"Any chance January ordered Amanda, or you, killed?" Mr. Salazar asked.

Mr. Thorne shook his head. "He had plenty of chances to kill either of us. And he gave me the artifacts because he wanted my help. He had to know that killing Amanda would be the worst way to get it."

"If not January, then who?"

"It had to be Judith," Miss Amanda said after a few seconds of silence. "She's the guard. She's the only one who had access to the garage. And it seemed to me like she had some kind of military training."

Astarte had once watched Judith lure a spider from the bathtub onto a stick and put it outside on a bush. She didn't seem like a mean person. But maybe she liked spiders better than people.

"Makes sense," Mr. Salazar said. "I bet this Judith was a plant, taking orders from the outside. Cam, did she even know about you?"

"I don't think so. There was a male guard at the front gate when I came in. The first time I saw this Judith woman was after January shot himself."

"So that's it. That's why they targeted Amanda and not you. My guess is Amanda learned something while she was at the compound. Something someone didn't want exposed. Judith was reporting back to some central authority, who then sent orders back how to handle it." Mr. Salazar paused. "Did the girl tell

Amanda any secrets? Or show her anything that was supposed to be kept secret?"

Astarte felt her face get hot. Was that why they tried to shoot Miss Amanda?

Miss Amanda nodded kindly. "Go ahead, Astarte, tell Mr. Salazar what you showed me."

Astarte turned away so Mr. Thorne wouldn't see her crying. But she couldn't keep from sobbing as she answered. "I showed her ... where my uncle kept ... the devil's rocks." Venus leaned over and licked the tears off her face. She buried her face in the dog's fur and closed her eyes. She never should have brought Miss Amanda to the bunker. Uncle Jefferson had told her bad things would happen if she showed the devil's rocks to anyone.

"The devil's rocks?" Mr. Thorne repeated.

Astarte took a deep breath and dried her eyes. Using her most grown-up voice, she explained how the rocks told the story of white people coming to America a long time ago just like the Book of Mormon said, and how the devil made some other rocks to confuse people and make people wonder if the Book of Mormon had the story right, and how Uncle Jefferson put the devil's rocks in a separate room, and how she brought Miss Amanda to see them. She lifted her chin. Maybe it wasn't totally her fault after all. "Did the devil try to kill Miss Amanda because she looked at his rocks?"

Miss Amanda bit her lip. "It wasn't the devil that did this, Astarte."

"That's right," said Mr. Salazar. "But whoever it was isn't going to be happy that you guys escaped with January's artifacts and that Clairvaux Codex. It was smart for you to get out of there. But this isn't over. Not by a long shot."

✚ ✚ ✚

Amanda tried not to let Cam see she was cross with him. They had more important things to do than bicker. But soon she would need to make it clear to him she had no intention of abandoning Astarte.

She and Cam were still unnerved from the gunshot, but Salazar had come up with a plan. They met him at a highway rest area and jumped into his minivan, abandoning the rental car. That would at least buy them some time.

"Hello, Amanda," Salazar said, turning as she jumped into the back seat with Astarte. "I never had a chance to thank you for being so kind to my daughter." His eyes, smoky brown and a bit sad, locked onto hers.

The last time she had seen him he had put a bullet in Cam's shoulder. But she had managed to outfox him so she and Cam could escape. Yet she had never forgotten his parting words: *I have a little girl, almost seven years old. I hope she turns out like you.* A strangely intimate thing to say to someone you had almost killed. But how normal a conversation could one have with a man who had been hired to assassinate you?

Amanda offered a polite smile. "This is Astarte. She's the same age as your daughter." It seemed premature to be discussing play dates.

Salazar extended a stuffed pink bunny toward the back seat with one arm while he steered the van back onto the highway with the other. "My daughter keeps this bunny in the car so she'll always have company in the back seat. I don't think she'd mind if you played with her."

"Thank you," Astarte said. "What's her name?"

"Rosalita."

Astarte cocked her head. "No, I meant the bunny."

Salazar chuckled softly. "Well, Rosalita got her for Easter." His eyes found Amanda in the rearview mirror. "So we named her Ishtar."

Ishtar was the pagan fertility goddess after whom the Easter holiday was named. Originally the Easter holiday was a spring fertility celebration, which is why eggs and grass and rabbits were its symbols. In the early centuries of Christianity the Church piggy-backed onto the festival and transformed it into a celebration of Jesus' resurrection. Salazar had learned all this from Cam and Amanda a year ago. "How very appropriate," Amanda said. "Even more so because Ishtar and Astarte are simply different ways of pronouncing the same name."

Cam cut the conversation short. "We need to figure out where we're going. And what to do with Astarte."

Salazar nodded. "I'm pretty sure nobody saw you getting into my van. But at some point the police are going to come looking for Astarte. And whoever fired that shot is going to come looking for you."

✠ ✠ ✠

The police had finally left, which meant Eliza could wipe the painted smile and dreamy look off her face, stand up straight and get to work. Jefferson had insisted that he had taken care of everything, that upon his death there would be no loose ends. Well, he always did overestimate his ability to control things. Now she would have to try to clean up his mess. Actually, messes.

Mess number one was the disappearance of Astarte. Eliza made a quick phone call. "The princess is missing. She's with Cameron Thorne and the Spencer woman." She described the car and stated the obvious. "We need her back."

Mess two was the failure of the CIA operative to carry out her assassination order. Had Judith simply botched the job? Or gotten cold feet? Or was it possible she had figured out that the assassination order was bogus, that Trey had intercepted Judith's communication with Hayek in Virginia and issued the otherwise-authentic kill code and confirmation? If so, Trey—and their entire operation—might be at risk. Whatever the reason for the failed assassination, the result was potentially catastrophic—the Spencer woman had seen the devil's rocks and lived to tell about them.

The third mess was the devil's rocks themselves. Jefferson should have destroyed them years ago—preserving them was an unnecessary risk. But her brother was a collector at heart, a sentimentalist who could not bring himself to destroy the pieces of history he had so laboriously collected and deciphered. The Vatican at least had the good sense to burn the documents that did not comply with the orthodox teachings of Catholicism.

Jefferson had locked them away, but he had not destroyed them. And now the Spencer woman had seen them.

Eliza retrieved the dynamite-filled suitcase from the kitchen, lifted the bulkhead door and descended the stairway to the underground bunker. She punched in the security code, turned on a light and strode into the main display hall, locking the entry door behind her. She examined the display cases—other than the artifacts Jefferson had packed up to show Thorne, everything seemed in order.

Now to the back room. She entered the security code a second time, opened a second door and flicked a second light switch. Tucked into the back corner of the room sat an old cast-iron bank safe about the size of a child's playpen. Wearing a pair of gardening gloves, she gathered the devil's rocks from the display cases and tossed them into the center of the safe. She counted them as she did so, mostly as a way to keep her mind focused and her thoughts organized. Twenty-one artifacts.

From the suitcase she pulled out a single stick of dynamite. For generations her family had worked in the mining industry so she had some familiarity with explosives—she rested the stick on top of the artifacts, struck a match, lit the fuse, slammed the safe closed and scrambled to the far side of the room, hopeful that there was enough oxygen in the safe to keep the fuse lit. Ten seconds later she had her answer as the room concussed. The iron safe bounced a few inches off the ground, belching smoke and dust before skidding to a stop, its door hanging on a single hinge.

Job done, she gathered the description cards from the display cases, planning to burn them in the fireplace. Out of habit she counted them as well. Twenty-two cards. She froze. She recounted the cards; twenty-two again. Had she miscounted the artifacts? Or was an artifact missing? She eyed the smoking safe. It was too late to find out.

She strode back across the room and peered into the safe. What was left of the artifacts lay in a clump of dust and rubble. Even the devil would have found them useless. And even the devil would have no way of telling if the rubble comprised twenty-two stones, or only twenty-one.

CHAPTER 10

Cam drove north on Interstate 95 in the early afternoon traffic. Astarte, traumatized by her uncle's death, had cried herself to sleep on Amanda's shoulder; Amanda tried to doze with her, though Cam doubted she would be able to sleep much after the gun shot. Cam tried to control his breathing, his body still trembling from the combination of adrenaline and trauma.

Amanda still didn't know she had been one sip of tea away from immortality. Nor did she know Cam had murdered January. Or at least killed him. Or maybe just caused him to die. Whatever the correct term, Cam couldn't help but replay the scene, wondering what he might have done differently. How was he even sure there was dynamite in the suitcase? Maybe the whole thing had been a bluff. And had he reacted more quickly, when he had the full 43 seconds, he might have had time to wrestle the gun from January and still disable the detonator. But he had been too slow to figure out January's plan. And no way was he going to put Amanda in danger, or even the threat of danger, to save a dying megalomaniac. Even if it meant he had blood on his hands.

They had dropped Salazar off at his home in Rhode Island, along with Venus, but not before stopping at Salazar's cousin's house and trading Salazar's van for the cousin's Ford Explorer. "Whoever is after you will find your rental car and figure out you didn't walk away from that rest area," Salazar explained. "At some point they're going to check your cell records and see you called me. If they have half a brain, they'll figure out I picked you up and lent you my van. Using the SUV should buy you an extra day or so."

He had lent Cam a wad of cash and instructed them not to use their bank or credit cards. "You don't know who's following you. They might have access to financial data bases." He then dropped their cell phones into a bucket of water. "My phone is untraceable but you need to get some disposable cell phones. You guys need to be totally under the radar. Get one for the girl also in case you get separated." He would rejoin them if necessary but for now they were heading to Boston—Salazar knew of a furnished apartment available on short notice where the owner would ask no questions.

Cam felt a pang of remorse at leaving the dog but was glad to be rid of the mercenary. It wasn't so much that Salazar outwardly flirted with Amanda; rather, he seemed to idealize her. It was unnerving. Cam had the sense Salazar thought him unworthy of Amanda.

Of course, they had bigger problems. When they arrived in Boston they would need to figure out what to do about Astarte and the artifacts. The obvious way out of all this was to just give the artifacts and/or the Clairvaux Codex back to whomever it was who wanted them so badly. But how were they supposed to do that? Who was it that wanted January's research to die with him? Cam doubted it would be enough to just offer the items up on eBay and hope January's enemies—who now were also apparently his and Amanda's enemies—popped up with a winning bid and a mailing address.

And even so, could Cam just let this go? In some kind of macabre, dying wish sacrament January had traded his very life for Cam's assistance. Sure it was a slimy, coercive trick, but the reality was that Cam was responsible for the death. The gun would not have fired but for Cam flicking the light switch. He clenched the steering wheel. What he had done was not murder. He owed the loony January nothing.

Amanda stirred, reached forward and caressed his cheek with the back of her hand. "Sorry I nodded off."

"Feel better?" He sighed and kissed her palm.

"Actually not. I had horrid dreams." No doubt he would be haunted by nightmares of his own.

He had already summarized his trip to the cave and his meetings with January for Amanda and Salazar. But she had not yet provided any details of the artifacts in the bunker. "What was it about the artifacts you saw that would make someone take a shot at you?"

"You know, I didn't really get much of a look at the devil's rocks. Other than the fact they were in black display cases rather than white ones, they mostly looked like the same as the others." She smiled coyly. "But I did pilfer one."

"You what?"

"I lifted one of the devil's rocks. It's in the trunk with the ones January gave you."

"Really?" He shook his head. "That was pretty ballsy. And pretty smart. What kind of artifacts were they?"

"Mostly carved stone. I was only in the room for a few minutes. I spent most of my time studying a stone which had a carving of Jesus on his knees, sort of praying to another man standing up. The figure standing was barefoot and had scruffy hair and a beard and was carrying a shepherd's staff. The description card said it was John the Baptist."

"Why is Jesus praying to John the Baptist? Are you sure it wasn't a baptism scene?"

"That's what I originally thought, but there was no water or even a bowl of any kind. And John was looking rather imperious."

"I wonder why January hid it away. What else did you see?"

"Next to the John the Baptist stone there was another carving of Jesus, on the cross. It had Latin writing on it."

"Then it may not have been a Burrows Cave piece." Though many of the Burrows Cave pieces did portray Jesus, based on what January had shown Cam none of them had Latin writing. "Maybe January found it up in the Catskills. Do you remember the Latin?"

"I made a point to memorize it. 'Ereptor Crucis.'"

Cam had taken four years of Latin in high school. "I'm pretty sure 'Ereptor' means thief. And 'Crucis' means cross."

"Odd. Did Jesus steal a cross or something? Or did someone steal his body off the cross?"

Cam shrugged. "Another mystery."

"I'll add one more. One of the description cards mentioned Prince Madoc. But I didn't get a good look at the artifact." Amanda summarized the legend of the Welsh prince—tired of fighting with his brothers over control of his father's kingdom, he sailed west to North America to colonize a new world.

"What year was that supposed to be?"

"I think 1170. My mum was Welsh so I remember hearing about it when I was a girl. That's why the card caught my eye."

Cam switched lanes. "That's about the same time as the journey in this Clairvaux Codex."

"You know most historians think the Madoc visit never occurred."

"Yeah, well I'm beginning to think most historians should find a new line of work."

✠ ✠ ✠

Trey Buckner had a lot of work to do to clean up the mess caused by January's suicide and the loss of the artifacts, but he couldn't just walk out of the ODNI meeting like a fourth-grader going to the nurse's office. Instead he stewed: How had the agent missed that shot?

Finally the meeting wound down. Jabil Hayek issued his orders. Trey was to work with Georgia Johnston, whom he knew from the Presidential campaign and didn't particularly care for— she had an anti-Mormon bias that no amount of political mumbo-jumbo could mask. They were to find Thorne and Spencer, and also the artifacts and medieval document. Hayek had looked directly at Trey, his meaning clear: "This needs to be contained."

What Hayek didn't know was that Trey had spent his entire career in the intelligence community angling and maneuvering and strategizing to put himself squarely at the center of the Burrows Cave mystery. The cave was a birthright, its secrets passed down through generations of the Buckner family for well over 100 years. He would work for Hayek, and he would even work with Georgia Johnston, but in the end his loyalty would be to his forefathers. And to the legacy he and his Aunt Eliza safeguarded.

✠ ✠ ✠

Salazar had done his job well. Just as dusk arrived, Cam pulled into the driveway of a Village Colonial-style home on a small lot in Boston's working-class Brighton neighborhood and punched the security code into a keypad mounted on a fencepost.

The garage door opened, the sophisticated security belying the commonplace appearance of the property. Inside an envelope taped to a plain oak door at the rear of the garage Cam found a key and a short note from the property owner: "Your friend has arranged payment. Stay as long as you want. For privacy, the door in the rear of the garage leads to a path which exits to a park. The apartment has WiFi. Call if you have any questions." The owner signed his first name and left a phone number. Clean, anonymous, efficient.

The oak door opened to a staircase leading to a suite of rooms above the garage. Amanda kept Astarte busy by exploring and unpacking while Cam checked out the path behind the garage. As the note said, the path—sheltered by thick shrubbery—led to a park containing a rusty swing-set and some benches. The park looked to be rarely used, which meant they'd be able to come and go without neighbors noticing. A three-minute walk brought him to a half-block retail area. He ordered a pizza and ducked into the CVS to get some insulin; while the pizza cooked and they filled his prescription he grabbed some snacks and breakfast food along with three prepaid cell phones. He also bought an elastic wrap and ice packs for Amanda to treat her rib injury and iodine to clean the cut on her wrist. He paid cash for everything and returned to the apartment.

"Pizza was Uncle Jefferson's favorite," Astarte sighed.

"Then we shall have it in honor of him," Amanda exclaimed, handing out slices. She was doing a good job not allowing the girl to wallow in her sadness.

"And I got ice cream for dessert," Cam said. He couldn't help but like the girl. She was earnest and sweet and sharp. And lonely. She had also caused a ton of trouble, but that wasn't her fault. Of course liking her was not the same as wanting to keep her, nor was liking her a valid legal defense to a charge of kidnapping. This would all be a conversation for later tonight, after the girl fell asleep. "I also got you a cell phone in case of emergency." He handed it to her. "Do you know how to use it?"

"Of course. I have my own at home. Uncle Jefferson taught me how to text also."

"Apparently January was a bit of a gadget freak," Amanda explained.

After dinner they found a Disney movie for Astarte on the bedroom television. "Will she be okay alone?" Cam asked.

"I think she'll be fine for a bit. I'll peek in on her."

Using his new disposable phone, Cam dialed Salazar's number. He had hoped to be done with the mercenary once they rescued Amanda. But now it seemed they needed his help more than ever. Cam put him on speaker and placed the phone in the middle of the round kitchen table.

"Something strange is going on," Salazar said. "You raced off with an eight-year-old girl seven hours ago right in front of the police and there's just … nothing. No Amber Alert. No news flashes. Nothing. It's like it didn't happen."

Cam's mind raced. Did they—whoever they were—want Astarte to be kidnapped? It made no sense.

"Another thing. I know a cop in Connecticut. He made some calls. The official word is that the sniper shot was a stray bullet from a hunter. No investigation. No crime. Again, like it didn't happen."

"So how do you explain it?" Amanda asked.

"It has to be the feds. CIA, FBI, Homeland Security, someone like that. They're the only people who can make stuff like this just disappear."

"The feds?" Cam said. "Why would they care about January and his artifacts?"

"No idea. But you guys better figure it out quick. Next time, I doubt Amanda is going to be so lucky—those guys usually don't miss when they shoot."

Cam and Amanda stared at the phone for a few seconds after Salazar hung up, Cam's arm around her shoulder.

"What in the world is going on?" she asked.

He replayed the events of the past few days in his head. "Crazy as it sounds, there must be something in these artifacts, or in the Clairvaux Codex, that affects national security."

"Well, if they'd bother to ask we'd be bloody happy to return the whole lot to them."

"I don't know if that's going to do it. What if we know too much already? They can't erase our memories, can't change what we know." He tried to keep his voice steady, as if they were talking about what to eat for breakfast.

"Oh, but they can. By eliminating us." She locked her green eyes on his. "I don't know how we got to this point. But it seems our only hope is to make the secret no longer a secret. Then eliminating us would be pointless."

Amanda was always good at cutting to the core of a problem. "What you say is logical. Hopefully we're dealing with logical people."

✛ ✛ ✛

Cam pulled the notebook containing the translation of the Clairvaux Codex from his bag. January's stone artifacts, including the devil's rock Amanda stole, could wait—the document seemed key to understanding the man's quest.

"January said the original parchment was carbon-dated to the twelfth century," Cam said as Amanda checked on Astarte and closed the blinds in their Brighton safe-house.

"Can I watch TV out here, with you?" the girl asked.

"Of course honey." Amanda found the movie, sat down on the couch next to Astarte and turned to Cam. "While you were out shopping I did a quick web search on Seborga, where the Codex was found. It's on the Italy-France border, near the French Riviera. Fancy this. The first nine Templar Knights, before they went to Jerusalem in 1118, were all ordained there."

"Not in Rome?"

"No. And over the next two hundred years, fifteen of the Templar Grand Masters were also given the titles of Prince of Seborga. That's more than half of them."

"And they kept this journal secret for over 800 years, hidden in some church. Can you imagine how much history is buried in these old churches?"

Cam read aloud from January's translation, with Amanda taking notes. As January had summarized, the document detailed the journey of the noblewoman Marie-Claire, her husband

Aragon, their 13-year-old son, and five other Templar Knights across the Atlantic. Interestingly, the group traveled from southern Europe first to Norway before crossing the ocean.

"Likely because the Norsemen knew the best route to America," Amanda observed.

"Makes sense. They probably island-hopped their way across the North Atlantic, just like the Vikings and Prince Henry did."

Cam continued reading. "Hey, listen to this. It says they departed from the north coast of Wales. I wonder why they didn't go straight from Norway."

"Maybe they had to get supplies. Does it say where exactly in Wales?"

"Hold on." Cam scanned the page. "The modern translation is a place called Colwyn Bay."

Amanda repositioned herself on the arm of the couch. "That's where Prince Madoc departed from."

"Really?" Cam put the notebook down. Again, too much coincidence. "Same date, same departure point. Maybe the Madoc legend was based on fact, based on the Templar trip." He let his mind drift. "Is it possible one of the Templar Knights was actually Madoc himself?"

"Could be. Many noblemen of the time were Templars. But one problem is that the Madoc legend has Madoc building forts along the Alabama River and further up into Tennessee. According to your document our Templars ended up in New York."

"Good point."

Amanda slapped the back of the couch. "Blimey. I forgot. The Madoc legend says he crossed the ocean and then returned to Wales to get more men for a second visit. So perhaps he journeyed with the Templars to New York before later exploring more to the south. I wish I had grabbed the Madoc stone from January's devil's rock collection," she sighed. "But I just grabbed a random marble piece."

Amanda came over to the table and typed in a series of Google searches on her laptop, chewing her lip as she concentrated. "Okay. Listen to this: In 1782 the Governor of Tennessee, a chap named Seiver, reports he had a conversation with a Cherokee chief asking about the ancient fortification works in the area. Here's what the chief said: 'It is handed down by the Forefathers that the works had been made by the White people who had formerly inhabited the country. . . They were a people called Welsh, and that they had crossed the Great Water and landed first near the mouth of the Alabama River near Mobile.'"

"This all makes sense," Cam said, pacing now. The idea that no Europeans set foot in America during the 500-year gap between the Vikings and Columbus strained credulity. No reason the Welsh couldn't have made the trip, with or without the Templars.

"Wait," Amanda interrupted, "I have more." Her eyes scanned the screen as her fingers worked the keyboard. "You're going to love this mural." She turned the screen toward him.

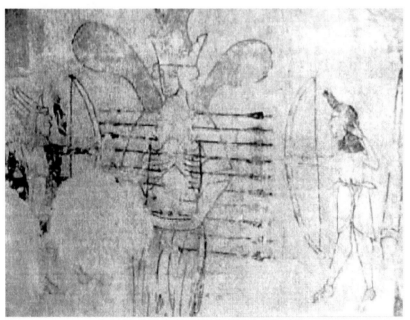

MADOC STOKE DRY MURAL

Cam studied a mural of a white-skinned, crowned figure being pierced by arrows shot by naked, dark-haired assailants, one of whom was wearing a headdress. "That looks like some European monarch being attacked by Native Americans."

"Precisely. It was uncovered during renovation of a church in England in the 1970s. The mural dates back to 1280." She paused. "I believe it shows Prince Madoc being killed by your natives."

He studied the image. How would the so-called experts explain this? Either the Europeans had traveled to America, or the Native Americans had crossed the Atlantic and attacked England.

"And get this," Amanda continued. "The church is in the town of Stoke Dry. Stoke Dry means 'Fatal Blow.'"

Cam grinned. "That's pretty cool." His mind sifted the evidence, trying to sort all the information. The words came slowly as his brain worked through the problem. "But if it was the Welsh who were here, and they were the ancestors of the Mandan people, then January's whole theory that the Mandan descend from Jesus' niece is bogus."

Amanda nodded as she followed his line of thinking. "Not necessarily. The stories are not mutually exclusive. Madoc and his Welsh friends could have settled in with the Mandans once they arrived here. If the Mandan remembered their history they would have been thrilled to have cousins visiting from across the pond. Especially ones who claimed to follow the teachings of their ancestor Jesus."

Cam smiled. "Cousins visiting. That's pretty much how this whole country was settled. But that doesn't explain why January hid the Madoc artifact away with the other so-called devil's rocks."

"Perhaps in his mind the Madoc legend muddies the waters unnecessarily."

"Okay." He shrugged. "So back to the Clairvaux Codex. According to January, the Templars buried some artifacts up in the Catskills. January found some of them, and he has a bunch of clues and maps leading to others, but he was too sick to get them. They also hid some ancient scroll, but January hadn't found that yet either. That seems to be the thing he was most interested in."

"So that's our job."

Cam nodded. "If we decide to pursue this, that'd be our first stop."

She took his hand. "I don't see that there's any 'if' here, Cam. I don't think we have any choice."

"You're probably right. And I think Salazar agrees with you. But then what do we do about Astarte? We can't drag her along."

Amanda sat straight in her chair. "And we surely can't dump her on the side of the road."

"Of course not. But we could drop her off at the local police station."

She took a deep breath. "Cameron, whatever secrets I learned Astarte knows as well. She's just as much a threat to these people as we are. Perhaps more. Whatever January was working on, whatever secrets he was intent on revealing, she's a crucial part of his plan—she's the Fortieth Princess. Can we be sure she'd be safe?"

Would they murder a little girl, whoever 'they' were? Probably not. But then again Cam never would have expected them to try to murder Amanda. And he also would have expected Aunt Eliza to have reported Astarte missing and for her face to be plastered all over the nightly news. Nothing seemed to add up. Until they understood the full ramifications of January's discovery it was impossible to predict what 'they' might do. "No, I can't guarantee that."

"Then it's settled. She stays with us."

✠ ✠ ✠

"Any sign of them?" Georgia asked. She and Trey were holed up in connecting rooms at a Holiday Inn outside of Hartford, Connecticut. One of her earliest memories was of a family vacation, her parents allowing Georgia and her sister to share a connecting room at the Howard Johnson's. Looking back, it was probably because her parents wanted to fool around. She, on the other hand, would be lucky to get a smile out of the tightly-wound Trey Buckner.

"Nothing." Trey sat in front of a desk, one hand working an iPhone and the other a laptop mouse. "We've been monitoring all the financial databases—no credit cards, ATM withdrawals, nothing. And he ditched his rental car. They must have someone helping them." Somehow his white shirt was still fresh and wrinkle-free after a long day of travel. As soon as the meeting with Hayek ended they had jumped in Trey's government-issued SUV and driven the six hours from Washington to Hartford, Trey using blue police lights mounted on the grill to weave through rush-hour traffic in Baltimore and otherwise cruise the left lane at 85. No doubt Hayek had made a call to clear their path.

"Do you think they're headed to the Catskills?" she asked. They were flying in the dark here—nobody had seen the Clairvaux Codex, so nobody knew what it said. All she had been able to glean through Internet searches was that January had hinted at artifacts he had found in the Catskills. They had chosen Hartford as a base of operations because it was essentially equidistant from Foxwoods, the Catskills and the Boston suburb of Westford, where Amanda and Cameron lived.

He shrugged her question aside and focused on his gadgets. He was the field agent—it was his job to track and deal with Spencer and Thorne. Georgia was an analyst, on board to interpret the artifacts and use them to try to anticipate their quarry's next move; she had no experience being out on a mission. Which meant for now she was pretty much useless.

"I'm going downstairs to get some food," she said. And a cocktail. "Want me to bring anything back for you?"

"I'm good."

"Okay. Call my cell if you hear anything."

She found an open stool at the bar and ordered a turkey wrap and a martini. The down time gave her a chance to muse about the possible Templar connections to this mission. She hadn't expected Jefferson January's artifacts to be tied to the Templars in any way, but it was possible—and in fact even likely—that all ancient explorers of North America had been following the same maps and were some way related to each other. So she shouldn't have been surprised. There always seemed to be connections, as if secret knowledge was handed down through the generations and centuries. Perhaps the Templars and other related groups like the Freemasons really did have their roots in ancient times and really did possess secret knowledge shielded from the masses.

Which led her to focus on the primary issue she had been wrestling with lately: What was it the Templar knights found in Jerusalem in the early years of the 12th century that allowed them to become so powerful so quickly? They must have returned to Europe with something truly extraordinary—some artifact or treasure or secret writing or ancient knowledge—that enabled the Order to become the most powerful entity in all of Christendom for almost 200 years. Some scholars believed it was the Ark of the Covenant, or the Holy Grail, or the treasures of King Solomon. But Georgia rejected these possibilities—these items would have been extraordinary finds, but whatever the Templars found gave them not only unsurpassed wealth and fame but more importantly unequaled power. Power to demand that Church leaders grant the Order complete autonomy and sovereignty at a time when the Church controlled almost every aspect of European society. And there was only one way to get that kind of power over the Church in medieval times: blackmail.

Which meant whatever they found must have been pretty damn earth-shattering. And perhaps heaven-shattering as well.

Had Jefferson January somehow stumbled onto the trail of this secret? And, if so, was it still as radioactive?

The buzz of her cell phone interrupted her musings. It was Trey. "I've got something. A couple of hours ago Thorne filled a prescription for insulin at a drugstore in Boston."

There was something unsettlingly Big Brother-ish about the government knowing when you bought birth control pills or herpes medication or Viagra. No doubt Thorne's name was in some electronic data base the pharmacist tapped into to fill the prescription. "Are we heading up there?" She eyed her cocktail.

"No. I don't want to race east and find out they passed us going west out to the Catskills. I've already got someone on the ground in Boston—he'll be at the drug store when it opens in the morning. Maybe someone will remember seeing him."

Georgia nodded. Once Amanda and Cameron reached the Catskill Mountains it would be difficult to track them—there were literally hundreds of trails covering dozens of peaks in the area. The best bet would be to intercept them on the way.

She sipped again at her cocktail. This was exactly the type of operation that would have slipped through the cracks before ODNI had been created. January had committed no crime, so the FBI had no reason to monitor him. The CIA might have viewed his research and artifacts as a threat to national security, but they had no authority to operate domestically. And Homeland Security would have ignored him since he was not a terrorist.

But, as Hayek had made clear in his briefing, that didn't mean January didn't have the potential to destabilize the entire Middle East.

CHAPTER 11

Amanda awoke in the middle of the night, her ears straining to hear the soft breathing of Astarte in the adjacent bedroom over the patter of rain against the roof. She had checked on the girl a couple of times, happy and a bit surprised to see the young princess sleeping comfortably with Ishtar, the stuffed pink bunny Salazar had given her.

She and Cam had not been so resilient. He snored now quietly next to her, his nightmares finally having exhausted him. Long after midnight they had huddled together in bed, Cam recounting January's death, she reliving the fear of the bullet whizzing past her ear. Her experience had been the more terrifying one, but it had come and gone quickly; the gory details of January's death seemed burned into the back of Cam's eyes, and the causal connection between his flip of the light switch and the gun being fired convinced Cam he had January's blood on his hands. She had read once about how policemen reacted to suicide- by-cop incidents, and it seemed like Cam was experiencing the same range of emotions. Intellectually, he knew he was not to blame. But emotionally he found it hard to get past the reality that he directly caused a death.

She had covered him like a blanket as they made love, her hands cradling his face and her body flat against his, shielding him from his memories and guilt while the rhythms of their breathing drowned the echo of the gunshot in her head. But when they curled up together afterward and he began to drift off to sleep, he startled awake, his hands raised to shield his face from a shower of blood and brain matter as his subconscious replayed the death scene. Finally she tucked his face into the crook of her arm and draped her nightgown over him, and he slept. She, on the other hand, had barely dozed, the memory of the bullet ricocheting off the car inches from her cheek buzzing in her head like an angry mosquito.

Even cuddled together under the blankets she could not warm her core—the fear of captivity had been replaced by the fear of being shot at. She quietly got out of bed, threw on a sweatshirt and pulled the blind aside, a sharp pain knifing her side from the motion of lifting her arm. The street was empty. Were they safe here? She didn't doubt Salazar's aptitude, but was it really possible to hide from the feds? There was that Boston gangster, Whitey Bulger, who had been on the run for almost 20 years before they finally caught him. But he had spent years setting up aliases and bank accounts and safe houses preparing for a life in hiding. She and Cam were just winging it. Not to mention they had a little girl in tow.

A night of reflection hadn't changed her thinking. Their best move—perhaps their only move—was to go to the Catskills and find the missing artifacts. Not that they could climb a mountain in this weather. But by tomorrow, Thanksgiving, it was supposed to clear. She turned back toward Cam; she'd let him sleep a bit. In the meantime she'd take advantage of their Internet capability. She made herself a cup of coffee and opened the laptop on the kitchen table.

Amanda focused first on the 'Ereptor Crucis' mystery, probably because it was a simple matter to type the terms 'Jesus,' 'thief' and 'cross' into a Google search. Most of the search results discussed the New Testament story of two thieves being crucified alongside Jesus. But once she narrowed her search she was astounded at what she learned. Apparently a Templar official, under questioning and torture after his arrest in 1307, admitted that the Templars referred to Jesus as "The Thief on the Cross." She found the specific Templar teaching on the subject: "*Jesus ... said he was God and the King of the Jews, which was an outrage to the true God who is in Heaven. When Jesus, a few moments before his death, had his side pierced by the lance of Longinus, he repented of having called himself God and King of the Jews and he asked pardon of the true God; then the true God pardoned him. It is thus that we apply to the crucified Christ these words: 'as God pardoned the thief on the cross.'*"

She and Cam would need to pursue this further. Did the Templars really see 'the crucified Christ' as some kind of thief? If so, it could only mean they believed Jesus had stolen the ... what, the claim to being the messiah? But stolen from whom? Was this the secret the Templars had used to blackmail the Church back in medieval times? Amanda shook her head: There had to be more to it than just this.

She checked her watch. Almost five o'clock. The Thief on the Cross research would have to wait. If they were going to trudge their way through the mountains, she preferred to at least know what they might stumble upon. She focused on the Catskills and the clues left by January.

An hour of Internet searching later she had some answers. She gently woke Cam. "Sweetheart, I think I found something." She kissed him lightly. "We need to wake up and get started."

He rubbed his eyes, smiling up at her. "I like it when your face is the first thing I see in the morning."

The sleep seemed to have done him good. "And it's a fine thing to see you smiling."

He threw the covers off. "Give me a minute to wash up and get a little food in me."

While he did so, Amanda tiptoed into Astarte's bedroom. The girl was already out of bed, half dressed. "You people sleep late."

Amanda raised an eye. "It's not yet six o'clock."

"I used to get up at five every morning to have breakfast with Uncle Jefferson."

"Well, then, you won't mind if we get an early start. Finish dressing; I'll fix you some breakfast."

"Where are we going?"

"To find some answers."

✛ ✛ ✛

They beat the Boston rush hour traffic out of the city, though Cam was surprised when Amanda directed him north out of the city rather than west. "I thought we were heading to New York?"

"We are. But we're not climbing any mountains in this weather, and I don't think we should just sit around the Catskills waiting to be found—no doubt that's where they're looking for us. So first I thought we could make a quick detour."

"Okay, where?"

"You said that January talked a lot about Phoenicians coming to America."

He sipped from a bottle of cranberry juice as Astarte chewed on a bagel in the back seat. "Right. Lots of his artifacts have Phoenician writing. And they were the best navigators in ancient times."

"Mr. Thorne is right," Astarte said, nodding.

Amanda smiled. "Thank you, Astarte." She turned to Cam. "Where were these artifacts found?"

"Mostly the Ohio River Valley."

"Well, the Phoenicians may have been in New England also. Perhaps even the Catskills."

He shrugged. "Okay. But that would have been, what, 1,500 years before the Templars and Prince Madoc and the Clairvaux Codex. So what's the relevance?"

Amanda stared out the window. "I guess that's the key point here. January found these artifacts, and he views them all while looking through his Mormon glasses. In his eyes, they all authenticate the history set down in the Book of Mormon. But we need to see them objectively. The artifacts can be authentic—they can tell the story of ancient peoples coming to America—and yet not be Mormon."

Cam considered her argument for a few seconds. "Great point. Maybe January's artifacts have nothing to do with the Mormons at all. But that doesn't answer my question: What's the connection between the Phoenicians and the Clairvaux Codex?"

"Just this: The Templars, or Prince Madoc, or whoever it was, did not just stumble across the Atlantic blindly. They must have followed ancient maps, or used ancient navigational devices—remember, the compass was not used in Europe until the early 13th century."

Cam drummed the steering wheel with his fingers as the wipers thwacked back and forth. "You think the Templars discovered ancient maps or navigational charts while they were in Jerusalem?"

"That is precisely what I think. And the Templars weren't only in Jerusalem. They were all over the Middle East. I believe they uncovered details of the ancient Phoenician travels to North America, and used that information to cross the pond."

He smiled. "And do you have any evidence for this theory?"

"I do. But I'd rather show you than tell you. So please just keep driving." She patted his knee. "And be careful, as everyone seems to be on the wrong side of the road."

✠ ✠ ✠

Jabil Hayek turned the car radio off. "Sorry, Farah, I have to make a call." If he waited he might miss his chance.

His daughter yawned. "Kay."

He hated to do it—he only had custody of her two days a week, and the morning car ride to school was one of the few chances they had to talk. And even that was tough—there was little conversational common ground between a 17-year-old girl and a middle-aged man. Last week he had taken her to the Kennedy Center to see "Mamma Mia," but they had talked that out. "You can listen if you want, or you can listen to that *i*-thing of yours."

She shrugged and stuck an earplug in her ear. Not a bad kid; a pretty good one, in fact. Solid grades, decent athlete, nice friends, no drugs or booze or weird piercings. But nothing outstanding, nothing that would get her that fat college scholarship. The knot in his stomach tightened—he had less than six months to figure out a way to come up with $50,000 for her freshman tuition, plus another $50,000 per year for three years after that. He wasn't looking forward to this phone call, but at least it might distract him from obsessing over the college conundrum. He recognized the irony—he was doing his best to keep the Middle East from igniting like a powder keg, but his real fear was the prospect of explaining to Farah—and his ex-wife—that she would have to go to a state college.

The digital clock flicked over to 7:00 AM. He pulled out a scrap of paper and dialed the number of the director of the Smithsonian Institution, officially known as the Secretary. He had wanted to make the call from his home office but he knew if he called any earlier the Vice President, a close friend of the director, would hear about it. Not the best career move.

The director, a sixty-something professor of history from Princeton, was not pleased to be contacted at home. "I'm sorry.

Your name was 'Hike,' as in something one might do on a mountain? Or perhaps to a football?"

"No, Madam Secretary. Hayek. As in Salma, the actress. And I'm sorry to bother you so early. But this is a matter of national security."

The director exhaled into the phone. "It always is. I'm amazed the Republic hasn't crumbled. What is it?"

He took a deep breath, one hand on the wheel. He didn't dare put her on speaker phone. "It's about the Bat Creek Stone."

She snorted. "A Masonic hoax. What about it?"

He craved a cigarette but knew Farah would disapprove. "Actually, that's an open question. I'm concerned that the Smithsonian is allowing the stone to be tested by a geologist. And also allowing DNA testing of the bones found with it."

"Mr. Hike. How in heaven's name is this a matter of national security?"

He hit the brakes as an SUV rushed through a red light and cut him off, the 12-year-old chassis of his Honda creaking and moaning from the torque. He took another deep breath, resisting the urge to lay on his horn. How could he keep the peace if he couldn't even make it in to work? "Madam Secretary. There is already strong scientific evidence establishing the Bat Creek Stone as an authentic ancient artifact. Technology has advanced to the point where the carvings in the stone can be dated based on the weathering of the cut faces. I also believe the DNA testing will show that the bones are of Middle Eastern origin."

"That is ridiculous. As I said, the stone was proven to be a fake. In fact, it was one of the Smithsonian's own men who planted it in the burial mound."

How convenient was that. And how absurd. "I believe the Smithsonian's man was made a scapegoat in this. There simply is no evidence he planted the stone. And why would he?"

"People do strange things, Mr. Hike. And they believe in strange conspiracies."

And some other people cling to the history they learned in second grade like a life raft. "The fact is that the wooden beams uncovered with the skeletons buried in the mound carbon-date to the first century AD. And the inscribed stone was found under the head of one of the skeletons. I believe further testing will show the stone and bones are equally as old."

She exhaled. "Even if what you propose is true, so what? The carvings are Cherokee."

"No. They are not. They are Paleo-Hebrew, from the first century AD."

"You're not proposing that some ancient Jewish voyagers stumbled their way across the Atlantic 2,000 years ago, are you? I suppose they were looking for good Chinese food? Or a sale at Macy's?"

Hayek bit back a retort. He loved his adopted country, but there were plenty of people, including more than a few governmental officials, who could benefit from some cultural immersion. How could the younger President Bush, with all his wealth and life of privilege, have never traveled outside North America before being elected President?

"That's exactly what I'm proposing. That and much more. And the ramifications extend far beyond the world of academia. Which is why I'm involved." If the Jefferson January artifacts, and their implications, became public, Hayek's people could strong-arm a bunch of academic types to pooh-pooh the whole thing as the work of amateur conspiracy theorists. But if hard science showed the reality of Middle Eastern explorers arriving here 2,000 years ago, a strategy of refuting January by painting him as a kook would be fruitless. Even the Catholic Church had been swept under by *The Da Vinci Code* tidal wave, powerless to squelch the theory of a Jesus bloodline once the idea of Mary Magdalene being his wife took root in popular culture. Hayek needed to stomp out the various brushfires before they joined together in a huge conflagration. "I need you to get that stone back from the geologist. And retrieve the bones as well."

She steeled her voice. "Mr. Hike. What you need and what I am prepared to do are two entirely different things. For the record, the bones are already on their way to the University of Tennessee and the stone is already there. As you know the bones and artifact belong to the Cherokee tribe. It is their legal right to test them, their time and money to waste. I believe they have retained Geraldo Rivera to announce their findings on national TV. Now good day."

Hayek rubbed his face. It would be anything but.

✝ ✝ ✝

They had been driving just over an hour when Cam pulled off the highway in southern New Hampshire. He recognized the exit—he and Amanda had visited the America's Stonehenge site only days after they first met. And, in fact, they later had been held captive by Salazar and his cronies there. He was not sure why Amanda saw the need to return.

She read his thoughts. "When I brought you here last year, we rushed through quickly. Do you recall that many believe ancient Phoenician explorers built the site?"

"Actually, no. My head was spinning with all the Templar stuff. But I do remember the Sacrificial Stone." The site consisted of a series of mysterious stone structures predating Colonial settlement. In the center of the complex, in what scholars believed to be the ceremonial area, stood the trapezoidal Sacrificial Stone. A priest, concealed in a nearby stone chamber, could have projected his voice through a stone conduit running under the slab, making it appear as if the gods were speaking through the bodies of the sacrificed offerings. It would be nice to come here someday when someone wasn't trying to make *him* a human sacrifice.

"Do you remember the astronomical alignments?" she asked.

They had also intrigued him. A series of boulders and standing stones were aligned to mark calendar events such as solstice and equinox sunrises and sunsets. The site, like its namesake in England, served as both ceremonial site and calendar for an ancient culture. He smiled. "Ah, I see where you're going with this. Whoever laid out those boulders knew a lot about astronomy. And we're back to our Phoenicians."

"Precisely. They were experts in navigation, due to their extensive knowledge of the solar system."

"But you didn't bring me here to see the stone alignments. I've already seen those."

She smiled and turned in her seat. "You see, Astarte, Cameron is clever in addition to being handsome."

They pulled into a muddy parking lot. A pet alpaca—a llama-like animal—waddled over and pressed a wet nose against Astarte's window. "Well," Amanda laughed, "apparently someone is glad to have company today."

"Can I pet him?" Astarte asked, rolling down her window.

"Perhaps offer him a piece of your bagel first."

Astarte did so, giggling as the animal nibbled against her fingers. Cam watched, wondering if the scene foreshadowed his future with Amanda. Assuming they had a future.

Amanda had cut holes in some garbage bags which they slipped over their heads to serve as rain ponchos. They left the car, the alpaca trotting along behind Astarte.

"Are they even open yet?" Cam asked.

"Probably not. But there's usually someone here early to feed the animals."

A few minutes later an accommodating staff member unlocked the door to the information center. "Make yourself at home."

Amanda led Cam to a display case. She pointed at a salmon-colored stone the size of baseball mitt. "The writing on this carving is Punic, an ancient Mediterranean language. It translates as, 'To Baal of the Canaanites,' and dates back to roughly 500 BC. Baal was the supreme god of the Phoenicians at that time."

148

BAAL STONE, AMERICA'S STONEHENGE

Cam studied the stone. "So this, along with the calendar alignments, is pretty good evidence the Phoenicians built this place."

"Or if not built it, at least used it and modified it. The Merrimack River is only about 6 miles away and a tributary runs right by—it would have been easy to get here."

"Wait. I think I read something recently about a Phoenician coin found at the mouth of the Merrimack River."

The staffer allowed Amanda to plug into the Internet; she did a quick search. "Indeed you did," she nodded. "A 2,000-year-old

Phoenician coin was found in Newburyport, Massachusetts during construction of a home." Skimming the article, she laughed out loud. "Some archeologist theorized that a seagull picked up the coin and flew across the Atlantic with it in its beak, dropping it in Newburyport." She angled her computer. "Here's a picture of the coin. If you look closely you can see the beak imprint."

PHOENICIAN COIN

Cam smiled and leaned over her shoulder. "Amanda, it says here the coin came from the city of Tyre." He shook his head. "You may not believe this, but Tyre is the name carved on a lot of January's Burrows Cave artifacts."

She grinned up at him. "That was one busy seagull."

"No kidding. But, seriously, there were dozens of major Phoenician port cities back then. Is it just a coincidence that the name 'Tyre' keeps appearing on artifacts in North America?"

"I don't believe in coincidences, Cam."

"Neither do I."

✠✠✠

Using her iPad, Amanda found a shopping mall off the highway near the America's Stonehenge site. "Whoever is looking for us is probably expecting us to be along the Massachusetts Turnpike somewhere, heading out to the Catskills," Cam said. "So let's get our supplies up here in New Hampshire. Then we can take back roads out to New York."

Amanda fitted herself for some hiking boots and a heavy fleece pullover before returning to the SUV and live-parking in front of a Starbucks; she wanted to access their WiFi while Cam and Astarte finished shopping. The forecast was for heavy rain the rest of the afternoon, clearing later that night. She cranked the heat, trying to stay warm. The wet leaves would no doubt make for a challenging Thanksgiving Day hike, but at least the sun would be out. Astarte seemed pretty hardy—hopefully she'd be able to keep up.

Amanda tried a couple of Internet searches with 'Templars' and 'Madoc' along with 'Catskills,' but came up with nothing. She modified her search to follow the Phoenician angle, which led her to a link to a presentation at a recent conference focusing on early exploration of the Americas. Amanda watched a video of a researcher explaining how carvings of the Phoenician goddess 'Tanit' had been found in both Vermont and New York. The Phoenicians, the researcher theorized, had originally crossed the Atlantic in search of copper to meet growing demand during the Bronze Age.

Cam and Astarte returned, Astarte's teeth clenched as she strained under the weight of her bags. "Boy," Cam announced as Amanda opened the door to help, "Astarte is a big help."

Amanda grinned. "I knew she would be." The girl was less weepy today. The key would be to keep her busy and active.

Astarte set down her bags and huffed. "Mr. Thorne says we're only going for one day. But he bought enough food for a week."

He ruffled her hair. "That's because I've seen how much you eat." Turning to Amanda he explained, "We have the SUV, and

I'd rather not go out in public more than we have to." He climbed into the driver's seat. "Let's get going."

"Before you drive, check out this carving. There's a researcher who found a number of stone artifacts that depict Phoenician goddess worship. This one was found in the Catskill Mountains. She calls it the 'Goddess Stone.'"

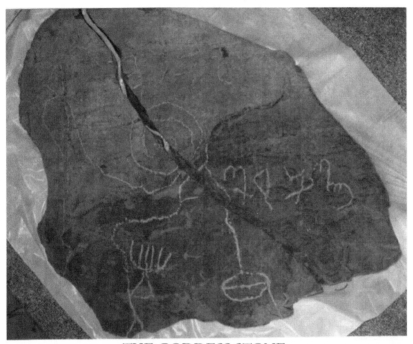

THE GODDESS STONE

Cam studied the images carved onto the stone—a spiral, a candelabra, some ancient script, a bird-like figure, an oval bisected by a horizontal line. He looked up at Amanda questioningly.

"Trust me. All these descriptions represented the goddess in ancient times. And all these symbols trace back to the eastern Mediterranean—what we now know as Israel and Lebanon but what used to be Phoenician trading ports."

"I'm not sure I see the relevance."

"For one thing Tanit was the consort of our friend Baal--"

"The god on the America's Stonehenge piece."

"Right. But beyond that I'm not sure either. It just seems like everywhere we look, the Phoenicians turn up."

"Sort of like the *Where's Waldo?* book," Astarte interjected. "Waldo is on every page."

"That's exactly what it's like," Amanda laughed. "Perhaps Waldo was Phoenician."

As Cam drove and Astarte napped, Amanda stared out the window and tried to organize her thoughts. "There are so many loose ends here; I don't know which ones to follow." Plenty of artifacts existed that showed someone had traveled to North America in pre-historic times. But for every artifact there seemed to be multiple possibilities as to who may have carved it and why they may have journeyed across the ocean. She hadn't even told Cam about her Thief on the Cross research yet, and they still hadn't figured out why Jesus was praying to John the Baptist, but for now she wanted to stay focused on the Phoenician angle. She pulled out a spiral notebook and she and Cam compiled a list of the artifacts, their age and who may have carved them.

- Burrows Cave (Illinois) stones (first wave). Circa 500 BC. According to January, they were carved by Nephites escorted to North America by Phoenician sailors. Many stones have the word 'Tyre' on them, a Phoenician port.

- America's Stonehenge 'Baal' piece (New Hampshire). Circa 500 BC. Probably carved by a Phoenician since Baal is a Phoenician god.

- 'Tanit' goddess figures found in Vermont and New York. Circa 500 BC. Probably carved by Phoenicians.

- 'Goddess' Stone (Catskill Mountains, NY). Circa 500 BC. Probably carved by a Hebrew-speaking people, influenced by Goddess-worshiping Phoenicians.

- Burrows Cave stones (second wave). 1st Century AD. According to January, they were carved by refugees from Mauretania who came to North America to join the Nephites. Some refugees supposedly descend from both Cleopatra and Jesus' niece, Anna. Many of the carvings, including a menorah, reference the Phoenician port of Tyre.

- Phoenician coin found along Massachusetts coast. 1st Century AD. Originally minted in Tyre.
- Bat Creek Stone (Tennessee). Circa 2nd Century AD. Translated as "Hail the Jews." Language is ancient form of Hebrew.
- Ohio Decalogue Stone. 100 BC-500 AD. Carved by Hebrew-speaking peoples who followed the Ten Commandments.
- Clairvaux Codex. Late 1100s AD. Written by Templars who traveled to Catskill Mountains. According to January, mission was to refortify Jesus bloodline.

"So," Amanda said, "there are some definite patterns emerging."

"Well, obviously the Phoenicians are a key part of this. Which makes sense. In addition to being expert navigators, they have ancient ties to the Templars and Freemasons. The Masonic rituals all trace back to the construction of the First Temple of Solomon around 960 BC. King Hiram was friends with King Solomon; he sent his craftsmen to Jerusalem to help Solomon build his Temple. That's why Hiram is such a key part of Freemasonry."

"Okay."

"So guess what Hiram was king of."

"Um, Tyre?"

"Exactly."

Amanda pulled her knees up to her chest. "Wow. That's sort of creepy." She rolled some possibilities around in her mind. "So, if we believe the Templars and the Masons are two sides of the same coin, it's possible the Templars knew about travelers exploring the New World even before they went to Jerusalem in the 12th century."

"Right. Maybe they didn't know the exact details, but they knew what to look for in Jerusalem. Ancient maps, charts, travel logs, that kind of stuff."

"Well, if that's the case—if the Templars were just following the Phoenicians across the pond—then this has nothing to do with the Mormons at all."

154

"Not necessarily. I've been thinking about this. What if Joseph Smith really did find golden scrolls up in New York that told of ancient voyages to North America? But let's say the scrolls weren't gold, they were copper. That's what people did in ancient times—they carved stuff on copper sheets, just like the Dead Sea Scrolls; and don't forget Smith found the scrolls right in an area the Phoenicians would have been mining for copper." Cam tapped the brakes as the rain intensified. "And let's say Smith embellished things a little, added a story about angels and visions and speaking to God. People believe him and pretty soon he's got himself his own little religion. The whole thing may be a lie, but the scrolls themselves could be real."

"I like your thinking. But I don't think January would."

"Yeah, well, screw him. The last thing I care about is authenticating the Book of Mormon. In fact, if we could prove it to be a fake, that'd be fine with me. Serve January right for dragging us into this."

✠ ✠ ✠

Astarte was pretending to be napping, but she heard what the adults were saying in the front seat. She didn't understand all of it, but what she did understand made her sad. Uncle Jefferson had spent his whole life trying to show people the Book of Mormon was real. And now Mr. Thorne was saying he wanted to prove the Book wasn't true.

She didn't quite understand how it all worked, but she knew the Book of Mormon was an important part of her becoming the Fortieth Princess. Mr. Thorne seemed nice, and she loved Miss Amanda, but Uncle Jefferson had told her that sometimes the devil sent people who seemed nice to do his work. She knew the devil would do whatever he could to stop people from reading the Book of Mormon and following God's words. And wasn't that what Mr. Thorne was trying to do when he said he wanted to show the Book was a fake?

It was all very confusing. But nobody ever said being princess would be easy.

CHAPTER 12

Trey barged into Georgia's hotel room without knocking. "Get your stuff together. We leave in ten."

"Where to?" She tossed the remains of an egg salad sandwich into the trash. So much for lunch.

"The Catskills. We're pretty sure they're on their way. And we have a plate number and description of their car. Maroon Ford Explorer."

"Good work. From your guy in Boston?"

"No, not from him. He hit a dead end. But it's reliable."

"What's the source?"

"Like I said, it's reliable."

She was getting used to Trey's evasiveness. But this was different: He was hiding something. "If we have the plate and vehicle, why not just have the police pull them over? Why go all the way to the Catskills?"

Trey shook his head. "No cops. This is our operation." He paused. "Hayek's orders."

"When did Hayek say that?"

He ignored the question. "I've got two of our guys from New York driving up. Plus us. Should be plenty."

"Plenty? For what? Do you think they're going to put up some kind of fight?" Georgia had assumed Trey would just flash his badge and that would be the end of it. Thorne and Spencer were not criminals, after all.

Trey shrugged. "You never know. And Hayek said to take no chances."

✟ ✟ ✟

As Cam drove, the rain pelting the windshield, Amanda stared out the window and allowed her mind to wander. Sometimes thinking about nothing was the deepest type of thought. It hit her between thwacks of the windshield wiper. "John the Baptist. That's the key."

"What?"

"You need to find me a Wi-Fi network."

Cam took the next exit and followed the signs to Panera Bread outside Albany, New York. While Cam and Astarte ran through the rain to buy sandwiches for an early dinner, Amanda logged on from the parking lot and pounded on the keyboard, bouncing from site to site, collecting stray bits of information and speculation and conjecture like a bird building a nest.

Twenty minutes passed, Amanda occasionally scribbling some notes on a legal pad, before she exhaled and smiled triumphantly at Cam. "Okay, Mr. Barrister, see if this floats your boat." She took a deep breath. "We know that for some reason the Freemasons venerate John the Baptist. They mark the beginning of the Masonic year on June 24, his birthday. And most Masonic lodges are dedicated to John the Baptist, with their cornerstones laid on June 24."

Water dripped from Cam's hair down his face. "Isn't June 24 also the date in ancient times pegged as marking the summer solstice?" They waited a couple of days after the solstice to make sure the sun had begun to ascend, just as religious Jews even today celebrate their lunar-based holidays on two consecutive days to ensure they hit the actual full moon.

"Brilliant, yes." Amanda clapped her hands. "That indicates some type of connection between John the Baptist and the ancient pagans who worshiped the sun and celebrated its solstices and equinoxes. And we know the Masons base a lot of their rituals on ancient pagan rites. So the circle completes itself. But why the focus on John the Baptist rather than Jesus? After all, aren't most Freemasons Christians?"

"Fair question."

"I kept thinking about that carving of John the Baptist in January's devils rock collection, with Jesus in a subservient role. If the Freemasons venerated John the Baptist, chances are so did the Templars. Did the carving indicate that someone—perhaps the Templars—worshiped John the Baptist over Jesus? So that's what I was just researching." She took a deep breath. "First I found that during medieval times the Grand Masters of the Templars traditionally took the name of John upon taking office. Then I found the clincher from a book called *Morals and Dogma*." She explained the work was a 19th century reference book given to every new Masonic initiate. *"Morals and Dogma* says that the first Templar grand master, Hugues de Payens, was secretly a Johannite—a worshiper of John the Baptist—and not a follower of Jesus and the Church. How could this be? How could the army of the Christian Church not be orthodox Christians?"

"Another good question. Does it have anything to do with that other stone you saw, with Jesus and the words 'thief' and 'cross' on it?"

She smiled. "It does, and I'll get to that. But first look at this." She turned the screen toward him. They studied a painting of two babies sitting with two women on a rocky outcrop.

VIRGIN OF THE ROCKS, LEONARDO DA VINCI

"This is called 'Virgin of the Rocks,' by Leonardo da Vinci. We know that da Vinci was initiated into the medieval secret societies and knew all about Templar beliefs and history—in fact, he was a leader of the Priory of Scion. Dan Brown was only scratching the surface when it comes to the secrets imbedded in da Vinci's works. The woman in black is the Virgin Mary; the other adult is not a woman but the angel Gabriel. Here's where it gets interesting: Which baby do you think is Jesus and which is John the Baptist?"

"Probably the one Mary has her arm around is Jesus."

"I agree. And I think that's what da Vinci intended. But in a later version of the painting someone added in a reed cross, which is the symbol of John the Baptist, and gave it to the baby with Mary. It's almost like they switched the babies."

"Why?"

"I think it's because the baby that was originally supposed to be Jesus is praying to the baby John, as if in a subservient role. Just like on the devil's rock. I wrote a paper about this at university, but could never make sense of it. Until now."

"That's good stuff, Amanda."

"Can I see?" Astarte asked.

Amanda lifted the laptop. "Of course honey."

"Yes," the girl announced. "That's the Virgin Mary with baby Jesus."

Amanda smiled. "So I think da Vinci originally intended Jesus to be praying to John the Baptist, but since the painting was in a church it was changed because it was considered heretical."

Cam nodded. "I can see why."

"I'll take it one step further." Amanda took a deep breath. "One of the crimes the Templars were accused of in the trials after 1307 was that they worshiped a secret idol, a human head--"

"Baphomet," he interjected

"Exactly. In fact, many members confessed to this heresy. Well, do you remember how John the Baptist was killed?"

Cam took a bite of his sandwich. "Ah, he was beheaded."

"Yes. King Herod had him beheaded at the request of Salome—they made a movie about it, *The Dance of the Seven Veils*.

Anyway, his body was put out to be eaten by the vultures, but his head was spirited away by his supporters and never seen again."

Cam nodded. "I see where you're going with this. You think John the Baptist's head became the Baphomet idol."

"Think about it, look at the words themselves. 'Baphomet,' 'Baptism,' 'Baptist.' The Templars were worshiping the skull of their patron, John the Baptist."

"But why?"

"Because the Templars believed Jesus stole the messiahship, or whatever you call it, probably from John the Baptist. They think Jesus lied when he said he was the son of God." She paused and waited until Cam turned to her. "The Templars used to call Jesus the Thief on the Cross."

✠ ✠ ✠

Cam rotated his neck, trying to ease the stiffness. The back roads and heavy rain and holiday traffic had turned a four-hour drive into a seven-hour one. Astarte had been an easy travel companion—other than insisting she was big enough to use the ladies room herself she made no demands and had not complained. Amanda kept her busy by searching for every letter of the alphabet, in order, on passing signs, which reminded Cam of family ski trips when he was a kid. Now, finally, they were approaching the Catskills region. The rain had slowed to a drizzle, and the forecast was for the storm to move off overnight.

"So, where to?" Amanda asked.

"I've been thinking about it." Actually, he had been thinking about the Thief on the Cross and the Templars worshiping John the Baptist until just recently. "Any major hotel is going to ask for a credit card."

"So we need to find a dump, is what you're saying."

"Pretty much. Sorry about that."

"I grabbed a map at the last rest area; it's full of advertisements. You want me to ring up a few of the motels?"

"Good idea. We can easily pass for a family traveling for the holiday. Try to find something close to the town of Phoenicia."

Amanda did a double-take. "Phoenicia? Really? As in the Phoenicians?"

He chuckled. "I thought you might like that. Maybe it's just a coincidence, but January says the mountain written about in the Clairvaux Codex is near the town of Phoenicia."

"I do like the Phoenician connection. I just hope we don't have to rise up from any ashes."

✠ ✠ ✠

Salazar sat in his Toyota at the far end of the motel parking lot and watched Cam, Amanda and the young girl unpack his cousin's SUV in front of the Cobblestone Motel. Someday a similar scene would unfold, with himself and Rosalita replacing Cam and Astarte. Or maybe Astarte would be with them. And also the dog.

The single row of flat-roofed efficiencies that comprised the complex ran perpendicular to the street, each with a lonely plastic chair on a cement slab next to the front door. It had not been hard to track them using a simple transponder he had tucked under the Explorer's back seat. Bullets would be flying and he wanted to make sure they found their proper marks.

As Amanda carried the last of their bags into the motel room, Salazar started the engine, followed the river back into town and parked. Phoenicia was a small town, especially during the non-summer months when the tourists were not around. If the feds had tracked Cam and Amanda this far, they shouldn't be hard to spot.

Downtown Phoenicia consisted of two blocks of Victorian-era buildings, many of them converted for use as inns, restaurants and shops. Most of them needed a coat of paint and a few more customers. Salazar parked on the main commercial strip, strolled into a Mexican restaurant and grabbed a table opposite the bar. He ordered a tomato juice and some quesadillas and studied the clientele: a few hunter-fisher types, a couple of families, a group of twenty-somethings home from the city for the holiday. Nothing out of the ordinary.

He paid the bill and entered an Italian restaurant next door. He sat at the counter and ordered a pastry for dessert. Same kind of crowd as the Mexican place, except for a guy about his age sitting with an older woman at a table in the corner. They didn't talk much—the guy spent most of his time on his smartphone as he picked at some lasagna. When they did interact they did so stiffly, strangers forced to share a meal together.

Ten minutes passed and a pair of clean-cut young men in khakis and windbreakers entered the restaurant, looked around, nodded to the guy in the corner and strode over. Salazar recognized the purposeful walk, the erect posture, and the pressed pants as ex-military. Which meant they were probably FBI or something. Self-righteous, arrogant pricks, most likely. The guy with the lasagna introduced himself as Buckner. After the waitress left the group huddled over a map and what looked like a rough drawing on a yellow legal pad, Buckner doing most of the talking and apparently issuing orders.

Salazar slipped off his stool and strolled toward the back of the restaurant as if looking for a restroom. The operatives were in hunter mode—it didn't occur to them that they themselves might be under surveillance, and they paid him no attention. He was not surprised to hear the words 'Thorne' and 'pre-dawn' as he walked by, but the words 'heavily armed' were unexpected. Why was Buckner lying about Cam and Amanda carrying weapons?

By the time Salazar had returned to his stool the answer had become obvious: Buckner wanted his team to treat this like a commando raid rather than a simple arrest. They didn't want Thorne and Amanda walking out of that motel room alive.

✠ ✠ ✠

Amanda and Cam stood over the map unfolded atop the chipped linoleum table. The motel had flooded during Hurricane Irene, and it still had a musty smell. "So this is the map January has been using," Cam said. It was a detailed topographic map of the Catskill Mountains, showing trails and ridge lines along with roads and waterways. "You can see he marked a few places where he's been."

162

"And presumably searched," Amanda said.

"Right." Cam pulled out a rough drawing from the stack of papers January had given him. "But he never got a chance to search here." Cam pointed at an X marked on the drawing. "Apparently the Clairvaux Codex references a bunch of carvings on boulders up on the mountain that serve as guideposts. January found most of the markings, right where they were supposed to be."

"What kind of markings?"

"One group of boulders arranged in a triangle had numbers in an ancient script carved on them; if you found the exact center of the triangle, there was another boulder with a bird carved on it. The bird's beak pointed in a certain direction, which led to the next marker. It was pretty elaborate."

Cam sipped some water. "Anyway, January couldn't figure out why he couldn't find the last cache of artifacts. It finally occurred to him he was using a modern compass, while the Templars were using a 12th-century instrument. Both point to magnetic north, but magnetic north drifts back and forth around the North Pole. Back in the late 1100s it was way over in Western Canada, about as far away from the North Pole as it's ever been. So he made some adjustments. He just never got a chance to get back here; the climb was too strenuous." Cam pointed at the X. "This is where we need to go."

Amanda studied the map. "Based on those ridge lines, that's going to be a tough climb. Especially with the ground so wet." She looked over at Astarte, propped up in bed watching a movie. "Do you think she can make it?"

"I remember hiking with my dad and uncle when I was a kid. In some ways it was easier for me because I was more flexible and lower to the ground. Plus I didn't get tired." He smiled. "So it wouldn't surprise me if she's the first one up the mountain."

Amanda grinned. "Well, then, she and I will just have to wait for you at the top."

✠ ✠ ✠

Salazar's room was two doors down from Cam and Amanda's, between them and the street. From his window he could see the entrance to the complex, and he had positioned his car so that he could look out his window and see the lights of their motel room reflected in his side view mirror.

He assumed the guys from the restaurant received the same training he had, which meant they would storm the motel room a few hours before dawn, when people slept the most soundly. And it also meant they had someone now conducting surveillance, probably in the wooded area facing the front doors of the motel rooms, making sure Cam and Amanda didn't leave. It would be easy enough to take the guy out, but doing so now would only arouse suspicion when the sentry failed to check in. But at some point Salazar might need to even the odds a bit.

Salazar phoned Cam's disposable cell. As much as he fantasized about sticking a knife in Cam's back, it would be difficult to arrange it without Amanda becoming suspicious. He had his chance in the woods, but once Amanda phoned and Cam told her they were together the moment was gone. But if Cam happened to take a stray bullet from one of the feds, well....

"I'm two doors down from you."

"At the motel?" Cam asked.

"It's what I do." Cam put him on speaker and Salazar described the operatives he had spotted in the restaurant. "At least two of the guys are ex-military. Probably special ops. And the guy in charge seemed pretty trigger-happy."

Cam exhaled. "Great. How did they track us?"

"Don't know. But they're here. And they're coming after you. Probably sometime pre-dawn, based on what I heard. Unless we act first."

"Act? What do you mean?"

"Well, I could take out one guy right now. But that would just solve part of the problem. We need to hunt them before they hunt you. There's only three of them, plus the woman. And we have the element of surprise. We could do it."

"Take them out." Cam's voice had raised an octave. "As in kill?"

"First we would need to talk about my fee. A thousand a day does not include murdering federal agents."

Amanda spoke. "Just wait a bloody minute. We haven't committed any crimes. What if they just want to arrest us, maybe scare us into keeping quiet?"

Salazar answered. "If they just wanted to arrest you they'd call the local police and send over a cruiser."

"What if instead we turned ourselves in to the local police?" Cam asked.

"Might work." Salazar paused. But then there would be no bullets flying. "But you'd have to get there first. And even if you did, I doubt they'd believe your story about federal agents trying to assassinate you. They'd just hand you back over to Buckner. He'd have to be a little more creative in the way he killed you— probably some story about you trying to escape—but he'd make sure you ended up in a ditch."

"Then what about going to the press?" Amanda asked.

Cam answered before Salazar could. "And tell them what, that federal agents are trying to assassinate us because of some ancient artifacts? I don't think they'd listen. Besides, it's the night before Thanksgiving, and we're in the middle of nowhere. When you say press, you're talking about a weekly newspaper. I don't think CNN has a bureau in Phoenicia."

Amanda nodded glumly.

Cam continued. "Back to your plan to go after these guys. I agree we have to do something. But I'm not ready to do the Rambo thing yet. Do you know where they're staying?"

"A Hampton Inn back by the highway exit."

"And you're sure their plan is to come after us pre-dawn?"

"Yes."

"So you think Amanda is safe until then?"

"Should be. As long as she doesn't try to leave."

"Okay then. I have an idea. I'm going to slip out the back window. Drive up to the gas station on the corner and meet me there in an hour."

✛ ✛ ✛

Georgia Johnston sat in her hotel room, mindlessly changing channels on the television. She called Hayek again, on both his hard line and cell. Straight to voice mail. And he had ignored her texts. She was beginning to think this whole thing might be a set up, with Hayek basically washing his hands of whatever Trey Buckner and his minions did so long as they made sure the artifacts and Codex remained buried. Which likely meant a couple of bodies would be buried with them. There was no direct order to kill anyone, just a generic set of instructions to complete the mission using whatever means were necessary and appropriate. Plausible deniability—Survival 101 for a Washington insider.

But that didn't mean she had to go along with this witch hunt. Big picture, she wasn't comfortable with erasing ancient artifacts and documents from the historical record—the Vatican had done this for centuries, and in the end half the world no longer trusted what its officials said. The truth had a way of bubbling to the surface no matter how hard humankind tried to suppress it. And even more egregious was the idea that her government was willing to rub a couple of young, innocent lives off the face of the earth with no more consideration than a driver clearing bugs off the windshield with the flick of the wiper button. Amanda and Cameron seemed like people—if the secret history they uncovered really was that explosive, no doubt they could be convinced to cooperate in how that information was eventually made public.

Somehow she needed to keep Amanda and Cam safe without arousing suspicion in Buckner. As far as she could tell Buckner didn't question her loyalty. In fact, he barely even acknowledged her presence, especially after the two operatives arrived from New York and the three of them put their heads together over the map like boys playing with little army figurines. Their plan was to storm the motel in the middle of the night and retrieve the artifacts and documents. Georgia's job was to wait in the Suburban, serve as look-out and coordinate communications. No doubt they would expect her to make sandwiches and clean up for them as well.

As Cam changed into dark clothing Amanda paced around the motel room, wondering how they had ended up in a cheap motor lodge in New York with a bull's-eye on their chests. "Are you really going out there? This is mental." Another wave of cold washed through her.

Cam pulled his shirt over his head. "It does seem crazy, and yet that bullet really did whiz by your ear, and unless Salazar is lying there really is a commando team ready to storm this motel room."

"Seriously, Cameron, this is the kind of thing that happens in Libya or North Korea or Iran. Civilized countries don't have hit squads." She stopped ranting as she saw the fear in Astarte's eyes.

"Are they really going to kill you and Mr. Thorne?" the girl asked, her knees tucked into her body as she pulled the blanket up.

Amanda sat on the bed next to her and grasped her hand. She forced herself to modulate her voice. "They may try, but Cameron has a plan, and we're going to be just fine. I'm just angry because some people are using their heads for nothing more than a place to rest their hats."

Astarte's eyes pooled. "This is all my fault."

Amanda hugged her. "No, darling, it is not. You are very brave, and very smart, and you will be a fine princess someday, but this is the fault of a bunch of grown-ups who need to have their ears boxed."

The girl spun away, her back now to Amanda. "No. It is my fault."

There was something in the girl's tone that resonated with Amanda. She rested her hand on Astarte's shoulder. "Why do you say that?"

Astarte sniffled and looked warily at Cam.

Amanda motioned to Cam. "Why don't you finish dressing in the bathroom." She paused as Cam complied. "Now, Astarte, you must answer me. I won't be cross with you if you tell me the truth."

The girl rolled over and faced Amanda, her dark blue eyes wet and sad. "When we stopped to go to the bathroom I used my phone and called Aunt Eliza. I told her what kind of car we were driving and the license plate number and where we were."

What? So much for the promise not to be cross. "Why in the world would you have done that?"

She lifted her chin. "Mr. Thorne said he was going to prove the Book of Mormon was a lie."

Of course. The girl had been taught the book was the story of not just the Mormons but the Mandan also. So both her religion and her culture were being attacked.

Astarte continued. "Aunt Eliza said she knew people who could stop him." She dropped her eyes. "But I didn't know they wanted to kill him. And you."

Amanda nodded. The poor girl had no idea whom to trust anymore. "Yes, I can see why you did that. It was very brave of you. Just like Mulan going off to fight the Huns even though the grown-ups didn't want her to. You indeed are a fine princess."

The girl nodded; apparently she had reached the same conclusion herself. "So you're not mad at me?"

"No, I'm not. But I do need you to trust me, to trust that we would never do anything to hurt you. But the people who are after us, the people your Aunt Eliza is friends with, are very bad people." She lowered her voice. "So I need you to make a deal with me. If I can get Mr. Thorne to promise not to tell people the Book of Mormon is a lie, will you promise not to call Aunt Eliza again?"

The princess weighed the offer. "Must it be a promise on the Bible?"

Amanda put her hand in front of her face to hide her smile. "Yes. On the Bible." She opened the drawer in the side table next to bed and pulled out a brown Gideon's Holy Bible. "You must promise on the Bible not to call Aunt Eliza again."

Astarte nodded. "All right then." She rested her hand on the book, closed her eyes and recited her vow. "But how will you get Mr. Thorne to agree not to tell people the Book of Mormon is a lie?"

Amanda grinned. "Because he's in love with me. Think about the men in *Anastasia* and *Mulan* and *Sound of Music* and *Little*

Mermaid—whenever men fall in love, they do whatever the women tell them to do."

Astarte thought about it for a couple of seconds. "Funny, they do, don't they?"

✠ ✠ ✠

Cam slipped into the passenger seat of Salazar's Toyota Camry as the mercenary finished filling the tank. The knife incident fresh in his mind, Cam didn't offer his hand. "I never asked. Why are you here?"

Salazar shrugged. "Job wasn't done yet. And I'm not rich enough to walk away from a thousand bucks a day."

Cam sensed there was more to it than that but he let it slide. "How's Venus?"

Salazar offered a rare smile. "Rosalita is wearing her out. When I left Venus was wearing a bonnet." He handed Cam a digital camera. "These are pictures of the feds I took at the restaurant. You and Amanda should study their faces. So what's your plan?"

"It's based on a story an older partner told me once when I worked at a law firm. He was pretty much a sleaze-ball but he liked to share his war stories with me. Apparently a business deal went bad for one of his clients. A couple of days before the trial he found out the other side had a surprise witness—his client's ex-girlfriend—who would destroy his guy's case."

"Want me to drive?" Salazar interrupted, "or just stay here?"

"Head out toward their hotel." Cam took a deep breath. It felt good to be doing something proactive instead of just reacting as best he could. "So, anyway, the night before the trial the partner called some guys he knew. They stole the girlfriend's car; she never made it to the courtroom. Another guy stopped short in front of the opposing lawyer's car—nothing serious, but enough to send him to the emergency room. The other side had some young associate in the courtroom but he had no idea what he was doing, and no star witness. The moral of the story is that the person who wins the fight is the person who picks the battlefield—instead of waiting for court, he made a preemptive strike."

Salazar shrugged. "Nothing earth-shattering about that. That's what the Japs did at Pearl Harbor. So what's your plan?"

"What kind of car are they driving?"

"Buckner and the woman drove up in a Chevy Suburban. The other guys have a Crown Victoria; the guy watching the motel is probably driving that."

"Where do you think their weapons are?"

"Other than their side arms, and whatever is in the Crown Vic, probably locked in the Suburban. They wouldn't take assault weapons into the Hampton Inn on a luggage rack."

"Okay then. This might work."

Five minutes later they pulled into the hotel parking lot. Salazar pointed to a black Suburban parked against a fence at the edge of the lot. "That's it."

"Good, it's not too close to the front door. Pull over in front of it; try to block the view from the hotel. And face the exit."

"What are you going to do?"

"You'll see." Cam slid from the car and pulled from inside his jacket a cheap hand-towel and wire coat hanger he had taken from the motel. He edged through the puddles and crouched next to the Suburban's gas tank. His hand was shaking so he flexed his fingers like he had seen safecrackers do in the old Hollywood movies and removed the cap. Things seemed quiet, but that probably didn't mean much when dealing with trained operatives. He dropped to his belly, his legs in a puddle, and peered under the Suburban. Allowing his eyes to adjust, he scanned the lot, looking for the movement of feet under the cars parked nearby. Nothing.

Rising to one knee, Cam twisted the towel and, using the coat hanger, forced one end of the threadbare fabric deep into tank. The taste of gas settled in the back of his dry throat; he licked his lips and swallowed. The gas wicked up the towel, eventually soaking a portion of the fabric hanging outside the tank. He waved away any fumes, pulled a lighter from his pocket and lit the unsaturated end of the fabric, holding the flame far from his

170

body. When he was sure the flame would not go out, he sprinted to the car.

"Drive. Fast. We have about five seconds."

As Salazar screeched out of the parking lot a thunderous boom concussed the night air. A few seconds later a series of smaller staccato pops cut through the echo of the first explosion as the ammunition in the Suburban ignited. An orange glow illuminated the low clouds in the night sky behind them.

Salazar nodded. "Nice work. But they're going to be really pissed off."

✛ ✛ ✛

Georgia waited until the sedan peeled out of the hotel parking lot before pounding on the door across the hall. "It's the Suburban," she yelled. "It's on fire." *Good for them.*

Trey pushed past her and peered out the window. Flames shot high into the sky as the inferno popped like a summer campfire. "Weren't you watching?" He glared at her.

"I was. I just looked away for a minute." She tried not to laugh as the vein on Trey's forehead throbbed.

"You didn't see anything?"

The hotel probably had a security camera, so she didn't want to push her lie too far. "There was a sedan driving around a minute or so earlier. Silver, I think a Honda." She made a show of scanning the parking lot. "I don't see it now."

✛ ✛ ✛

As Salazar drove, pushing the speed limit but not so much that they would get pulled over, Cam phoned Amanda. He put her on speaker and recounted how they blew up the Suburban. "Pack up our stuff. We'll be there in fifteen minutes."

"What about the guy watching our room?"

Salazar responded. "My bet is we see him racing past us in a few minutes. They'll reestablish surveillance in a few hours after they assess damage. Right now they're pretty much unarmed."

"Hey, I know how they tracked us." Amanda recounted her conversation with Astarte. "So Eliza must be somehow linked to Buckner and his hit squad."

"Eliza?" Cam said. "You mean the whole Mormon spinster thing is an act?"

Salazar nodded. "Makes sense. There had to be someone inside that compound who had a hidden agenda."

"But what is that agenda?" Cam asked. It didn't make sense. "Why would January coerce me to take his artifacts and go finish his mission, and then his sister turn around and try to stop us?"

"Not just his sister," Salazar said. "It's the feds also. Buckner is following someone's orders." He paused. "Or he's gone rogue and is working with Eliza clandestinely, maybe taking this further than his orders allow him to. That would explain why he's trying to take you guys out."

"I think it all goes back to me seeing the devil's rocks," Amanda said. "January wanted us to follow the bread crumbs and find some kind of Holy Grail. But there must be something in the devil's rocks that leads us, I don't know, down a different path." She paused. "Or maybe further down the path than they want us to go."

"Don't you have one of these devil's rocks?" Salazar asked.

"It's still in my pack. There's been so much going on we haven't had time to examine it closely."

A dark blue Crown Victoria with a single male driver sped past. Cam spoke into the phone. "We just passed the guy who was watching us, going the other way. So you're okay to pack the car. See you in ten."

✠ ✠ ✠

Amanda watched as Cam finished packing the SUV, the last item being Astarte's softly snoring body wrapped in a sleeping bag. "Boy, when she sleeps she sleeps."

Amanda smiled. "Only two speeds on that one—off and full."

Salazar followed for a couple of miles as they ascended the mountain road; the mercenary pulled onto a side street to stand sentry in case Buckner and his cronies somehow tracked them. Cam found an old logging road near where they would be beginning their hike in the morning, pulled deep into it and covered the car with branches and underbrush.

"Now what?" Amanda asked. "Where do we sleep?" She was wide awake, but they had a long day ahead of them.

"I don't want to make a fire," Cam said, watching the steam from his breath in the moonlight. At least the weather had cleared. "And it's too cold to sleep under the stars."

She shivered again. "Agreed. We could fold down the rear seat and sleep side-by-side in the back."

"Okay. We can stack our supplies on the front hood. But not the food—I don't want to attract bears. We'll leave that in the front seat."

Twenty minutes later they had arranged themselves atop a blanket under a pair of sleeping bags in the bed of the SUV, Astarte huddled between them in the nook of Amanda's arm.

Amanda shifted and turned, her mind racing. Cam's breathing told her he was awake also. "You thinking what I'm thinking?" she whispered.

"What, you want to fool around?"

She reached over Astarte and cuffed him. "No. I want to look at the devil's rock."

"Sounds good to me."

While Amanda retrieved the stone and a flashlight, Cam cleared the food off of the passenger's seat. She sat on his lap, shifting until she found a position that didn't hurt her ribs, and rested the paperback-sized slab of white marble on her thighs. She ran the light beam across the carved surface of the marble. A female figure knelt naked beneath the sun, her hands upraised as if accepting the sun's rays. The figure was simple but graceful.

BURROWS CAVE ISIS STONE

"The description card said this is supposed to be Isis. She usually has wings, but not always," Amanda said. "But why would this be one of January's devil's rocks?"

Cam studied it. "I assume this is a Burrows Cave piece—lots of them have Egyptian themes just like this, especially the white marble ones. And stylistically it's similar. I really don't see anything wrong with it." He paused. "What about the fact that she's kneeling? Or naked? Assuming it is Isis, would that be historically inaccurate?"

174

"No, Isis was often displayed kneeling or naked. And sun worship was an important part of ancient Egyptian religion. Whoever carved this knew their Egyptian history, or at least knew enough to copy something authentic."

"Maybe there's something about the stone itself? Maybe this kind of marble isn't found in North America?"

She shook her head. "Even so, the piece could have been brought here. Ancient travelers often carried religious icons with them. Or the slab could even have been part of ship ballast and the carving made after they arrived."

"Flip it over. Maybe there's something on the back."

Amanda held the light at a low angle to the stone, slowly moving it along the rough surface. "Bloody hell, look at that." She pointed at a couple of carved characters, faded but still visible. "That's manmade."

She snapped a digital photo of the characters, downloaded the image to her laptop, magnified the marks and drew a red box around them.

BURROWS CAVE ISIS STONE (back side)

"It's cursive writing," Cam said. "Looks like an 'h' and an 'e.'"

"And I see a 't' before the 'h'. So we have 't-h-e.'"

"Clearly not ancient writing. But the word 'the' isn't much of a clue."

"No, but 'the' as part of 'mother' or 'father' is. As in 'dearly departed.' Dear old mum or dad, buried under a marble slab."

Cam chuckled. "You're right. It's part of an old tombstone. Probably from some abandoned frontier cemetery."

"So someone took an old grave slab, roughed up the epitaph, turned it over and carved an Isis figure on the reverse face. And then left it for Russell Burrows to find, not realizing they botched the job and didn't completely erase the backside."

"Or Russell did it himself."

"Either way, it's a fake. And that calls into question the whole Burrows Cave lot."

Cam nodded. "That's why January hid this one away. It undermines his whole theory."

She put the marble slab on the car floor and leaned back against him. "So all this is for nothing? These stones are fake, the Codex is fake, the secret history is fake?"

"Maybe. But we don't know the Codex is fake. And don't forget January knew about this fake carving and still thought the other stones, at least some of them, were authentic enough to devote his life to them. I don't think the John the Baptist stone is fake—why would January fabricate something like that?"

"January was delusional." She sighed. "It's one thing to get shot at over something truly remarkable." She gestured at the Isis carving. "But this is just rubbish."

"Unfortunately the guys chasing us don't know that yet. Or if they do, they don't care. I don't see how this really changes anything. I think we still have to go up the mountain tomorrow and figure this all out. They're going to hunt us down, fakes or not."

"Jolly wonderful." She turned and kissed him gently, allowing her body to sink further into his. She felt his manhood stir beneath her. But he often allowed her to set the tone and pace for their lovemaking, and he waited for her to determine whether the kiss was meant as the cap to the end of a long day or rather the prologue to one final climax.

There was no doubt in her mind—they might be dead by tomorrow, and fat chance she would waste her last night on sleep. Lucky for them Astarte was such a deep sleeper. She moved her lips slowly up his jaw line, nibbled an ear, then tongue-flicked her way down to his neck and chest. He moaned lightly, his eyes closed, and she slipped off her jeans as she moved her lips back up to his face and opened her mouth to his.

They kissed for a few minutes before she shifted her body and unbuttoned his pants. He entered her slowly, their mouths still together, their eyes open and focused on some spot deep within each other's soul. Quietly they moved together, a slow, sweet dance at the end of a long day. The music climaxed and then stopped, but they held each other for another few minutes, a dance without music, until she felt herself drifting off to sleep.

She considered just staying in the front seat, atop Cam, for the entire night. But they needed at least a couple of hours of real sleep. "Come on, darling."

Five minutes later they nestled together in the back of the SUV. But the walk around the car had taken the edge off her fatigue, and her mind raced. She was frightened of the assassins pursuing them, and angry at the stone being a fake, and anxious about the climb tomorrow. But being with Cam made it somehow bearable. She laughed to herself—'bearable' probably was a bad choice of words. "You were joshing about the bears before, right?"

"Hopefully they're hibernating by now," he mumbled. "But these mountains are probably full of them."

She sighed and rested her head on his shoulder. "That's okay. Astarte and I don't have to outrun the bears." It was a favorite joke of theirs, dating back to when they had first met and were being chased by Salazar and his henchmen. "We just have to outrun you."

CHAPTER 13

Eliza turned down the volume on an old John Wayne movie as the phone rang. With Jefferson dead and Astarte missing and the security staff dismissed, she didn't have to keep up appearances and watch those stupid preachers all day. "It's two in the morning, Trey. I assume this is important."

She didn't like this, didn't like having to sit by the phone and wait for updates while the men did the dirty work. But it had always been this way with the women of her family—they controlled things quietly, subtly, puppeteering behind the scenes while the men blustered about thinking they were in charge. Obviously God did not oppose the idea of female control; he allowed the family matriarchs to hatch a plot after the Civil War to both prove the validity of the Book of Mormon and elevate a female into a position of worldwide spiritual authority. The Age of Aquarius dawned. Just as the Age of Pisces had ushered in King Jesus so too would this new age usher in the reign of Princess Astarte.

"It's important," Trey said, "but it's not good news."

"Tell me." Trey was Eliza's sister's son, one of the few men entrusted with secrets the matriarchs of the family kept. Brigham Young himself had approved the matriarchs' original post-Civil War plan, which gave the women of her family more power than was normal in Mormon society. In the intelligence community Trey was an accomplished operative. But within the family he took his orders from Eliza—even if those orders ran contrary to those he received from Langley.

"They escaped." Trey described the attack on the Suburban. "I'm assuming they're up in the mountains now. But we've lost the trail. I could ask for help from the locals—"

"No," she interrupted. "We need to keep this quiet. We've involved too many people already." She paused. There was no sense being cross with Trey; he was loyal and competent, and sometimes God scuttled even man's best plans. "I assume you can control your team?"

"They have no idea what's going on, only that we need to retrieve some stolen contraband. The only issue is the Johnston woman. Hayek insisted she come along. She's an expert in Middle Eastern history and politics. So far she hasn't been a problem, but obviously she doesn't share our sense of urgency that this be kept quiet."

"Yes, urgency. Which brings us back to our lovebirds. It may not be the worst thing to let them climb the mountain and find the scroll and artifacts. It actually saves you from having to do it." Perhaps that was what God intended; perhaps it was Astarte's destiny to retrieve her family heirlooms. Imagine the headlines: *Eight-year-old princess recovers 800-year-old artifacts deposited in mountain cave by her ancestors.* If that didn't capture the world's attention, nothing would.

"So I'm just supposed to wait for them, hope they come driving through town on their way home?"

"Of course not. There is no more room for error. They must not leave the Catskills alive—they know too much, and they have one of the devil's rocks. You have a team of trained operatives. Go find them. But make sure Astarte is not harmed. I don't think God would appreciate it." She paused. "Apparently he has big plans for her."

✝ ✝ ✝

Cam didn't sleep much, his ears tuned to any break in the rhythm of the forest and his body wedged against the side door of the SUV. At 4:30 he crawled out the back hatch to boil water for their dehydrated breakfast, shielding the small propane stove with a blanket. No doubt Buckner and his team would be on the road at first light; Cam wanted to stay ahead of them. It was a seasonally cold November morning, and the ground was still wet from the rain, but at least it would be clear.

Astarte woke up cheerfully, as she always seemed to. "What's for breakfast?"

"Turkey, stuffing, all the fixings. It's Thanksgiving."

She rolled her eyes. "Really, what are we having?"

"Well, the package says scrambled eggs and bacon."

She scrunched her nose. "In that bag?"

"Yup."

"Are you a good cook?"

"The best." He handed her a plate as he drained the excess water from the pack.

Amanda hugged him from behind and kissed his cheek. "Actually, he's a horrid cook. But he can boil water with the best of them."

They ate quickly by the light of the fire. Cam glanced at the eastern sky. "We need to get moving. I told Salazar we'd meet him at 5:30." They had discussed ditching the mercenary, as Cam didn't trust him and he gave Amanda the willies. But what chance did they have against Buckner and his team without him?

The plan was to meet Salazar at a trailhead five miles down-mountain from the trail they actually planned to climb. After abandoning the SUV Salazar would drive them in his Toyota to the trail shown on January's map. Hopefully Buckner would find the SUV and fall for the ruse.

The plan required Cam to carry the stone artifacts and the Clairvaux Codex, adding about 65 pounds of weight to his pack. The items were too valuable to leave in one of the vehicles, and Salazar couldn't take them, even if they did trust him with them, as he needed to stay nimble to conduct surveillance and perhaps even track the operatives. Amanda, her ribs wrapped, would carry the other supplies necessary for a day hike, but at Cam's body weight of 175 pounds the 65-pound pack exceeded the recommended pack weight by almost a third.

"Why not just hide them at the base of the trail?" Amanda asked.

Cam was tempted. January had died for them—he'd rather not meet a similar fate. "The problem is if we have to make a run for it, we're not going to be able to circle back and get them. I think I'd rather deal with the extra weight."

They met Salazar at the base of a public trail and pulled their packs from the SUV, Salazar carrying Amanda's pack for her. Salazar suggested Cam drive the SUV into the underbrush and cover it with branches and leaves. "Make it look like we don't want them to find it."

After doing so Cam climbed into the front seat of the Toyota. "Follow the road higher up into the mountains," Cam said. He consulted January's topo map. "From what I can see, there used to be a trail heading up along that ridge line." He pointed out the window. "It's on private property now, but hopefully some of the trail still exists."

"That's a steep climb," Salazar said. "Even with a trail it's going to be tough after all the rain. Why not come up the backside of the mountain? It'd be easy to follow one of the ski trails to the summit."

"I thought about that, but all the orientations and directions in January's notes are based on coming up this way. I don't want to miss the landmarks."

"Then why not send Amanda and the girl up the backside with me? We can meet you at the top."

"Thanks, we'll stay together," Amanda answered quickly.

Salazar stared hard at Amanda for a few seconds before shrugging and handing Cam a walkie-talkie. "Not sure you'll have cell reception up there. Check in every half-hour."

Cam nodded. "Over that ridge there's a dip into a saddle between this and the next ridge line. Somewhere up in the saddle is a cave marked by a carving on a rock. According to January that's where the artifacts are." He didn't want to go into too much detail about the exact location.

"You're talking 800 years ago. Would the carving still be there?" Salazar asked.

Amanda said, "If they carved it into a hard rock it would be. We have plenty of artifacts older than that in Great Britain." She bit her lip as she peered up the mountain. "But I'm more concerned with finding the cave in the first place. That ridge line goes on for hundreds of yards; that's a massive area we'll need to search."

Astarte patted her hand. "Don't worry, Miss Amanda. I can find the artifacts. It was my ancestors who hid them."

✚ ✚ ✚

Twenty minutes later, just as the sky was beginning to glow in the east, Amanda, Cam and Astarte piled out of Salazar's car, slipped on their packs and hats and gloves and began trudging through the woods along an old logging road. It felt surreal to Amanda—how did a simple girl from the London suburbs end up chasing Templar secrets while being pursued by United States military operatives? Her first few years in the States had been deathly boring. Now here she was the fulcrum of some national security crisis, hunted by assassins for the second time in just over a year.

As if reading her mood, the miner's lamp strapped to Cam's forehead illuminated an orange 'No Trespassing' sign, complete with skull and crossbones, nailed to a tree. Cam smiled. "The Templars are the ones who first used the skull and crossbones. Maybe that's a signal we're on the right path."

"The Templars used it as a symbol for death," Amanda said. "Hardly an auspicious sign."

Wet, fallen leaves covered the ground; once off the main road the trail ascended sharply up the mountain face. Amanda glanced up the steep ridge: What were they doing? The Isis piece was fake—didn't that make this whole quest quixotic? She sighed. Not necessarily. As Cam pointed out, just because January linked the Codex to the Burrows Cave artifacts didn't mean the link was an actual one. The Isis stone could be fake and the Codex still authentic....

The trail split, the wider path leading off to the left while a scar-like serration on the mountain face climbed upward. Cam studied January's map. "Unfortunately, we take the road less traveled."

"Hopefully that will make all the difference," Amanda exhaled.

They ascended carefully, their vision limited by the range and direction of Cam's lamp. Amanda and Cam each carried hiking sticks; Cam led the way, using his stick as a third leg, planting it deep into the path and transferring part of his body weight over it with every step. With his free hand he grabbed hold of tree branches to pull himself forward; Amanda did the same, but stayed a few yards behind him so the branches didn't slap back in her face. Astarte scampered along rabbit-like, using her gloved hands as another pair of feet and following the indentations in the trail made by Cam and Amanda ahead of her. She hummed the "It's off to work we go" song from Snow White as they climbed. Cam kept his head bowed, careful that the light not serve as a beacon for their pursuers. So far there had been no sign of Buckner. The sun at their backs occasionally filtered through the forest, but for the most part they proceeded in the near-dark.

Amanda watched Cam. He did a lot of mountain-biking and jogged a few miles almost every day, but not with a 65-pound load on his back. After about fifteen minutes he was breathing hard, sweat moistening his forehead. Amanda's pack was lighter, and she worked out regularly herself, but he refused her offer to share his load. Especially with her injured ribs. There was a bit of macho in him, which she actually found endearing as it did not cross over into chauvinism. In fact, she sensed he secretly liked it that she regularly beat him on the tennis court.

Not that this climb was any kind of a game. She arched her neck; the entire mountain face loomed above her, mocking them. The trail, or what was left of it, angled upward, bypassing the sheer rock faces but otherwise making no accommodation to the mountain's incline. Cam shifted his pack, reaching back to push at some protruding artifact that dug into his shoulder blade.

She came up next to him, breathing hard herself, which only made the pain in her chest more acute. "My kingdom for a chairlift."

He sipped at some water. "No wonder all the trails up here are called Devil's Path, and Devil's Tombstone, and Devil's Acre."

"They are?" Astarte asked, her eyes widening.

"Don't fret," Amanda said. "It's just a name."

Astarte chewed her lip. "You said these mountains are called the Catskills. Is that because the devil kills all the cats?"

"No," Cam said. "It's an old Dutch name, like where the windmills are. 'Kill' is the Dutch word for creek. So it just means cats lived near the streams."

"I haven't seen any cats. Have you?" the girl asked Cam.

"No. But did you know the story Rip Van Winkle was set in these mountains?"

The girl would not be distracted. "Is there another name, different than Catskills?"

Cam gave Astarte a funny look. "I think the Native Americans called this area Onteora. Why?"

Astarte swallowed. "I knew it. This is where the evil spirits live." She explained that Onteora was a spirit who terrorized the ancient peoples of the area. The great god Manitou captured Onteora and created these mountain ridges to imprison him. "He lives here still," the girl concluded. Apparently January made sure she was well-versed in her Native American culture. Even the darker parts.

Amanda crouched in front of the girl. "Astarte, those are just legends. There's no such thing as evil spirits."

She raised her chin. "You're wrong. Have you seen any animals this morning?"

Amanda and Cam exchanged glances. Other than a few birds high in the trees, and some insects, she hadn't seen anything. No squirrels, no chipmunks, no rabbits, no deer. Peculiar.

"Well," Amanda said, "that may be because it's getting close to winter."

"No. There are no animals here because Onteora eats them. That's why all the cats get killed here." She glanced back down the trail, her voice now a whisper. "My people know they are not supposed to come up here. I think we should go back down."

Amanda peered again into the woods. Why were there no animals up here?

"Go back down?" Amanda forced a light laugh. "This story you just told us about Onteora is actually very good news. I think Manitou gave Onteora a job when he imprisoned him here, and that job was to guard the artifacts in the caves. Manitou knew someday the Fortieth Princess would come looking for the artifacts, and he wanted to make sure people stayed away from here until she did. Until you did."

Astarte looked at her uncertainly.

"Tell me, Astarte, is it your destiny to save your people?"

She nodded.

"Well, then," Amanda said, clapping her hands together, "this gives us a huge advantage over the men chasing us. It's like King

184

Arthur and Excalibur—only the Fortieth Princess is destined to find these artifacts. Others who try will fail, just as no other knight could extract Excalibur. And Onteora is here to make sure of that, just as the wizard Merlin helped Arthur. Onteora is a spirit, but his evil is directed at those who would defy Manitou, would defy the destiny of the Fortieth Princess." She stood up from her crouch. "I, for one, welcome Onteora's help. It's about time we had a bit of good luck."

But as Astarte mulled over Amanda's placating words, Amanda edged closer to Cam. "Cam, why are there no animals up here? The girl's spot on. It's bloody unnatural."

✠ ✠ ✠

They continued climbing, the post-dawn sun illuminating the trail but not drying it. Cam and his pack outweighed Amanda by well over a hundred pounds; every few yards the moist earth gave way and he either fell to one knee or slid down the trail into Amanda, who learned quickly to brace herself so they both didn't snowball down onto Astarte. The sharp edges of the stones jabbed into Cam's back every time he slipped or lunged.

Astarte kept up, but her chipper mood had turned reflective as she, like Cam and Amanda, listened in vain for the sound of wildlife in the woods. At least the thought of evil spirits took Cam's mind off the strain of the climb.

After an hour of climbing he turned to Amanda. "How about a break?" Sweat streamed from his armpits and back and pooled along his waistband.

"Fine with me."

He sat on a rock and removed his ski hat and lamp; he had already unzipped his jacket. His shirt was drenched, and he guessed his pulse was in the 150 range. Not dangerous, but quite a workout. "We're about halfway. Looks like the toughest part of the climb is just ahead."

As Amanda removed water bottles and energy bars from her pack, Cam checked in via walkie-talkie with Salazar, who was driving up and down the mountain access road watching for Buckner.

"No sign of them yet," Salazar said. "My guess is they're waiting for it to get light enough to get some aerial surveillance."

"Like, military satellites? Looking for us?" Cam glanced skyward involuntarily. He remembered the new clips showing U.S. drones assassinating terrorists in the hills of Afghanistan. Was that same technology being marshaled against them now?

"Satellites, or maybe a surveillance aircraft. This is the feds. And they want to stop you guys pretty bad."

Cam guided Amanda and Astarte under an overhang of vegetation. He hadn't heard any airplanes this morning, but a satellite or high-flying military plane would be out of his hearing range anyway. As they snacked he angled his chin toward a rivulet flowing past them. "According to the map, the trail runs parallel to that stream. If for some reason we get separated, just follow the water back to the road."

Amanda looked hard at him and slipped her arm over Astarte's shoulders. "We're not getting separated."

They hadn't really discussed an escape plan, or what do to if confronted by Buckner and his men. If Salazar was right about the satellite surveillance they had less than a two-hour head start on the agents, with the trained operatives likely able to close the gap quickly. And that was assuming they fell for the wrong-trail ruse. Cam scanned the slope below them, as he had done dozens of times already. He hoped Amanda was right, that they wouldn't be separated, but the sobering reality was that if Buckner's men found them Cam would have no choice but delay them and hope Amanda and Astarte could escape. He had no desire to be a hero or a martyr; in fact, he desperately wanted to live long enough to have children with Amanda and grow old together and hopefully spend the next 50 years rewriting American history. But it made no sense for all of them to die on this mountain. His death would force the police to believe Amanda's story and protect her from Buckner if she and Astarte were somehow able to get back to town. Suddenly all the Thief on the Cross stuff seemed pretty unimportant....

There wasn't much of a trail anymore so they navigated up a series of steep rock outcroppings on all fours, using weeds and bushes and crevices in the slick, wet rock as handholds. Astarte, again, had little trouble scurrying up the slope. But Cam and Amanda struggled, their higher centers of gravity and the weight of their packs hindering them.

"Cam, this is bloody foolish. Someone's likely to get hurt."

He found a foothold and turned his head. "I don't know that we have much choice. There's no other way up to this ridge line."

She snorted but didn't argue. Cam resumed, his eyes focused on the rock just ahead of him, making sure his upper foot was firmly secured before shifting weight off his lower foot. As he neared the top of a particularly slick outcrop, he gripped a small birch tree rooted in a crevice where the rock had split. As he tugged he swung his back foot forward. *Snap.* The birch sheared in his hand. Instantly he knew he was in trouble. He was falling backward with nothing to break his fall except air and whatever rocks he might finally crash against.

Desperate, he waved his hands, trying to propel his body weight forward, using his arms to counterbalance his weight the way a tightrope walker used a pole. But it was too late. He could not defy gravity, could not overcome the weight of the pack and the slope of the mountain. A voice in his head told him to relax his body, reminded him of stories of drunken college kids surviving falls from balconies because their intoxication kept their muscles flaccid....

"Cam!" Amanda screamed. She lunged for him, hooked a couple of fingers around a strap on his pack and yanked. It was just enough to partially rotate his body. Now instead of his back facing down the mountain, he was angled across the fall line. Milliseconds before his feet lost contact with the outcrop, he thrust himself sideways, directing his fall away from the steepest slope of the outcrop. He soared, his body now in a prone position, his hands and feet splayed outward like a pouncing cougar. The outcrop rushed up to meet him. He braced and landed chin first, the weight of the backpack driving his chest into the stone. Bouncing and skidding, he slid down the slope as he clawed at the wet rock, willing to let the fall tear his fingers from his hands if necessary. Finally he came to a stop 30 feet down the slope.

He was alive. He knew it because his body was screaming out in anguish.

✠ ✠ ✠

"No!" Cam teetered backward on the rock ledge, just an arm's length from Amanda's grasp, her fingers unable to hold their grip on the strap of his pack. And then he fell. No, no, no, no. She dropped to her knees, paralyzed, and watched him bounce down the slope. The sight of his body sprawled on the rocks below, twitching, sent a jolt of adrenaline through her. "Cam! Are you all right? Cam?"

She threw off her pack and crab-crawled down the outcrop. "Astarte, stay here," she yelled over her shoulder. She knew she needed to focus on her descent but she couldn't take her eyes off of Cam's crumpled body. And tears clouded her vision anyway. She skidded the final few feet to his side. "Cam, can you hear me?" He stirred, shifting his head a bit. She exhaled. He was alive. "Don't move."

She touched him lightly on the shoulder. Blood pooled under a nasty gash on his chin. "Astarte," she called, "get the first aid kit from my pack and toss it down here." She removed her glove, folded it in half and pressed it against his chin. "Can you tell me what hurts?" How would she get him down if he had serious injuries?

He moaned and blinked. "Chest. Knee. Chin. Everything."

"Can you move your fingers and toes?"

He blinked again and nodded.

"Okay." She slid his pack off. "We need you to spin around, get your head uphill to stop the bleeding. And also get you onto your back." He grunted and eased himself around.

"Good. That better?"

He spit some blood; hopefully he had bit his lip or tongue. How in the world would she know if he had internal injuries? He could bleed to death and she would never see it.

"Can you breathe okay?"

"I think I just got the wind knocked out of me." He took a deep breath, exhaled slowly. "I feel like I fell off a mountain."

"Funny that." She smiled and kissed him gently on the cheek. Astarte tossed her the kit, and she taped a bandage to his chin. "Now look at me." She had some first aid training and experience with head injuries from her days as a gymnast. Cam's pupils were dilated and he shaded his eyes as he turned toward the filtered sun rays. "Do you remember what we were talking about before you fell?"

He paused. "Um, no."

"Do you know what day it is?"

He stared off in the distance. "It's Thanksgiving, right?"

"Good. Do you remember what Astarte was saying about the wild animals on this mountain?"

"She's afraid of bears?" He furrowed his brow. "No, wait, that was you last night. I don't remember."

"What did you have for breakfast?"

"I can't remember."

"Do you feel like throwing up?"

"A little. I'm nauseous." He swallowed. "And light-headed."

"It sounds like you have a mild concussion. You have some short-term memory loss. I don't think you lost consciousness, at least not for long, so hopefully it's not too serious." Normally he would be on his way to a hospital. Instead he was going to have to finish this climb.

Bending gingerly, he reached down for his pack. She braced him as he staggered. "Yeah, well, that rock will think twice before going 10 rounds with me again."

✝ ✝ ✝

Hayek still hadn't called her back, and she knew he was usually in the office by 8:00, so Georgia played her final card as she sipped her coffee at a corner table in the hotel lobby. "I know you're dodging my calls. If you don't return my call in five minutes, my next call is to the Senate Intelligence Office. I'm sure they'd love to hold hearings on why our Homeland Security agents are assassinating U.S. citizens." She would need to act quickly—it wouldn't take Trey and his posse long to track their prey.

Two minutes later Hayek phoned. To his credit, he didn't lie about not getting her messages. "I was hoping you wouldn't push this."

"Too late. Unless you're trying to stop a world war there's no way you can justify this mission."

He exhaled; Georgia pictured a cloud of blue smoke engulfing the phone. "Maybe not a world war. But close."

She had been in the intelligence business long enough to know the mindset at Langley—every loose end was the thread that, if pulled, would unravel the entire fabric of Western civilization. Hayek wasn't a bad guy, but you couldn't spend a career in the CIA and not develop paranoid tendencies. "Mr. Hayek, with all due respect, the whole world is not a nail."

"I get that. And I'm not just a man wildly swinging a hammer. I'm trying to deal with this surgically, quietly. Before it escalates."

"Hammer, rifle—it's all the same to the nail. And to Amanda Spencer and her fiancé." She paused. "There must be another way to handle this." She was at a disadvantage, since she didn't really know what 'this' was. She softened her tone. "Can you at least give me a little more info? You assigned me to this case presumably because you valued my expertise."

"Fair enough. This goes back to the Knights Templar."

She chuckled. "Doesn't everything these days?" The Templars and their secrets fascinated many of her friends in academia; they also knew admitting to that fascination was tantamount to academic suicide. Studying the Templars had become like viewing pornography—many did it, few openly.

"The reality is that the Templars, along with the Catholic Church, were the most powerful entity in the world for almost 200 years. To ignore them is to ignore history."

"And, like the Church, they kept secrets."

"Which brings us to the Clairvaux Codex." Hayek explained that though the Templars were technically the fighting arm of the Church and beholden to the Pope, Templar leaders were educated noblemen who often butted heads with the Church and its orthodox doctrine. Georgia knew all this but let him continue; her grandmother told her that God gave her two ears and one mouth, and to use them proportionately. "The Templars spent a lot of time in the Mid-East and forged relationships with many groups in the Arab world. More importantly they acquired knowledge from these Arab sources, knowledge that had been lost in Europe during the Dark Ages."

"Lost, and also suppressed by the Church."

"Exactly. The Church didn't want common folks to read or be educated."

Again, Georgia knew all this. It was why masses were held in Latin, and women healers hung as witches, and science viewed as blasphemy. Knowledge—whether in the form of science or medicine or culture—threatened a church based on blind faith and obedience. Curing disease through the use of herbs rather than by a donation to the local priest undermined both their authority and their financial health. The Church thrived amidst the ignorance of the Dark Ages. "But the Templars weren't buying it," she said.

"Right. They learned about medicine and architecture and astronomy and navigation and alchemy, and they brought that knowledge back with them to Europe. The Church wasn't happy, but the groups were able to coexist for a couple of hundred years because they had other common interests, most prominently the Crusades. But one thing the Church could not abide was the Templars acquiring knowledge about the true history of early Christianity."

"Are you talking about Jesus being married to Mary Magdalene?"

"That, and things perhaps even more inflammatory. The Church had for centuries whitewashed the history of early Christianity—writings or records that did not correspond to orthodox doctrine were either burned or buried deep in the Vatican archives."

"And any person brave enough to question that doctrine was slow-roasted at the stake. So what does all this have to do with January's artifacts and the Catskill Mountains?"

"I'm getting to that. This whitewashing covered all of Europe. But even the Church's tentacles couldn't reach to the Middle East and northern Africa. Or, for that matter, southern Spain, which was controlled by the Moors. In these areas the

Templars learned of ancient writings and artifacts that revealed the true history of the Church. And suddenly the soldiers of the Church learned that the Church was built on a foundation of lies."

"Again, are we talking *Da Vinci Code* stuff, or is there more?"

Hayek sighed. "I don't know the specifics, but apparently these revelations undermine the entire foundation of Christianity. From what I've been able to learn, the Templars created a half dozen scrolls which record the true history of Christianity."

The true history of Christianity. What would be the ramifications if ancient texts called into question the New Testament? Would Christians riot in the streets? Probably not. But the Middle-East was a different story. "Things could get ugly. The entire dynamic in the Middle East—all the pilgrimages and holy wars and Crusades and intifadas—it's all based on competing claims to sacred religious sites and shrines. What would happen if the justification for those claims turned out to be false?" She honestly didn't know. And neither did anyone else. But it was her job, and the Agency's job, to assume the worst and work to prevent it. She suppressed a shiver. "As if that pot needs to be stirred any more than it already is."

"Exactly. Anyway, the Templars knew at some point the Church might turn on them, so they hid these scrolls in remote locations for safe keeping. They wanted to make sure the truth survived."

Georgia's political instincts kicked in. "And they also wanted leverage in case things got ugly."

"Yes, that too," Hayek said. "But what you call leverage others call blackmail. And things, indeed, got ugly. As you know, in the early 1300s the Templars were outlawed and their leaders imprisoned and tortured."

"The date was October 13, 1307. The famous Friday-the-thirteenth. Unlucky for the Templars."

"But what the Templars hadn't counted on was that the Church would be so efficient in rounding up the Order's leaders. Under torture, the location of all of the scrolls was revealed. And, of course, all were destroyed."

"Let me guess. All except one."

"All except one."

She exhaled. "What, exactly, are Trey's orders?"

"They were purposely inexact. You know how this works."

"So basically his orders were to make sure the last scroll stays buried."

"Yes."

"Did it ever occur to anyone that maybe the world has a right to know the truth?"

He lowered his voice. "There is no such thing as truth, Georgia. You should know that."

CHAPTER 14

Cam's head throbbed. The gash on his jaw dripped blood through the saturated bandage. His left knee supported only a fraction of his body weight. His left middle finger smoldered in purple and blue. His entire torso ached from belly-flopping onto the rocks with sixty-five pounds of stone strapped to his back. And it was only nine o'clock in the morning.

But the mountain didn't give a damn.

Neither would Buckner and his team.

Unfortunately, it was possible Amanda's scream had given away their position despite the echoing effect of the mountain ridges. Cam tried to check in with Salazar; either he had wandered out of range, or the rocky terrain blocked the signal, or, well, their situation had turned even more desperate.

They made slower progress now, Cam forced to use his arms to propel himself up the slope while his good leg served as a brace. He almost wished his plummet had destroyed some of the artifacts so he could lighten his pack, but they had survived intact, as had his insulin pump, his torso cushioning their fall. Fortunately the mountain leveled off a bit near the top, and after another hour of climbing they neared the summit of the ridge.

"Are we almost there?" Astarte asked.

"Yes, almost," Amanda answered. "You can do it. And you too, Cam," she said lightly.

Normally he didn't like to be babied. But he probably deserved it with all the moaning and groaning he was doing. He clenched his teeth, recoiling as his molar bit into the swollen cut on the inside of his mouth. At least the cut accounted for the blood he was spitting out—Amanda had been concerned he was bleeding internally. Swallowing a curse, he hoisted himself up the last few feet of the trail and collapsed to the ground. He lowered his voice so only Amanda could hear. "Did I mention I really hate Jefferson January?"

✤ ✤ ✤

They rested for a few minutes along the back crest of the ridge line, snacking on energy bars while studying January's map. Amanda glanced at her watch. Nine o'clock. And she was already exhausted.

They overlooked a mini-valley, a saddle between two ridge lines. Cam had some trouble focusing, but he had studied the map the night before so was already pretty familiar with it.

"We need to climb down to the low point in the saddle and find a boulder that is flat on top, like a table," he said.

"Do you want to rest more?"

"Yes. And I want a recliner and a cold beer. But I'm not going to get any of it."

They hiked down the slope, skidding on the wet leaves and slick rocks. In some ways it was more treacherous than the climb up. After a few minutes Astarte plopped onto her butt and slid. "It's like sledding," she announced. "When you get going too fast, just put out your feet."

"Works for me," Cam said as he and Amanda dropped to the ground. It might be uncomfortable to sit in a hard chair the next day, but they made good time down the ridge and in ten minutes reached the base of the valley.

Amanda pointed to the left. "There's a cluster of boulders over there."

Five minutes later they found a large stone with a perfectly flat surface. "Wow," Astarte said, "it is like a table."

"It must be a glacial erratic," Cam said, "something the glaciers picked up and dropped here during the Ice Age. Look how the rock is different than others. That's why it's so flat and the others are rounded—it's like a slate, which breaks off in layers." Weird how he was able to remember details from a college geology class but couldn't remember what he had for breakfast that morning.

"Okay, what next?" Amanda asked.

"We go 40 paces due north of the table rock and look for another boulder," Cam said. "That was the problem January had—he was using magnetic north as it exists today, which at this latitude is about twenty degrees off from what it was in the 12th century. So we need to angle twenty degrees to the west."

Cam stood with his heel against the table rock and, using his compass, marched 40 paces through the brush, forcing his injured knee to extend to a full stride as he dodged trees in an attempt to keep a straight line. Amanda and Astarte fanned out to either side in case his angle was wrong. At 40 paces he stood in the middle of a wooded area. Plenty of small rocks and trees, but no boulder. Was he so foggy-brained he counted wrong? "Amanda, did you count along with me?"

"Yes," she smiled. "I knew you'd run out of fingers and toes."

He couldn't help but grin. "Seriously, even if I was a bit off, there's nothing around here that looks like a boulder."

Cam dropped his pack at the 40-pace mark as they trudged around, exploring. Was it possible the forest floor had covered the boulder during the course of 800 years? A foot of organic material could accumulate in that time, but not enough to cover a boulder. He kicked at the leaves and dirt with his good leg as he walked, hoping to strike a buried stone.

A few minutes passed and Amanda jogged over. "I think I might know what's wrong. I'm pretty certain a pace in ancient times was a stride with each leg, not just one leg."

"Really? How would you know that?"

"I used to date a surveyor. Handsome bloke." Cam smiled, familiar with her humor. She shrugged. "It's the type of stuff they teach us in primary school."

"Good enough for me." He reached for his pack. "So we're only halfway there."

Forty more strides brought them up the incline of the opposite ridge line and to a cluster of a dozen boulders. "Bingo," Cam said. "Supposedly there's a carving of a bird on the side of one of these rocks."

Astarte nodded. "It's not a bird, it's a dove."

"How do you know?" Amanda asked.

She shrugged. "I just do."

"Okay then, we're looking for a dove." Cam smiled.

Amanda knelt in front of the nearest stone. "There's a lot of moss on the face of this stone."

"Hopefully the carvers were smart enough not to carve on the north side."

"And also smart enough to carve into a hard rock. If not, it will have weathered away."

They split up, studying the surfaces of the boulders, Cam trying not to bend over too much because the blood rushing to his head throbbed like a thumb in an old Saturday morning cartoon gag. He looked up as Astarte marched toward a pyramid-shaped stone far off to one side. "Astarte, don't go too far away please."

She ignored him and dropped to one knee in front of the boulder, her fingers running across the rock's surface as if reading Braille. "Here it is," she called.

Amanda jogged over, Cam hobbling behind. "She's right. It's a bird, a dove." Amanda hugged the girl. "Well done, Astarte." Someone had carved a hand-sized bird near the top of the pyramid on the stone's eastern face. Just as the 800-year-old map described. The carving appeared old—lichen growth obscured parts of one wing, and the edges of the carved surfaces had worn smooth. A geologist could estimate the age of the carving based on a microscopic examination of the weathered surface, but even Cam's untrained eye told him the carving was not modern.

He pulled out the map and January's notes. "The bird is like an arrow. We're supposed to follow its beak. It leads us up to a cave, just below the opposite ridge line." Cam knelt on his good knee and sighted up the ridge line as the bird's beak directed. Were they really following in the footsteps of medieval warrior knights? "The beak points to a spot about three-quarters of the way up the slope."

"You should take a compass reading, matching the direction of the bird as best you can."

He did so. "Got it. The brush doesn't look that thick up there; we should be able to hold our line pretty well."

His head throbbed, but the prospect of finally reaching the cave brightened his mood. He took Amanda's hand. "This is pretty cool."

She smiled. "It'd be even cooler if nobody was trying to kill us."

"Good point."

Cam began to climb, but Amanda stopped him. "Wait. Let's take a picture of the ridge line from here, focusing on the target spot. Then as we get closer we can use it to try to find our way."

It was a good suggestion, even more so because they probably couldn't trust Cam to remember exactly where they were headed. Sighting along the bird's beak as Cam had done, she took four shots, starting with a panorama and progressively zooming in. She also took a few pictures of the bird carving and surrounding topography in case they needed to backtrack and find it again. "Done. Let's climb."

The mid-morning sun had climbed high enough to both cut the chill and illuminate the hillside. A few birds chirped in the trees but they still had not seen any wildlife along the forest floor. The slope of the ridge line rose less steeply than during their early morning climb and they made good time despite Cam's injured knee. It helped that the forest had thinned, fewer trees able to thrive at the higher elevation. After twenty minutes they approached their target area.

Amanda compared the camera images to the landscape ahead. "I think I see a tree a bit up the way that may be spot on."

Astarte, energized, jumped in front of Cam and scampered ahead. A half minute later she called down. "I found a cave. Hurry!"

"Don't go in, Astarte," Amanda said. "There may be animals inside." She raced to join the girl, leaving Cam to limp along and contemplate what they would do if they found a bear hibernating in the cave. Maybe the evil spirit Onteora had chased the bears away along with the other wildlife.

Cam joined Amanda and a bouncing Astarte in front of a 15-foot-high and 50-foot-wide cliff face tucked just below the ridge line. Astarte pointed to a phone-booth-sized fissure in the cliff. "Can we go in and look?"

"Not yet," Cam said, dropping his pack and removing a flashlight. He approached the entrance slowly, swinging the arc of light along the cave walls near the entrance. The beam illuminated dust and cobwebs along the cave floor, but no animals. At least not in the front area.

He stepped back and examined the cliff face. From the ridge line above it would have been impossible to see the cave, as the opening was literally under the feet of any climber. So the only way to find the opening was to climb up from the saddle via the opposite ridge line after making the same treacherous ascent Cam, Amanda and Astarte had just made. Not a path a hiker would likely choose.

Salazar's voice crackled from Cam's walkie-talkie. "Better hurry. You have company."

Cam and Amanda traded a quick look. "Where are they?" Cam asked.

"Following your trail. Buckner and two friends. They're two-thirds of the way to the first ridge line, moving fast. I see them once in a while through the trees. Where are you?"

"Near the top of the second ridge line, still in the saddle, maybe 100 yards west of where the trail ended on the first ridge line."

"I'm another 200 yards further west, where the two ridge lines come back together. I'll wait here for you."

"Astarte, you stay here and keep watch," Cam said.

She scowled. "I want to come in and find the artifacts."

"Sorry, it's too dangerous," he said. "There may be wild animals in the cave."

She glared at him. "I'm the fortieth princess. It is my destiny to find them."

"And you did, Astarte," Amanda said. "You are the one who found the cave. But there is another important job for you. We need a look-out, someone with really good eyes. Call to us if you see anyone approaching."

They were running out of time. Buckner and his men were probably only 20 minutes away. And Cam and Amanda had made no effort to conceal their tracks. Cam ducked into the cave, Amanda behind him. "Yuck, bats," Amanda said, her light shining on a pulsating cluster of rodents in a corner of the cave ceiling.

"They're hibernating. They won't bother you if you keep your light off them." His light showed the cave to be the size of a large bedroom.

"What, exactly, are we looking for?" Amanda asked.

"January thought there's an ancient scroll up here, probably in a clay container. And maybe also an urn with the ashes of Marie-Claire, the princess."

"Astarte's ancestor."

"Right."

Starting on opposite sides of the entryway they walked the perimeter of the cave. A few seconds later they met along the back wall. "Whatever might have been here is gone now," Amanda said.

A waist-high, tunnel-like opening along the back wall led deeper into the mountainside. Cam shone his light into the tunnel. Water dripped from the roof of the tunnel and flowed back toward them, pooling at Cam's feet. "Unless they hid the stuff in here."

"Well, there's no way to find out now. That tunnel is too steep to crawl into, especially being slick with water. And I don't think they would have put a scroll up there anyway. It's too wet; the scroll would be ruined."

Cam nodded, secretly relieved that her logic meant he wouldn't have to crawl into the fissure. He let out a long sigh. It was probably too much to expect that an ancient scroll would go undiscovered for over 800 years. But after having such good luck finding all the clues, he actually thought they were on track to find the artifacts. "Let's look for a few more minutes, then get out of here."

"Maybe the scroll is buried," Amanda said.

They continued their perimeter walk, probing the base of the cave wall with their walking sticks. Cam found nothing and moved to the middle of the cave, kicking at the ground with his boot. All he unearthed was bat guano.

"If we had time, we could dig," she said.

"I'm not sure it would do much good. The Dead Sea Scrolls were in caves but weren't buried. Same with all these Burrows Cave artifacts, assuming they're not all fakes. The cave itself was supposed to be the hiding spot."

"Well, it apparently wasn't a very good one. Someone beat us to it."

With a final arc of his flashlight, Cam followed Amanda out of the cave. Astarte sat on a rock outside the entrance, her back to them. She did not turn to them as she spoke. "I knew you wouldn't find them. You're not the princess."

"We'll come back another time and have another look," Amanda said. She glanced over her shoulder. "But for now we need to leave."

They arranged their packs and began trudging westward along the upper edge of the saddle toward Salazar, staying below the ridge line to avoid being silhouetted against what had become a bright blue mid-morning sky. As had been the pattern all morning, Cam led with Amanda behind him and Astarte trailing. For the first few minutes he picked a path through the dense growth to stay concealed from Buckner and his men. Then he angled up the ridge line, where the growth was thinner, dragging his bad leg behind him.

"What next?" Amanda asked, panting.

"Find Salazar." The exertion made his head pound. "Hopefully he can help us get off this mountain alive. If we have to maybe we can bluff Buckner into thinking we found something." With every step the pack bounced against his back. "Then I think we need to go public or something. Bring attention to ourselves so people will notice if we end up dead."

"It's a bit of a cliché, but maybe we should write up a summary of everything we know and send it to someone we trust. Then threaten to let it go public if anything happens to us."

He turned his head. "Might work. Hey, where's Astarte?"

Amanda spun. "I don't know. She was just right behind me." She called for the girl. Nothing.

Before she could call again, Cam put a hand on her arm. "Not too loud."

They waited a few seconds, but no response. "She went back to the cave," Amanda said.

"Shit. I bet you're right."

Amanda sprinted toward the cave. Cam took two strides, dropped his pack and hobbled after her. "Drop your pack," he called.

She ran gazelle-like through the brush, her gymnastics training evident in her balance and agility. Even healthy he would have trouble beating her in a sprint. He ignored the pain in his knee and managed to keep within sight of her, while at the same time noting their path so they could find their way back to their packs. "Head more to the right," he called.

A hundred yards further, his face raked raw by branches and brush, he reached the cave. A faint light emanated from within the enclosure. He ducked inside, his head throbbing.

"Look what Astarte found, Cam."

The little girl stood along a side wall of the cave, her pink Disney flashlight aimed slightly upward. Cam dropped to his good knee and followed the light beam—the cave wall overhung a shelf-like cavity about three feet off the ground. The cavity was not visible from adult eye level, but Astarte's eyes were the perfect height to notice the cavity behind the overhang.

She turned to Cam. "Sometimes you have to be small to do big things."

✠ ✠ ✠

Amanda carefully reached under the overhang in the cave wall, her hand probing for objects resting on the shelf-like ridge in the cavity. She was so excited she almost didn't think about the possibility of spiders or snakes viewing her fingers as lunch. Almost.

Cam had retreated to the front of the cave to stand watch, while Astarte stood next to her, video camera held steady. How odd to be eight years old and so sure of your life's destiny. And then to have that destiny fulfilled. Hopefully the girl would find happiness along with her fate.

Her finger brushed against a hard, rounded object. Ducking her shoulder under the overhang, Amanda encircled the cold orb with her fingers and pulled it gently forward. The object felt fairly light, but she did not want to take any chances and reached her second hand into the cavity to help support its weight. Moving slowly, she grabbed the cylinder and eased it off the shelf and out of the cavity. She held it out it to Astarte, a kind of royal offering.

The girl nodded somberly and together they eased the cylinder to the ground. Astarte bowed her head over the object and waited as Amanda shone the Disney flashlight on it.

The light revealed a beige clay canister a bit larger than a one-liter soda bottle. A ceramic lid, matching the canister, covered the open end and was held in place by some kind of wax seal. Fighting the urge to pop open the top, Amanda slid the canister into Astarte's Little Mermaid backpack and returned to the cavity.

Working quickly, Astarte still holding the camera, Amanda found another object, a round clay vessel about the size of a cookie jar with a narrow opening topped by the same type of clay lid. January said they were looking for a scroll and a funerary urn, and it appeared they had found exactly that. "Okay," Amanda said, "let's go."

"Wait. There might be something else."

So far the girl's instincts had been spot on. Amanda reached in again, searching with her fingers. From the far recess of the cavity she extracted a rectangular stone the size of a paperback book. She grabbed it and blew the dust away—someone had carved into its brown face a series of Roman numerals plus the words "IN CAMERA." Amanda stared at the object. What could it mean?

Amanda cushioned the pieces in the backpack with a sweatshirt and an extra pair of socks and zipped the pack closed. She lifted the pack, swinging it by a strap to make sure the artifacts didn't shift. Did finding the objects, and thereby fulfilling Astarte's destiny, somehow ensure they would survive today's ordeal? After all, what kind of destiny would it be if the bad guys ended up with the little princess' treasure? Then she recalled the sound of the gunshot whizzing by her ear. "Time to go, Astarte."

The girl placed her hand firmly on Amanda's and lifted her chin. "Okay. But I shall carry the artifacts."

✛ ✛ ✛

Cam's walkie-talkie buzzed as Amanda and Astarte emerged from the cave. Their wide smiles conveyed the good news.

Salazar's words tempered it. "Buckner's team is less than a hundred yards from the cave."

"We're leaving now." He motioned for Amanda and Astarte to follow as he retraced their original escape route, his full concentration needed to remember the path.

"I'll try to buy you some time. Don't be surprised if you hear a gunshot," the mercenary said. As unbalanced as Salazar was, out here in the field he was a trained pro.

Cam reached for Astarte's pack as they jogged through the woods but the girl shook her head. She was keeping up, so Cam didn't press the point. Ten seconds after the walkie-talkie conversation a rifle shot rang out and echoed off the mountain peaks.

It would take the agents a while to figure out where Salazar's shot came from, and Salazar would be smart enough to limit his shots so as not to let them home in on his location. But the strategy would only buy them a few extra minutes. At some point the trained agents would overtake an injured and overburdened pair of civilians hiking with a young child.

They retrieved their packs and worked their way toward Salazar at the front of the saddle. The fear of Buckner's men so close, and the sobering reality of Salazar's gun shot, should have given Cam a burst of adrenaline. But the exertion of their escape had sapped him. He felt light-headed and lethargic. Amanda must have noticed—she took his hand and led the way, adjusting their course in response to another gunshot from Salazar.

"I see you guys," Salazar said over the walkie-talkie. "Angle up toward the ridge line on your right."

"Where's Buckner?" Cam murmured.

"They're tracking you, but they're staying low and ducking behind trees. So they're not really gaining on you. But I can't give you much more cover; at some point they're going to find me and start shooting back."

Five minutes later Salazar called down to them; he had climbed halfway up a pine tree. A rifle lay across his waist and a pair of binoculars hung around his neck. His eyes shone—he was enjoying this, like a kid playing cowboys and Indians in the woods with his friends. He gestured to five pear-sized rocks piled at the base of the tree next to his pack. "How's your throwing arm?" he asked Cam.

Cam leaned against a tree and gulped some water. "Pretty good. I pitched in high school."

"You've got five chances to hit that outcrop over there." He pointed to a bald ledge of rock along the ridge line, in the general direction of the cave. "A stone hitting it will sound like a gunshot. Should slow them down and redirect them." He dropped his rifle to Amanda and began to climb down.

Cam grabbed a couple of rocks, bending slowly to avoid the nausea. The outcrop was less than a football field away, slightly downhill. Not much different than throwing out a runner at the plate from the outfield. Fortunately the injuries were to his left middle finger and left knee; as a righty he would push off with his right leg. He moved a few feet to his left to clear some trees, wound up, and heaved. The rock skidded into the trees, well short of the target. Obviously he had lost a bit off his fastball. He took a deep breath and weighed the second stone in his hand, blinking a couple of times to focus on his target, and wound up again and threw. This one was a strike, the impact of rock on rock splintering the air like the sound of a wet towel being snapped poolside. Not exactly a gunshot, but close.

"Nice, Cameron," Amanda smiled.

A gunshot from deeper in the saddle answered his volley, erasing her smile.

Salazar leapt from the tree and grabbed his pack. "When they stop to shoot they lose time. But they're not far behind. Follow me."

As he led them down the backside of the mountain, he turned and smiled at Amanda. "I think you're going to like this."

✠ ✠ ✠

Salazar bounded his way through the woods, swallowing a smile. Thorne was in rough shape. He would have trouble keeping up.

The more he thought about it, the more convinced he was that Thorne must be brainwashing Amanda. Or drugging her even. She was vulnerable, alone in a strange country, with no family to protect her. Thorne had preyed on her like a predator. And now she didn't even know better, didn't remember what it was like to have free will. Battered wife syndrome. Cognitive dissonance. He had seen enough shrinks lately to pick up on some of the terminology. They said the pressure of being a mercenary was getting to him. Bullshit. All he needed was a loving wife, someone who appreciated him.

As he stopped quickly to adjust course, Amanda brushed against him. Even her sweat smelled fresh, as if the morning dew of Mother Nature flowed from her pores. *Did he really just think that?* He laughed at himself—love turned even a soldier into a poet. He lingered next to her for a few seconds.

"Are you able to keep up?" he asked.

"For now. Astarte seems more rabbit than girl. Cam hurt his knee, and he's lagging a bit, but he'll bully through."

Salazar resumed the trek, Amanda and the girl on his heels and Cam lumbering behind. Salazar's strategy now was to play defense; he passed on a handful of chances to take out their pursuers because he preferred not to deal with the fallout from killing a federal agent. Plus he needed them to do his dirty work. Like lions hunting a herd, they would cull out the ailing Thorne and take him down. Then he could rush Amanda and the girl to safety. It was the perfect scenario—she might never forgive him if she suspected he killed her lover, but she would be forever beholden to him if he saved her and the girl before they met the same fate.

Ten minutes passed, the distance covered perhaps a half mile through the thick brush. In a clearing ahead, he spotted a raised wooden platform. "That's where we're going," he said to Amanda

"What is it?"

He increased the pace. "Our escape." And their future.

✛ ✛ ✛

No way was Cam going to ask the group to slow down, but there was also no way he would be able to continue at this pace all the way down the mountain. When he walked his knee joint alternately buckled and locked—he had felt the ligaments snap like elastic bands when his knee twisted during his fall. He had wrapped the knee with an ace bandage; the bandage, his jeans and some connective tissue felt like the only things connecting his femur to his tibia. As hard as climbing had been, descending was far worse as every other step shifted his entire body weight onto the frayed joint.

At some point he would let the others go ahead and take his chances on his own. He considered dumping the artifacts to ease the strain on his knee—the really good stuff was in Astarte's pack anyway. But Buckner didn't know that, and the artifacts might be the only bargaining chip he had once they caught him. By threatening to destroy them he might be able to barter for his life.

His knee buckled again; this time he couldn't catch himself and he tumbled forward, skidding to a stop as his head slammed against a tree. A sharp whistle pierced his ears and the objects in the forest danced and swayed. He closed his eyes. It would be nice to just lie there and take a short nap....

The whistle began to fade. In fact, the forest had turned silent. And his head didn't hurt so much anymore. A little nap would do him good. Just a few minutes....

Amanda's face. *Wake up,* she commanded. *We have a life together. Don't you dare screw it up.* He jolted. Panicked at how close he had come to letting go, he lurched to his feet. Staggering, he vomited, chunks of energy bar and trail mix splattering his boots and littering the forest floor. He held a tree for support and wretched a few more times. Finally he steadied himself and splashed some water on his face. It felt wet, which told him he must be alive.

If only he had thought to ask Salazar for a weapon—he could have found a defensive position and held off Buckner long enough to allow Amanda and Astarte to escape. And, sappy as it was, it would have been nice to have thought ahead and kissed Amanda goodbye.

Stumbling, he bounced from tree to tree down the trail, using his arms to grab at branches to arrest his fall. The pounding of the descent was causing his already concussed brain to bounce around the inside of his skull, destroying his equilibrium. He lost track of time, one tree looking like the next, only vaguely aware that he was following the path of broken branches left by his companions. At any moment he might lose his balance one final time and end up crumpled at the base of some tree, the backside of the mountain finishing the job started by the front face.

And then Amanda appeared from behind a tree like some medieval forest fairy, floating toward him. At first he thought he had fallen asleep again. But she slipped her arm around him and removed his pack, whispering in his ear. "I'm here, Cam. I've worked too hard to train you to just leave you up on this mountain."

✠ ✠ ✠

Amanda tried to keep her tone light, but the reality was Cam's condition had deteriorated rapidly. His pupils were fully dilated and his breathing light and irregular. She should not have allowed Salazar to push them so hard.

He leaned away from her and vomited. "Water, please," he gasped.

She handed him her bottle, supporting him as he rinsed his mouth. "Salazar and Astarte are just ahead. If you can make it a bit further, Salazar has found a way for us to escape."

They shuffled along, Amanda staggering under the weight of both Cam on her side and his pack on her back. His chin rested on his chest, his eyes half-closed. She grabbed her water bottle with her free hand and splashed water in his face. His eyes flew open. "Cam, you need to stay awake."

"Okay," he mumbled.

She spotted the wooden platform through the trees and angled toward it. "Listen. There's one of those Zip Line rides on this side of the mountain. That's how we're going to get out of here." From her summer camp days she remembered the Zip Line—a steel cable strung tautly between trees to provide children a gravity-propelled ride through the woods; apparently the ski industry had turbo-charged the concept as a way to draw thrill-seekers to the mountains in the off-season. Salazar had broken into the equipment shed and secured the harnesses and handlebars they would need for their descent.

Salazar stood atop the raised platform, peering through his binoculars. "Hurry," he said. "They're not far behind." He tossed Amanda a harness as she staggered up the stairs of the platform. "You go first, Amanda. We'll send Astarte next."

Breathing heavily, Amanda slipped on the harness and tightened the straps. A half-inch thick steel cable attached to a massive steel stanchion above the platform descended into the woods and down the mountain. Salazar had mounted four sets of handlebars on the cable. He positioned her under the cable and attached her harness to the first set of handlebars. "You can hold on, but even if you let go the harness will hold you up."

"What do I do?"

"Nothing. Just run to the end of the platform and jump. When you get to the bottom, disconnect yourself and wait for Astarte."

She nodded. "Astarte, you help Cameron get into his harness, okay?"

The girl, already wearing her harness, began to climb off the platform, ready to dress Cam like one of her Barbie dolls. Cam smiled weakly. "Thanks, Astarte." Wobbly-kneed, he climbed the platform stairs. Some blood had returned to his face. Just standing still for a minute or two had allowed his brain to stop bouncing around inside his skull. But he still looked like a boxer just getting off the canvas after a knock-out punch.

Amanda leaned toward Cam and embraced him, lingering for a few seconds until Salazar interrupted. "No time for that."

"I love you so much," she whispered in his ear. And then louder: "Okay, I'm off. Astarte, I'll be waiting for you." She smiled. "Just think. You'll be like Wendy on her first flight with Peter Pan."

She took three running steps and raised her feet, allowing the cable to take her weight. The handlebars connected to the cable via a pulley wheel, and she accelerated quickly. Dangling only a few body lengths off the ground, the cable sagging slightly above her, she rocketed down the slope of the mountain, the wind bringing tears to her eyes as the trees flew by. It was like flying along the highway without a car. Frightening, yet also exhilarating.

Suddenly the mountain fell completely away. She soared now, birdlike, hundreds of feet above a steep ravine, the noon-time sun high above her. While enclosed by a canopy of trees the cable had seemed substantive and solid, but framed now against the expanse of blue sky it appeared thread-like. She kicked her feet, the movement meaningless when weighed against the enormity of the mountain peaks around her. She was a single leaf fluttering in the forest, a ripple in the river.

A line of trees on the opposite side of the ravine rushed at her, the cable somehow finding a gap in the forest wall. She sliced through the foliage, again only a few body lengths above the ground. In the distance a raised wooden platform blocked her path. But as if by magic her descent slowed, the sag in the line expertly bringing her to almost a complete stop as the platform floor rose up to gently meet her feet. She took a couple of quick steps to arrest her momentum, unclipped her harness, let out a whoop of relief, and turned to wait for the young, flying princess.

✝ ✝ ✝

Cam leaned against a support beam on the platform next to Salazar. His head pounded but he no longer felt so lightheaded—there was no way to put the egg back in its shell, but at least the yolk had stopped sloshing around in the mixing bowl. He watched Salazar send the nervous but stoic Astarte whirring down the line. The question was who was to follow her.

"My plan was for you to go last," Salazar said. "I need to get into position to cut the cable on the far side so Buckner and his men can't follow." He had disabled the other handlebar sets, but that wouldn't stop the trained operatives from improvising a makeshift device to drape over the cable and pursue them. "I can climb up there with my tools and get ready while you're on the line."

Cam blinked. "Okay."

Salazar handed Cam his rifle. "In case you have company. It's semi-automatic. I saw three men come over the ridge line. They're not far off."

The weapon felt cold in his hand. He was pretty sure semi-automatic meant the gun would reload itself after every shot. He blinked again. "How many rounds?"

"Eight. The safety lock is off. Just point and shoot, like a camera."

There was something Cam wanted to do. He searched for the thought; it was like waking up and trying to remember a dream that had faded. But this was more important than some dream. Finally it came to him. He handed Salazar his pack. "You take these." Now that Amanda and Astarte were safe there was no need to use the artifacts as a bargaining chip to buy time, and he didn't want Buckner to get them.

Salazar loosened the straps, slipped the pack over his own and clipped his hunchbacked form onto the cable. "The instructions in the equipment shed said to wait at least 90 seconds between riders. Otherwise the engineering of the cable sag gets messed up and we both crash to the ground. If I get there quicker than that, I'll call you on the walkie-talkie." Salazar pushed off without a look back.

Cam checked his watch and attached his harness to the cable. Shivering despite the sunshine on his face, he eyed the narrow path leading down from the ridge line, the rifle dangling by his side, and began a steady count to 90. By the time he reached 91 he would either be in flight or dead.

✠ ✠ ✠

Salazar soared through the wind, oblivious to the sights and sounds and speed of his ride. Buckner and his men had already crested the ridge line and might easily overpower and capture the injured Cam before he could embark. That would be the easiest solution to this mess. Salazar would explain to Amanda that Cam had heroically fought off the operatives for long enough to allow Salazar to escape but had eventually succumbed. And that in order to complete their escape they needed to cut the cable immediately. He looked far into the future, visualized a home with Amanda in the suburbs, Astarte and his Rosalita playing together in the yard, Cam only a sad but distant memory. She was drawn to him, he was certain, even if she herself didn't realize it yet due to the psychological damage Cam had inflicted upon her.

His mind raced, matching the pace of the trees whipping by. Life was really nothing more than an aggregation of the choices one made, and the next few choices he made would forever alter the path of his. As he broke through the woods and out over the ravine, a gunshot pierced the wind and echoed around the canyon below. He heard Amanda scream in the distance, or perhaps his mind was playing tricks on him. But the gunshot was real. Cam was defending himself. Little did Cam realize that the gunshot would end up being a self-inflicted wound, validation of Salazar's lie that Cam had been captured after a heroic final stand.

He pictured Amanda's face, her easy smile, the way she arched an eyebrow when making a point. He recalled how she interacted with the girl, caring and doting yet playful and light. He imagined how her body, young and lithe and toned, would mesh into his. And he pulled his knees into his chest, making himself as aerodynamic as possible.

✞ ✞ ✞

Salazar unsnapped his harness even before he stopped moving. He tossed Cam's pack aside and slipped off his own.

"Is Cam behind you?" Amanda asked.

Salazar hated to see the anguish in her eyes. "I heard a shot." He dug in his pack for the bolt cutters, welcoming the excuse to look away. Lying to her was nearly impossible. "He held them off long enough for me to get away. But I don't see how he's going to make it."

"Why didn't you help him?"

He tried not to sound defensive. "He told me to go, to make sure you and Astarte were safe. And he's right. There's no reason for both of us to die in some shoot-out. He gave me the artifacts, told me they would keep you safe."

He climbed a short wooden ladder at the end of the platform, reaching for the cable line. She looked up at him, her eyes wild. "What are you doing?"

Someday she would have the same loyalty toward him. "Cutting the line. Otherwise they'll come after us."

"But what if Cam fought them off? If you cut the line, you'll kill him for certain."

"He's not coming, Amanda. It was three against one." He leaned back and slid the mouth of the bolt cutter over the cable.

"Stop." She sobbed. "Please stop. At least try to raise him on the walkie-talkie."

He held her stare. "There's no time. They might already be on their way across. My job is to save you and the girl." He forced the arms of the cutter together, the blades digging partway into the steel cable.

She ran at him, screaming, and grabbed at his foot. "Stop." She yanked, forcing him to release one hand from the bolt cutters to stop himself from falling. This was not going as planned. He shook his leg, but she held tight. Did he really want to begin their romance by kicking her in the head? If he waited much longer, Cam would come whizzing back into their lives.

With his free leg he kicked, catching Amanda above the ear. She staggered, loosening her grip, and he tore his foot away. Before she could recover he scampered higher up the ladder and swung his legs away from her. He slid the bolt cutters over the cable a second time, found the cut he had made, and snapped the arms together. The teeth ground into the cable, fraying the individual fibers. One more cut should do it....

A voice on the walkie-talkie cut through the forest. "Eighty-eight, eighty-nine, ninety. Ready or not, here I come."

"Cam!" Amanda exclaimed. She spun and glared up at Salazar. "Don't you dare cut that cable."

CHAPTER 15

Cam didn't remember much of their trek down the mountain. Salazar carried his pack and Amanda supported his body. Salazar's Toyota waited, chariot-like, at the bottom.

Salazar and Amanda must have come up with a plan while he slept in the back seat, because when he awoke two hours later they were double-parked in front of a crowded Port Authority bus terminal in New York City. "What are we doing?" If he remembered correctly, they weren't far from Times Square.

Amanda turned in the front seat and smiled. "Glad to see you're awake. How do you feel?"

"Better, actually." His head ached but did not throb, and the nausea had dissipated. "But I thought you weren't supposed to let someone with a concussion sleep."

"Old wives' tale—a couple of hours at a time is okay," she responded. "Anyway, Salazar is going to take a bus back to Rhode Island and leave us with his car. I thought the city would be a good place to hide out for a few days."

She walked around the front of the car while Salazar grabbed his gear from the trunk. Cam rolled down his window as the mercenary approached. "Thanks," Cam said. "Obviously I owe you a lot of money."

Salazar shrugged. "We'll settle up later." He looked somber, almost sad.

"Hey, sorry you missed Thanksgiving with your daughter."

"Actually, if I catch this bus I'll be home for dinner." He turned toward the front seat. "Take care, Amanda."

She barely glanced back. "Yes, you as well."

Amanda put the car into drive before Salazar had even begun to back away. Obviously Cam had missed something while he slept. And just as obviously Amanda did not want to discuss it.

"We actually don't owe him money," she said.

"Why not?"

"I stopped at an ATM machine outside Phoenicia. I figured the feds already knew where we were, so why not? I used my bank card and a couple of credit cards. Paid Salazar and we still have cash to spare."

"Okay." Again, he seemed to be missing something. But Amanda apparently wanted to cut ties to the mercenary.

"So," Amanda said, changing the subject, "we never heard the story of how you escaped from Buckner's men."

"We heard a gunshot," Astarte said. "Did you kill one of the bad guys?"

"No, nothing that exciting. I saw them coming so I fired one shot over their heads just to slow them down, then I jumped on the Zip Line and flew away. I never even saw their faces."

Amanda nodded. "In that case I'm glad to be rid of Mr. Salazar."

It seemed a strange response, a bit of a non sequitur, but Cam's head throbbed and he didn't have the energy to try to figure out why.

✛ ✛ ✛

Amanda chewed her lip as they sat at a traffic light. She turned up the heat. Why had Salazar claimed Cam would not escape the mountain? His insistence on cutting the cable over her protestations could have been chalked up to panic or even poor judgment. But based on what Cam had just described, Salazar kicked Amanda away and tried to snap that cable knowing Cam was alive and in need of the Zip Line escape route. This went far beyond poor judgment.

Was Salazar working for the feds? If so, why had he not finished the job and cut the cable even after hearing Cam's voice on the walkie-talkie? Or betrayed them once they reached the base of the mountain? Or turned them over to Buckner on any number of different occasions? The more she tossed it around in her mind, the less it made sense.

But for now at least Salazar was gone. She needed to concentrate on finding a refuge. Cam needed more rest and they all could use a meal and a shower. And they needed to examine the ancient scroll—hopefully whatever secrets it contained could somehow be leveraged into securing their freedom.

While Salazar drove she had used her iPad to find a list of cash-only hotels in New York. She drove by one, rejected it as too seedy, and headed downtown toward the East Village. The second choice looked better—stately and solid, the neighborhood bustling with activity despite the holiday. She phoned and inquired about rates and availability. Not cheap, which was good—they wanted safe not squalid, with enough room for the three of them to spread out for a few days.

They parked in a garage ten blocks away just in case somehow Buckner tracked Salazar's Toyota. After stuffing their camping gear in the trunk, they consolidated everything in their packs and took the subway back to the hotel. Thirty minutes later they opened the door to a tired but clean room on the third floor with a queen bed and a high-speed Internet connection. A door in one wall connected to a second, smaller room with a single bed.

Amanda looked deep into Cam's eyes, trying to determine if his pupils were still dilated and, more importantly, whether he had his wits about him. "I'm thinking we should take you to a hospital."

"Why? There's nothing they can do to treat a concussion."

"What if there's something else going on inside that head of yours?"

He smiled. "There's nothing going on inside my head, trust me. I'm actually feeling better. If there was internal bleeding or something, I'd be getting worse. And if we go to the hospital, that just gives the feds another chance to track us."

"You could give a fake name."

He shrugged. "Really, I'm fine. If I feel worse, I'll go in."

"What about your knee?"

"I'm pretty sure I heard the ligaments pop. But I'm not going to have surgery, so what can they do for me?"

"It's going to be tough to outrun that bear." She kissed him gently on the mouth. "Astarte, you come with me—we're going to get some pizza. Cam, you get the first shower." She kissed him again. "Remember to check your blood sugar. When I return I'll change the bandage on your chin. I'm also going to get you a knee brace; I saw a drug store around the corner."

216

"See if you can find a Latin dictionary also. The Codex is written in Latin, so I bet the scroll is also. And some more Advil, please."

"Maybe I'll even find you some chicken soup." She smiled. It might help warm her as well. "And while we're gone, no looking at the scroll."

✠ ✠ ✠

They had eaten a late lunch and showered and found a Disney movie on TV for Astarte, and Amanda had nursed Cam's wounds as best she could. Amanda eyed Astarte's backpack. "Do you feel up to examining the scroll?" she asked him.

Astarte snapped off the television. "I do!"

Cam smiled. "Me too. Just don't expect me to be too quick on translating the Latin."

"Hey, you're the lawyer." Amanda reached into the back. "Speaking of Latin, take a look at this. It was in the cave with the scroll and urn." She handed him the carved stone from the cave cavity. He turned the stone over in his hand, examining it, and laid it on the bed so Amanda could snap a photo of it.

IN CAMERA STONE

"Do you know what 'IN CAMERA' means?" she asked.

"It's a legal term. It means 'in secret,' or 'in hiding.' And these Roman numerals across the top look like they could be latitude and longitude coordinates," he said.

She was glad to see Cam was thinking clearly. "So maybe something secret is hidden at those coordinates?"

"Good guess. Let's take a look at the scroll—maybe it'll tell us what we're looking for."

They had set up the smaller adjoining room as a work area, with a pair of chairs on either side of a simple desk. Amanda covered the desk with a white sheet and handed out rubber gloves she had purchased at the drug store. She had also purchased a humidifier, which had been running for the past hour to moisten the air and help keep the parchment from cracking. Using his pocket knife, Cam cut the wax seal and removed the lid from the canister as Amanda videoed the process.

"Put the wax in here," Amanda said. She opened a sandwich bag with her free hand. Someday they would carbon-date the wax.

"Here," Cam said, "you pull the parchment out. Your fingers are smaller. I'll take the camera."

"Ready then." Hands shaking, Amanda gently tugged on the parchment. Hopefully, sealing it in the clay canister had maintained a constant humidity and preserved the animal skin. The scroll slid slowly toward her, a small cloud of dust and the scent of old leather escaping from the tube with it. She exhaled slowly, the dust wafting away from her. "Could this be real?" she breathed.

"The parchment looks like a Torah scroll." Cam's voice was thick and low behind the video camera.

She laid the beige-colored scroll on the desktop. It unrolled only slightly, unable to retake its original shape after an 800-year confinement. Gently she spread the parchment, working slowly as the humidifier moistened and softened the ancient animal skin. "I'm surprised it's still so supple." She didn't force it completely flat, unrolling it only enough to view the writing. The black, block letters were neat and even, the scroll about the size of a tabloid newspaper.

"It's Latin, like the stone," Cam said.

"Uncle Jefferson could speak Latin," Astarte said.

Amanda nodded. "I'm not surprised." But she was on guard. In light of the Burrows Cave Isis piece anything associated with January needed to be examined critically—these scrolls might be fakes as well. The parchment looked—and smelled—ancient, and the cave hiding place felt authentic, but that didn't mean the whole thing wasn't an artful ruse. "Notice how the words extend all the way out to the margins. Parchment was expensive, so they wrote on as much of the surface as possible." Would a hoaxster know this?

Cam peered at the Latin, which was the language of most religious orders during medieval times. "My Latin's pretty rusty. But I bet we can translate it with the dictionary." He turned off the camera.

Amanda handed Cam a pad of paper and a pen as he bent low over the scroll. He translated slowly, word by word. Finally he looked up. "The heading reads, 'The True History of the Church, as Discovered in Jerusalem by the Poor Knights of Christ and the Temple of Solomon.'"

"That's what the Templars called themselves," she said. But what the document might reveal? "The true history of the Church? As in, no virgin births or resurrections or walking on water?"

"Apparently." He studied the writing. "It's dated 1129."

"That's the year the Templars left Jerusalem and returned to Europe. They had been digging and exploring for about ten years, then they came back to Europe and became instantly powerful and wealthy. At the time, there were only a few dozen of them. Nobody's ever been able to answer what it is they found in Jerusalem that made them so bloody influential."

Cam smiled and tapped the parchment. "Until now."

"But this doesn't sound like something that's going to validate the Book of Mormon, does it?"

"Good point. I don't think January knew exactly what was in the scroll. He assumed it was some kind of Holy Grail for the Mormon Church—that's the term he used. But you're right; it would be pretty ironic if the scroll had nothing to do with the Mormons at all."

"Okay, I'll hush up. You translate."

Cam worked for another ten minutes, scratching notes on the pad, his body taut with concentration.

Amanda couldn't wait any longer. "I need an update."

He rubbed his face. "Sorry, this is hard with my head pounding. But I think I've got most of it. Apparently the Templars were brought to a burial chamber by some locals. This is in 1129, in Jerusalem. The Templars had helped rescue the locals from some hostile Saracens, and this was their way of thanking them. They knew the Templars were interested in finding ancient Christian relics. The chamber was about three miles south of Jerusalem. That's as far as I got."

Amanda grabbed for her laptop. "Are you thinking what I'm thinking?"

"Um, what? I'm not really thinking at all right now."

"Keep translating—I'm going to check something." Amanda typed 'Talpiot' into a Google search. "I knew it," she whispered. The Talpiot site was 5 kilometers, or about three Roman miles, south of historic Jerusalem.

"What?"

"Nothing. Keep at it." If her hunch was right, Cam would know soon enough.

A minute later he dropped his pen. "Holy shit." He looked up and swallowed. "They found the bones of Jesus."

CHAPTER 16

Georgia expected Trey and his henchmen to come marching back to the hotel victorious, smiles on their faces, artifacts in their satchels and a couple of dead civilians buried in some remote mountain ravine. Instead Trey's jawbone pulsed in anger as he pushed by her in the hallway. Swallowing a smile, Georgia retreated to her room.

Amanda and Cam were safe, for now. But Trey and his team were skilled and tenacious. Georgia wanted to reach out to the young couple, to offer them help, to try to negotiate safe passage for them. And, yes, to learn what kind of amazing history they had uncovered. But they did not want to be found.

Georgia pondered the problem, staring at the distant mountains in the fading afternoon light. The solution crept up on her like the lengthening afternoon shadows: Trey Buckner and Jabil Hayek couldn't find Amanda and Cam because they were thinking like men. A woman knew that sometimes the best way to pursue something was to let it come to you.

She opened her laptop and signed on to a medieval history discussion forum she belonged to. She clicked on the "new post" tab and crafted her message carefully. She read the message a second time and hit enter, transmitting the lifeline into cyberspace. But would Cam and Amanda grab for it?

✝ ✝ ✝

Cam drank some water, careful not to drip onto the ancient parchment. Parchment that threatened to undermine 2,000 years of world history. If January only knew what he had unleashed....

Cam had finished translating the Latin—as Amanda had guessed, the scroll detailed the discovery by the Templars of the Talpiot Tomb outside Jerusalem. According to the Templar account, the tomb not only contained the remains of Jesus, but those of his family as well. His mother, Mary. His brother, Joseph. His wife, Mary Magdalene. Even a son named Jude, perhaps named after his brother. Collectively the discovery told the story of a wealthy man named Jesus who lived, married, had a child and died a very human though perhaps painful death, his bones secreted in a family tomb like many of his neighbors. Hardly a unique story. And surely not the story of a god, resurrected from the cross.

"Well," Amanda said. "At least we know why they're trying to kill us."

"Stop us, yes. But kill us?" Cam massaged his forehead. Even with a clear head the ramifications of their discovery would have been difficult to comprehend. "Would proving that Jesus was mortal really be such a bad thing?"

"It's not such a big deal to you or me because we're not Christians. But the most powerful religion in the world is built upon Jesus' immortality. And that religion shapes and influences our entire society and culture. When you yank on a thread—and this is a major thread—the entire tapestry starts to unravel. I suppose now we know why the Templars called Jesus the Thief on the Cross. They knew he wasn't divine, knew he usurped the role of the messiah by letting his followers believe he was." She paused. "And if the story of Jesus is fake, what about Moses and Abraham and Solomon? Are we to just throw out the Judeo-Christian ethos?"

Cam shrugged. "I guess. It just seems like people are more resilient than they're given credit for. The whole idea of Mary Magdalene being the wife of Jesus seemed earth-shattering a decade ago; now it's not such a big deal."

"Yes, but this is different. This is like saying God is not really God. It's the type of revelation that could redirect history." She swallowed. "I don't think the authorities can allow this to just drop down and engulf the populace—it's too risky. They will do anything to ensure the scroll remains buried. Including burying us along with it."

Translating the scroll from Latin to English had taxed his injured brain. He turned the desk lamp off and sipped more water. "As important as the scroll is, there's something even more momentous."

"The bones themselves."

"Right."

"Where do you suppose they are?"

"I don't think they were in that cave—the Templars wouldn't have just stuck Jesus' remains in a hole in the wall. They would have built some kind of tomb or monument, someplace to keep them dry so they wouldn't decay or be dragged off by animals. Jesus may not have been a god in their eyes, but he was still considered a prophet and a king. Not to mention the bones gave them incredible leverage over the Church." He lifted the IN CAMERA stone. "So we're back to this. The carving must be a clue."

"I like your idea that the Roman numbers are latitude and longitude coordinates."

"If so, it would make the stone more modern than medieval times. Longitude readings weren't used until the 15th century."

"Okay then. So the stone wasn't carved by our Templar friends. But it still might be important. Maybe the bones were moved at a later date—say during Colonial times—and whoever moved them left the stone as a signpost where to find them." She turned the stone toward her. "Reading left to right, we have latitude 45 degrees, 30 minutes north and longitude 75 degrees, 53 minutes west." Amanda typed the coordinates into Google Earth. "It brings us close to Ottawa, a bit northwest of downtown. Looks like a wooded area, with a lake."

Cam peered at the satellite image. "I've never heard of any Templar sites out there. The Templars were in Quebec, and New England, but not Ottawa as far as I know."

"Again, perhaps someone retrieved the bones at a later date and moved them to Ottawa, maybe some early settlers."

"But why Ottawa? If you're right, and some of the early settlers had Templar roots, they would have brought the bones to an important Templar site—maybe the Newport Tower, or near the Westford Knight carving, or maybe Montreal. Ottawa just doesn't fit."

They stared at the stone for a few minutes, each trying to decipher some meaning hidden within the carvings. It was a good distraction—a puzzle to piece together, a riddle to solve. Unlike the ramifications of proving Jesus' mortality, which made Cam's head throb when he thought about it....

Suddenly Amanda jumped off the bed. "Of course it doesn't fit." She clapped her hands. "How long has Greenwich been the prime meridian?"

"Maybe a couple hundred years."

"Exactly. And whoever carved the IN CAMERA stone probably did so long before 1800."

Cam nodded. "You're right. We need to adjust the coordinates. They would probably have been using Paris as the prime meridian."

Amanda tapped at the keyboard. "Okay, Paris is two degrees, twenty minutes east of Greenwich. So if we make the adjustment we end up…" She stared at the screen, her eyes wide.

"What?"

"You're not going to believe this. When I typed in the coordinates, an image popped up."

She turned the screen toward him. The ornate Basilica of Notre Dame, in Montreal's Old City, peered back at him. "Of course," he whispered. The Basilica was one of the most majestic religious structures in North America. An ideal repository for the bones of Jesus.

✜ ✜ ✜

Amanda spent twenty minutes researching the history of the Notre Dame Basilica in Montreal, built originally in 1672, while Cam rechecked his translation of the Latin scroll.

Amanda felt Astarte's eyes on her and turned to the young princess. The girl had sat silently for the past hour, listening to Cam and Amanda translate the scroll. Her cobalt eyes were wide and sad. Finally she swallowed and spoke. "Are you certain Jesus is not the son of God?"

Damn. They should have been more careful about what they said in front of her. Just what the little girl needed to hear after losing the father figure in her life. "Not certain, honey. But the Templars may have found his bones, which would mean he wasn't resurrected as Christianity teaches."

"And the Templars were smart men. My Uncle January said they knew all the secrets. They knew about the Mandan people and the bloodline and everything. That's why they came to America."

"I think your uncle was correct about that."

"But if Jesus was not God, then how can I be the Fortieth Princess?"

How indeed. "Well, just because Jesus was not God does not mean he was not a king. Which he was—he was the King of at least some of the Jews and later of course of the Christians. That's actually what the word 'messiah' means. It does not mean god, it means king. And you still have Jesus' family blood in your veins, along with that of King David and Cleopatra and Mohammed and even Joseph Smith." She took the girl's hand. "So you are still the Fortieth Princess."

"But it's not the same. The Book of Mormon says Jesus is the son of God. It says he is our savior. And I am supposed to bring his word to the peoples of the world."

January sure had burdened the little princess with a Tiger Mom's load of responsibility—no pressure, honey, just grow up to unite the world's religions, and then reign over them. And now for the first time it was dawning on Astarte, at the ripe old age of eight, that she might fail in her quest. "Listen, you can still spread the word of Jesus to the peoples of the world. In fact, they will need it more than ever if the truth comes out. Jesus may not have been God, but he was a great man, and the things he taught us— to take care of the poor, and to love our neighbors, and to heal the sick—are lessons that are very important still today. You can still be the princess who brings righteousness to the world."

The girl offered a doubtful smile. "But it won't be the same."

"No, it won't." Amanda looked deep into ocean-blue of the girl's eyes. "But it's the truth. And it might be even better."

The girl stared back at her, her dark blue eyes a mystery.

✝ ✝ ✝

Amanda and Astarte had gone out in search of Thanksgiving dinner, leaving Cam alone in the hotel room. He lay down on the bed and turned the lights off. But his mind was revving too fast to even consider napping.

His initial reaction had been that the discovery of the bones of Jesus would be hugely significant from a historical perspective, but he didn't agree with Amanda's conclusion that it could destabilize the Middle East and perhaps even Western society. But the more he mulled it over, the more he was coming around to her way of thinking. The Middle East was already a powder keg, a house of cards, dominoes ready to fall—pick your cliché. The last thing the world needed was something to trigger more turmoil and uncertainty in the area.

Cam recalled a YouTube video of a Texas evangelical church choir belting out a country version of Hava Nagila, the Israeli folk song, at a rally to raise money for Israel. The main American supporters of Israel, in addition to the Jews, were the fundamentalist Christians, who often took pilgrimages to the Holy Land and wanted the area—and its numerous Christian shrines—secure and in friendly hands. This mirrored the primary justification for the Crusades during medieval times—to keep the Middle East safe for religious pilgrims. But if the story of Jesus was revealed to be a ruse, how devoted would Christian groups be toward safeguarding religious sites in Israel?

Even more fundamentally, Islamic extremist groups had become increasingly successful in attracting adherents from among the pool of disillusioned young males in both American and European inner cities. Especially in America, the primary counterbalance against Islamic spread was the inner city Christian churches. Again, undermining the foundation of these churches would only empower recruitment efforts of the Islamic extremists. Hardly a recipe for stability, either in the Middle-East or the Western democracies.

Cam rolled out of bed. He did a Google search and found an article arguing that the roots of modern-day Islamic hostility toward Christianity took hold in the 19th and 20th centuries, when Protestant leaders began questioning Christianity's core teachings. If, the argument went, even Christian leaders conceded that the words of the Bible were not to be accepted literally, the religion itself must therefore rest on a false foundation. As a false religion, it should be destroyed and replaced by the "true" word of God, as set forth in the Koran. In fact, the article continued, the perceived fallibility and weakness of Christianity is what has fueled the push by radical Muslims to replace democracy in Europe today with Sharia religious law.

Cam stared out the hotel window at the lights of New York. The Twin Towers had fallen not far from where he stood. Clearly, anything that might empower Islamic extremism threatened Western security. And calling into question Jesus' divinity might do just that. Was it a sure thing, would these revelations topple the precarious balance of geo-political factors that kept a modicum of peace in the Middle-East? Perhaps, perhaps not. In the fog that was the Mid-East it was impossible to see across the street, never mind around the corner. But the stakes were too high, the danger too extreme. Nobody would want to risk it. Those charged with arresting the spread of Islamic extremism would think nothing of sacrificing a couple of busybodies like Cam and Amanda—it would be like paying pennies for a million-dollar insurance policy.

If Cam and Amanda wanted to survive, they needed to face reality. The stability and security of the Western democracies was at stake—apparently because Jesus wasn't really resurrected after dying on one.

✝ ✝ ✝

Amanda and Astarte had found a take-out restaurant serving Thanksgiving dinner. In many ways Amanda missed England and hadn't really taken to American culture. And she found the Thanksgiving holiday a bit insensitive to Native Americans. But she enjoyed the emphasis on family and giving thanks. Plus she was a glutton for the stuffing.

Astarte refused to eat until they had said grace, so Amanda took the girl's hand and Cam's as well and closed her eyes. "We offer thanks this day to Mother Earth for supplying us with food and sustenance, and for sharing her bounty with our fellow citizens and the animals of the world. And we promise to protect our environment for future generations. Amen."

Astarte opened one eye and whispered. "Aren't you going to thank God?"

"I just did."

"No, you thanked Mother Earth."

Amanda smiled. "True. Let me explain. Some people believe Mother Earth and God are the same thing." Amanda had never verbalized this before, but it was a concept that had been fermenting inside her ever since she and Cam began studying the Templars and concluded that the monastic warriors secretly worshiped the Goddess, or Mother Earth, as an equal partner to the male godhead in the hierarchy of the heavens. Amanda was a bit surprised to hear herself describe her beliefs in a way that reflected a pagan or even Wiccan mind-set, but she didn't choke over the words as they escaped her mouth.

"But God is in heaven. And Mother Earth is … in the ground."

Cam jumped in. "Maybe another way to think about it is that God and Mother Earth are partners, sort of like a husband and wife." Amanda squeezed his hand. "Mother Earth gives life to the world, just as the mothers of all species give life to their young. The female is the giver of life—what would a male god rule over if there was nothing living?"

"So that's why you thank Mother Earth for the food, because it comes from the earth?"

Close enough. It was not fair to the little girl to try to change her religious beliefs. "Yes," Amanda said. "But we can also thank God for creating the world if you would like."

Astarte closed her eyes and held her hands together in prayer. She was obviously trying to think of a correct prayer. She sighed. "Thank you God for helping Mother Earth give us this food."

Amanda bit back a smile. "Amen," she responded.

✝ ✝ ✝

Astarte worked on a jigsaw puzzle they had bought while Cam cleaned up after their makeshift Thanksgiving dinner. "How's your head?" Amanda asked.

"It throbs." He bent over slowly to pick up a napkin off the floor. "And sometimes I get dizzy. But at least I can function."

Amanda took his hand. "Come. Sit with me." She guided him to the room's only easy chair and sat on his lap, avoiding his injured knee and positioning herself so she could twist toward him without straining her cracked rib. "We need to figure out what to do next."

"You mean other than get X-rays?"

"Yes, other than that." She kissed him, lingering with her lips on his for a few seconds.

He sighed. "I guess it's the same choices we've always had. Choice one is to turn ourselves in."

"To whom? Not the feds, obviously."

"Probably the New York City police; they're probably as sophisticated as any."

"I've been considering that," she said. "But here's what the feds are going to tell the locals: First, we kidnapped a young girl. Second, you blew up their SUV in the Catskills. Third, you fired a shot at their agents on the mountain. And that's just the true stuff; who knows what else they might fabricate? How long do you think it will take for the locals to hand us over?"

"Good point. Within 24 hours we'd probably find ourselves on some water-board in Guantanamo Bay."

"So what's our second option?"

"Go to the press with the scroll and hope the publicity protects us."

"And I'm tempted by that. But the problem is that we need to convince some reporter to convince some editor that this is a legitimate story. And then the editor needs to convince his publisher to run with it, despite knowing the government wants it stifled. It might take weeks. Do you think we can remain hidden that long?"

Cam shook his head. "No. A couple of days, maybe. Not a couple of weeks. Especially because we'd have to expose ourselves to make contact with the press."

"So we have choice number three--"

"Go to Montreal. Find the bones, or whatever it is that's buried at Notre Dame Basilica."

She played along. "Very well, but how does that help us? Won't we just be having this same conversation again in a couple of days?"

Cam blinked, weighing his response. "Well, for one thing we'll be in Canada, which might give us some protection. It might be a little tougher for U.S. agents to assassinate innocent people across the border. Also, if we have the bones of Jesus ... well, we could call a press conference and get a ton of publicity right away. The bones of Jesus are different than some scroll, no matter what it says."

She played the devil's advocate. "But who's to say the bones are authentic?"

"They don't have to be. Just claiming to have them is enough of a news story to get press attention that day. Especially if we have the scroll and the IN CAMERA stone to back up the story. Look at all the attention the Discovery Channel special about Talpiot Tomb got."

She had reached a similar conclusion. Finding the bones would improve their odds, even if that meant improving only from a long-shot to an underdog. "Okay, I agree. Montreal is our best bet. Now we just have one problem: How do we cross the border?"

Cam smiled. "That's actually an easy one."

✝ ✝ ✝

Cam sat on the bed and studied a map of Lake Memphremagog from a road atlas Amanda had borrowed from the front desk. He had spent many boyhood summers boating on the lake, which straddled the Vermont-Quebec border. The area possessed a long history of contraband smuggling, and as a teenager he and his cousin often snuck into Quebec to buy fireworks and beer to try to impress the local girls. As long as the old trails hadn't changed, and as long as he could secure a boat, crossing the lake into Quebec should be fairly simple....

Amanda interrupted. "Have a look at this." She had repacked the scroll in its clay canister and double-sealed the canister in a pair of large Ziploc bags. She angled the laptop screen toward him. "It came up when I did a Google search using the words Templars and Catskills."

Cam leaned in and read a chat room message: "*Wondering if anyone knows anything about a Templar document called the Clairvaux Codex. Also interested in knowledge of Templar artifacts in the Catskill Mountains. Perhaps related to Burrows Cave artifacts, and also to pieces held by collector JJ. A and C, I have a feeling you can help with this. And I can help you as well. Here is my email if you prefer privacy.*"

Cam whistled. "When was this posted?"

"This afternoon. By a woman named Georgia Johnston."

"Who is she?"

Amanda turned the screen back to herself. "Let's find out."

She tapped the keyboard as Cam contemplated the message. Obviously it was not random—the details were too specific. But who was the writer and what kind of game was she playing?

"Okay," Amanda said. "This Georgia Johnston is a political consultant. An older woman, based on her photo. Looks like she's working on the Presidential campaign."

"Her candidate is a Mormon. Just a coincidence?"

"You know I don't believe in coincidence. This must somehow involve January." She scanned a few more websites. "But I can't find anything more about her."

"Wait. Salazar saw Buckner sitting with an older woman the other night at a restaurant in Phoenicia. He took pictures of them and showed them to me so I could recognize anyone following us."

Amanda angled the computer screen toward him. "What do you think?" she asked.

"Bingo. That's her. So the political consultant thing is just a front. She's a fed, probably trying to trick us into coming out of hiding. I say ignore it."

Amanda cocked her head. "I don't know. There's something about the message that rings true. Mind if I give her a little test?"

Cam shrugged. "Okay. It's not like we have a lot of options."

Amanda flexed her fingers over the keyboard. She typed a response to Georgia's post: "*What did people in Phoenicia eat during Thanksgiving?*"

Cam studied it before Amanda hit send. "Sort of cryptic. But I like it. It gives her the chance to be honest with us. Any chance it can be traced back to us?"

"I don't see how. I'm just posting to the website."

The response came a minute later: *When they had to work, they ate Italian. Then they watched some fireworks. Of course, the thanks they give is to Baal and Asherah.*"

Amanda chuckled. "Well played. The fireworks are a reference to your little trick in the parking lot of the hotel. So she's admitting she's working with the feds. And the reference to Asherah, which is another name for Astarte, tells us she is a student of ancient religions. So she's not just some goon sent to track us down. She's a scholar."

"But the question remains, can we trust her? Or is this just a ruse?"

"I have an idea. Presumably she's in the Catskills still. I'm assuming you want to head up to Montreal first thing in the morning?"

"Actually I'd like to leave tonight. I'll need time and daylight to get us across the border tomorrow."

"Okay. Here's my plan." She typed a response to Georgia. *"Meet us midnight in middle of O'Neill Plaza, Boston College campus. Come alone. Wear no hat and carry 2-liter soda bottle."*

Cam arched his neck. "I don't follow."

"Have a look," she said. She turned the laptop screen toward him again. "This is the Boston College webcam; it runs 24-7. The campus is empty tonight because of Thanksgiving. But it's still lit, and the moon is bright, so we can see the entire area surrounding the plaza."

"I get it. We can watch the plaza from now until midnight. If she calls in back-up, we'd be able to see them getting into position. Which means we can't trust her." It was simple but ingenious. He smiled. "Remind me never to try to cheat on you."

She rolled her eyes. "As if."

"Okay, why the soda bottle?"

"So we can be sure it's her. The image isn't great at night. I want to make sure we're not watching some janitor or something."

Cam checked his watch. "It's just after eight. Assuming she's still in the Catskills, she can get to Boston by midnight if she leaves right away. But that's a long drive just to get stood up."

"Yes, well, I've got a cracked rib and you've a concussion and torn up knee and nasty gash on that pretty face of yours that makes it hard for me to kiss you. I'm not feeling particularly sorry for her."

✠ ✠ ✠

Georgia resisted the urge to push 90 on the interstate; she would make Boston by midnight even at 75. But her heart was racing, and somehow the Grand Am she had commandeered from Trey Buckner wanted to race with her.

It had been relatively easy to make her exit. She had convinced Hayek that she would be of more use in Boston with all her reference materials, and Trey—still sulking over losing his prey in the Catskills—was happy to be rid of a stodgy academic who couldn't even stand guard over a few cars in the hotel parking lot.

She had been fairly certain Amanda and Cam would grab for the lifeline she had cast them—they might not trust the captain of the rescue boat, but their only other choice was to drown. That they wanted to meet in Boston meant they must have returned to familiar ground after their escape from the Catskills. Perhaps they were holed up near Westford, north of Boston, where they lived.

Just before 11:00 she hit the Charlton toll plaza, 45 miles outside Boston. She ran in and purchased a 2-liter bottle of Diet Coke and some trail mix. Finally she would be doing something productive, something worthwhile. She wanted to help Amanda and Cam not just because it was the right thing to do, but because the history they had uncovered fascinated her.

The one problem she hadn't yet solved was what to do with her intrepid historians once she had gained their trust. For a day or two Hayek would not suspect her of harboring them. But at some point the truth about what they had discovered would need to come out, preferably before Hayek charged her with treason.

What they had discovered. That was the most fascinating part of this. Did the Templars discover something that convinced them the teachings of the Church were a lie, that the entire religion was built on legend and bluster? She couldn't help but picture the scared little man behind the curtain proclaiming his greatness and power to the citizens of Oz. Were Amanda and Cam about to pull the curtain aside?

CHAPTER 17

Amanda drove, following the Connecticut River north through Vermont on Route 91. She and Cam had shared the overnight drive while Astarte slept in the back with the stuffed bunny. Cam reclined in the passenger seat, an ice pack wrapped around his knee and a warm compress on the back of his neck. They discussed the ramifications of the hidden history they had uncovered as the first glow of dawn brightened the sky out Cam's window.

Cam said, "I think the Templars saw Jesus as important because he was part of the kingly bloodline of David, and also a kind of prophet. They probably even venerated him. He just wasn't a deity."

"Jesus not a deity." Amanda chuckled. "We say it so matter-of-factly." She glanced to the sky. "I'm surprised lightning bolts haven't smitten us."

A good theory often provided explanations for unanswered questions. "This also explains why the Templars always fought in the name of the Virgin Mary," Amanda said. "It never made sense to me before—why not fight for Jesus?"

Cam nodded. "Getting back to the thief thing: Isn't there some story in the New Testament about a pair of thieves being crucified with Jesus?"

"Yes. When I first Googled thief and Jesus and cross that's what came up." She had actually been thinking about this while Cam napped. "And it fits the pattern perfectly of the Church co-opting local legend, modifying it slightly and incorporating it into the 'official' record. It's like Christmas." The December 25th holiday originally marked the rebirth of the sun after the winter solstice. Early Church leaders co-opted the pagan festival and turned it into a celebration of Jesus' birth—never mind that Jesus was really born months later. Amanda sipped at a Diet Coke. "In this case, there must have been contemporary accounts of Jesus' crucifixion in which Jesus was described as the thief on the cross. The Church dealt with it by adding a pair of new thieves to the story, just to fog things up. Jesus was not the thief, the new story goes; the men crucified next to him were. It's really quite brilliant. Hide the lies deep inside the truth."

In St. Johnsbury, fifty miles from the Quebec border, they found a truck stop for an early breakfast. While they waited for their food Amanda emailed Georgia Johnston: *"Sorry to miss our meeting. Thanks for coming alone. You have gained our trust. More later."* Amanda felt a bit guilty standing the woman up—she had waited, alone in the abandoned plaza, huddled against the night air. When they left their Greenwich Village hotel at 12:30, the operative was still pacing in a small circle in the courtyard of the abandoned college campus.

By 7:00 A.M. they had freshened up in the restrooms and were heading north again. "Are we going to swim to Canada?" Astarte asked. She must have heard Cam talking about crossing the lake.

"Actually, only Amanda is going to swim. You and I will be using a boat."

It took the girl only a second to realize Cam was teasing. Amanda said, "Tell Mr. Thorne you think *he* is the one who is all wet."

The girl grinned and repeated the words. She really was a bright, sweet kid. Amanda opened her window. It would be an unseasonably warm November day. "Actually not a bad day for some boating."

"I'm a bit worried about the wind. Otherwise we should be fine."

"Are you certain you'll be able to find a boat?"

He nodded. "My uncle keeps his bass boat in the water until the ice comes, usually mid-December. And if he pulled it out already, I'll just drop it back in. They're away for Thanksgiving, visiting my cousin in Boston."

"Yes. If I recall correctly we had plans to join them for dinner tonight in the North End."

"I had forgotten. Seems like a different lifetime."

"Or a different life."

Hopefully Cam's family wasn't worried about them, but there was no way they could risk a call or email. He took a local exit to Newport, Vermont. "Newport, huh?" Amanda smiled at him.

She had followed him to Newport, Rhode Island when they first met.

"Maybe it'll bring us good luck again."

✛ ✛ ✛

Cam followed the local highway into Newport, the road hugging the western shore of the lake. The lake, shaped like a backward comma, ran north-south with only the southern tip within U.S. borders. "My uncle's place is a few miles up. It's usually pretty quiet up here this time of the year, especially on the American side where most of the properties are summer homes."

Five minutes later he turned down a dirt road. They bounced along for a couple hundred feet through the woods. "Any chance they might track us here?" Amanda asked.

Cam shrugged. "I doubt it. I haven't been here in probably five years. Besides, we're not staying long."

He pulled into a clearing and a stone, A-frame chalet rose up to meet them. "How quaint," Amanda said. "It looks like something you'd see in the Alps."

"Actually, the guy who built it is from Austria. He came over to teach skiing in Vermont and kept busy in the summer building ski chalets. Wait till you see the deck in the back."

Cam parked and found the key his uncle kept hidden under a bird bath. "Go on in. But don't disturb anything; I don't want them to know anyone was here."

He let himself out the sliding door onto a large mahogany deck overlooking the water and peered out at the dock. A gray bass boat, its raised fishing seat mounted on the front and outboard motor protruding off the rear ruining its otherwise sleek lines, bobbed in the early morning mist. His uncle would not be happy to learn it had been stolen and driven to Canada.

Cam found the boat key hanging on a hook near the sliding door, attached to a starfish-shaped wedge of Styrofoam designed to float in case someone dropped the key overboard. "Amanda, do you have any old keys with you?"

She dug through her purse and handed him her ring.

He held up a small copper-colored one that approximated the size of the boat key. "Is this replaceable?"

She shrugged. "It fits the padlock on my gym locker."

He switched the two keys, leaving Amanda's hanging on the hook attached to the starfish. "I don't want them to notice the key is missing. I want them to think someone hot-wired the boat."

He limped down the back steps, grabbed some life jackets from the shed under the deck and threw them into the boat along with a couple of fishing poles—if they were stopped by the authorities, he at least wanted to have a plausible story that they were out fishing and had inadvertently crossed the border. Fortunately his uncle had left the gas tank almost full. "This didn't take as long as I thought. Let's get going. It'll be chilly on the lake, so we should bundle up a bit."

"What about the car?" Amanda asked.

"Here's the plan. I'll lock the house and stash our packs in the boat. You and Astarte drive back south, toward town. Follow the lake road around the southern tip of the lake until you get to the Eastside restaurant." He handed her a map. "Park in the parking lot and come out onto the pier. I'll pick you up in the boat. Then we'll head north." He checked his watch. "It's just after nine. I'll pick you up in half an hour. Keep your cell phone on."

She kissed him firmly on the lips. "Make it 45 minutes. Not that Astarte and I don't trust your fishing skills, but I'm going to fetch some sandwiches for lunch."

"Grab some worms also." They would add authenticity to the fishing story.

Astarte crinkled her nose. "Worms?"

Cam grinned. "Of course. They're delicious on sandwiches."

✝ ✝ ✝

Jabil Hayek had been at his Virginia office for two hours already. The only thing he had to be thankful for was that the Friday-after-Thanksgiving traffic allowed for an easy commute. He had spent an uncomfortable Thanksgiving with his ex-wife and her new boyfriend, dodging questions from both her and Farah about college tuition. To make matters worse, Buckner and his team had failed; somehow Amanda Spencer and her fiancé had evaded them and vanished. With the little girl and the Clairvaux Codex no less. He squished his cigarette into the ashtray. Unbelievable.

His foot brushed against an object beneath his desk, which reminded him there was actually a second thing to be thankful for. The Bat Creek Stone, and the skeletal remains excavated with it, sat in a lockbox at his feet thanks to a Thanksgiving-day burglary at the University of Tennessee science center. As high-tech as the spy game had become, sometimes an old-fashioned break-in was just what was needed. Hayek couldn't bring himself to destroy the objects, and the human bones under his desk gave him the willies, but he didn't know what else to do with them other than stick them in his wall safe once he had a free minute. Perhaps when this all blew over he could arrange for the artifact and bones to be anonymously returned to the tribe.

He dialed Georgia Johnston's cell. Yesterday he had briefed her on details of the Clairvaux Codex only because she had threatened to go public with the mission and he wanted to shut her up. He had brought her onto the team because he thought she might be of use after the quarry was captured. Now, with Buckner having failed, she might be their best hope.

He didn't bother with pleasantries. "I know you're up to something, Georgia. What is it?" The agency had tracking devices in all its agents' cars; he received a written report twice a day with a summary of all movements.

She didn't miss a beat. "You're wrong. I just wanted to get back to my office to check on some sources. I wanted to follow up on this Clairvaux Codex. Besides, I wasn't doing anyone any good sitting in that hotel room playing den mother."

"Then why did you spend a half-hour in the middle of the night at the Boston College campus?"

"An old colleague of mine is a professor there. I wanted to pick his brain a bit."

Hayek let it go with an exasperated sigh. By letting her know he didn't believe her she would be less likely to follow it up with another lie. "I'm not going to ask you to break any confidences, or even remind you about the consequences of insubordination. But tell me this: If our lovebirds were to contact you, what would you give them for advice?"

She did not hesitate. "I'd tell them to stay on the run. I don't trust Buckner. I'm not sure if he's following your orders or if you're just turning a blind eye, but he wants them dead."

"He wants them dead because they are a runaway train. Millions are in their path."

"Perhaps so. But nobody has even bothered to ask them to just pull the emergency brake. Maybe they'd say yes."

Hayek stared at the phone for a few seconds even after his agent hung up. She had a point.

✠ ✠ ✠

After picking up Amanda and Astarte, Cam hugged the eastern coast of Lake Memphremagog, his left hand on the steering wheel and his right on the throttle, stopping occasionally to drop a fishing line into the water in case anyone was watching. Eventually he angled his way out to Province Island, a 100-acre landmass separated near its southern tip by the international border. They were not far from his uncle's house on the opposite shore; he anchored and dropped his line again while Amanda scanned the shore with a pair of binoculars.

"No activity at your uncle's property."

He nodded, put the engine back into gear and puttered up the western side of the island into Canada. They waved at an older couple in a canoe and Cam motioned to Astarte and Amanda to hold tight. "I'm going to see how fast we can go, okay Astarte?"

She grinned and nodded, her little face framed by the wide neck brace of the orange life jacket. Cam raced into Canada, angling toward the western shoreline a mile north of his uncle's camp. He cut obliquely across the waves, keeping the bouncing of the light boat to a minimum—Amanda had cushioned the artifacts and canister as best she could in his pack, and he had further cushioned them with a life jacket in the boat's bilge, but he didn't want to damage them. The boat responded to his touch on the throttle and pressure on the steering wheel, a welcome sense of control after days of feeling like a leaf in the wind. They rode silently, the noise of the outboard and the wind making it impossible to talk. Cam extended his leg, keeping his knee straight and elevated to try to control the swelling. At least his head wasn't throbbing so badly, thanks to a few Advil and a pair of sunglasses to fight the mid-morning glare. Yesterday he felt like a dead man walking; today was more like a man getting over a hangover. As they approached the shore he tapped back the throttle and the boat's bow sank off its plane.

"So we're in Canada. What happens next, Cam?"

"Um, I thought we agreed you would call me 'Captain Cameron' while I am piloting this vessel."

Amanda grinned. "Captain Crunch is more like it."

He feigned disappointment. The few hours sleep while Amanda drove had given him some energy, and being on the lake made him feel elated despite his injuries. "How about you, Astarte, will you call me Captain Cameron?"

A smile crept across her mouth. "Only if you eat one of those worms."

"Really, that's all it takes?" He reached into the small jar Amanda had purchased, arched his jaw and dangled a night crawler above his open mouth. A flashback hit him: He had done the same thing to impress a girl a couple of decades ago on this same lake. He dropped the worm into his mouth and swallowed quickly, fighting back a gag reflex. What the hell.

"Ewww," Astarte proclaimed, leaning away.

"We'll not be doing any snogging today, I'm sure," Amanda said.

"Bummer," Cam said, smiling. "I had hoped to snog on Memphremagog."

Amanda rolled her eyes and tossed a worm at him. He shook his head: The worm trick hadn't worked when he was a teenager either.

✝ ✝ ✝

Cam and his passengers had navigated their way up the western edge of the lake and were cruising along the shoreline not far from the lake's northern tip. The tree line along the shore sheltered them from the wind and kept the chop from tossing the boat. "That's the town of Magog up ahead. Technically it's not illegal to cross into Canadian waters as long as you don't actually step on land. So, so far we haven't broken the law."

"You mean not today," Amanda said.

"Good point." He angled the boat back across the lake, which had narrowed to less than a mile. He kept his speed down—just a young couple and their daughter out for a day on the water, proceeding carefully in the rougher waters of the open part of the lake. "Local legend is there's a sea serpent in this lake, sort of like the Loch Ness Monster. They call her Memphre." He kept it light so as not to frighten Astarte. The reality was that the Native Americans refused to swim in the lake out of fear of the serpent. "But she's a friendly monster."

"Have you ever seen her?" Astarte asked.

"No, but my uncle knows a guy who swears he saw her one day." Cam shrugged. "The lake is really deep, so who knows what might live down there."

He pointed to the far shore. "Up ahead there's a wooded area with a snowmobile trail that leads to the lake. When we were kids we used to beach our boat and walk to town. Hopefully it's still there."

He approached the shore line and handed Amanda the fishing pole. They puttered around for a few minutes, creeping in to shallower waters and the shelter of the trees, until they were sure nobody was watching. "There it is," Cam said, pointing to a narrow, sandy path between the trees. He cut the engine and coasted onto shore, lifting the outboard before the prop caught in the sand. Scanning the lake a final time, he stepped onto land and dragged the boat up with him. "Okay, all ashore. Welcome to Canada."

✠ ✠ ✠

Sitting on the porch swing in the noontime sun, the compound empty after Jefferson's death and Astarte's abduction and Judith's flight, Eliza reread the incendiary text. "The scroll says Templars have Jesus bones. Miss Amanda says Jesus not son of God. This makes me sad. I have been saying my prayers. Bye." Was it possible? Did the Templars really find the bones of Jesus? Perhaps the girl had it wrong. Or perhaps the Templars only thought they had the bones. It was just too outlandish to be true. She shook her head. She couldn't take the risk; she had to assume the girl was telling the truth.

The message had come in late last night, apparently when Astarte was alone in bed. Trey had traced the call back to Manhattan and had agents scouring the city. Thank God the little princess remained loyal to her people—the years of indoctrination, of emphasizing the importance of duty and sacrifice over self, had paid off. No doubt the little girl saw herself as Belle in *Beauty and the Beast*, sacrificing her happiness out of loyalty to her family.

Eliza stared into the woods. It had never occurred to her that the scroll hidden in the Catskills might actually *undermine* the Book of Mormon. Jefferson had been obsessed with retrieving the ancient scroll because he believed the parchment would somehow validate the sacred Mormon text. And she had no reason to question her brother, which is why Trey's mission to retrieve and safeguard the scroll was so important.

But important had suddenly become essential: If the scroll was authentic and its contents made public, the entire foundation of Christianity—built on the cornerstone of Jesus' physical ascendancy to heaven—could crumble. And smack dab in the middle of that rubble, broken and shattered, would lie both the Mormon Church and her family's dream of Astarte uniting the religions of the world at the foot of her throne.

As if on cue Trey phoned. "We found their hotel, but they left late last night."

"Curse it." She sighed. "Any idea where they went?"

"No. They did a good job sanitizing the room before they left. Assuming a 12-hour head start, they could be anywhere in the northeast quadrant of the country."

244

"Can you trace Astarte's cell phone?"

"Only if she uses it again. Have you tried responding to her?"

"I sent a text. But I can't just call—if they see her talking to me they'll take away her phone."

"Well, keep trying. Even a short text should be enough to track."

"Trey, I don't need to tell you how important it is to retrieve that scroll."

"No, you don't."

She told him anyhow. "If things blow up, the Christian right-wingers are going to look for a scapegoat. And they're going to find one in Jefferson. He's the one who let Pandora out of her box; he's the one who caused that scroll to be found. And because he was Mormon, they're going to blame all of us. They're going to say it was all because the Mormons are obsessed with proving the validity of their precious Book of Mormon. And they'll be right." She exhaled. "We have a rare opportunity to win the Presidency, to gain control of the most powerful nation in the world. We may never have that chance again. You must not fail."

"Like I said, you don't need to explain. I get it. Loud and clear."

✠ ✠ ✠

Astarte lifted her backpack and put it over her shoulder. She had never been in a foreign country; she was surprised it didn't look any different than the United States. "Are the people in Canada the same as us?"

Miss Amanda smiled and took her hand. They were following a path up from the lake through the woods. Mr. Cameron was limping and using a stick to support himself so they were walking pretty slowly, like Uncle January walked after he got sick. "Some of them speak French, but otherwise they are the same. You'll meet them when we get to the village, called Magog. From there we'll board a bus for Montreal."

"Montreal? How do you spell that?" She didn't want to confuse Aunt Eliza. Hopefully Miss Amanda and Mr. Cameron wouldn't be angry with her when they found out she had texted her aunt—she had promised not to *call* Eliza, so texting wasn't really a lie. Astarte had been thinking about their conversation before Thanksgiving dinner. Miss Amanda said God was really Mother Earth. And then Mr. Cameron said God and Mother Earth were married. It seemed to her that they were both wrong. Yes, Mother Earth gave life, but that didn't make her a god. God created everything, including the earth. And how could God be married to something he created? It just didn't make sense. And if they were wrong about that, they were also wrong about Jesus not being the son of God. Uncle January used to talk to her a lot about people who were good people but who were not good Christians. He said we should love them and try to teach them the error of their ways, but not to be led astray by them. Aunt Eliza, on the other hand, wasn't a very nice person. But she was a good Christian. And she would know what to do with the scroll Mr. Cameron was carrying in his pack that said Jesus wasn't really the son of God.

☩ ☩ ☩

The phone call to Georgia came from Hayek rather than Trey Buckner, who apparently no longer even thought of her as part of his team. "Buckner just called. He's tracked them to Montreal. He's in pursuit."

Georgia was eating lunch in her Cambridge condo while waiting for Amanda and Cam to contact her again. "His team has clearance to operate in Canada?"

"I'm working on it now. If we have to, we'll get the President to make a call."

"Why are you telling me?"

"Georgia, you're still assigned to this mission as far as I'm concerned. A lot of what you said this morning made sense. But I'm not willing to call off Buckner and his hounds—that scroll and those artifacts are too explosive, the risks too high. So you've got less than six hours to get up there and diffuse things before Buckner and his team start throwing their elbows around."

"They're driving?"

"Yup. You know Trey. Can't go on a mission without a trunk full of weapons and gear. Like I said, you have six hours."

✠ ✠ ✠

They had hiked to the town of Magog and, less than two hours later, boarded an early-afternoon bus for Montreal.

"Okay," Cam said, "what next?" He sat across the aisle from Amanda, with Astarte in the window seat.

"I think we need to contact Georgia Johnston again," Amanda said. The bus had Wi-Fi, though the service was sporadic.

"Can we trust her?"

"At some point we might have to risk it. We can't run forever."

Had they reached that point? Now that they had crossed into Canada he felt a bit safer—it would be difficult for Trey Buckner and his team to gun down civilians on the streets of Montreal. Maybe they could blend in and disappear for a while. "Let's wait until we get settled first. I'd like to figure out a way to contact Salazar and see what he thinks."

"I'm not sure we can trust him either," Amanda said. "He seemed a bit too willing to leave you hanging on that Zip Line."

Cam shrugged. After the outburst in the woods when Salazar almost stabbed him, he didn't doubt it. "Bottom line is we don't know who we can trust right now." He patted his pack, containing the Templar scroll. "And our Templar friends are a bit too old to be much help."

✠ ✠ ✠

Georgia had grabbed her passport, thrown together an overnight bag and hailed a cab. Within minutes of ending her call to Hayek she raced to Logan Airport, searching the web on her phone for the next flight to Montreal as the taxi sped through Boston. Fortunately traffic was light on the day after Thanksgiving, and her ODNI credentials allowed her to bypass the security lines. She jogged to the Air Canada gate and boarded the plane minutes before its 1:20 departure.

Another cab ride from Trudeau Airport deposited her at the main bus terminal in downtown Montreal just before three o'clock. She had perhaps a three hour head start on Trey Buckner and his team. She scanned the monitor of arriving buses. Hopefully her hunch was correct.

CHAPTER 18

The size of the St. Lawrence River amazed Cam. As an American he never heard much about the waterway. But it was immense. Just crossing it on the bus took almost five minutes.

Once across the St. Lawrence the bus exited the highway and snaked its way through the streets of Montreal. "It's just a regular Friday afternoon rush hour here, no holiday," Amanda observed.

"When we arrive, I think we should split up. If the authorities are looking for us, they're expecting a man, woman and little girl. Let's not make it easy for them."

"All right then. Astarte and I will wait for a bit on the bus. You push on ahead and we'll meet in the lobby."

Cam shouldered his pack, careful not to jar the artifacts and scroll, and moved toward the front of the bus. He pulled his baseball hat down over his eyes and left his sunglasses on. He hadn't shaved since the morning at the museum, but that was only two days ago so his beard wouldn't help disguise him. He pushed through the terminal door and into the station lobby, where he milled around and waited for Amanda and Astarte. He didn't see Buckner or his men. But that didn't mean they—or their friends—weren't here.

A few minutes later Amanda and Astarte approached slowly from across the lobby. He scanned the area one more time and moved to meet them. As they converged a big-boned woman in her sixties carrying a 2-liter bottle of soda marched over. "Welcome to Montreal," she said. "I'm Georgia Johnston." She held up the soda bottle as a form of identification.

Amanda stammered a reply. "How ever did you find us?"

"That doesn't matter. But if I found you, you can be sure the posse is not far behind." She shifted her glance between Cam and Amanda, her brown eyes intelligent and kind. "I know you didn't trust me completely before, and I can't say I blame you. But now you have no choice."

✠ ✠ ✠

Georgia surprised Cam by taking charge of the situation. She issued orders immediately. "Cameron, you walk with Amanda. I'll take Astarte. Let us get a half block ahead before you follow. We'll be taking a left out the front door."

The girl looked up at Amanda, her eyes wide. "I don't fancy letting the girl out of my sight," Amanda said. She hugged the little princess to her.

Georgia responded before Cam could. "I'm sorry, but we don't have time to argue. Astarte walking with only one of you is not going to fool anyone. But nobody expects her to be with an old woman like me." She took the girl's hand, bending low to look her in the eye. "I knew your Uncle Jefferson. He was a very smart man. Now please come with me. And please don't look back." She glanced at Cam and Amanda. "Comfort Inn, room four-two-six," she said. "But wait a few minutes before entering the building."

Amanda gripped Cam's arm as the little girl walked away with Georgia. "Either she's telling the truth," Cam said, "or she is just trying to get Astarte out of the way and this is where Buckner and his team take us out." If so, it was best that Astarte not be in the line of fire.

"Which is it?"

Cam scanned the crowd. "We'll know soon enough."

They waited ten seconds, Amanda digging her nails into Cam's arm. Finally he could not hold her back any longer and she pulled him outside into the dimming late afternoon light. Georgia and Astarte marched along less than half a block ahead. Amanda took a deep breath and they followed. At any moment Cam expected a car to screech to a halt next to them, or a pair of strong arms to grab him from behind, or a ring of police to emerge from some doorway and surround them. But nothing.

Georgia took a left at the corner and walked another half block before ducking into a door under a Comfort Inn sign. Cam and Amanda circled the block to kill a few minutes before entering; two minutes later they stood in front of room 426 and knocked twice.

"Who's there?" Astarte responded cheerfully. Clearly Georgia had succeeded in calming the girl.

"Know any knock-knock jokes?" Amanda whispered to Cam.

No reason to stress her out further—she'd had a tough few days as it was. "Ice cream," he responded.

"Ice cream who?"

"Ice cream if you don't let me in."

Astarte giggled as Georgia pulled the door open and peered up and down the hall. "This room looks down over the street. I was watching; I don't think you've been followed. That's why I told you not to come in right away." She moved aside; the suite contained a work area along with two queen beds. "But we only have a three-hour head start. I need to see the scroll and those artifacts, and I need you to tell me everything you can as quickly as you can."

"Okay," Cam said, "but first tell us why you are helping is."

"Simple. I don't like seeing innocent people killed."

"Especially by their own government," Cam added.

"Actually, I don't think the feds are necessarily trying to kill you. I think they just want to keep this all quiet."

"Um," Amanda said, "a bullet whizzing by my ear is more than is needed to keep me quiet."

"Yes. I think the agent on this case has gone rogue. I'm just not sure why."

"So why doesn't your boss call this rogue agent in?" Cam asked.

"Again, killing you is not the purpose of the mission. But if there is so-called collateral damage, so be it. As long as the secrets remain secret."

"Bloody great," Amanda said. "Well, who is this agent, and why would he want us dead?"

Georgia looked straight at Amanda. "I don't know. Obviously it has something to do with the Clairvaux Codex and whatever you found in the Catskills. But I can't figure it out until you fill in all the blanks for me."

Amanda and Cam exchanged a nod. Amanda and Astarte crossed the room and leaned against the heat register while Cam sat in a desk chair to rest his knee. Cam and Amanda took turns recounting their past couple of days. When they got to the part involving the IN CAMERA stone and the scroll, Cam pulled the objects from his pack and laid them on the bed.

Georgia bent low over the scroll, asking Cam to repeat his translation from the Latin. She whistled. "So the Templars found the bones of Jesus. I knew whatever they found had to be monumental."

"We think they had rejected Jesus and were secretly worshiping John the Baptist," Amanda said.

Georgia nodded. "That makes sense. I've been studying this stuff for years. Perhaps I can fill in some of the gaps in your research." She folded her hands behind her back like a college professor and paced between the beds. "The first thing you need to know is that the Templars inherited and followed the teachings of the Essenes, a Jewish monastic order living outside of Jerusalem in the first century A.D. You've probably heard of them because they wrote the Dead Sea Scrolls."

Cam nodded.

Georgia continued. "According to these Scrolls, the Essenes believed that the arriving messianic era would be ushered in by two messiahs rather than one. A kingly messiah, descended from the line of King David, would rule the people. Meanwhile a priestly messiah, descended from Moses' brother Aaron, would lead the people in spiritual matters." She explained that when Jesus, a descendant of King David, and John the Baptist, a descendant of Aaron, rose to leadership positions in the first century, the Essenes along with other Jewish sects welcomed the two young men, who happened to be first cousins, as a fulfillment of these prophecies. "In fact, both Jesus and John the Baptist lived and studied with the Essenes in their youth. The two messiahs were meant to rule jointly, together ushering in the Kingdom of God. Upon their deaths, the priestly messiah would ascend and sit by the side of God."

"Wait," Cam said. "John the Baptist was supposed to ascend, not Jesus?"

Georgia smiled. "Precisely. The place of dominion of the high priestly messiah was to be in heaven, while the royal messiah resided on earth."

Amanda chuckled. "How the story has changed."

"So that's probably where the Thief on the Cross name comes from," Cam said. "Jesus stole the seat in heaven next to God. The Templars knew Jesus was not really divine. Based on this Essene prophecy, John the Baptist is the one in heaven. Not Jesus."

Georgia stared out the window, apparently weighing and processing the revelations. A few seconds passed. "Suddenly everything makes sense. As I said, historians knew whatever the Templars found had to be monumental, had to be something so earth-shattering that they could blackmail the Church into doing pretty much anything they wanted. The pieces fit together perfectly."

"How so?" Cam asked.

"Well, picture this: The Templars take Jesus' bones back to Europe and threaten to expose the great big lie that is Christianity. Jesus wasn't resurrected, we have his bones, he had a wife, he had children, blah blah blah."

"But would people have believed them?" Cam asked.

"Perhaps, perhaps not," Georgia said. "But the Church couldn't risk it. Remember, these Knights were French Noblemen, well-educated from respected families--"

"Actually, bloodline families," Amanda interrupted. "They probably went to Jerusalem with the express purpose of proving that Jesus had children and they were his descendants. Descendants of a king, if perhaps not a god."

"Exactly. As I said, the pieces fit together. So the Church couldn't risk it. The Templars had the bones and the tomb, plus all the local legends about Mary Magdalene bringing Jesus' baby to southern France. The entire foundation of the Church would have been undermined."

Cam jumped in. "So the Church cut a deal: Keep your mouths shut and we'll leave you alone."

Amanda nodded. "Not just leave them alone, but cut them in. The Templars became equal partners, sharing in the power and wealth of the Church."

"But the Templars didn't trust the Church," Cam said. "Which is why they made multiple copies of the scroll, in case the Church ever turned on them--"

"Which it did," Georgia interjected. "In fact, the Church murdered tens of thousands of Christians in the Albigensian Crusades in southern France in the early 1200s. Many who died were of the bloodline families. And then finally the Church turned on the Templars in 1307, imprisoning and torturing and executing thousands."

Amanda swallowed. "And we stand to meet a similar fate."

Georgia seemed lost in thought. "Nobody could ever figure out how the Templars got so powerful so quickly," she whispered. She looked out the window, the traffic and bustle of Montreal a stark contrast to the ancient history revealing itself in their sterile hotel room. "Now we know." She turned back to Cam and Amanda. "As I said, the pieces fit together so perfectly now that we know the secret. Once you know the answer to the mystery—that the Templars found Jesus' bones—it's easy to find all the clues."

Cam raised an eyebrow, inviting her to continue.

"For example, this explains the Templar use of the skull and crossbones as their banner. Once the Templars found Jesus' bones, they would have brought them—probably his skull and thigh bones, as was the custom in medieval times—back to Europe. So they put their great secret out in the open on their banner, hidden in plain sight. Every time the Church leaders saw the Templar battle flag they were reminded of the threat the Templars posed."

Amanda nodded. "Same with their veneration of Mary Magdalene. They had proven the existence of the bloodline, and in fact were part of it, so they worshiped the matriarch as well as the patriarch of their family."

Georgia continued. "Even the Templars' worship of John the Baptist makes sense in this light. The Templars worshiped John the Baptist as a reminder to the Church that they did not recognize the Pope as the voice of the priestly class—the true priests descended from Aaron, as John the Baptist did. Worshipping John was like a shot across the Church's bow."

Cam paused, pensive. "The irony of all this is that the scroll—which January was obsessed with finding—totally undermines his quest. The entire Mormon religion, like all of Christianity, is based on Jesus being a deity."

Amanda gently patted the parchment. "You're right. The joke's on him. In trying to prove the authenticity of the Book of Mormon, he uncovered a scroll that proves the whole religion is based on a falsehood."

"This is all fascinating," Cam said. "But back to the big picture: We have a medieval scroll which undermines Christianity. So what do we do with it now that we've found it?"

Georgia lifted the IN CAMERA stone. "In order to answer that, I think we need to find out what's buried at the Notre Dame Basilica."

✠ ✠ ✠

The Notre Dame Basilica was less than a mile from their hotel, but Amanda wanted to make a quick detour. They hailed a cab.

"I keep wondering why the bones would have been brought to Montreal," Amanda said from the front seat as the taxi navigated the narrow streets of Old Montreal. They had left the stone artifacts in the hotel room, but Cam was unwilling to leave the scroll and carried it in his pack. "Well, I did some research on the bus, and it turns out the earliest settlers of the city had Templar roots. The city was founded by the Sulpicians, a French Catholic order. And many historians believe the Sulpicians were closely connected to the outlawed Knights Templar."

"So where are we going?" Georgia asked.

"Right there." Amanda pointed ahead. "The Bon-Secours Chapel." A narrow, cobblestone structure with a soaring center spire rose up in front of them along the shores of the St. Lawrence River.

"We don't really have time for this," Georgia said.

"Ten minutes," Amanda responded. "What we see here may save us hours once we get to the Basilica."

Using a side door they entered a modern gift shop. Amanda bought tickets and led them down a staircase into a round stone crypt with an arched ceiling. "The original chapel burned down and was rebuilt in 1771. Down here is the original foundation. It's a museum." A number of exhibits displayed the history of the chapel and the city through the centuries. "I think behind that door is an ongoing archeological dig site." She scanned the room. "But what I want to see is over here."

She strode across the room and stopped in front of a tombstone-sized slab of gray stone. "That's an ancient cornerstone for the chapel. It was the first church in Montreal, built back in the 1670s."

BON-SECOURS CHAPEL CORNERSTONE

"Look at the crosses on the front and sides," Cam said.

"Exactly. That's what I wanted to see," Amanda said. "Those are Templar crosses—they look like plus signs rather than a lower-case letter 't.' They tell us a lot about early Templar influence, and power, in Old Montreal. And that's the kind of stuff we need to look for at Notre Dame."

She led the group back up to the street. They walked a few blocks along the cobblestoned Rue Saint Paul, the main passage in Old Montreal; brick and stone buildings, many dating back to the 1700s, lined the way. Amanda stopped and pointed through a gap in the skyline at a massive gray Gothic Revival-style structure looming in the distance. "That's Notre Dame Basilica."

✠ ✠ ✠

Astarte had never seen anything so fabulous. She stood in the back of the soaring basilica, a small butterfly alighting within the most amazing flower garden in the world. The Mormon Temples Uncle Jefferson often brought her to were soaring structures themselves, with marble and fine woods and thick carpets and snow-white spires that reached to the heavens. But the Basilica of Notre Dame was different. The sanctuary blazed with vibrant blues and glowing golds—with oranges and reds and greens mixed in as well. It was as if God was a princess designing a palace for himself. Or herself—this church was not a place a man would chose to live; it was more like something out of a fairy tale. Perhaps Mr. Cameron was right, perhaps God was married to Mother Earth and she helped him build this....

Astarte began to walk the perimeter. She recognized many Bible scenes portrayed on the stained glass. But the churches Uncle Jefferson took her to didn't have nearly so many windows devoted to the Virgin Mary and Mary Magdalene and other women. In fact, many of the women displayed were Native American—she had never seen that before. For every man with a beard there was a woman wearing a dress or Native American clothes, as if the builders of the church wanted to make things even. Like picking teams for kickball—one for you and then one for me. One for the boys and then one for the girls. One for the

Europeans and then one for the Native Americans. She sighed. She liked this church. It made her proud to be a girl. And proud to be Mandan.

Miss Amanda interrupted her musings. "Everyone, come here," she called out in a stage whisper. She was in the left-hand pews, looking up at a raised pulpit. The pulpit rose midway between the rear of the church and the front altar, approximately 25 feet in the air, upon which a priest could stand over his flock and preach.

NOTRE DAME BASILICA PULPIT

"Look at the very top, that triangle inside a starburst on the ceiling of the pulpit," Miss Amanda said. "That looks to me like the Delta of Enoch."

Mr. Cameron joined her. "You're right. But it looks like there's a letter missing." He took out his camera and zoomed in closer. "Yes, the Yod is missing from the far right."

Astarte had no idea what they were talking about. Apparently neither did Miss Georgia. "Who is Enoch, and what in the world is a Yod?"

✠ ✠ ✠

Cam studied the triangle of gold embedded on the ceiling of the pulpit. It was clearly the Delta of Enoch, or at least most of one. He pointed out to Georgia the triangle surrounded by golden rays of light that symbolized the divine presence. "Usually the Hebrew letters Yod, Hey, Vav and Hey are inscribed within the triangle. Together the letters comprise the Tetragrammaton, the secret, unspeakable name of God as used in the Hebrew Bible—what we now pronounce as Yahweh or Jehovah. According to the Book of Enoch the name of God was revealed to the prophet Enoch, the great-grandfather of Noah, who then inscribed it into a triangle of pure gold." He explained that though the Delta of Enoch was an important part of Masonic ritual, the Book of Enoch was not considered an authoritative text within either Judaism or mainstream Christianity. So why was the Delta of Enoch prominently displayed in a Catholic church? And why was the letter Yod missing?

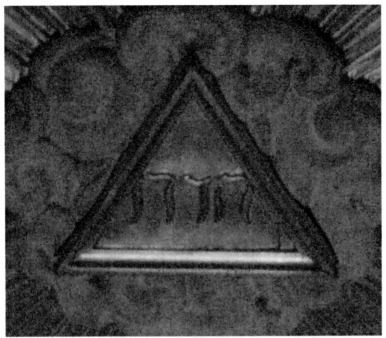

NOTRE DAME BASILICA DELTA OF ENOCH

Cam motioned to one of the basilica tour guides. "Excuse me, can you tell me how old this pulpit is?"

The woman smiled. "The church you are standing in was built in the late 1800s. But the original structure dates back to the 1670s. This pulpit was salvaged from that structure."

Cam nodded. So Notre Dame Basilica was built at the same time as Bon-Secours Chapel, no doubt by the city's Sulpician founders. The name was not surprising—the Templars almost always dedicated their churches to "Our Lady," Notre Dame. The use of the Delta of Enoch, on the other hand, astounded him. The Delta was far more telling than the Templar crosses at Bon-Secours—at least the Templar cross was a Christian symbol. The Delta of Enoch, on the other hand, clearly evidenced Sulpician ties to the ancient Gnostic secrets and traditions. It was the type of thing that could get oneself burned at the stake.

Cam looked again at the letters, turning his head to orient himself to read them better. With the first letter missing, the Hebrew read Hey, Vav, Hey. He zoomed in close with his camera to see if the fourth letter had faded away or been covered by the Delta's wooden frame. But based on the spacing there was never a letter Yod there. He stared at the symbols for a few seconds, trying to make sense of them. Suddenly his neck burned. "Chava," he whispered.

"What was that?" Amanda asked.

"It says Chava. The three letters. They spell Chava. And Chava is Hebrew for Eve."

Amanda's eyes lit up. "Inside the sacred Delta!" she exclaimed.

Georgia didn't follow. "Guys, slow down."

Amanda explained. "Whoever built that pulpit changed the name of the divine being inside the sacred triangle from 'Yahweh' to 'Eve,' the name of the first woman. They did it very subtly, by just removing a single letter which is really no larger than an apostrophe. But there's no doubting their meaning: They are saying that they worship the female aspect of our creator along with or even more so than the male." Amanda motioned around her. "Look at all the female imagery in this church, all the tributes to Mary Magdalene and of course the Virgin Mary. This church is a veritable shrine to the sacred feminine. These people were carrying on the old Gnostic traditions, the very teachings the Vatican was trying so hard to suppress."

Georgia nodded. "The very teachings the Templars believed in."

"Bloody amazing," Amanda breathed.

"This is all very interesting," Georgia said after a few seconds, "and it tells us we're on the right track, but what about the bones?"

A tall, gray-haired priest in a long black robe appeared as if by magic from behind the wooden pulpit. He smiled kindly, his large brown eyes on Astarte and his hands clasped behind his back. "Yes, what about the bones?" he repeated, his English refined behind a French accent. "We have been asking ourselves that same question for many centuries."

✠ ✠ ✠

Father Jean led the group down a side hallway toward the back of the massive basilica, speaking over his shoulder as he did so. Amanda noticed that, somehow, the massive stained glass windows glowed even in the dimming late-afternoon light. "I make a point of coming out to meet visitors who study the Delta of Enoch. It is, as you deduced, quite a unique feature of our church. For those who have eyes that see, it reveals much of our history. And of our secrets."

Eyes that see. What did he mean by that? In any event, Father Jean had a commanding presence—it apparently didn't occur to him that his guests would do anything other than fall in line behind him. She took a deep breath. "Excuse me, Father, but where are you taking us?"

Father Jean smiled; his face reminded Amanda of the handsome priest played by Richard Chamberlain in "The Thorn Birds" television miniseries she and Cam recently watched. Father Jean no doubt broke a few hearts when he joined the seminary. "Well, where would you like to go?" he asked.

Amanda responded. "I suppose we'd like to see whatever's left of the original structure of the church."

"Of course you would," Father Jean said. "And that is precisely where I am taking you." The priest stopped and turned. "And perhaps once I've earned your trust you'd be willing to show me that ancient scroll of yours?" He raised an eyebrow.

Cam blurted out a response. "How do you know about the scroll?"

Father Jean turned up both palms. "How else would you know about the bones?"

✠ ✠ ✠

Astarte liked Father Jean. He spoke to her like an adult, and when he smiled his eyes twinkled like he really meant it. Plus he was a priest in the most beautiful church in the world.

But it surprised her that he seemed to agree with Miss Amanda and Mr. Cameron that Jesus' bones were not in heaven. In fact, it was almost like he was expecting someone to show up looking for them here at his amazing church. How could he be a priest if he didn't believe Jesus ascended? Astarte knew that when Jesus was resurrected it was his whole body, not just his soul, that went to heaven.

Father Jean led them down a narrow staircase and into a hallway. Three red steel doors lined the passage; the priest unlocked the one at the far end. He pulled it open, flicked on a light switch and stepped aside. "After you," he said. The room looked like other basements Astarte had been in, with a cement floor and pipes on the ceilings. Plus lots of cobwebs and the smell of a furnace.

Mr. Cameron went first; Miss Amanda held Astarte's hand and followed, with Miss Georgia behind. "Is this the original foundation?" Mr. Cameron asked. He bent low to examine the stone walls; perhaps he thought they would find more Templar crosses or other writings.

Father Jean stood by the door. "Yes it is. In fact, during your Revolutionary War prisoners were held in this very room." He backed away. "I regret that I am going to have to use it for that purpose again."

Mr. Cameron leapt for the door but Father Jean was too fast for him. He slammed it quickly and locked it. "I hope you will forgive my poor hospitality."

CHAPTER 19

Cam paced the square cement room, ignoring the throbbing in his left knee. "I can't believe I let some old priest sweet-talk us into a jail cell." They had been in the room a half-hour. Long enough to learn the door was thick and the walls thicker. And that there was no cell coverage.

"This is my fault," Georgia said. "I'm supposed to be the trained operative." She, Amanda and Astarte sat on a plank they had set between two old paint cans.

"This is nobody's fault. We all trusted him," Amanda said, rubbing her hands together.

"Not very smart of us." Cam ran his hand through his hair. "Why would Father Jean want to help us? He's a priest. And we found evidence his whole religion is based on a fat lie." He turned to Georgia. "Any chance you have a weapon?"

"No. I knew I couldn't fly with it." She smiled. "Besides, I didn't plan on having to shoot you."

Astarte spoke, her head on Amanda's shoulder. "What do you think he's going to do with us?"

The poor kid had been through so much in just three days. Cam didn't want to scare the girl and tell her what he really thought: The priest was going to turn them over to Buckner and his goons and leave it up to them to make sure the secret stayed buried. So he lied. "Maybe he just wants to make sure we are who we say we are. Then he's going to let us out."

Astarte pondered this. "No, I think he doesn't want you telling people Jesus wasn't really the son of God. That's why he locked us in this room."

Amanda smiled. "That's a good theory, Astarte. But I think Mr. Cameron is probably correct this time."

✝ ✝ ✝

Another half-hour passed in the cramped, damp basement of the church. Cam had been busy fashioning a weapon—he pried a section of two-by-four off of a workbench and, using a piece of scrap iron as a hammer, drove some old nails through the wood

264

so that the points extended out the back side. He also held a rag against the light bulb until it flamed, then let it smolder on the cement floor, occasionally blowing on it or adding sawdust to keep the weak flame alive. "I don't want it to burn too strongly or the room will fill up with smoke," he said. "But there's a can of paint thinner we can use to make a mean fire bomb if we have to." He appreciated that Amanda didn't ask how he planned to use it without blowing them all up.

Footsteps in the hallway. They all froze. Cam pulled the paint thinner closer to the smoldering rag and hoisted the spiked two-by-four. He motioned for everyone to move to the back of the room and unscrewed the light bulb with another rag. The world turned black. Perhaps the only thing worse than being locked up down here was being let out—who knew what kind of violent death might they face?

A key slid into the lock. Cam wasn't sure of an exact plan. All he knew was he wasn't just going to allow Amanda and Astarte to be dragged away to face some staged death. The first guy would get a face full of nails. After that it would be a street brawl. And if he needed to set himself afire and throw himself at the enemy, well, so be it.

The door creaked open a few inches. The outside hall was dimly lit. Cam waited—he needed a bigger opening to swing his club. He counted to three. Still nothing. Slowly he reached out and pushed on the door. No resistance. He took a deep breath, shoved the door open and swung the club wildly, straight down like an axe man. Whoever was standing beyond the threshold didn't stand a chance.

The two-by-four swished through the air and crashed against the cement floor. Cam stumbled behind it, his momentum propelling him through the doorway. His knee gave way and he skidded to the floor. A flashlight flicked on, partially blinding him. "Easy, Mr. Thorne." Father Jean's voice. "Put down your weapon. I am alone. I've come to get you. It is time to see the crypt."

✝ ✝ ✝

Astarte wasn't sure Mr. Cameron wasn't going to try again to hit Father Jean over the head, but Miss Amanda put her hand on his shoulder and Mr. Cameron lowered the piece of wood. Astarte had never seen anyone try to hit a priest before. But she had never known a priest to lock people in a prison either.

Father Jean led them to the steel door at the opposite end of the hallway. "I apologize for having to detain you," he said. "But I needed to make sure your story checked out. The girl referred to you by name; I quickly found your images on the Internet. And your works. You have done some fine research." He had turned his back on Mr. Cameron, apparently not afraid that Mr. Cameron would attack again. Astarte wasn't so sure—he looked pretty angry still. "And I needed to be sure I was following proper protocol. You must understand, I have been waiting for this day for decades, and my predecessors for centuries before me. But I also never thought it would come."

"So you locked us in some … dungeon?" Miss Amanda was also pretty angry.

"My dear. We are talking about the greatest secret in … well, in the history of the modern world. An hour locked in a basement is inconsequential. I do apologize, but I'm sure you see my point."

As he pushed open the door a wave of cool, dry air washed over them. "We keep the room climate-controlled." He flicked on some lights and ushered the group into a square room that reminded Astarte of Uncle Jefferson's underground bunker with its white walls and dark blue carpet and lack of furniture.

A round, stone building sat in the middle of the room; it looked like something a rich person might build for his dog to live in. Astarte counted eight pillars holding up the domed roof of the little house, but the area between each of the pillars was filled in with stone so she couldn't see any way to get inside. Each of the pillars had a Templar cross carved on it, the kind that looked like a plus sign with flared ends.

The grown-ups all stared at the stone building and Miss Georgia's face seemed paler than normal. Finally Miss Amanda spoke. "How long has this been here?" She didn't sound angry any longer.

"From the earliest days of the Basilica, sometime in the 1670s. As soon as the original church was built, this crypt was constructed here in the basement. As you know, the Sulpician order had—and still has—strong ties to the Templar families and legacy. The story that has been passed down is that two men on horseback arrived in the middle of the night carrying a satchel containing a skull and a pair of thigh bones. They deposited the bones in the crypt, the crypt was sealed, and here we are." He smiled. "The crypt has never been moved, though as you can see we have renovated the room around it. Behind the white walls and ceiling the room is encased in thick stone. This is all that remains of the original church foundation; in fact we are not even under the existing church, we are under the street."

Astarte listened intently. Uncle Jefferson would have been fascinated by all this. Even if it did ruin his plans to have Astarte unite the world's religions. But … maybe the bones didn't ruin his plans....

She pulled on Miss Amanda's sleeve.

"One second, honey."

"I'm sorry, but it's very important."

Miss Amanda crouched to look her in the eye. "Okay, what?"

"Uncle Jefferson taught me about DMA--"

"Do you mean DNA?"

She sighed. She wished she were smarter. "Yes. DNA. If these really are Jesus' bones, would DNA prove that I am his descendant?"

Miss Amanda blinked and then nodded. "Yes, yes it would. In fact, not only could it determine if you are his descendant, but it also could determine how closely related you are."

"Uncle Jefferson said I have as much of Jesus' blood in my veins as anyone else alive."

"If that is so," Amanda said as she raised an eyebrow, "then DNA testing could tell us that as well."

"Okay. Thank you."

Astarte edged away as the adults continued to talk. Turning her back, and typing as quickly as she could, she sent a text to Aunt Eliza; it would transmit as soon as they left the basement.

Hopefully Miss Amanda and Mr. Thorne wouldn't be too angry if they found out.

"What about security?" Mr. Cameron asked, motioning toward the door. "That's not much of a lock."

The priest shrugged. "Nobody knows what's down here, so what's the need for security? We tell people the bones of the architect who built the church are buried in the crypt. If we had an elaborate security system, it would just make people curious about what we might really be hiding." He paused. "And if they did know what we were hiding, no amount of security could keep it safe."

✝ ✝ ✝

Cam circled the crypt. "Is there any way to open it?" he asked. He meant it as more of a rhetorical question, but Father Jean answered nonetheless. "I am not a Templar Knight, so it is not for me to say."

Amanda turned on the priest. She was obviously still peeved about being locked up. "But it's in your church. You've been its caretakers for over 300 years." She didn't bother to mention that neither Cam nor she were Templars either.

"Yes, caretakers. But not owners. The only instructions that have been handed down to us through the centuries are, first, to preserve the crypt and second, to allow access to the crypt to those who have eyes that see." He paused. "As far as I know, you are its first visitors. The first who have eyes that see."

"So you wouldn't stop me if I took a chisel and tried to pry it open?" Cam asked.

"Stop you, no. I might counsel you not to be rash, to perhaps think about the ramifications of your actions. But presumably if you are wise enough to have discovered its location, you are wise enough to ... well, to not need my counsel." He clasped his hands behind his back again and took a small step backward.

Cam smiled at Amanda. "Well, no pressure on us, is there?"

"If I may," Georgia said. "I have some experience in public relations and in working with the media. I think, with Father Jean's help, that we could pretty quickly put together a press conference that would bring enough attention to you that it would prevent Trey Buckner from … doing anything stupid." She exhaled slowly. "But the question is, do we … or I should say do you … really want to let this cat out if its bag?"

"Yes, that is precisely the question," Amanda answered. "What's that line Mary Magdalene sings from *Jesus Christ Superstar*? 'He's a man. He's just a man.'" She looked at Father Jean. "Is the world ready for Jesus to be just a man?"

✠ ✠ ✠

"Unless you plan to attack the crypt now with your pocket knife, I suggest we go back upstairs and discuss your next move," Father Jean said. "And, yes, my motives are partly selfish: I am anxious to examine that scroll of yours."

Cam nodded. On the one hand the priest had locked them in the basement. On the other hand he had then freed them, and also showed them the crypt. And his story seemed to make sense—he wanted to make sure his visitors' story checked out before giving away the Basilica's centuries-old secrets. Cam decided to trust him. "Okay. And I'd like you to see the scroll. We're not one hundred percent convinced it's authentic—my guess is you might help with that."

Father Jean smiled. "You are correct. Part of the legend regarding the crypt is that the scroll will, within its text, contain a hidden authentication code."

Cam glanced at Amanda. This was actually good news, as it would be a check against another January hoax. Amanda was with him, plus one step ahead. "We'd like to film you examining the scroll," she said. "No doubt later on there will be those who question both its authenticity and its provenance."

He bowed to her request. "It's settled then." He paused and smiled. "I'm sure Astarte is hungry. And my hospitality has clearly been subpar. I will order some dinner and we can spread out comfortably." He turned to Astarte. "We have excellent French fries in Montreal, and also excellent pizza."

The girl bounced. "Can we have both?"

Smiling, Father Jean took her hand and led the group back up the stairs, bypassing the Basilica interior and leading them to a large conference room attached to the function hall in the rear of the church. A light knock on the door announced the arrival of the food as Cam and Amanda carefully unpacked the scroll and IN CAMERA stone on the conference room table. Amanda held up a pair of rubber gloves. "Food or artifacts, not both."

Father Jean reached out. "I'll feed my brain first. My stomach can wait."

Georgia also held out her hands. "Me, too."

Cam set Astarte up with some pizza on a side table far away from the artifacts as Amanda used her digital camera to film Father Jean examining the scroll, his lips moving as he silently read the Latin to himself. When he finished his eyes were moist and wide. He shook his head. "I had hoped the legends were incorrect. The bones of Jesus. It is a difficult thing to accept. But the words are clear, and the code authenticates the document."

Cam gave him a minute to compose himself before handing him a piece of paper. "This is my translation. Did I get it right?"

The priest shifted his eyes back and forth from the paper to the scroll. Finally he nodded. "Yes, perfectly." He took a deep breath. "May I ask where you found the scroll?"

"In the Catskill Mountains of New York," Amanda responded.

The priest nodded. "As our legend proclaims. And the stone was found with it?"

"Yes," Cam said. "We figured out that the Roman numerals were coordinates. Once we adjusted for the Paris prime meridian, the stone brought us right here."

"Father, you said there is a code which authenticates the scroll?" Georgia whispered. She was almost as stunned as the priest.

He nodded again. "The Church used to use simple codes and ciphers hidden within its messages to prevent forgeries. The Templars used more elaborate ciphers, but my guess is they resorted to something simple in this case because they anticipated they would be dealing with non-Templars." He pointed a rubber-gloved finger at the Latin text as together they leaned over the scroll. "Let's look at the first letter of the first line, the second letter of the second line, and so on." Amanda pulled out a pen and pad of paper as Father Jean called out the letters. "N, O, S, T, R, A, M, A, T, E, R." He looked up. "The next letter is an X, which usually means to stop."

Cam scrunched his face. "Nostramater? Sounds a bit like Nostradamus."

Father Jean smiled at Amanda. "Do you care to give it a try?"

A few seconds passed as she stared at the paper, the camera still running. "I get it. Nostra Mater. Our Mother. Notre Dame."

"Yes. A simple authentication cipher. And perhaps an explanation for the name of this Basilica."

Amanda turned to Cam. "Is there any way January would know about these codes?"

"I supposed he might. But why would he forge a document that undermined Christianity?"

"Okay, then who else might have forged it?"

Father Jean held up his hand. "My dear, there is no doubt in my mind as to the scroll's authenticity. As I said, we have been awaiting its arrival for almost 350 years."

A steely voice cut through the room. "That's a long time to wait. I'm sorry we're going to have to cut your visit so short."

✝ ✝ ✝

Cam spun to see Trey Buckner and his two henchmen, weapons drawn, shoulder to shoulder in front of the conference room door. Father Jean straightened himself slowly. "Put your guns away. This is a house of God."

Buckner lowered his revolver but motioned to his subordinates to maintain their positions. "You should know, Father, that I am here under the authority of the President of the United States, with the consent of the Prime Minister of Canada." It was an audacious claim, but Cam didn't doubt it.

Father Jean nodded. "And you should know I take my orders from a higher authority."

Buckner showed his teeth. "In this case, I actually think we could get the Pope on the phone."

"I wasn't talking about the Pope."

Buckner shrugged. "No matter." He slid his revolver into the holster inside his jacket and turned to Georgia. "I had a feeling we shouldn't trust you. But thanks for leading us here. We tracked your cell phone."

"But I powered it off," Georgia exclaimed.

Trey smirked. "Even with the power off the new cell phones can be tracked. Anyway, I need all of you to move away from the table. Go stand with the girl, over in the corner there." Cam thought about resisting but the numbers and weaponry were simply too one-sided. Buckner approached the table and examined the parchment.

"If you damage that scroll I'll make sure you spend the rest of your life in a Canadian jail," Father Jean said.

Before Buckner could respond his cell rang. It must have been a special ring tone because he answered the call right away.

✠ ✠ ✠

Eliza hissed into Trey's phone. "The scroll is a fake, a copy. The real one is at some lake house in Vermont. Get out of there, quickly. If you create an international incident over a fake scroll, there's going to be hell to pay."

Trey gently touched the brittle parchment. "Really? I'm looking at it now. It looks pretty old."

"Yes, and we all know how much archeological training you have."

His aunt could be a real bitch. He took a deep breath. "How do you know?"

"The girl texted me. I've been trying to call you for fifteen minutes."

They had lost reception inside the Basilica's stone walls. He stared at Astarte, huddled against Amanda's leg. "Could she be lying?"

"Trey, she's eight years old for God's sake." Eliza raised her voice. "Now get out of there. And bring the girl."

✠ ✠ ✠

Buckner removed his gun, bounded across the room and grabbed Amanda by the arm. Cam moved to intercept him but froze as the operative put the gun barrel to Amanda's head.

"Here's the deal," Buckner said. "I'm taking the girl. If you try to stop me I'll kill your fiancée. Very simple, choice A or choice B. There is no choice C."

What did the feds want with Astarte? It didn't make any sense, but Cam didn't have time to think about it now. His eyes swept the room, searching for a weapon or a plan or a quick escape. But Buckner was right; there was no choice C.

Buckner motioned for one of his cohorts to grab Astarte. The girl clutched Amanda's leg. "Don't let them take her, Cam." Amanda's eyes bore into him. How could he deny her? And would she ever forgive him if he did?

But they were checkmated. Buckner would not hesitate to kill Amanda; he had almost done so a few days ago. Amanda was of no use to him. But apparently Astarte was. Cam tried to buy some time. "I understand why the government wants to keep the Jesus bones stuff quiet. But what do you want with the girl?"

Ignoring the question, Buckner motioned to his underling, who pried a crying Astarte away from Amanda. Amanda made a move to stop him but Buckner pressed the barrel hard against her head, holding her in place. He likewise froze Cam with his eyes. Buckner's operative tucked the girl under his arm like a running back carrying a football, her feet kicking and arms flailing as he loped across the room.

It happened so fast that Cam almost missed it. Astarte purposely reached into her pocket and, still kicking and screaming, gently dropped her cell phone onto a chair as she was carried past.

Even more surprisingly, Buckner and the third operative rushed from the room without taking the scroll.

✠ ✠ ✠

Amanda dropped into a chair and covered her face with her hands. They took Astarte. The poor girl must be terrified. She knew she shouldn't be cross with Cam but she couldn't help herself. She pushed his comforting hand aside. "We should have stopped them." Her body convulsed as she sobbed, the chill spreading deeper into her than it had even during her kidnapping.

"There was no way, Amanda. He would have shot you. I saw it in his eyes. And then they would have taken Astarte anyway."

She nodded glumly. Father Jean had already phoned the local police; he was speaking rapidly in French, apparently trying to get them to pursue Buckner. But if what Buckner said was true, that his mission had been cleared by Canadian authorities....

"Now we need to focus on getting her back," Cam said. "And to do that we need to figure out what game Buckner is playing."

Georgia spoke. "I have no idea why he didn't take the scroll. That was the entire basis for our mission."

Cam reached down and grabbed Astarte's cell phone. "This might be a clue. Astarte dropped it here as she was being carried away. I'm pretty sure she did it on purpose."

Amanda lifted her head. "Really?" Cam handed it to her. She punched a few keys. "She texted someone less than an hour ago. A Connecticut number."

"Eliza," Cam said.

Amanda nodded. "Here's the message: *Scroll is fake. Real scroll is hidden in house on lake in Vermont.*" What was the girl up to?

"So that's who Buckner was talking to," Cam said. "Buckner is taking orders from Eliza."

"Wait," Georgia said, "Eliza is the girl's aunt?"

"Yes. January's sister."

"Then this must all have something to do with the Burrows Cave pieces," Georgia said.

"Astarte must have been helping Eliza help Buckner track us." Amanda paused. "But then something changed her mind and so she double-crossed her aunt with this text." She shook her head. "There sure is a lot going on inside that little brain of hers."

"Well, she bought us some time with the fake scroll lie," Cam said. "But at some point they're going to come back looking for it."

Amanda pictured the little girl being tossed into the trunk of a car. "That point needs to be now, Cam. We need to call Buckner and tell him the girl was lying, that the real scroll is here. And we need to somehow convince him to trade Astarte for the scroll. It's the only leverage we have over him."

Georgia weighed in. "If you give him the scroll he's going to bury it."

"Well, that's better than burying Astarte."

✛ ✛ ✛

Cam dialed Buckner's number.

"I'm listening, Thorne."

"The scroll is real. The one here with us."

"You really aren't very good at this."

"I'm serious. Astarte lied to Eliza. We know about the text. Which means we also know who you're working with."

Cam heard a catch in Buckner's voice. "Why would a little girl lie to her aunt about something like that?"

"It doesn't really matter why. The fact is the scroll here is the real one. Why else do you think we were showing it to Father Jean?"

Buckner didn't respond.

"You saw it. If it was a fake, it was a damn good one. And how would we have pulled that off? You think I carry a fake medieval scroll around with me? Face it. You got duped by an eight-year-old girl."

Cam heard Buckner giving hushed commands to his cohorts. Probably telling them to turn around. "So why are you telling me this?"

"We want to make a trade. The scroll for Astarte. We have no idea why you even took her."

"Did you think maybe her aunt wants her back?"

"What, so she can continue to brainwash the poor girl into thinking she's some kind of messiah? I don't think so."

"Sorry, no deal. We keep the girl. I'll just come back and take the scroll by force if I have to."

Cam played a bluff. "I wouldn't try that. Father Jean has some pretty close friends on the Montreal police force."

"Not buying it, Thorne. The police have been ordered to stay out of this."

"Well, before you say no to our offer, you might want to run it by Eliza. And you can tell her we'll throw in the devil's rock also. Somehow I don't think she'd like it if we proved to the world that Burrows Cave is a hoax."

"It is not a hoax."

"Whatever. Call me back in five. Otherwise we go public with the scroll and the bones and the Burrows Cave fake piece. I'm not sure what you and Eliza are trying to prove but I have a feeling that kind of publicity would not help your cause."

✠ ✠ ✠

Trey checked his watch. It had been only twenty minutes since they raced away from the Basilica the first time. Damn Montreal traffic. It had taken ten minutes just to go one mile. He should have trusted his instincts about the scroll and not listened to Eliza. The thing was old.

"Pull over right in front," he ordered. He sat in front with the long-nosed operative, whom he called Falcon. The other, whom he called Python because he had a slight lisp, sat in back with the girl. The men had performed well over the past three days—tireless, efficient and unquestioning. He hadn't even tried to learn their names.

As Falcon edged alongside the curb a movement near one of the Basilica's arched doorways caught Trey's eye. The church was supposed to be closed. "Hey, check out that person near the front door. Is that the Spencer woman?"

As he asked the question the young woman peered at the car before scampering back into the shadows. Astarte let out a short gasp. The bells of the church sang out.

Python had his binoculars out in a flash. "I think that is her. And she's carrying some kind of canister."

"The scroll," Trey said. "And she's trying to get away. Python, go!"

As Python opened the door the woman bolted, sprinting across the church plaza before cutting down a side street toward the waterfront, the operative less than half a block behind.

"Do you want me to go with him?" Falcon asked.

"No, stay with me. Python should have no trouble catching her." While they were here Trey wanted to get whatever other artifacts they might have. And he wouldn't mind getting the bones out of the church crypt also. Might as well end this nightmare once and for all.

Trey stepped out of the car. "We'll leave the girl here." They had tied Astarte's hands together and tightened her seat belt in the middle of the back seat—she wasn't going anywhere.

"Don't you need her to trade for the scroll?" Falcon asked.

Buckner rolled his eyes. "I'm not trading anything."

✠ ✠ ✠

Amanda ran down the narrow street, the Basilica looming on her right. The thwack-thwack-thwack of her pursuer's footsteps mixed with an occasional burst of anger from a pedestrian as he plowed after her. As she turned left down a brick-lined pedestrian walkway she tossed the funeral urn into a garbage can. Now unburdened, the urn having fooled the operatives into believing she carried the canister and scroll, she pumped her arms and shifted into a sprint. *Let's see how long this guy can go full speed.*

Two blocks later she risked a glance back. Khakis and a dark blue windbreaker. He had kept pace but was not gaining. Obviously she did not want to get caught. But nor did she want to totally lose him—her job was to keep him away from the Basilica. Despite her fear she smiled at the street sign ahead: Rue Saint Jean Baptiste. Perhaps a good omen. She cut right onto Jean Baptiste in front of a Marriott hotel tucked amid the old stone buildings, the road more alley than street, angling again toward the riverfront.

Her fear propelled her—her shoes flew across the pavement; her lungs sucked in the cool night air; her blood rushed oxygen to her muscles; even her ribs didn't throb. There was no way he could catch her. Not tonight.

And then a scream echoed off the stone buildings. Through the shouts in French one English voice stood out: "Watch out! That guy has a gun!" Amanda hunched and swerved reflexively. The blood pounded in her ears, muffling the sound of the shouts and her pursuer's footsteps.

Back at the Basilica, when Buckner had put a gun against her forehead, her fear had made her lightheaded and woozy. But she had understood, at least on an intellectual level, that even the CIA couldn't just waltz into a Canadian church and gun down five innocent people, including a priest. But here, on the street, where the assassin could take her out and disappear into the alleys of the city, she was incredibly vulnerable. Woozy could get her killed.

She needed to get to a more major thoroughfare. Sprinting, she leapt off the curb and cut left onto a cobblestone-paved road. She recognized historic Rue Saint Paul from their earlier walk from Bon-Secours Chapel. Now the street teemed with pedestrian and vehicular traffic. Good. Maybe there would even be a cop around.

Accelerating once more, she weaved her way along, her ears tuned to the sound of shoes clopping on pavement. If he slowed, or stopped, that might mean he was positioning himself for a shot. But she couldn't hear anything over the street noise so she risked another glance back. Still there. His face pink with exertion, he kept pace less than a half-block behind.

She glanced at her watch. She had been running for just over five minutes. So almost a mile. Too soon to stop. Cam needed more time. But he also might need help.

She kept her pace, her lungs beginning to burn. But fear was a wonderful motivator. Ahead, on the next block, a crowd massed outside a nightclub. She broke into a full sprint, hoping to buy a few extra seconds, slowing only to push her way through the pack. Shielded from view by the wall of people, she cut left into a restaurant, ducked behind a hostess station and peered out onto the street. "Angry boyfriend," she whispered to the startled hostess.

Five seconds later the operative sprinted past. Shivering despite her exertion, Amanda counted to ten. She stood, planning to step through the entryway and peer around the corner of the building. The hostess placed a protective arm on her shoulder. "Allow me," she said in a French accent as she trotted outside. "He is gone," she called through the door.

Exhaling loudly, Amanda smiled in thanks. Back on the street, she reversed direction, pushed through the wall of people and began to run once more.

If Cam could hold out another five minutes, she'd be there to help.

✙ ✙ ✙

Georgia waited in the shadows along the perimeter of the sanctuary. From her vantage point she would be able to both see Buckner enter and also make a quick dash to the staircase leading to the basement. While she waited she doused herself with some spray perfume she kept in her purse.

Cam leaned against a pew in the church nave, not far from the ornately-carved wooden staircase leading to the elevated pulpit containing the Delta of Enoch. Facing the rear of the church, he nodded to Georgia. Father Jean had rung the church bells, sending Amanda racing way. It wouldn't be long now.

Buckner and the one he called Falcon pushed through the front door and marched toward them, guns drawn. Good, there were only two of them. They must have taken Amanda's bait. Cam waited until they saw him. As they adjusted their course, Cam called out in a voice just loud enough for Buckner to hear, "Georgia, get the bones!" It was a childish ruse, but Buckner couldn't very well ignore it.

She bumped around to get their attention before yanking open the door to the basement stairs and bounding down. From above she heard Buckner's orders. "Follow her, Falcon. Don't let her do anything with those bones." Chauvinistic and cocky, Buckner would never suspect his operatives were being neutralized by women.

Heavy footsteps followed her down the stairwell. The hallway remained dimly lit. She pulled open the door to the prisoner room and slipped in, closing the steel door behind her. She held her breath and tried to control her breathing, the key grasped tightly in her sweaty hand as she pressed her back against the wall next to the door, her body partially concealed by a thick wooden post.

Five seconds later Falcon jumped down the final few stairs and froze in the hallway. Georgia could picture him, his gun drawn, evaluating the situation. Which of the doorways to explore first? He sniffed the air and grunted. He had her scent—not many women wearing perfume in the church basement.

He tiptoed toward her door, pulled it open and slipped into the room, his gun drawn. He crept forward slowly, the gun arcing in front of him, drawn to the flickering candle Georgia had placed at the far side of the room. Georgia waited until he had fully entered the room before spinning off the wall and scurrying out into the hall. She slammed the door closed just as a shot rang out, the bullet pinging against steel. Fingers shaking, she aimed the key at the lock, knowing she had only one chance at the target before the operative kicked the door back open. Her eyes wide, she shoved the key in the lock and turned. Click. Falcon's foot smashed into the door a split-second later.

✠ ✠ ✠

Buckner waved the gun as he approached Cam. "Where's Astarte?" Cam asked. He remained leaning against the pew, his body language relaxed and non-threatening. But his heart was racing.

"In the car. Where she's going to stay."

"Then you're not getting the artifacts."

Buckner aimed the gun at Cam's chest. "I think I am."

Cam forced his eyes away from the barrel and shrugged. "Amanda took the scroll, and no way is your man catching her. And the priest himself is long gone with the Burrows Cave artifacts; good luck finding him." Actually they were in Georgia's hotel room, which would no doubt be the next place Buckner looked once he left the Basilica. "So I've got nothing for you."

"That wasn't very smart of you. The scroll and the artifacts were your only bargaining chips."

"But like you said, you have no intention of freeing Astarte. So my bargaining chips weren't worth much."

"They might have saved your life."

"It seems to me they might have cost me it. At least now you need my help to retrieve them."

Over Buckner's shoulder Cam saw a movement in the vestibule of the church. A shadow edged up the side aisle, ducking behind the large statues that lined the perimeter of the church nave. "Enough games," Buckner said. "I want the artifacts. All of them."

Cam chewed his lip. Buckner hadn't demanded the scroll and he hadn't demanded the bones—he must have believed Amanda and Georgia were no match for his operatives. "We're just going in circles here. It's a stalemate."

Buckner leered at him. "Actually not. At this point I have not given orders for my man to kill Amanda, though he has captured her already." Was he bluffing? Buckner tapped the cell phone strapped to his belt. "But I will order her killed if necessary. I don't believe you that the priest has fled with the artifacts. Take me to them. Or your pretty fiancée dies."

Apparently Cam didn't answer quickly enough because without warning Buckner whipped his gun through the air, catching Cam on the cheek with the barrel. It was more a slapping impact than a crushing blow, but Cam staggered sideways and landed on one knee. Blood oozed from the side of his face and he spit out a piece of tooth. His cheek burned. It took a second but thankfully his head cleared. "Fuck you, Buckner. Put the gun away and let's see how tough you are."

"No time for that." The operative waved the gun. "Now, like I said, take me to the artifacts."

Being on the floor gave Cam a different sightline; he glanced toward the side aisle again. More movement. A candle flickered, illuminating a lithe female form. *Amanda.* She was okay. Thank God. She caught his eye, motioned with her head for Cam to come toward her. She must have heard their conversation as it echoed through the empty basilica. He made a show of glaring at Buckner before nodding and sighing. He pulled himself upright. "If I give you the artifacts, nobody gets hurt, right?"

"Once I have the artifacts you are of no threat to me."

"Amanda will be pissed if I let you keep Astarte."

"If Amanda is dead it won't matter how pissed she is." He tapped his cell phone.

Cam ground his teeth again to make it look good. "Okay," he hissed. "Follow me."

Cam limped across the nave and turned left along the aisle toward the front altar of the Basilica, as Amanda had motioned. Buckner trailed him, the gun held loosely by his side. Cam exaggerated his injury, hoping to further lure his adversary into a false sense of overconfidence. In the shadows ahead, Amanda disappeared through a doorway.

"Where are we going?" Buckner asked.

"The artifacts are back here," Cam said.

They pushed through an oak door into a smaller chapel area, built end-to-end with the Basilica. Cam made conversation, hoping to buy some time. "They built this chapel to accommodate smaller crowds. The Basilica is too big for regular services."

"Whatever. Just make it quick."

Cam limped down the center aisle of the chapel; a massive bronze sculpture loomed above them against the altar wall in the front of the chapel. A door panel set flush into the altar wall was slightly ajar, a rim of light visible around its frame. Cam began to head toward it but another movement in the shadows ahead redirected him. Again exaggerating his limp, he turned right as they approached a rope barrier in front of the altar. "I need to go around," he said.

Buckner followed close behind as they detoured around the rope, now approaching the altar from the side. The door loomed ahead. On their right a statue of John the Baptist stood above them atop an ornate wooden side altar, the bearded, barefoot figure clothed only in a sheepskin wrap with his normal shepherd's staff fashioned into a cross. *John the Baptist.* Draped across the statue's shoulder was a silk scarf. What was Amanda up to? Cam slowed.

As he passed the statue a voice, small but strong, cut through the silence from the main altar area. "That wasn't a very good knot." Astarte stood up from behind the chapel pulpit, her cobalt eyes ablaze with indignation. Amanda must have freed her.

Buckner turned toward the little princess. "How did you get out of the car?" He raised his gun.

As Buckner glared at Astarte, the John the Baptist statue and the side altar upon which it stood rocked, teetered and finally toppled toward him. Buckner turned and raised his arm to protect himself but the massive fixture crashed onto him, driving him to the ground and pinning him. His gun clattered away.

Amanda stepped out from behind the side altar, Georgia and Father Jean with her. It had taken the strength of all three to tip the fixture. Buckner moaned, shifting under the weight of the immense altar, the horizontal bar of the Baptist's crossed staff impaled partway into his shoulder. Cam grabbed the gun.

"Sorry about your statue, Father," Amanda said, her cheeks still red from her run. Her green eyes shone with excitement. She never looked more beautiful.

The priest smiled as he brushed the dust off his robe. "My guess is he was getting bored just standing there all these years. It was time for him to join the other Templars in battle."

CHAPTER 20

The Montreal police had refused to officially intervene in Buckner's mission, but they had no problem with Father Jean handling things as he saw fit. He made a phone call to a desk sergeant who served as a church deacon and within fifteen minutes a half dozen off-duty cops, many of them well into their Friday night beer, had arrived. They bound Buckner, corralled Python when he finally returned empty-handed from his pursuit of Amanda, and lastly retrieved Falcon from his cell.

"Please escort our three American guests to the border," Father Jean said. "And give this one something for the pain in his shoulder." He turned to Buckner. "I promise if you return to Montreal we will not be nearly so hospitable next time."

Father Jean accompanied the sergeant out to the street as the off-duty police deposited Buckner and his posse into the back of a windowless van. "Did they really bring guns into the Basilica?" the sergeant asked.

The priest nodded.

The sergeant kicked the ground and shuffled his feet for a few seconds before looking up at the priest. "Mind if we take the long way to the border?"

✝ ✝ ✝

Cam, Amanda, Astarte and Georgia had reassembled in the function room of the Basilica while Father Jean gave final instructions to the police sergeant. Amanda tended to Cam's wound, dabbing at the gash with a cloth napkin they found in the kitchen. Her ribs throbbed from the exertion of her run; she held an ice pack to her side with her free hand.

"I'm getting a bit tired of nursing you. Can't you take better care of yourself?"

Cam held up a piece of his tooth, which Astarte had found under one of the pews. "How are you at dentistry?"

The priest walked in and examined the gash on his cheek. "You're going to need stitches. Otherwise you're going to have a nasty scar."

"Like Frankenstein?" Astarte asked.

"Worse," Amanda said. "At least Frankenstein had a nice smile."

The priest nodded. "And I suppose we should try to get that tooth repaired as well. I'll make a call."

"And don't forget his knee," Amanda said.

Cam held up his hand. "We've got more important things to deal with. My boo-boos can wait."

"Nonsense," the priest said. "We can talk in the car. I'll drive. I have a good friend who's the team doctor for the Montreal Canadiens. They're playing tonight at the Bell Center, not too far from here. He can fix you up in no time. And there will be a dentist at the rink as well."

Amanda turned up her lip. "He's not going to look like one of those toothless hockey players is he?"

✙ ✙ ✙

They piled into Father Jean's Audi, the two men in the front. The priest had removed his black robe, but kept his clerical collar on over his black dress shirt. Amanda made a point of sitting behind Cam so she could see at least part of the priest's face as they talked—she didn't want to misread their conversation. Cam brought the ancient scroll; leaving it unguarded—in a Catholic church of all places—didn't seem like the wisest move.

The priest drove expertly, cutting down side streets and weaving his way through traffic. "This car is my one earthly indulgence, though I did buy it used. When I was a young man," he explained, "I used to race Formula One cars." He shrugged. "Now I'm in a race to save souls." He shook his head. "I'm sorry; that sounded sanctimonious."

Amanda smiled. "Perhaps what you meant was you try to steer people in the right direction."

He grinned and slapped the wheel. "Yes, yes, very good."

She turned serious. "Speaking of the right direction, what's our next move?"

"Good question," Cam said. "I sort of feel like the dog that caught the mail truck. What are we supposed to do now?"

The priest nodded. "As I said, in some ways we have been preparing for this moment for centuries. But at the same time we never believed it would arrive."

Amanda turned to Georgia. "You're the expert on this. Can the world handle the truth? Can the world accept Jesus' mortality?"

Georgia bit her lip. "I think people are more resilient than we give them credit for. So I think over time this kind of revelation might be okay."

Father Jean nodded again. "That is my belief as well. I believe the truth is holy, and must be honored as such. It is the cover-ups and the lies that undermine faith. And I believe there are those in the Vatican who agree with me on this."

"But how do you reveal something like this over time?" Cam asked. "Jesus was either immortal or he wasn't. There's not much middle ground."

The priest responded. "Sure there is: Jesus could be deemed immortal spiritually but not physically. And there are ways to pave the way for this type of revelation. An admission that he and Mary Magdalene were married and had children, for example. And then an emphasis placed on Jesus' siblings, to make him seen more human. And also perhaps a recognition that Mary and Joseph had a normal marriage that included sexual relations. Then, eventually, an admission that when Jesus was resurrected his soul ascended to heaven but his bones did not." The priest shrugged. "If this is done in small steps, I don't see it causing such a crisis."

"But doesn't Jesus' mortality undermine the entire basis for Christianity? How can a god be mortal in any sense?" Amanda asked.

"For those who look at religion in a purely rational sense, I suppose it might. But the part of our brain that deals with reason and logic is different than the part that deals with faith. So a physicist can still believe in heaven and a medical doctor can believe in a soul—as the doctor who is about to repair Cam's face does—even though there is no scientific basis for either. The discovery of Jesus' bones, even if proven conclusively through DNA and other evidence, will resonate in the 'reason' side of our brain. But for most people the 'faith' side will still believe in the things taught them at their parents' knee on a snowy Christmas morning."

"Despite all the evidence," Cam said.

"Yes, despite all evidence," Father Jean replied. It was an uncommon concession for a priest to make, but Father Jean was proving himself to be an uncommon member of the Catholic clergy. "And you need to realize: As compelling as the evidence is, it is not 100 percent conclusive. The science may prove that the bones belong to a 2,000-year-old Middle Eastern male, and that the scroll is an authentic 12th-century writing, and even that Astarte is a direct descendant of the person buried in the ossuary. But there are those who will still argue that this is all just circumstantial."

"But why would the Templars go to such trouble if the bones didn't belong to Jesus?" Amanda said. "They risked certain death if the Church found out what they were doing."

The priest shrugged. "I agree with you. But skeptics will say the Templars simply made a mistake. They got the wrong bones."

"And they just happen to be 2,000 years old, and from the Middle East?" Cam said. "And they happen to match Astarte's DNA? The odds on that being a coincidence are pretty long."

Father Jean smiled. "And that's why faith is such a powerful force. Faith ignores the odds."

The priest turned into the players' lot at the downtown arena and exchanged a few words with the guard, who bowed and waved him in. The game was at its midpoint, so there was little traffic around the sports complex. "Let me ask you a question, Cameron. Actually, two questions."

"Okay."

"First, do you believe in God?"

"Probably not in the way you mean, no."

Father Jean nodded. "But when you first saw Amanda in the Basilica tonight, and knew she was safe: What was your first thought?"

Cam smiled. "*Thank God.*"

The priest nodded again. "I thought as much. As the saying goes, there are no atheists in a fox hole. Your faith is strong even though you claim to have none. Faith is potent, and it is resilient. Most of all, it is not rational. The story of Jesus is powerful and it is instilled in Christians at an early age: God sent us his son to suffer on our behalf and lead us to salvation. If the Church announces it made a mistake, that the actual bones of Jesus did not ascend, that it was only a spiritual ascension rather than a physical one ... well, that changes a detail of the story but not the story itself. Perhaps to religious historians the revelation would be cataclysmic. But the average Christian would see it as a few buckets of sand removed from the beach. Jesus would be no less our Savior."

Father Jean parked the car. "And another thing, Cameron." He put his hand on Cam's shoulder as they walked toward the arena's side door. "You know that moment when the doctor takes out that big needle and brings it up close to your face and you get that queasy feeling in your stomach?"

"Yeah...."

He smiled. "Well, I better not hear you asking God for any mercy."

✠ ✠ ✠

The Novocain numbed Cam's face but at least the hockey doctors had closed his gash and capped his tooth. The knee would have to wait.

"I'll drop you back at your hotel," Father Jean said. The hotel was booked; they would get cots and share Georgia's room.

The group piled back into the Audi. "I am hoping you will join me at the Basilica for breakfast," the priest said. "The Vatican is sending an envoy by private jet. I have briefed them but not provided details. I'm certain he will be interested in your find."

Cam worked his tongue around the inside of his mouth, trying to get feeling back. "Of course we will listen to what the Vatican has to say. But this is not going to be like the Dead Sea Scrolls, with the Vatican trying to control and filter the information."

"I understand," the priest said. "You have custody of the scroll. And the bones are the property of the Basilica, not Rome. But I think you agree the Vatican deserves a seat at the table."

"As does the U.S. government," Georgia said. "And probably the Canadians as well." She had updated Hayek. Langley had already shifted to damage control, claiming Buckner was acting on his own. "Obviously we do not want to cause unrest or turmoil in the Middle East."

Amanda rolled her eyes. "The U.S. government can pound sand as far as I'm concerned."

Cam smiled. "I'm with Amanda on that. But I think we'd be okay if Georgia joined us for breakfast."

Amanda said, "And let's not forget that Astarte needs to be part of any decisions we make." The girl leaned against Amanda's shoulder, barely awake. "She found the scroll, and she is the Fortieth Princess. None of us would be here were it not for her."

Father Jean stopped in front of the hotel. "Very well then," said the priest as he stepped from the vehicle. "I will see you all at eight o'clock at the Basilica." He smiled at the girl. "Astarte, I would appreciate it if you would sit next to me. The men from the Vatican often wear funny-looking clothes; you will have to keep me from laughing."

✠ ✠ ✠

Amanda felt exhausted. And she wanted a shower. And a glass of wine. And maybe a big bowl of popcorn. And a massage. Yes, definitely a massage. But at least cold fear no longer numbed her core.

They requested the cots and took the elevator to the fourth floor. Amanda immediately opened the closet to check on the artifacts. She gasped. The closet was empty. "That's where we left them, right?" she said. The blanket they had covered them with lay crumpled on the floor. Amanda lifted it, knowing nothing lay beneath. They stared into the empty closet. "Damn it," she breathed.

"It had to be Eliza," Cam finally said. "Buckner and his men are in the back of some van—Father Jean just spoke to the sergeant twenty minutes ago. And nobody else knew about them."

"What about Georgia's boss?" Amanda asked. She plopped onto one of the beds; she was tired and frustrated and angry and … well, just ready to be done with all of this. Astarte sat next to her and patted her knee while Cam and Georgia plopped into chairs. The room smelled stale. Or maybe it was them.

"Hayek is trying to wash his hands of this," Georgia said. "Besides, he doesn't care about the Burrows Cave pieces or even the urn with the ashes. He cares about the Clairvaux Codex and the scroll, which we still have. And of course the bones themselves, assuming they are in the crypt."

"Again," Cam said, "we're back to Eliza. She wants to keep the Isis piece quiet—obviously the writing on the back reveals it as a fake. But why should she care so much?"

"I would think that is fairly obvious." Eliza appeared in the foyer of the room, gun drawn, her hair pulled tightly into a bun above the high collar of a blue, long-sleeved house dress. Amanda lurched off the bed. Eliza waved the gun at her, her small teeth visible beneath her sneer. "They are called the devil's stones for a reason."

✝ ✝ ✝

Eliza considered her options. She had hoped to make a quick escape with the artifacts before they returned. But this might work out for the better. "I will take Astarte, of course. And Thorne, you will come along also; you will carry the artifacts. They are in the bathtub. I will need the scroll as well."

"But why, Aunt Eliza?" Astarte asked. "I would like to stay with Miss Amanda. And Mr. Cameron. I think we could all be friends once you get to know them."

"Nonsense. They have become a liability to us. And to you. You will never take your role as the Fortieth Princess if you remain with these fools."

"I don't understand."

Eliza sighed. "I suppose you have the right to know." And it would be better if the girl came voluntarily; she had already shown how resourceful she could be. "Everyone sit on the bed. Hands behind your head." She motioned with her .38 Smith and Wesson, equipped with silencer.

She focused her words on Astarte, but watched the others for any sudden movement. "This all begins back in the 1870s, just after the Civil War. Many of the Mormons had gone to Utah with Brigham Young. But my family stayed in Illinois. My great-great-grandmother Sarah was a teenager at the time." The story had been told dozens of time, mother to daughter, over the decades. "She was walking in the woods near the family farm with her younger sister. They stumbled upon an underground cave filled with carved stones. They brought a few of the stones home to show their mother, who showed them to her sister, Sarah's aunt. For the next few months the four of them returned to the cave every chance they got, studying the artifacts. There were many rooms in the cave complex, and thousands of artifacts in them."

Usually the story was told to girls on their tenth birthday. But this was not a usual circumstance, and Astarte not a usual girl. Eliza continued. "Sarah was a brilliant girl, and very spiritual. One night the prophet Joseph Smith came to her in a dream and gave her instructions which he said were crucial to the survival of the Mormon Church. He ordered Sarah and her mother to travel to Salt Lake City to tell Brigham Young about the cave and her dream, which they did."

"What was the dream about?" Astarte asked. She had always loved these kinds of stories, and her curiosity outweighed her apprehension at seeing her aunt wave a gun at her new friends.

"I'll get to that." Eliza cleared her throat. "The carvings on the stones supported many of the stories in the Book of Mormon. But a few of the carved stones contradicted the Book, and other parts of the Book described events which the stones didn't mention."

The Spencer woman interrupted. "Imagine that? And here all along I thought your Book of Mormon was the word of God."

Eliza ignored her. "Brigham Young had heard legends of the cave from some of the Mandan elders—their oral history told of a cave holding artifacts and gold of an ancient people. But so many of the Mandan had died that the cave's location had been lost. So he was very excited about Sarah's discovery, and about her dream." She spoke to Astarte. "So Sarah did all the things Joseph Smith told her to do in her dream. She removed the artifacts that did not agree with the stories in the Book of Mormon. And she was artistic enough and knowledgeable enough about history and the Bible to create other artifacts that filled in the gaps. She also created pieces that supported the claims of the Mandan Fortieth Princess—this had become part of Brigham Young's vision for the Mormon Church. Not that Mormon leaders today wanted anything to do with it. She even put bars of gold that Brigham Young gave her in the cave to make it seem even more authentic—who would bury gold as a hoax? Then, as Joseph Smith instructed, she sealed the cave back up."

"Why did she close the cave?" Astarte asked.

"Because the artifacts needed time to age and weather. Joseph Smith told Sarah that her descendants needed to wait a hundred years before the cave could be discovered. And the person who found it should not be a Mormon. So beginning in the 1970s the women of our family—I was a teenager at the time—exposed the cave opening." By that time nobody in Salt Lake City had any memory of the matriarchs' plan—and if they did they never would have supported it. The Mormon leaders had turned conservative and timid, a bunch of momma's boys. Heck, Jefferson couldn't even convince them to take his research seriously.

Eliza continued. "We tried to lure treasure-hunters to the area with rumors of valuables hidden in the woods. It took a few years but eventually Russell Burrows found the cave in 1982." She paused. "It might have been better if the cave had been discovered by someone else. But the Lord works in mysterious ways."

"The Lord has nothing to do with this," the Spencer woman said.

Eliza had ignored the first snide comment. But it was time to put the uppity Brit in her place. "Brave words." She waved her gun under the tart's nose. "But God seems to have brought us to this point—me with a gun and you cowering on a bed." She paused. "Things have not proceeded exactly as we planned. But Jesus' bones will prove Astarte's royal lineage through DNA testing—we hadn't counted on that piece of good fate. And even if the Vatican buries the bones, the ancient scroll you found proves the validity of the Clairvaux Codex, which proves the story of Burrows Cave and the artifacts. All we need to do now is destroy the devil's rocks. Then the evidence proving both the Book of Mormon and Astarte's royal lineage will be one hundred percent convincing."

Eliza had been watching for Thorne's reaction as she spoke. He had seen the actual cave, studied the artifacts. He knew how compelling they were. As a historian, he would argue for the artifacts' authenticity even if he didn't like the result. She turned to him. "Jefferson was smart to find you. You have finished his quest." After decades of work and planning things were finally coming together.

Finally Thorne responded, his voice little more than a whisper. "So the Burrows Cave pieces are authentic...."

"Yes, other than a few dozen pieces carved by my family. Like the Isis Stone. We needed that one to demonstrate the connection between Astarte's bloodline and the Egyptian royal line of Cleopatra. Thankfully Jefferson pulled the Isis piece from the collection before anyone discovered its flaw. But the other pieces—thousands of them—are authentic."

Thorne shook his head. "That is amazing. In some ways more amazing than the bones of Jesus. To think ancient explorers were in America's heartland more than two thousand years ago...."

"Not just any ancient explorers," Eliza said. "We know exactly who they were. And why they were here. God describes it all for us right in the Book of Mormon."

The Spencer woman rolled her eyes, her hands still atop her head. "You just admitted you cooked the books. Or cooked the book, as it were. The artifacts tell an entirely different story."

Eliza had had enough. She fired a quick shot, aiming for the triangle between the crook of the sassy Brit's elbow and her ear. The bullet nicked her sleeve and thudded into the wall above the headboard—well away from Astarte, of course. The Spencer woman screeched. "I'm getting sick of your mouth," Eliza hissed.

Astarte began to cry. "Come with me, Astarte," Eliza said. "This instant. You too, Thorne." She glared at the Brit cowering on the bed. "I won't miss next time."

✠ ✠ ✠

Cam scrambled to obey Eliza's order to retrieve the pack she had stashed in the bathtub. Anything to get the crazy woman and her loaded gun away from Amanda. He exhaled as the hotel room door latched shut behind them, his only farewell a fleeting glance at his fiancée, wide-eyed in fear on the bed.

"Take the stairs," Eliza ordered. He limped ahead, with Astarte walking alongside her aunt stoically. She had hugged Amanda before following her aunt, but the echo of the gunshot in the room had ended any debate about whether Astarte would accompany her aunt.

Cam exaggerated his limp, the pack of artifacts draped over one shoulder, hoping to slow their pace to buy some time. He considered trying to overpower Eliza, but she was a large-boned woman who wasn't afraid to use that gun. And she had, smartly, left herself unburdened by the heavy pack. In her shoes, Cam would just use himself as a pack mule to reach her car and dump him at the hotel curb. If that was the case, he'd better do something quickly or the artifacts—and Astarte—might be lost forever.

Eliza would not harm Astarte, at least not in the physical sense. But she would destroy the artifacts. Part of him remained numb at the realization that the Burrows Cave carvings were authentic. Every history book in America would need to be rewritten.

And if Eliza had her way, every Bible would need to be rewritten as well.

✠ ✠ ✠

They approached the stairwell. Eliza had a decision to make. She had made a deal with the love-struck mercenary, Salazar—he had tracked Thorne and Spencer and supplied her with a master pass-card that would unlock the hotel room door. Was she ready to betray him? No, it was too soon. She might still need his help. Already outnumbered, she didn't need another enemy.

"Astarte, wait here," she said as Thorne, ahead of them, reached for the stairwell door. She pushed the girl into a gap between the ice machine and the wall, the whir of the machine masking the noises of the hotel. The recent gunshot had numbed the usually-irrepressible girl into obedience. As Thorne pushed open the stairway door a pair of hands reached out and ensnared him in a chokehold. Eliza grabbed for the strap of Thorne's backpack and lifted the pack off of him as he writhed to the floor. She allowed the door to close behind her as she stepped back into the hallway, the sound of the men scuffling muffled behind the thick door.

As she had promised Salazar, the girl hadn't seen—or heard—a thing. "Come with me, Astarte. We will take the elevator after all."

✚ ✚ ✚

Salazar's right arm encircled Thorne's neck, pressuring and constricting his enemy's windpipe. But somehow Thorne had managed to slide his arm inside the choke hold, partially blocking it. This was taking longer than Salazar had planned. Didn't Thorne realize who the true alpha male was?

Salazar's plan required him to make quick work of Thorne on the stairwell landing before rushing to the street below to rescue Astarte from the crazy Mormon woman. He would blame Thorne's death on the Mormon woman's "accomplice"—he would need to kill her as well to keep the story from unraveling—and return the young girl to an appreciative Amanda. The plan was far from perfect but in the field you improvised as best you could. And it was worth the risk. With Thorne out of the way, he and Amanda would finally be able to build a life together.

But first he needed to subdue Thorne, who was much stronger than he looked. And who apparently felt he had a lot to live for.

☩ ☩ ☩

Instead of surprise or even fear Cam's first reaction at being grabbed around the neck was anger. Hadn't he gone through enough today? But when he realized his assailant was Salazar his anger turned to rage. "What the fuck are you doing?" he gasped.

The mercenary did not respond verbally. But the extra pressure on Cam's windpipe was answer enough. Rage turned to panic. Cam had already lost strength from the lack of oxygen; a few more seconds would be fatal.

Cam writhed, aiming his free elbow at the mercenary's face while simultaneously trying to spin away. But Salazar held—he was stronger than Cam, and he had the advantage of the dominant position due to his surprise attack. But Cam wasn't going to die without a fight.

The red railing atop the landing gave Cam an idea. Under the guise of trying to spin away Cam worked himself closer to the rail. He threw another wild elbow, forcing Salazar to duck. In the next instant Cam lifted both feet, planted them against the railing and pushed backward. Salazar, slightly off-balance from ducking the elbow, had no leverage to defend the maneuver and the two men careened back into the cement wall, Salazar absorbing the force of Cam's body against his. The mercenary grunted, his grip loosening, and Cam threw another elbow. This one connected to Salazar's jaw, catapulting his head back a second time against the cement wall. He staggered as Cam broke free.

Eyes wild, Salazar shook his head clear and snorted. Bellowing with fury he charged at Cam like a rhino meeting the challenge of a young bull. Cam rose up to engage him, inviting the charge, two bucks replaying the timeless primeval struggle over male domination. Who would fertilize the herd, whose genes would live on?

But Cam was not a beast. At the last instant before shoulders and chests collided he ducked and spun from Salazar's charge like a matador avoiding a bull. As Salazar's momentum carried him past, Cam shoved him in the back, propelling him even more violently toward the railing. Up and over the barrier the mercenary went, somersaulting, his fingers clawing at the rail. Cam spun to watch his adversary fall, his body rag-dolling off the steel railings lining the central stair well. Three stories later Salazar's body finally thudded off the cement landing on the ground floor.

Cam had no interest in descending to see if his motionless adversary had survived the fall.

✝ ✝ ✝

Amanda took a second to fight back the tears, wrapping her arms around herself to stop from shaking and to allow the echo of the gunshot to fade. Eyes closed, she took three deep breaths. She could actually smell the gunpowder residue. But enough of that. Cam and Astarte were in danger. She jumped off the bed.

Her first inclination was to run after them. But Georgia put a hand on her arm. "Hold on, cowgirl. If you step into that hallway and she sees you, she'll shoot you."

Amanda nodded. "You're right."

"I'll call Father Jean and ask for help. Look out the window and see if you can spot them."

Less than a minute passed before Amanda saw Eliza pulling Astarte into a grey SUV. But where was Cam? Amanda gave the plate number to Georgia and sprinted from the room. She plowed through the stairwell door, shocked to see Cam standing there. His face was red and scratch marks ran up and down his neck. Panting, he smiled weakly. "Are you okay?" she asked.

"Fine." He took her hand and spun her gently. "But not this stairwell. Salazar's down there."

"Salazar?"

"Long story—I'll tell you later. But let's find Astarte first."

"They got into Eliza's car. Hurry!"

"Eliza has the artifacts also," Cam said.

The ding of the elevator bell drew them, racing, back down the hallway. Amanda arrived first and jabbed at the buttons. She took the opportunity to embrace Cam as the car descended. His heart pounded against her. "Are you okay?" she asked again.

"Yes. But Salazar isn't."

She shuddered. "Is that how Eliza found us? With Salazar's help?"

He nodded. "He tried to kill me."

She kissed him. "I think this is my fault. I think he has a crush on me."

He rubbed her cheek with the back of his hand. "Some crush. Not that I blame him." The elevator slowed. "How was the traffic out there?"

"Quite heavy, actually."

"Good." Cam glanced at his watch. "The hockey game just ended. Hopefully it was a big crowd."

✠ ✠ ✠

The elevator door slid open as they hit the first floor. "Go," said Cam. "I can't run. I'll try to follow but this is going to have to be you. "

Amanda nodded and kissed him again quickly. "I'm off."

"Just follow," he yelled. "Don't get too close!"

She bolted through the hotel lobby and turned right out the front door. Fortunately most Canadians drove sedans so Eliza's gray SUV should be easy to spot. Amanda raced to the next intersection. No sign of the SUV. Traffic flowed straight and right, the street to the right being the larger road. Without hesitation Amanda cut right and sprinted. Astarte needed her.

As she approached the next block traffic clogged outside the main bus terminal. She pictured a map of the city in her head. Straight would put Eliza deeper into the hockey traffic. A left on Rue Berri would take her toward Old Montreal, from where she could merge onto Route 720 and head south to the United States. Assuming the woman had a GPS or even a good map, that would be the choice.

Was it only a few hours ago she had sprinted these same streets? Ahead in traffic she glimpsed a gray roof protruding above the line of cars. She pumped her arms, her eyes glued to the metal of the SUV. The light changed and the car jerked ahead, the flashing of its brake lights betraying the driver's impatience. It had to be them.

Slowing slightly she pulled out her phone and directed Cam to her route. "I think she will be getting on Route 720. Perhaps Father Jean can do something." Sprinting again, she closed the gap to half a block. But traffic was thinning a bit. And of course once they reached the highway there was no way Amanda could keep pace.

The light ahead flashed yellow and then red. This was her only chance. Using the pedestrians to shield herself, she dodged her way forward, reaching the car just as the light turned green. Now what? The doors would be locked, and she had no weapon. Her only hope was the crowd around her. She raced from the sidewalk and leapt onto the hood of the car. "Help," she yelled. "This woman is kidnapping my daughter!"

Eliza reacted immediately. She spun the wheel and, screeching forward, U-turned into the opposite lane of traffic. Still on the hood, Amanda gripped the rim beneath the front windshield, her legs swinging from the centrifugal force of the turn. Horns honked as Eliza raced up the incline, Amanda barely hanging on. Her heart pounded as her fingers dug into the metal. Now what?

✝ ✝ ✝

Cam dragged his left leg along the route Amanda had given. She had far outdistanced him but he couldn't just stand there and wait for her at the hotel. Maybe he'd see a policeman or an idling cab....

Or a scooter. A young man, probably a college student, hopped off an electric scooter in front of a pizza parlor. Cam jumped in front of him. "Do you speak English?"

"Yes, a little."

Cam pulled out his wallet. "This is an emergency. I need your scooter. Here is all my money and my credit cards and my driver's license. I'll be back soon." Without waiting for a response he pulled the cycle to him, mounted it and sped off.

Barely slowing, he raced through an intersection. From the far end of the block a gray SUV careened toward him, a blanket or some other debris atop its hood. He slowed. *Amanda.* The crazy Eliza was swerving and braking, trying to dislodge her. No way would Amanda survive if she fell under the tires.

Cam had only a few seconds to react. Bending low so Eliza wouldn't recognize him he edged the scooter toward the road's center line, slowing as the SUV bore down on him. At the last second he cut hard to the left, the scooter skidding into the opposite lane as he leapt free and rolled to the pavement.

✝ ✝ ✝

Amanda had never been so frightened in her life. The gunshot in the hotel room had whizzed by her ear, death only inches away. But the danger was fleeting. This, now, clutching the rim of the hood with every ounce of strength while a madwoman tried to dislodge her, was like being on a never-ending carnival ride without a safety harness. She couldn't hold on forever—at any instant she might soar through the air and splat onto the pavement like a bug on a windshield. If only she could get a better grip with her feet....

The SUV swerved suddenly to the right. Amanda strained to maintain her grasp. She barely heard the blare of the horn only inches from her ear. The vehicle thumped and skidded, metal grinding against metal as the SUV collided with something. Whatever it was had lodged itself into the vehicle's undercarriage, apparently causing the swerve. Amanda glanced over just in time to brace herself and swing her legs away before the SUV crashed into a sign post.

The sudden stop ripped her fingers away, catapulting her forward off the hood. She flew toward the sidewalk, mitigating the impact of the fall by forcing her body to roll and tumble with it. She thumped to a stop against the front wall of a brick building. Blinking, she did a quick survey of her body. Scrapes and bruises, but nothing seemed to be broken. Or the adrenaline was masking it.

She rolled to her knees just as Eliza pulled Astarte from the SUV. Holding the girl in front of her, Eliza marched toward her, gun in hand. "Idiot," the woman screamed. "The hand of God is directing me. Who are you to try to stop me?"

Amanda pointed her chin at the scooter wedged under the SUV. "Apparently God isn't much of a driver."

"I'm tired of your insolence." She raised the gun and closed one eye, the other eye cold and hard. "And your interference." Amanda froze in fear. Would Eliza really shoot her here on the street, in front of the girl and all these witnesses?

Amanda said a silent prayer. Father Jean was right—in moments of peril faith overcame reason.

✠ ✠ ✠

Cam was getting really sick of jerks pointing their guns at Amanda. He probably could have disarmed Eliza with a simple karate chop to the back of her wrist. But he didn't want to take any chances. Plus four days worth of rage had built up in him. He rushed up from behind and, two hands clasped over his head, clubbed Eliza across the back of the neck. She crumpled to the ground, her gun skidding away as the skirts of her house dress bunched at her knees.

Astarte edged away from her aunt but not all the way to Amanda, torn between her destiny and her desires. After a few seconds she swallowed and lifted her glistening blue eyes to Amanda. "I guess God doesn't want me to be the Fortieth Princess."

From her knees Amanda reached out and took the girl's hand. "On the contrary. God has cleared the path for you. He wants you to be anything *you* want to be. Including the Fortieth Princess."

CHAPTER 21

Cam had awoken early, dreams of gunshots and skeletons and needles haunting his sleep. Not to mention the lumpy cot in Georgia's room. But at least the worst was over for him, as well as for Amanda and Astarte. Eliza, on the other hand, languished in a Montreal jail while Salazar remained unconscious in a hospital with a fractured skull and internal bleeding. And some poor Vatican envoy, who had just taken the red-eye across the Atlantic, faced the prospect of some unpleasant conversations with his superiors in Rome later today.

As requested, Astarte sat at the right hand of Father Jean during the 8:00 breakfast. Amanda sat next to Astarte with Cam positioned to the priest's left and Georgia next to him; the envoy sat at the foot of the table. Along the side wall a representative from the Canadian government and an assistant to the envoy sipped at coffee, observing. The scroll and the artifacts, cushioned carefully in Cam's pack, sat under the table at his feet.

As the priest had predicted, the Vatican envoy—a younger, heavy-set man with ruddy cheeks—looked a bit silly in his red-buttoned black robe and cape, complete with pink satin sash and skull cap. "He looks like one of the Russian soldiers in *Anastasia*," Astarte giggled as the envoy consulted with his aid. She had surprised Cam by waking up cheerful and energized; Amanda explained that children who viewed themselves as heroes rather than victims tended to be very resilient. No questioning which category Astarte fell into.

"Yes," the priest responded to Astarte in a whisper. "All he would need is a taller hat and a sword."

They made small talk for a few minutes, Cam taking the opportunity to finish his French toast. It seemed like the first meal he had actually savored in weeks. Father Jean theatrically put down his fork and wiped his mouth with his napkin. "So," he said, "we have some decisions to make."

The envoy responded immediately. He smiled a lot as he spoke, with just a hint of a German accent. The Vatican had chosen well—the envoy was warm and likeable, the chubby boy at school who was always sharing his candy and helping the other kids with their homework. He spread his hands. "We thank you for your extraordinary efforts. Your research is truly remarkable, as is this discovery." He continued on for a few more minutes, praising Cam and Amanda as well as Father Jean. "You should also know we are not entirely surprised by your discovery." He paused. "This revelation was hinted at when the Templars were first put on trial in the early 1300s. One Templar knight in particular taunted the Pope with this information just before his death."

"So the Church knew about the bones?" Cam asked.

"Again, it was hinted at. The Templars were nothing if not resourceful. We had hoped that the bones, and the ancient scrolls recording the story behind them, had been lost to history. But now that they appear to have been found we must face reality. To that end, we would like to take the scroll and the bones back to Rome for further study."

Cam nodded. The envoy knew they would never agree to that; he was hoping to negotiate back to some middle ground. Cam didn't blame him, but the reality was that he and Amanda didn't trust the Vatican no matter how charming its emissary. He cleared his throat. "I want to make it clear that neither Amanda nor I are anti-Church. We understand how important your works are to millions of people around the world. We do not want to do anything to alienate Catholics from their faith."

The emissary bowed. "Thank you, for that. There are some who are passionate in their opposition to the Church for personal or even historic reasons. We are not perfect, but on balance our good works outweigh the harm we do." He smiled sadly. "Perhaps that was not always the case. But it is so now."

Amanda nodded. "And Cameron and I agree with that." She looked at Cam. "But we also feel that the truth must be paramount. This story must be told."

Cam continued. "And because of that we are not comfortable with the scroll and the bones being taken back to Rome." He didn't need to insult the envoy by stating the obvious—that the temptation to alter the test results or even destroy the evidence would be too great.

Father Jean knew his job was to facilitate discussion and eventually compromise. "Perhaps the Vatican could send its experts here to Montreal." He glanced at the Canadian official who nodded slightly. "Especially as I don't think the national government would approve of the artifacts leaving our jurisdiction."

They went back and forth like this for an hour, Cam trying not to get frustrated by the positions taken by the Vatican representative. The scroll and bones would have a huge impact on the Catholic faith and the Vatican clearly wanted to take steps to mitigate the damage. And Cam was willing to give those concerns due weight. But giving the Vatican a seat at the table was different than letting them call the shots.

"You must understand," the envoy said, "we cannot have information like this made public until it has been verified beyond the slightest doubt. What is your expression? We cannot put the toothpaste back in the tube once it is out."

"We get that," Cam said, motioning to include Amanda and Georgia. "We really do. But we fear that your definition of 'beyond the slightest doubt' is a standard that no amount of science will ever satisfy. The Vatican will be tempted to bury this forever." Cam sat up straight in his chair. "Over the past few days we've been shot at, locked up, kidnapped, hunted down, beat up … you name it. All because of this scroll. So we think we've earned the right to determine its fate. We agreed to meet with you because we agree the Vatican should have a say as to how and even when this information will be revealed. But the question of *if* it will be revealed is not negotiable. And I think the Vatican needs to acknowledge and accept this before we are going to get anywhere today."

Before the envoy could respond Father Jean stood. "I think it is time for a recess." He smiled at the envoy. "I'm sure the Emissary would like to consult with his superiors." He turned next to Cam. "Perhaps you and Amanda would join me? I'm sure Georgia would be happy to watch Astarte for a few minutes."

"Where to?" Amanda asked.

He smiled. "Sometimes things must be seen, must be felt. Sometimes words are not enough." He nodded to Cam. "And of course you may bring the artifacts and scroll with you."

✠ ✠ ✠

Father Jean led them back to the nave of the Basilica. The massive sanctuary was almost full. "This is a funeral," the priest whispered. "A young boy, Serge, seven years old, died in a tragic accident. He fell through some thin ice and drowned."

"Why are we here?" Cam asked.

The priest focused on a spot high on the altar. "Over the years I have had many doubts about my calling, about the Church. So much wickedness has been done in its name." He sighed. "The recent sexual abuse incidents are the most troubling. Such wrongdoing, such arrogance, such ... evil." He shook his head. "But then there are days like today when I see how much comfort we offer at times of death. Look around. Observe the mourners. Nothing can make up for the loss of a child, but families are comforted by the thought that their loved one is sitting by the side of Jesus in heaven." He smiled sadly. "In moments like this I believe strongly in the goodness of the Church."

Cam and Amanda sat in a pew not far from the pulpit emblazoned with the Delta of Enoch. Holding hands, they observed. A burly man in the pew in front of them crossed himself and dabbed at his eyes with a tissue. An old woman across the way dropped to her knees and prayed, her hands clasped around rosary beads. A young girl leaned against her father's leg, wide-eyed at the majesty surrounding her. When the priest declared that young Serge had gone to heaven to be with Jesus, a collective sob erupted within the Basilica, Cam and Amanda included.

As the service came to a close Father Jean leaned over. "This is a good thing, the succor we give. As I said before, I believe truth is holy. And I believe the Church keeping secrets from its parishioners is wrong. But I also realize that in the real world change takes time." His eyes were moist as he scanned the crowd of mourners. "So please think long and hard before you do something rash, before you do something that undermines our ability to provide comfort and solace to our flock. Jesus may not have been resurrected, but the idea of him welcoming and caring for little Serge is perhaps the only thing keeping his family from jumping into that frozen lake to join him."

The priest clasped his hands in prayer. "It may be true what you say, that the Templars called Jesus the Thief on the Cross. But if you take Jesus from these people it is you who will be stealing something truly irreplaceable."

✛ ✛ ✛

A half-hour later they gathered again in the function room of the Basilica. Cam and Amanda had huddled with Astarte and Georgia. They were all in agreement, brought to a compromise position by Father Jean's heartfelt words. Cam addressed the Vatican envoy. "This is what we are prepared to do. We think it will allow the Vatican to manage the fallout from all this but also ensure that the information is not buried."

"Please proceed," the envoy said, adjusting his pink skull cap.

Cam outlined their proposal: He and Amanda would maintain custody of the scroll, which would be tested in Boston. The bones would remain in Montreal at the Basilica, with Father Jean overseeing the DNA testing. Astarte's DNA would also be tested and compared to the bones. "We are nearly certain the scroll will be found to be authentic. And we expect the DNA will show a close genetic connection between Astarte and the bones. The DNA will also likely show the bones belong to a 2,000-year-old Middle Eastern male." Cam paused. "However, out of respect for the Church, we will agree to wait until Astarte's eighteenth birthday before making any of this public. At that time we will announce we have found the bones of Jesus and, if she chooses, also introduce Astarte as the Fortieth Princess and lay out her lineage. Here's the part you're not going to like: The Vatican will confirm our findings at that time."

"Confirm them? Why would we do that?"

Father Jean responded. "Because it is the truth, Emissary. And the truth must be made holy."

The group sat in silence for a few seconds, considering Father Jean's words.

Cam continued, his voice lower now. "The delay gives the Vatican ten years to prepare its parishioners for these revelations, to begin to turn the ocean liner. I suggest you adopt Father Jean's recommendation and begin by acknowledging Jesus' marriage to Mary Magdalene. But that is up to you."

The envoy nodded, again adjusting his skull cap. "We appreciate the offer of a ten-year delay. And though I and others may agree with Father Jean about the importance of truth, there are many in the Vatican who will never acknowledge Jesus' mortality no matter how strong the science or how long the delay."

Cam nodded. "Thank you for your candor. And that's why we can't let these bones go back to Rome with you. As for the hard-liners, in some ways our giving you an ultimatum should help you deal with them. You can present it to them as a take-it-or-leave-it scenario. If they reject our proposal, we will go public immediately."

The envoy rubbed his fleshy chin. "Yes, that might help." He gazed up at the ceiling. "I am also concerned that some in the Vatican might order the Basilica to cede the bones to the Vatican immediately. It would be a difficult order for Father Jean to ignore."

Cam smiled. It was a subtle threat, well-played. "I am curious how the argument to turn the bones over would be made," Cam said. "Clearly the Vatican would have a valid claim to the bones of Jesus. But how would the Vatican assert that claim without first acknowledging the possibility that the bones existed? Either the bones ascended to heaven or not—they can't be in two places."

"Well-argued, Mr. Thorne," the envoy said, smiling.

Amanda jumped in. "There are two more things, Emissary. First, Cameron and I would like free and complete access to the Vatican archives."

He took a deep breath and sighed, making a note on a legal pad. "I believe that should be acceptable."

"And second, we will be providing a complete report of all of our research to a dozen high-ranking Freemasons in both Montreal and New England." She and Cam knew they couldn't trust the Vatican, and they didn't relish the thought of spending the next decade feeling like they had a bull's-eye on their backs. "In fact," she continued, "a handful of local Freemasons have this material already." Cam sipped at his juice to cover his surprise; this last statement was a flat-out lie. Not that he blamed Amanda. There was no reason to make anyone feel like this whole mess could be wiped away in the next couple of hours. "These Freemasons can be counted on to keep these secrets, just as Father Jean and his predecessors have done through the centuries. However, should anything happen to Cameron or myself, they will make our findings public immediately."

"I understand," the envoy said. He stood, using his arms to lift his mass from the chair. "I will need to consult with my superiors. Personally, I appreciate the concessions you have made. Eventually this decision will be made by the Holy Father. As you know, he answers only to God."

Father Jean smiled and offered a half-bow. "With all due respect, Emissary, it seems like God is telling him pretty loudly what he needs to do. Hopefully the Holy Father is listening."

✠ ✠ ✠

The envoy returned to the function room a few minutes before noon. Amanda noticed a bounce in his step. "The Pope has agreed," she whispered to Cam.

"How do you know?"

She smiled. "I just do."

"The Holy Father has accepted your proposal," the emissary announced, smiling. He turned to Father Jean. "Apparently he was listening to God."

Father Jean bowed. "Well done, Emissary."

"He has one concern, however," the envoy said.

"Yes?" Cam responded.

"How are we to be sure that there are no others who know of your … findings? We must be sure there are no leaks. We will need the ten years to prepare the parishioners."

"Fair enough," Cam said. "I'm pretty sure Salazar won't be saying anything, assuming he survives. Not that he even knows what we found here in Montreal."

Amanda added, "And Eliza and Buckner still have much to gain. They'll keep quiet because in the end it will help Astarte fulfill her destiny."

"Not to mention Eliza is looking at some jail time here in Canada," Georgia said. She looked over to her Canadian counterpart, who nodded. "My guess is she'll be amenable to cutting a deal." Georgia continued. "My boss in Virginia is the only other one who knows about this."

"Can he be trusted?" Amanda asked.

She shrugged. "That's his job. He keeps secrets. And the whole reason for this mission was to keep all this quiet."

The envoy nodded. "Are there any other loose ends?"

Astarte cleared her throat. "Excuse me, but may I ask a question?"

Father Jean looked to the emissary, who nodded. "Of course, Astarte," Father Jean said.

"The Pope is very powerful, right?"

The Emissary gave her a funny look. Probably not too many little girls running around the Vatican. Finally he bent low and smiled at her. "Yes, very powerful."

Astarte turned to Georgia. "And your boss is very powerful also, right?"

Georgia also smiled and nodded.

The girl took Amanda's hand. What was the young princess up to? Astarte put her mouth against Amanda's ear. "I would like them to use their power to make it so I can live with you and Mr. Cameron. There's no place else for me now. I don't want to live with Eliza. And Uncle Jefferson is dead. I would like to live with you." She backed off and looked up at Amanda with wide eyes, the same imploring cobalt eyes that had lured Amanda into the bathroom four days earlier. "If you want me to, that is," the girl said. Amanda dropped to a knee and clutched the girl to her chest. The little girl's heart thumped against hers. "Of course, of course we do," she breathed.

"What?" Cam asked.

Amanda smiled at him, tears pooling in her eyes. She took his hand and held it to her cheek, Astarte's soft breath warming their joined fingers. "We're going to need to make room in our little castle for a young princess."

EPILOGUE

A light snow had fallen overnight and the morning sun glistened off the powdery crystals sprinkled atop the flat edges of the round stone tower. Cam brushed the snow off a bench with his glove so Amanda, Astarte and he could sit. They sipped hot chocolate in the cold December air, staring at the fieldstone structure. He never got tired of studying the Newport Tower.

A month had passed since their adventures in Montreal. Cam had knee surgery, their other injuries had healed and, at least so far, nobody had taken any shots at them. Georgia had arranged for an agent to retrieve Venus for them while Salazar recovered from his injuries in a rehab center in Montreal.

"I thought the tower would be taller," Astarte said as Venus tugged her to her feet and sniffed at the snow.

Amanda responded. "At one point it might have been. In any event the tower is probably the oldest structure in North America. It was built long before Columbus arrived, we think by the Knights Templar or their followers."

The girl cocked her head to one side. "Why is there no roof?"

"There probably was at one time, a domed one," Amanda said. "And also a wooden structure built around the tower, called an ambulatory. But this is all that is left." A group of amateur archeologists had recently uncovered the remains of ancient wooden posts that would have supported the ambulatory. The structure probably originally resembled London's Temple Church, built by the Templars in the late 12th century.

Cam limped around the tower to the west side, opposite the sun. He snapped a picture just as the sunrays burst through one of the narrow tower windows. He returned and showed the image.

NEWPORT TOWER WINTER SOLSTICE SUNRISE

"It looks like a starburst," Astarte gasped, clapping her hands joyfully.

"It does," Cam laughed. He had been hesitant about Astarte moving in with them—most couples did not assume guardianship of an eight-year-old girl before planning their own wedding. But now, a month later, it seemed as if she had always been part of their lives.

"How long before the ... illumination?" Astarte asked. She had just learned the word and was pleased to use it correctly.

"Another couple of hours," Amanda said. She pointed to a window on the east side of the tower. "At a little before eight o'clock the rising sun will pass through that window. As the sun rises higher in the sky and moves to the south, the light beam it casts through the window will shine on the opposite wall of the tower, moving lower as the sun gets higher. Do you see what I mean?"

Astarte nodded.

"Now, in ancient times the people feared that the sun was going to disappear every December as it sank lower and lower in the sky and the days got shorter and shorter."

"And without the sun people would die."

"Right. So when the sun finally began to climb again and the days began to get longer, the people held a big celebration. Today we call it Christmas, but in ancient times it had nothing to do with Jesus Christ. It was a celebration of the rebirth of the sun. The sun is reborn every year on the winter solstice."

"That's today, right?" the girl said. "December 21."

Cam stood and led Astarte to the tower. He pointed to the archway joining two stone pillars on the far side of the structure. "See that egg-shaped stone at the top of the arch?" She nodded. "That's called a keystone—it actually holds the arch up and prevents it from falling. But see how it is a bit off-center, and also a different color than the other stones?"

"Yes. It's orange."

"Now I want you to look around the entire tower and tell me if you see any other stones the same size and shape."

Astarte slowly circled the structure, dutifully peering between the archways linking the eight pillars which supported the tower. She shook her head. "That's the only one."

Amanda had wandered over with Venus, her jacket unzipped despite the weather. Lately she seemed never to get cold. "This is called 'having eyes that see,' Astarte," Amanda said. "The men who built this tower were very smart. And they were excellent masons. The fact that the stone is slightly off-center is no accident—it is a sign, calling attention to itself. And its unique shape and color are also signs. Again, we are supposed to pay attention."

Astarte pondered this for a few seconds. "The shape is an egg. Is that important also?"

Amanda smiled. "Yes. But you'll have to wait to see why."

A small crowd had begun to form—in recent years the winter solstice illumination had become popular among Freemasons, New-Agers, Wiccans, Native Americans and generally anyone with an interest in history or religion. On a sunny day like today there would likely be hundreds of people viewing the spectacle.

"We still have an hour," Amanda said to Cam. Astarte made friends with a young boy; together they began to build a snowman while Venus rolled in the snow. "This is a good chance to show you what I've learned." They had been so busy coordinating Cam's knee surgery, arranging for testing of the scroll, consulting with Father Jean regarding the DNA testing on the bones, and making arrangements for gaining custody of Astarte that they had little time to follow up on the research that led them to the discovery of Jesus' bones in the first place. But Amanda had made some discoveries last night she was anxious to share.

"Okay," she said. "I think Leonardo da Vinci knew all about Jesus usurping John the Baptist and not really being immortal. His paintings are full of clues."

"Someone should write a book," Cam said.

Amanda tossed a mitten-full of snow in his face. "Just listen." She took a deep breath. "First, let's start with Salome. Remember, she's the one who asked King Herod for John the Baptist's head after she got Herod and his guests all aroused with her dance of the seven veils."

Cam nodded. Herod had married Salome's mother, Herodias, who had been married to Herod's brother. Herodias and Salome were upset because John the Baptist condemned the marriage as illegal under Jewish law. "Nice family. The stepdaughter seduces the stepfather, who also happens to be her uncle, and convinces him to behead the chief rabbi."

"So back to da Vinci. The Italian word for Salome is Salomina." She wrote out the name on a small pad of paper. "Salomina is an anagram for Mona Lisa." She sat back against the bench. "See that?"

"Okay," Cam said. Interesting, but hardly earth-shattering.

"And what does the name Mona Lisa mean?"

Cam shrugged. "I don't know. I don't think it means anything."

"Exactly. For centuries scholars have been trying to figure it out. Nobody's come up with a good answer. I think it was da Vinci's way of saying, 'Hey, pay attention to Salome. Pay attention to John the Baptist.'"

"Okay. We know da Vinci used anagrams and word plays a lot. And he was definitely an initiate." Most historians believed he belonged to one of the ancient secret societies. "But I'm not sure the anagram is enough proof...."

Amanda smiled. "Don't worry, I have more." She shifted on the bench. "Do you remember the name of John the Baptist's mother?"

Cam shook his head. "Mrs. Baptist?" He ducked another mitten-full of snow.

"His mother was Elizabeth. In Italian that's Elisabetta, spelled with an 's' instead of a 'z.' And mother in Italian is Madonna. So look at this." She wrote out MadONnA eLISAbetta on the pad, with certain letters capitalized. "So Mona Lisa could be code for Elizabeth. Another tie back to John the Baptist."

"Hmm." This could still all be a coincidence, except for da Vinci's reputation for wordplay and imbedding secret meanings in his paintings.

"So here's where it gets really interesting." Amanda smiled and opened her laptop. "This is a picture of the Mona Lisa. What are the two things you notice right away?"

MONA LISA, LEONARDO DA VINCI

"I would say the smile—it looks like she's keeping a secret. And also she looks sort of ... androgynous."

"Spot on. That's what most people notice. Let's focus on the androgynous part first." She clicked at the laptop. "Now take a look at this. This is a da Vinci portrait of John the Baptist."

ST. JOHN THE BAPTIST, LEONARDO DA VINCI

"Wow. He looks almost feminine—look how delicate his hand is. And where's his facial hair?" Almost every portrait of John the Baptist portrayed him with a thick beard, to show his hermetic lifestyle.

"Now look at the smile."

Cam nodded. "Same smile as the Mona Lisa. Like they are keeping a secret."

"Now look at the two faces. What do you see?"

Cam studied the features. "Holy shit. The features are almost identical. Same nose, same mouth, same skin tone. And look at the chin. It's like they were brother and sister."

Amanda waited until he looked up at her before responding. "Or mother and son."

Cam couldn't help but chuckle; the entire past month had been so surreal and sometimes downright bizarre. "Oh my gosh, you're right. That could be it. The Mona Lisa is supposed to be John the Baptist's mother."

Amanda smiled. "Mona Lisa. Madonna Elisabetta. Mother Elizabeth."

Cam mulled it over a few seconds. "So why are they androgynous? And what's the secret they know?"

"I'm betting the secret they know is the same one we just discovered: Jesus is not divine, and he usurped half the godhead from John the Baptist. And it's not just the smile—look how John the Baptist is pointing up to heaven, as if to say, 'I'm going up.' In fact, whenever da Vinci painted John the Baptist, he is pointing to heaven."

"Wow. Good stuff, Amanda."

"You know, the divinity part is a big deal to us today, but I think back then what was really important was the concept of duality: The godhead is supposed to be both male and female, sun and earth, yin and yang, Mars and Venus, king and priest. The Baptist is shown with feminine qualities as a counterbalance to the male-dominated Church. God is supposed to be both male and female. That was a key part of Gnostic belief. The Templars knew the truth. And so did da Vinci." She gestured toward the images. "Da Vinci painted these portraits so that people with eyes that see would know all this. That's the secret behind their smiles."

Cam nodded. "Duality. You're right, that's it." He studied the images. "And that might be another reason why John the Baptist is always pointing up to heaven. As above, so below. Heaven and earth. More duality."

Amanda leaned over and kissed him lightly. "Well done. No wonder I love you so much." She pulled up another image on her laptop. "We looked at this on our drive to the Catskills. It's da Vinci's Virgin of the Rocks."

VIRGIN OF THE ROCKS, LEONARDO DA VINCI

Cam studied the painting. There was a lot going on here. They had already noticed the oddity of Jesus praying to John the Baptist. Cam noticed that the rocks were all phallus-shaped, which was probably da Vinci mocking the idea of the Virgin Mary truly being a virgin. "The babies are the same age—isn't John supposed to be six months older than Jesus?"

Amanda nodded. "Supposedly, yes. But I think da Vinci is showing them here as twins. Equals. In other portraits they are shown as light-haired and dark-haired twins. Again, duality."

"And look at baby John holding up two fingers."

"Right. Duality once more. He's saying, 'There are two of us.'"

Cam sat back on the bench. He had been so engrossed in their discussion that he hadn't noticed the park filling with people. In about twenty minutes the illumination would begin. He shook his head. "Da Vinci was really good. He had to reveal all this without getting himself killed. If the Church knew what he was really up to...."

"It wasn't just him. Other initiates kept the secrets also."

"Why do I get the feeling you're going to show me another painting?"

She grinned. "Just to close the loop on all this. And also to prove how brilliantly insightful I am--"

"Oh boy. Here it comes."

"I often wondered why so many of the paintings of Mary Magdalene depict her with a skull. The conventional explanation is that the skull represents death. But if that's the case why is she so often portrayed staring longingly at it, like this?" She turned the computer screen toward Cam.

MARY MAGDALENE WITH A SKULL, GUSTAVE DORE

"Could the skull represent Jesus himself?"

"How could it? He was resurrected; his skull is in heaven." She smiled. "Supposedly."

"Good point. So what's your explanation?"

"I think the skull represents John the Baptist, just as it does for the Templars."

"Okay. But then why is she looking longingly at it?"

"That's a bit harder to explain. But consider this: In the patriarchy of the Church, Mary Magdalene cannot take her rightful place alongside her husband Jesus. Instead, she is relegated to the role of a prostitute. So perhaps she is looking longingly at the skull because only once duality is restored to the godhead can she be reunited with her lover and take her rightful seat by his side. The priest rules alongside the king, as does a queen. But they both require a system of dualism to do so. She longs for dualism."

Cam grinned. "You're pretty good at this stuff. I'm impressed."

She shrugged. "Once you get clued in it all sort of fits together."

"Speaking of clued in, we're getting close to the illumination."

They walked over to admire Astarte's snowman and then found a good vantage point along the cast iron fence that surrounded the tower. The box of light formed by the sun passing through a rectangular window in the tower's east side had already begun its diagonal march down the interior tower wall. "See the light box, Astarte?" Amanda asked.

"It looks like a flashlight beam. But it's not round."

"That's because the window the light is passing through is not round." Amanda rested her arm on the girl's shoulder. Somehow she knew exactly how to speak to Astarte, how to explain complex things to a confused, vulnerable eight-year-old girl. Albeit a very bright one. "You asked about the egg shape of the orange stone. Well, the egg is a symbol of fertility; it is where life starts in the womb. What we are going to see happens only today, on the winter solstice. And that is not an accident—the window and the egg-shaped stone were carefully placed so this happens only once during the year. In a few minutes the sun will illuminate the egg. This is symbolic of rebirth—the sun is not dying but instead is being reborn. The light beam is fertilizing the egg just as the sun fertilizes Mother Earth and gives life to everything on it."

"So the sun is the father and the earth is the mother?" Astarte asked. She was a quick study. And the Native American culture taught children about the facts of life at a young age.

"Brilliant," Amanda said, smiling. "And that's why we believe God is both a man and a woman, not just a man. It takes both the male and female to create life. Since we are created in God's image, God must have both male and female characteristics. The people who built this tower understood that."

"And celebrated it," Cam added. "That's how we know it was built by the Templars or their followers."

"Look, the sun is approaching the egg now," Amanda said.

The crowd watched in silence as the light box crept across the interior tower wall. Cam marveled at the technology and science that must have gone into placing both the window and the egg-shaped keystone in exactly the right spot to mark the winter solstice. The fact that the keystone was slightly off-center testified to how difficult it must have been to construct the tower in perfect accord with the illumination.

Cam took Astarte's hand. "Okay, it's close. Watch how the egg stone lights up."

Astarte gasped and covered her mouth with a gloved hand as the beam of light, which showed only as a dull gray glimmer against the darker stones of the tower, glowed bright and gold as it enveloped the yellowish orb. "Oh my," the girl whispered.

NEWPORT TOWER WINTER SOLSTICE ILLUMINATION

"So," Amanda whispered. "Life is reborn for yet another year."

Astarte stared at the illumination for a few more seconds. "Thank you for showing me this," she said as she grasped Amanda's and Cam's hands. "If I am to be the Fortieth Princess I will need to learn about these things." She set her jaw. "I will need to teach the people how to have eyes that see."

THE END

AUTHOR'S NOTE

Inevitably, I receive this question from readers: "Are the artifacts in your stories real, or did you make them up?" The answer is: If they are in the story, they are real, actual artifacts.

It is because they are real that I have included images of many of them within these pages—I want readers to see them with their own eyes, to be able to make at least a cursory judgment as to their age, origin and meaning. Are they authentic? Do they evidence ancient exploration of this continent? I hope readers will at least consider the possibility that they do.

Specifically, in regard to this story, I expect to receive inquiries regarding many of the artifacts and themes written about in these pages. I offer the following background information and sources for readers curious about these questions (topics are listed in order of appearance in this story).

Templars in America

Much has been written recently about the possibility of the Knights Templar traveling to North American during medieval times. My prior novel, *Cabal of the Westford Knight: Templars at the Newport Tower* (Martin and Lawrence Press, 2009) offers a good overview of this subject, specifically focusing on the New England area sites and artifacts. For a non-fiction summary of this research, I highly recommend Scott Wolter, *The Hooked X: Key to the Secret History of North America* (North Star Press of St. Cloud, 2009), and also the DVD, *Holy Grail in America* (History Channel, 2010). The Newport Tower winter solstice illumination is featured in both of these books as well as the DVD.

The Burrows Cave Artifacts

As related in this story, thousands of artifacts were removed from this cave in southern Illinois by Russell Burrows beginning in the late 1980s. The artifacts shown in this story are all actual Burrows Cave artifacts. Recently, geologist Scott Wolter discovered the cursive writing on the back side of the Isis Stone, indicating that this particular artifact, at least, is a fake. The question as to whether the other artifacts are more than a modern-day hoax remains an open one. I recommend Frank Joseph, *The Lost Treasure of King Juba* (Bear & Company, 2003) as a good background source.

The Mandan Indians and Prince Madoc

The Mandan, the so-called "White Indians," sparked much debate among the early pioneers regarding their origin. Many, including President Thomas Jefferson, believed they descended from Welsh explorers (this is usually tied to the Prince Madoc legends). Others believed the Mandan were one of the Lost Tribes of Israel. Most historians believe the Mandan were wiped out by a smallpox epidemic. For more information on the Mandan, I recommend the works of George Catlin, who lived with and wrote about the tribe in the early 1800s. I also recommend Rick Osmon, *The Graves of the Golden Bear: Ancient Fortresses and Monuments of the Ohio Valley* (Grave Distractions, 2011), which contains background information on many of the ancient sites and artifacts found in the Ohio River Valley; this book also discusses both Prince Madoc and the Burrows Cave saga.

The Clairvaux Codex

Researchers recently uncovered remnants of a 12th-century Templar document purportedly journaling a Templar voyage to what we now know as New York's Catskill Mountains in the 1170s. I have renamed this document and left out many of the details surrounding its discovery per the request of the researchers who uncovered it. I was, however, present when the IN CAMERA stone was dug up in the Catskills in accordance with instructions and clues contained in the document. The latitude and longitude readings on the IN CAMERA stone do, indeed, mark Old Montreal. For more information regarding the Clairvaux Codex, look for a forthcoming book to be published by researchers Zena Halpern and Donald Ruh.

The Bat Creek Stone

Geologist Scott Wolter has performed some fascinating research on this artifact, and has concluded it is not a modern

326

hoax. Unfortunately, the Smithsonian seems to have misplaced many of the bones and artifacts found alongside the stone in the burial mound (you can't make this stuff up). If these objects and remains are found, they can be tested to perhaps determine age and origin. Many believe that this is the artifact that will conclusively prove trans-Atlantic exploration in ancient times. For more information regarding the Bat Creek Stone, look for a forthcoming book to be published by Scott Wolter.

Templar Religious Beliefs
I have long suspected that the Templars discovered something truly earth-shattering in Jerusalem in the early 12th-century that they used to blackmail the Church. One possibility, which I explore in this story, is that they stumbled upon Talpiot Tomb and the bones of Jesus and his family (this was suggested to me as a possibility by author and researcher Margaret Starbird). If so, they would have learned that Jesus did not ascend in the physical sense to heaven. This may have caused them to doubt the divinity of Jesus and the religious foundation upon which the Church was built, which in turn might explain many of the practices and rituals ascribed to the Templars, including: 1) the practice of spitting on the cross; 2) the worship of the head, Baphomet; 3) the veneration of Mary, Mary Magdalene, John the Baptist and many other Christian figures other than Jesus himself; 4) the observation of ancient pagan religious practices involving Mother Earth and astral alignments; and 5) the willingness to acquire knowledge from, trade with and even befriend the "heretical" Muslims the Templars encountered in the Middle-East. Not to mention, of course, that the discovery of Jesus' bones would also explain the Templar teaching referring to Jesus as the Thief on the Cross. The teaching quoted in the story, in which the Templars explain why they refer to Jesus as the Thief on the Cross, is based on testimony from the Templar trials.

Notre Dame Basilica
The Notre Dame Basilica was, as stated in this story, built by the Sulpician sect in the 1670's. This sect is believed to descend from or at least share religious values with the Templars. The

images of the Basilica shown in this story are real, including the Delta of Enoch on the ceiling of the raised pulpit. The bones of the Basilica's architect are purportedly buried in a crypt in the church basement; of course, the assertion that the bones in the crypt are those of Jesus is fictional. For an excellent overview of Sulpician influence in the settlement of Montreal, see Francine Bernier, *The Templars' Legacy in Montreal, the New Jerusalem* (Frontier Publishing, 2001).

Just as the artifacts displayed in this book are real, so too are the works of art. Again, I display these artworks because I want readers to perform their own analysis—what hidden message, if any, is the artist trying to convey? During medieval times, artists (such as Leonardo da Vinci) who had been initiated into the secret societies often communicated ancient knowledge considered blasphemous through their art. The expression "eyes that see" applies to those who knew how and where (including inside churches themselves) to look for these messages.

It is, then, these artifacts, sites and works of art that are the raw materials for this story. From them I have crafted a narrative that offers one plausible explanation for why they exist in the form they do. The key word here is 'plausible'—to use an analogy from our system of jurisprudence, it is not essential that a fiction writer prove his or her case beyond a reasonable doubt. But the writer must present a credible, believable scenario. The writer cannot simply make things up, fabricating history to suit his or her needs. I am cognizant of that, and have made every effort to craft a story that is consistent with the historical record. For inquisitive readers, perhaps curious about some of the specific historical assertions made and evidence presented in this story, I offer the following substantiation (in order of appearance in the story):

- For a summary of Samuel Eliot Morison's dismissal of the accuracy of the Vinland Sagas, see Samuel Eliot Morison, *The European Discovery of America: The Northern Voyages* (Oxford University Press, USA, 1971), at pages 52 and 55.

- For the assertion that the ancient Cherokee name for their divine spirit is 'Yo-He-Wah, almost identical to the Jewish Yahweh, see *Cherokee Beliefs and Practices of the Ancients,* by James Adair (Cherokee Language and Culture, 1998), at page 50.

- For the assertion that Egyptian and Roman hieroglyphs were found carved on the wall of Cave-In-Rock, see http://www.midwesternepigraphic.org/sMap01.html .

- For the assertion that Jesus' niece Anna married into the ancient Mauretanian royal family of King Juba II and Queen Cleopatra Selene (the daughter of the famous Cleopatra and Mark Anthony), see *The Knights Templar of the Middle East,* by HRH Prince Michael of Albany (Weiser Books, 2006), at page 11.

- For the assertion that Jesus descended from Abraham by 40 generations on his mother Mary's side, see http://en.wikipedia.org/wiki/Genealogy_of_Jesus (referencing The Book of Matthew).

- For the assertion that more than half of the Templar Grand Masters were also given the title, "Prince of Seborga," see http://seborga.net/history/index.html .

- For substantiation of Tennessee Governor Seiver's recount of a Cherokee chief stating that the ancient Welsh landed near the mouth of the Alabama River, see http://www.walesdirectory.co.uk/Myths_and_Legends/Prin ce_Madoc.htm .

- For the assertion that Prince Madoc traveled to America, see http://www.slideshare.net/JudyMJohnson/the-case-for-prince-madoc-and-king-arthur-in-america-revision-8-23-10 .

- For the assertion that a Templar teaching resulted in the Templars referring to Jesus as the Thief on the Cross, see http://tikaboo.com/library/Masonry_-_The_Knights_Templar.pdf .

- For the assertion that the inscription at the America's Stonehenge site is ancient Punic that translates as, "To Baal of the Canaanites," and dates back to roughly 500 BC, see

David Goudsward, *Ancient Stone Sites of New England* (McFarland & Co., 2006), at page 86.

- For information about an ancient Phoenician coin found in Massachusetts (and that archeologists speculated it was carried across the Atlantic in the beak of a seagull), see http://www.gloucestertimes.com/local/x124780161/Shekel-in-the-sand-How-did-2-000-year-old-coin-end-up-in-Manchester .

- For the assertion that the first Templar Grand Master, Hugues de Payens, was secretly a Johannite—a worshiper of John the Baptist—and not a follower of Jesus, see Albert Pike, *Morals and Dogma* (various publishers), 30th Degree, Knight Kadosh, at pages 816-819.

- For the assertion that the roots of modern-day Islamic hostility toward Christianity took hold in the 19th and 20th centuries, when Protestant leaders began questioning Christianity's core religious teachings, see http://www.messianicassociation.org/ezine26-usn.are-christians2blame.htm .

- For the assertion that the Essenes prophesized that the place of dominion of the high priestly messiah was to be in heaven, while the royal messiah resided on earth, see http://www.dhushara.com/book/yeshua/apoc.htm (approximately one-third of the way down the page).

- For the assertion that the removal of the first letter Yod in the Tetragrammaton at the Notre Dame Basilica, thereby changing the name "Yahweh" to "Eve," indicated that its worshipers venerated the female aspect of the divine, see Francine Bernier, *The Templars' Legacy in Montreal, the New Jerusalem* (Frontier Publishing, 2001), at pages 185-188.

Out of all this, then, comes a story that hopefully both educates and entertains. Were ancient explorers secretly visiting North America? If so, were they doing so to preserve ancient secrets or hide ancient knowledge? These are the questions that keep me up at night. Hopefully you've lost some sleep over them as well.

PHOTO CREDITS

Images used in this book are provided courtesy of the following individuals (images listed in order of appearance in the story):

BURROWS CAVE ROMAN SOLDIER, courtesy Scott Wolter

THE BAT CREEK STONE, courtesy Scott Wolter

BURROWS CAVE URSA MINOR STONE, courtesy Ancient Waterways

BURROWS CAVE MAP STONE, courtesy Scott Wolter

MADOC STOKE DRY MURAL, courtesy Lee Pennington

THE GODDESS STONE, courtesy Zena Halpern

BURROWS CAVE ISIS STONE, courtesy Scott Wolter

BURROWS CAVE ISIS STONE (back side), courtesy Scott Wolter

IN CAMERA STONE, courtesy Scott Wolter

BON-SECOURS CHAPEL CORNERSTONE, courtesy Scott Wolter

NOTRE DAME BASILICA PULPIT, courtesy Chris Devers

NOTRE DAME BASILICA DELTA OF ENOCH, courtesy Scott Wolter

NEWPORT TOWER WINTER SOLSTICE SUNRISE, courtesy Richard Lynch

ACKNOWLEDGEMENTS

Much of the research involving ancient exploration of North America rests on the ever-growing foundation of scientific evidence compiled by geologist Scott Wolter and his wife, Janet. They have truly become giants in this field, and their dedication, courage and intellect in studying the ancient artifacts that exist on this continent are the greatest factors forcing historians and academics to reconsider the question of "Columbus First." In addition to the great work they are doing, they have taken time out of their busy lives to help me research and formulate this story. Their assistance and their friendship have been invaluable.

Others who have assisted in my research include (in alphabetical order): Steve St. Clair, Chris Finefrock, Irene Gordon, Zena Halpern, Virginia Kimball, Gerard Leduc, Richard Lynch, Wayne May, Rick Osmon, Rabbi Shoshana Perry, Judi Rudebusch, Donald Ruh, Margaret Starbird and Dennis Stone (inclusion on this list does not in any way indicate approval or support of the conclusions reached in this story). I am grateful to you all.

I also want to thank my team of readers, those who slogged their way through early versions of the story and offered helpful, insightful comments, even if they did not necessarily agree with some of the themes of this story (readers listed chronologically): Lynn Keltz, Allie Brody, Richard Meibers, Spencer Brody, Richard Scott, Jeanne Scott, Jeff Brody, Shelley Kline, Tom Coffey, Renee Brody and Carolyn Metcalf.

For other authors out there looking to navigate their way through the publishing process, I can't speak highly enough about Amy Collins and her team at The Cadence Group—real pros who know the business and are a pleasure to work with.

Lastly, to my wife, Kim: Thanks for your unending patience, support and wise counsel. You inspire me.

CPSIA information can be obtained at www.ICGtesting.com
Printed in the USA
BVOW020500110412

287388BV00001B/8/P